ON WINGS OF EAGLES

The Story of Ferdinando Stanley and Alice Spencer

by

Lizzie Jones

**Grosvenor House
Publishing Limited**

This book is published by
Grosvenor House Publishing Ltd
28-30 High Street, Guildford, Surrey, GU1 3EL.
www.grosvenorhousepublishing.co.uk

A CIP record for this book
is available from the British Library

ISBN 978-1-78148-163-9

*Dedicated to all my relatives and
friends in West Lancashire and to the
memory of those places no longer visible
and the people who once lived there.*

CHAPTER 1

The Wedding

The soft flakes of snow fluttering like goose feathers were cosseting Althorp Manor in a coverlet of tranquillity, curling comfortably around the gables and chimneys and spreading a thin sheet over the moat. But the impression of protected slumber was an illusion belied by the hustle and bustle within the house as the hours slipped by all too quickly on the shortest day of the year 1574. In every room all the members of the large household were occupied with some task, trying to make the best of the fading light before candles had to be lit.

Alice Spencer was sitting on the bed in the chamber she shared with her sister watching the tailor put the finishing touches to the wedding gown.

"I wish I were getting married," she said, gazing enviously at the magnificent creation, the shimmering brightness of which illuminated the room more than the silvery snow-flecked light piercing the casement.

"Is the stomacher too tight, Mistress?" the tailor asked anxiously, aware of his responsibility for this momentous occasion. "I can let out the ribbons."

"No, I want my waist to look as small as possible," replied Elizabeth Spencer, turning from side to side but restricted from further movement by the stiff bell-shaped farthingale over which the dozen yards of silk velvet rippled like a summer lake with the swaying motion, shading from light to dark. "What does it look like, Alice? Oh I wish there was a large enough glass for me to see myself properly."

"It is the most beautiful dress I have ever seen," breathed her sister, lost in admiration at the gathered skirt of lapis lazuli blue latticed with silver thread, open in the centre to reveal a kirtle of white silk closely embroidered in a stylised design of blue flowers, with a matching pointed stomacher reaching below her waist and tied with silver bows. The tight sleeves of the same stuff as the gown were decorated with seed pearls and over them swung wide hanging sleeves of white velvet edged with white fur.

"My head tire is going to be splendid, though I have only seen the designs – silver wire with seed pearls and sapphires with a little veil – and my ruff will be edged in like manner, framed in a supporter."

Alice had never considered her elder sister particularly beautiful but looking at her now with her thin features animated with excitement and imagining the head tire on her dark hair, she had to admit that Elizabeth was going to be a beautiful bride.

Her thoughts were interrupted by the bustling arrival of their mother whose quick nervous movements and sharp commands to her daughters contrived to make the spacious bedchamber shrink to her presence. Lady Spencer inspected the gown with a critical eye, pulling and tugging and examining the stitches with exact observation whilst Master Hopwith looked on in apprehension, only nodding his head because his mouth was full of pins. Then giving her approval she ordered the tailor to pack up the gown and make the final adjustments, with the strict reminder for him to have it delivered to the manor with time to spare before the celebrations of the next few days.

"When you have helped Elizabeth to undress you may come to my chamber to try on your own gown, Alice. I will await you there."

She swept away, snagging her long sleeve on the door handle as she did so, her sharp face beneath her lace coif creased with the concentration of one who has a multitude of tasks to accomplish and not enough time to see to them all. The sisters breathed a sigh of relief. When the tailor had carefully packed away all the various pieces of his creation into a large box he followed her.

Elizabeth was standing in her shift and said to her sister, "Can you call Joanna and ask her to help me dress again."

None of the maids had been allowed to see the gown in its making in case they should inadvertently reveal its secrets.

But Alice climbed down from her perch saying, "No, I will do it, I won't have you with me much longer. I shall be lonely with you and Anne both gone, especially at night in this great bed on my own."

The tester bed with its four carved posts holding up the canopy of fringed rosy brocade (termed maiden's blush) with matching drapes and counterpane, was the one she had shared with her sisters since they left the nursery.

"Not for very long, I don't suppose. Your turn will be next," Elizabeth said confidently.

Alice picked up the discarded skirt and bodice from the floor and began to tie her sister into the more serviceable daywear of wool and linen.

"Will you invite me to Court when you are married then I can meet some-one rich and important. But he must be handsome too," she added.

Her eldest sister's husband might be Lord Monteagle but he was old and grey, Anne being his second wife, whilst Elizabeth's prospective husband George Carey, though he was son to the Lord Chamberlain and young, was small and stout.

"I don't think you are old enough at present for the Court," Elizabeth replied with all the superiority of her twenty years. "You are scarcely fifteen."

"Some of the Queen's ladies are not much older than I. And all George Carey's sisters are maids to the Queen and greatly in her favour I believe. Perhaps they could speak for me if you suggested it."

"Alice, I have to find favour for myself first," laughed Elizabeth. "Just because George is second cousin to the Queen does not necessarily mean that I will find favour with her. She is known not to look too kindly on those women who steal her courtiers."

After finishing lacing up her sister's bodice Alice went to stand by the window. "The Spencers have done well for themselves," she said, looking out over the knot garden, the sprinkling of snow making the yew hedges look as if they were glistening with diamonds. Paths alongside led to the rose arbour, bare of blossoms now but in summer a riot of colour. A stone terrace encircled the formal gardens surrounding the house, beyond which a moat separated the house and grounds from the orchards and fields of the estate.

"Sheep farmers not so long ago and now you are marrying with the Queen's kin and your children will carry Tudor blood in their veins."

"Don't exaggerate, Alice, George's father is only cousin to the Queen, son of Mary Boleyn."

Alice laughed and said gleefully, "Mary Boleyn and King Henry most probably, it's no secret. Few people believe Lord Hunsdon's father was Mary's husband. Look at his red hair and if rumour is true he has the same eye for the ladies. That means your children will have royal blood. And Lord Monteagle is of the family of the Earls of Derby who have also royal connections."

"I think Anne exaggerates her husband's lineage," Elizabeth said, pulling a wry face. "Lord Monteagle's grandfather was brother to the first Earl of Derby who was only stepfather to King Henry VII and that's a long time ago."

"But our family have done well for themselves you must admit. Only three generations ago the Spencers were Warwickshire farmers and mother's family modest merchants," Alice insisted.

"It's true," her sister concurred. "But only the other day I heard John say this was not unusual in this day and age, that the Earl of Leicester's grandfather was also a farmer and the grandfather of the great Lord Burghley only a Welsh squire."

Alice smiled, thinking how typical was such a statement by their eldest brother. John considered the Spencers equal to any of the new nobility and was as excited as anyone by the possibilities of this new age when money, personal charm and audacity could carve a path to the highest echelons, no longer the sole prerogative of noble lineage. It was a belief shared by their parents, especially their imperious mother Lady Catherine. The Spencers (and her own family the Kitsons) might be nouveau riche but rich they were. This was the reason she had been determined to have the wedding celebrated at their own house, Althorp Manor. The splendid house, built of red brick in characteristic Tudor style with gables, mullioned windows and many chimneys, was a new building when it was purchased by their grandfather from the Catesbys who were in financial difficulties. Two subsequent generations had endowed it with all modern conveniences and the finest furniture and possessions that money could buy. Lady Catherine welcomed the opportunity to display the Spencer wealth and good taste to all the important and titled guests who would throng to her daughter's wedding so that they would be in no doubt that in taking the hand of Elizabeth Spencer the Queen's kinsman George Carey was in no way marrying beneath him.

The Yuletide season this year was going to be enhanced by the approaching nuptials. Christmas was a popular time for weddings but Lady Spencer was determined that the household and the neighbouring poor would in no way lack the usual festive celebrations so eagerly awaited by them, and was combining the events with her customary efficiency, harrying her large body of servants into an orgy of activity. There was constant movement and bustle in the house - already festooned with holly and ivy, sweet scented rosemary and laurel - as servants rushed hither and thither, polishing wood and silver, dusting tapestries, renewing chambers with freshly swept floors, beeswax candles and lavender strewn sheets. Fires were constantly replenished with logs and the pungent scent of applewood mingled with the aroma of baking emanating from the kitchens so that the manor seemed to breathe out enticing smells. Vast quantities of poultry, game, beef and veal had been cooked, and pies and tarts made for the venison and calves' tongues as well as the sweet fillings of custard and fruits (carefully preserved since the autumn), but also dates, figs and raisins. Lady Spencer's own personal stock of spices, pepper, ginger, cloves as well as sugar had been carefully checked, enough white flour ensured for the manchet bread while the confectioner cooks were busy with the elaborate banquet sweets. The centrepiece of sugar, pastry and fruits was to represent an enchanted forest with strange beasts and creatures, all of which would finally be dismantled and taken as souvenirs by the wedding guests.

The elaborate feasts and culinary displays were to be accompanied by a consort of professional musicians and the magnificent show was intended to demonstrate to all and sundry the wealth and growing importance of the Spencer family, whom some of the older nobility considered upstarts. Set within this scene of ambitious display Sir John and Lady Spencer and their family were to be as richly clothed as any of the more noble guests.

"You had better go and see to your own gown in mother's chamber or she will be sending someone to find you. She considers she has no time to waste," Elizabeth reminded her sister.

"It's to be of popingay-green velvet to show off my hair," Alice said excitedly. She was immensely proud of her hair which was naturally and fashionably red, not a product of henna dye but glowing like firelight on copper and falling in lustrous waves to her waist. "I do hope she won't make me cover my hair with a cap."

"Of course she will," Elizabeth replied, then seeing her sister's pout added, "but it will be a very fine cap decorated with jewels no doubt."

"When I am being married with my hair flowing loose I shall look like the Queen, especially if I am marrying some-one of royal blood like you," Alice smiled in satisfaction.

Elizabeth regarded her young sister with resigned exasperation. "Alice, I think you should be aware that marrying some-one with royal blood in their veins does not make for an easy life," she said. "The Queen looks with great suspicion on any she considers rivals, look at how she dealt with all the Grey sisters – Lady Jane executed and Lady Catherine and Lady Mary imprisoned. I think that a husband with even the smallest tinge of royal blood is to be avoided. George's ancestry is mere rumour and no-one dares say openly that his grandfather was anyone other than William Carey."

Alice said nothing. But later she lay in bed thinking of all the excitement of the coming nuptials. The house breathed anticipation, in the lingering scents of herbs and spices, in the creaking of the roof timbers, in the warmth of the crackling logs in the grate, the gentle rattle of the casement from the wind outside. She turned her back on Elizabeth and pulled the layers of blankets tight around her, curling up her knees inside her nightshift and burying her head in the soft feather bolster. Within the confines of the drawn curtains she imagined she was awaiting her own wedding – to a young handsome courtier who might also be a prince.

On Twelfth Night, when Elizabeth Spencer and George Carey had been married with all the necessary pomp, some miles away in the same shire of Northampton Sir Edmund and Lady Agnes Brudenell were completing their Yuletide festivities by a gathering of family and friends at their home Dene Park. They had hired a group of musicians and the younger members of the family, three sons and four daughters, had arranged for games and masking together with the asking of forfeits as the customary merry-making for the night. Their eldest son John was a student at the University of Oxford and one of his fellow-students there, Ferdinando Stanley, was patron of a trio of tumblers. John Bredenell had persuaded him to bring them to Dene Park as a novelty suitable for the occasion of the night of the Lord of Misrule.

Young Ferdinando had agreed with pleasure saying proudly, "They are tumblers and jugglers second to none. One of them does the most amazing tricks with baubles, sleight of hand, and another is such an acrobat that his limbs seem to be made of wire. I think your guests will find great amusement in their performance."

"I'm sure they will," John said, "and no doubt they will be rewarded handsomely afterwards as well as having the added incentive of partaking of the feast."

The evening was a great success, the company of tumblers were roundly praised by the assembled household and their guests, and John Bredenell's standing with his siblings substantially improved. But afterwards he asked his companion, "Why do you give patronage to some tumblers? It must be a drain on your purse."

Ferdinando's lively face was thoughtful for a minute. "I like performers," he said. "I like the way they defy convention to try and earn a living doing what pleases them, I admire their skill and I enjoy their company. They are a change from the kind of people I usually consort with. And their life is so precarious, evading the strictures of the law, dependent on being able to find employment and not knowing where their next penny is coming from. Their life is especially dangerous since the recent laws declaring all players and entertainers as rogues and vagabonds if they do not have the protection of a patron. I like to help them along because I believe that giving pleasure to people by entertaining them and making them forget their worldly cares for a while is an important service."

John studied him in bemused amusement, only half understanding his enthusiasm.

"What I would really like is to be the patron of a company of travelling players, a company of actors," Ferdinando said. "I hope I shall be able to do that one day."

CHAPTER 2

The Jewel

"Alice, my dear niece, how delighted I am that you have been able to join our company," Thomas Kitson said, striding from the entrance to Hengrave Hall with arms outstretched to embrace her.

"Surely, sir, you did not think I would miss an occasion to meet the Queen," she replied mischievously, kissing him warmly on the cheek. Then she added, "And Queen or no, I would never pass by the chance to come and visit you."

Thomas Kitson, her mother's only brother, was her favourite relative and her affection for him was mutually returned. He held her at arm's length, studying her admiringly.

"Well little Alice, it seems you are now a grown lady, and a very beautiful one too. We shall have to protect you from the lascivious attentions of all the Queen's young courtiers."

"Not too much protection, uncle, please," she laughed, her vivacious face alive with mischief and her eyes sparkling. Thomas could never decide whether they were blue or green

He took her arm and led her into the Hall saying, "Come and meet your aunt, she is almost out of her mind with worry about the Queen's visit." He beckoned the waiting menservants who had followed his departure into the courtyard saying briskly, "Have Mistress Alice's chests conveyed into the chamber made ready for her."

Alice felt a surge of excitement as she accompanied him into the Hall. It wasn't often she got the chance to visit her mother's family house - Suffolk was too far away from Northamptonshire for regular visits - but she relished the rare opportunities. Hengrave Hall, like her own home, was a relatively new building, less than fifty years old and illustrating the same fact of new money making itself known. It was larger and more luxurious however and had taken fifteen years to build - an imposing edifice of brick and stone surmounted by gables and countless chimneys and flanked by four octagonal towers, in each of which five sets of huge mullioned windows soared upwards through three storeys. The estate was large and prosperous with a long curving gravel drive leading through formal gardens and arbours to the entrance where above the porch an oriel window set with three rectangular mullions bore a colourful representation of the family arms, though some critical visitors wondered how accurate it was.

Thomas was already calling for his wife as he led Alice into the magnificent hallway with its pargetted ceiling, no longer the dining hall as in the old houses but now a room in which to welcome visitors with tall-backed chairs and chests and small tables set against the linenfold oak panelling. Eliza Kitson appeared immediately at the top of the wide dog-legged staircase, eager to welcome her niece, though her plump good-natured face was creased with worry beneath her lace cap.

"Oh my dear, you cannot imagine in what straits you find me," she cried. "There is so much to be done, I fear we shall never be ready. Though it is a great honour for us I wish with all my heart the Queen had not chosen our house for a visit."

"Nonsense my dear," Thomas laughed. "You would have been mortified if she had visited all the other Suffolk gentry and excluded us. Look how everyone has been vying for her attention ever since we learnt she had chosen Norwich for this year's summer progress and intended a leisurely drive through Suffolk. This is our opportunity to show ourselves equal with the old nobility of the shire."

"That is what I am so afraid of, Thomas. I am afraid that I shall not be able to compete with those who have more experience in this matter."

Thomas laughed again, putting his arm around his wife. "Have no fear, am I not in charge of all things and I intend that our entertainment of Her Grace will be surpassed by none in this shire, or in Norfolk." Turning to Alice he said, "I have expended so much money already that I fear I shall be poverty stricken for the rest of the year. At least she is only honouring us with her presence for dinner and not for the night, or longer. I know for a fact that those who have been chosen to entertain her for board and lodging for several nights have been bankrupted for the rest of their lives, even great lords."

"There will be at least a hundred people," Eliza Kitson said, "and besides the feast we must provide suitable entertainment for a few hours."

"All arranged," Thomas said airily. "We have servants enough. All you need do is look wealthy and elegant, but not so that you outshine the Queen. Show her great reverence when she arrives then keep discreetly in the background and leave everything to me."

Alice laughed out loud. Thomas was much younger than her mother, in fact he had been born after his father had died, only five years before his eldest sister Catherine had married Sir John Spencer. He was still not forty years old, tall and handsome with thick dark hair, which though receding at the front served to emphasize his high intelligent forehead, a bushy beard and long curving moustache.

"Yes it's well known the Queen prefers the company of men to that of women," Eliza said ruefully, knowing that for the time Elizabeth was with them she must relinquish her husband to the monarch's attentions and not object to his fawning over-effusive compliments. "However what you said about the servants is not strictly true, Thomas. They may well do the work but I must supervise and arrange everything and the responsibility is weighing heavily on me. I swear I shall not sleep a wink in the next two nights. At least I have Alice to help me now. But come, dear, let me show you to your chamber."

"When does my sister Elizabeth arrive?" asked Alice as they mounted the stairs.

"She and Sir George are already in the company of the Queen," her aunt replied, "but we have several guests who will be staying for a few days so I am afraid I must give you one of the smaller chambers."

Alice proclaimed her satisfaction, especially when she saw the light airy room with matting on the floor and curtains and bed linen of cream wool embroidered with crewel work, while from the open window wafted the rich musky scent of the roses in all their summer glory in the gardens below.

"No doubt you will soon be interrupted by Margaret and Mary, the children cannot wait to see their cousin again," her aunt said as she left with a promise to send a maid immediately to see to her needs.

Left alone Alice felt a great surge of exhilaration. For the space of a few days she was away from the controlling influence of her mother, she was to have a rare meeting with her sister Elizabeth who was now ensconced in London, she was to wallow in the luxury of her uncle Thomas's hospitality and she was at last to achieve her ambition of seeing the Queen.

The days before Queen Elizabeth's arrival sped swiftly in a whirlwind of organised activity laced with a potent mix of excited anticipation and nervousness, a spur to filling the long summer hours with untiring labour. By the time the appointed day arrived the whole household was in a state of nervous exhaustion so that Thomas had to speak sternly to the assembly, including his wife and two young daughters, gathered now in readiness. Only Alice stood with apparent composure, bubbling inside with excitement but youthfully confident about new challenges, smiling at her uncle when he caught her eye and nodded approvingly.

The Queen's arrival was delayed by a half-hour which increased the atmosphere of nervous tension, although this was a probability for which they had been forewarned since she was known to make frequent pauses on her journeys as her subjects lined her path to greet her and present small gifts which she would receive personally and return a few words of thanks.

"The dinner is going to be spoilt," Eliza Kitson fretted, walking backwards and forwards and rubbing her hands nervously, "I had planned the timing so carefully."

"Do not trouble yourself, Mistress," the head cook soothed her, "I have allowed for such a leeway," and looking up into his calm face she was somewhat reassured.

Suddenly the expectant silence was shattered by a blare of trumpets that tore through the mellow breeze and sent a bevy of birds flying from the trees, followed by the sounds of clattering hooves. Thomas took a final glance around then went to stand with his family in readiness at the front of the Hall. He was splendidly dressed in velvet and satin but of a discreet pigeon grey while Eliza was visibly shaking in her stiffly splayed gown of claret brocade with a matching close-fitting hood and lace ruff. The fanfares grew louder, brassy and bold in their imperious announcement, and round the curve of the drive appeared a dozen trumpeters in golden livery followed by a huge procession led by the Queen herself on horseback and escorted by a group of her favourite courtiers. The elaborate open carriage in which she progressed through the towns had been left behind in Bury St. Edmonds. One of the courtiers, whom Thomas knew to be Robert Dudley, Earl of Leicester, helped the Queen to dismount as Thomas approached her and bent low on his knee, hat in hand. The women curtseyed deeply and when Alice lifted up her head she was able to study Elizabeth as the monarch listened graciously to her uncle's prepared speech of fulsome welcome heavily overlaid with gratitude at the great honour accorded to him. The Queen was wearing a riding habit of deep brown velvet but the skirt was heavily ornamented by gold wire braid and the bodice, cut like a man's doublet, tight and high-necked, was embroidered in gold thread with a score of gold buttons flashing shafts of light brighter than the sun's rays. Her small neat ruff was of the finest gauze threaded with gold wire and on her red hair she wore a jaunty brown velvet riding hat styled like a man's, small-brimmed and high-crowned with a cluster of feathers and a band of gold and amber jewels.

Thomas then presented his wife and daughters and finally his niece Alice, to whom the queen afforded a brief smile and nod before turning her attention elsewhere. She was then escorted into the Hall, surrounded by her chosen favourites in their peacock finery, to partake of wine and sweetmeats, (of which she was inordinately fond,) before sitting down to dine.

The assembling of the company of some hundred or so richly dressed courtiers and their ladies took a considerable time, while the horses were led to the stables to be attended by their own grooms and Thomas's servants. Room had to be found for the forty carts which had accompanied them, the three hundred remaining carts and their horses being already on their way to the next port of call where the procession was to spend the night.

At last the company was seated in the impressive dining hall liberally decorated by tapestries of the seasons, with branched candelabra hanging from the ceiling pargetted in an intricate design of scrolls and lozenges. Alice saw the Queen studying the new oil portrait of Thomas and his wife displayed in pride of place above the mantled fireplace and wondered what was going through the Queen's mind for when she had earlier teased her uncle about aspiring to the nobility he had boasted that it had been done by the Queen's own sergeant-painter, George Gower.

The Queen was seated at the head of the high table with Thomas on her right and Robert Dudley, to whom she constantly turned in a show of intimacy, on her left. Trestle tables had been set up to complement the seating, all laid with white cloths of fine damask and supplied with silver plates, bowls and serving dishes as well as Venetian glass goblets. Alice knew that her uncle had borrowed some, not an unusual custom as her own family had done so for Elizabeth's wedding, but most of them he had purchased himself and she wondered how he was going to afford this expense. The meal itself consisted of every type of meat and game, roasted, boiled and cold, as well as numerous fish dishes, all served in a variety of sauces and flavoured with herbs, together with pies, tarts, fricasees, cheeses, and elaborate sallets decorated with flowers. The Queen's companions ate with gusto but Alice noted how little she herself ate, choosing small portions and eating slowly and daintily, all the time complementing her hostess Eliza Kitson on the excellence of the board. During the meal a consort of musicians played in the minstrel's gallery running along one side of the hall and Alice noted how the Queen often stopped to listen appreciatively, sometimes gently tapping her fingers to a tune she knew.

Alice herself was too excited to eat much, and too interested in studying the company. She had been able to meet her sister Elizabeth, now Lady Carey and the mother of a small daughter, also called Elizabeth. What a lot of Elizabeths, she thought crossly – her sister, her aunt and now her niece, all named in honour of the Queen herself. A lot of the women also had red hair, dyed with henna, in imitation of the Queen. Alice smiled to herself in the satisfaction that her bright hair colour was natural. She had only had a brief space of time to speak with her sister but had been assured that all was well, determining to seek her out again before the company left to remind her about the possibility of an invitation to Court. Seeing the Queen and being in this renowned company had sharpened her appetite to be a permanent part of this society herself.

When the lengthy meal had finally drawn to its close the Queen held up her hand for silence and publicly thanked Thomas Kitson and his wife for the splendid hospitality she had received in their home. Thomas bowed his acknowledgement then taking a small box from the leather pouch on his belt he presented it to the Queen asking that she might graciously accept this small gift as a token of his undying loyalty and the honour he had been given by her presence in his house. The Queen smiled with pleasure for she adored gifts but when she opened the box and removed its contents there was a gasp from all those in a position to see. It was an enormous jewel, a blue diamond on a pin, surrounded by sapphires (a stone she loved) and surmounted by the royal crest in gold inlaid with diamonds, sapphires and rubies. A look of childish glee crossed the Queen's face for she adored jewels but the Earl of Leicester looked decidedly put out. Alice's eyes widened in astonishment. This must have cost her uncle nearly all of his fortune.

The Queen stood and turned to Thomas. "Sir Thomas Kitson," she said slowly and deliberately. "From this time forward this will be your title. Come to Court on Accession Day and I will formally give you your knighthood."

There was a chorus of polite applause as Thomas vowed his undying gratitude.

After the formal meal had ended the Queen and Sir Thomas Kitson, as he now was, led out the company to the sweet banquet which had been prepared in a pavilion in the gardens at the rear of the house. There sweetmeats and delicacies of custards and fruit pies with creams and sugar confections of ingenious manufacture had been laid out with a selection of fruit and sweet wines. To Alice's surprise she found herself called to her uncle's side while he was in conversation with the Queen and she curtseyed low as Elizabeth commanded her presence.

"Alice Spencer," she said peremptorily. "Daughter of Sir John Spencer of Althorp."

Alice replied nervously, wondering what was to come next.

"Sister to Lady Carey. How old are you?"

"Eighteen, Your Majesty," she replied, her throat dry as the small bright eyes bored into her. She could feel the critical gaze travelling over her but she stood her ground proudly. She had dressed with care in an open green gown of the lightest wool with a cream linen kirtle closely worked with green and blue flowers. The undersleeves beneath green puff sleeves with braided epaulets were of the same flowered stuff. The effect of youthful simplicity enhanced her slender figure. Her ruff was small and neat but of delicate cambric edged with lace and she saw Elizabeth's eyes settle on the red hair tumbling in waves beneath the green cap decorated with tiny pearl beads.

"Your uncle has requested you a place at Court. I would like to know your feelings on this matter for I have a mind to oblige him," Elizabeth said sharply.

Alice's surprise and excitement overcame her intention to be decorous and a wide smile spread across her face as she cried impulsively, "Oh I would like that so much, Your Majesty."

A fleeting smile crossed the Queen's face as she replied in a softer tone, "Attend Sir Thomas at the Accession Day formalities and we will arrange for your appointment also."

Alice continued to stammer her gratitude and her promises to be a loyal servant but the Queen had already turned away, leaving her with the feeling that her greatest dream had come true and this had been the most wonderful day of her life.

Later when the Queen had left and the household returned to normal, if that was possible for they were all exhausted and emotionally drained, Alice went to find her uncle. The new knight was sitting in the parlour with his feet, now encased in velvet slippers, carelessly propped on a walnut table bearing a brimming goblet of wine and indulging in the new fashion of smoking a pipe.

"I cannot thank you enough, Uncle Thomas," she cried impulsively, planting a kiss on his cheek. "I am amazed that you could even find time to think of me in all the worry and excitement of this day."

He looked at her quizzically and gave a lopsided grin. "I don't know if my sister your mother will thank me for this," he said. "But this knighthood has cost me greatly, more than I can really afford, to be honest. I might as well get what advantage I can for the family out of it."

Alice was to stay at Hengrave for a few more days after the Queen's visit and as other guests were also enjoying the Kitson hospitality - there was still a great mountain of left-over food to be consumed - Sir Thomas entertained them with his usual gusto. Hunting parties were arranged, games of bowls and skittles on the greensward before the house and a good-natured archery competition at which

Alice, to the amusement of her uncle, acquitted herself very competently. In the evenings they played chess and cards, one evening they were entertained by a group of local waites and on the day before Alice's departure for Althorp her uncle invited a troupe of players who had been amusing the Withipolls of Christchurch Mansion in nearby Ipswich to come and play at Hengrave.

The small company of five players arrived in the early afternoon to begin their preparations, for they were to commence their presentation at four o' clock so there would be no need of candles to light the dining hall where they were to perform. Imbued with her usual curiosity Alice went to see what was happening and stood in a corner of the hall watching with interest. Firstly the men discussed amongst themselves which direction to play from. The obvious choice seemed to be the back of the hall with two doors from which they could make their exits and entrances, but one of them pointed out the large oriel which distinguished the top of the room. After some discussion they decided to make use of this, a decision further prompted by an adjacent small ante-chamber that could serve as a tiring room. They carried into the hall a wicker basket and a set of poles which they fitted into wooden bases to hold a cloth painted with a sylvan scene which they placed before the entrance to the small chamber. Then they were pacing the floor so that instructions could be given to servants on how far away to place the chairs and benches for the spectators. They had not donned costumes, which Alice supposed were contained in the wicker basket, and were wearing faded old-fashioned doublets and ill-fitting hose. The one who appeared to be their leader, middle-aged and squat with a brown mobile face and eyes that were like black beads, wore his long hair tied by a colourful kerchief. He rapped out orders and the players started to go through a series of rapid movements which involved much changing of places and coming and going at a frenetic pace from behind the painted cloth

Then another man joined them and they stood still as he approached. He was very young, plainly dressed though wearing a small starched ruff and with a clean white shirt showing through the slashes of his doublet, and when he spoke they paid great attention to what he was saying.

"I trust you have all committed to memory the words I have written specially for this evening."

"We have had little time but we have incorporated the new scene into the interlude," the squat brown-faced man replied. "And Tam has fashioned the property as you ordered."

"Well done," the young man replied. "Now go through your paces once more. This is a special performance tonight and I want it to be word perfect."

Alice did not want to spoil the surprise of the performance by watching it in rehearsal so she crept away to change her gown and call for a maid to dress her hair in anticipation of the evening's enjoyment.

The evening was a great success and none was more satisfied than Sir Thomas. To his surprise the action of the play had incorporated within an old tale of romance and knightly prowess a scene where the hero presented to the monarch a rich jewel gained at great cost to his life and had been rewarded by the accolade of knighthood and the hand of the King's beautiful daughter. The young boy in a long blonde wig and blue silk gown held up the great pasteboard jewel for all to see, the brightly painted stones transfigured into gems by the sun's rays which poured unerringly through the oriel window.

The applause was enthusiastic and Sir Thomas warmly thanked the players, not only for making the journey to Hengrave but also for their ingenuity in presenting so topical an allusion to this memorable occasion. "You will find refreshment a-plenty awaiting you in the servants' hall," he said. Then he gathered together his guests to enjoy a cold repast and flagons of wine, now being laid out on the dining table which had been set at the back of the room during the entertainment.

Alice was helping herself to a slice of game pie and a glass of canary wine when she noticed her uncle in conversation with the young man whom she had seen giving instructions to the players and whom she had first considered to be the chief amongst them. When he had not appeared on the stage however she realised he must have been the writer of the improvised interpolation and guessed Sir Thomas was thanking him personally for his ingenuity. Seeing her uncle called away she seized her chance and approached the young man before anyone else could.

"I thought the piece about the jewel really imaginative," she said impulsively. "Did you write it yourself in such a short time after you had been invited here?"

He smiled at her warmth and replied, "Yes, I thought it would be a good idea to include some reference to the occasion once I heard what had so recently taken place. It didn't take me long but I did not know if the actors could learn it in time."

Alice judged that he could only have been about her own age and liked what she saw. He was of medium height and slightly built but his body looked firm and strong as if he exercised it well. His chestnut hair waved from his high forehead onto his shoulders and the grey eyes set in an oval face showed both intelligence and sensitivity. A thin moustache curved around a mouth that seemed set with good humour and his chin with the small pointed beard looked firm and determined.

Spurred by the admiration in her eyes, though unable to decide if they were blue or green, he said, "I wrote one of the songs also, 'I fain would win my heart's desire', sung by our boy heroine."

"He had a beautiful voice," Alice said, adding, "And it was a beautiful song. You are very gifted."

He smiled again at her obvious admiration and decided he liked this young girl with her vivacious face framed in a cloud of glowing copper hair, while Alice was pleased with her decision to wear the gown she had worn for the Queen's visit. She knew it flattered her and she was glad it did not make her look too extravagantly rich before this companion of players.

"My name is Alice Spencer," she offered, holding out her hand.

"And mine is Ferdinando Stanley," he replied, taking it and brushing his lips against her palm. Her eyebrows arched at the unusual name and he laughed as he explained, "After the Holy Roman Emperor. My father has ambitions of grandeur."

Alice wished she could have stayed longer in conversation with this handsome young man, a companion of travelling players, but considered it might not be judged in her best interests. She could already in her mind's eye see her mother's disapproving face and tomorrow she must return home in any case.

"I saw you talking with the Lord Strange," her uncle Thomas remarked later when the company was dispersing and flurries of farewell had been exchanged.

That must be his name with the troupe, she thought. She appreciated the novelty of such a whimsical name for a travelling player, highly suitable to his fanciful imagination. "A very apt name," she laughed. "He is certainly very talented, and so young too."

"That is certainly true. I did ask him to stay the night here, I thought you might have enjoyed talking with him further, but he said he must return to London. No doubt you might meet him again there in the future."

Alice suddenly recollected with a flurry of excitement that she would soon be bound for London herself, and not only London but the royal Court. She had to return to Althorp Manor on the morrow but come Accession Day in November and she would be leaving her home, perhaps for ever. She was uncertain as to how enthusiastic her mother might be about her promised Court appointment but she knew she would have the full support of Uncle Thomas, and perhaps Lady Catherine would be too gratified by her brother's newly-acquired knighthood to make much opposition. Alice fell asleep on her last night at Hengrave Hall dreaming of how she might indeed meet a rich noble husband at the Court but wishing he could be like the young handsome strange young man whose attractive face flitted involuntarily into her thoughts.

CHAPTER 3

Courtship

"Do you think the Queen is serious about marriage with the Duke of Anjou?" Alice asked her new friend Eleanor Bridges.

"There are rumours about it," Eleanor replied. "Why else should the Duke's representative and close friend Monsieur Simier be here at the Court and so extravagantly entertained."

"But the Queen is well past forty."

"Not yet too old for child-bearing, we know that of a fact," said Eleanor. The Queen's ladies were privy to the most intimate facts concerning their mistress.

Alice pulled a face. "I wouldn't like to think I had to wait until I was forty to marry. And what about the matter of he who shall be nameless."

"Ssh," Eleanor giggled. "Walls have ears and you never know who's listening. Gossip is rife here and everyone so keen on their own advancement that no-one scruples to get you into trouble if it serves their interests."

Alice looked nervously around her as they made their way down Whitehall Palace's Stone Gallery, so named because of the classical sculptures adorning the walkway, meeting other ladies and courtiers strolling along its length and talking in groups in the many window bays.

"Besides I vow the Queen herself can hear anything that is said within a hundred yards," Eleanor continued. "You're new here but you must learn your only duty is to please the Queen and not to trust anyone else."

"Is she a hard mistress?" Alice asked. It was her first week at the Palace of Whitehall and everything was new to her.

"In some ways. She demands absolute obedience and utter efficiency. When you are on duty you must pay no attention to anything other than her needs. You are expected to be able to converse with her on any topic she chooses, even religion and philosophy as well as poetry and music, you must know whatever dance she asks you to dance and whatever tune she wants you to play on the lute or the virginals. She will encourage you to gossip freely with her about Court life but not to anyone else under pain of death, she hates her maids chattering, and under no circumstances whatsoever must you return the attentions of young courtiers." Even as she spoke, Eleanor was casting admiring glances at the groups of young men sauntering along and eyeing the girls with interest. "But she genuinely cares about our wellbeing and is sympathetic when we are ill or homesick. And at least we are not on duty all the time, we have our days and hours free because as there are so many girls who crave a position at Court it means we work on a rota of service." Eleanor spoke with the authority of long experience although she herself had only been a maid of honour for less than a year. "Do you think you will be happy here?" she enquired.

Alice replied with certainty. "Yes, I have always wanted to come to Court. And pleasing the Queen and working hard is only what I have been used to with my mother for all my life."

She didn't confess as much to Eleanor who was still a new acquaintance but she relished being in the company of important people, watching them carefully and seeking opportunities to make herself known. She didn't mind sharing the maids' bedchamber with others, the lack of privacy, or having to wear simple white gowns all the time they were in attendance on the Queen. Of course everything was still a novelty to her and Whitehall Palace still a confusing warren of twisting passages and connecting rooms where she needed a guide. Every nook and cranny was of interest to her, every scrap of news fed her curiosity, and participation in the rituals of the Court excited her. No doubt the time would come when familiarity and fixed routines would make for boredom just as at Althorp.

As they reached the end of the gallery they were met by a group of four young men dressed in the height of fashion with tight doublets, padded hose, starched ruffs and feathered hats, talking loudly and laughing together. Suddenly Alice gasped in surprise for one of them was Lord Strange of the company of players. Eleanor noted her sharp intake of breath but made no comment and in some confusion Alice carried on her way, though the young man's eyes had briefly met hers and registered a spark of recognition. She continued to the stairs leading to the privy gardens but then was compelled to turn her head and found that he too had stopped and was looking back. To Eleanor's surprise Alice turned and was retracing her steps while he came to meet her.

"Lord Strange?" she asked, noting how different he looked from the last time she had seen him.

"Lady Fantastick," he quipped, admiring the way her bright hair and flushed cheeks showed to advantage in the simple gown of white damask while her eyes looked decidedly blue. "I did not know you were at Court."

"I am come here only recently to serve the Queen as a maid," she replied.

"I thought I could not possibly have missed you at the Yuletide festivities." He was aware of the interested stares of his companions, one of them whistling softly under his breath.

"No doubt we shall see more of each other." He made an extravagant bow, removing his hat with a flourish, and Alice found herself replying with a brief honour.

Eleanor had been watching the interchange with interest and noted Alice's flushed face when she rejoined her. "How do you know Lord Strange?" she asked with curiosity.

"I met him at my uncle's house, Hengrave Hall in Suffolk, in the company of a troupe of players."

"Yes he does keep players," said Eleanor airily. "In keeping with his usual extravagances."

Trying not to sound too interested, Alice asked off-handedly, "What is he doing at Court?"

Eleanor shrugged, "He's usually at Court. Part of a group of young men who try to impress the girls with their fine clothes and extravagant ways. They say he's always in debt, living above his income."

Alice tried not to show disappointment that she might not be the only girl in whom he showed interest and asked in puzzlement, "But why does he use the name of Lord Strange at Court?"

Eleanor's expression was one of incredulity at a stupid question. "Because that's his title. It's the title of the heir to the Earldom of Derby. Didn't you know that Ferdinando Stanley is the eldest son of Lord Derby?"

Alice did not know whether to laugh or cry. He must think I am such an idiot, she moaned to herself, trying to remember what she had said to him. But then she felt a flicker of excitement deep inside her. Ferdinando Stanley was not a travelling player. Not only was he handsome, interesting and her own age but he was also rich and titled and heir eventually to an earldom. But then an icy tremor replaced the flame burning inside her. Eleanor had hinted that he was a teaser of girls and she was most likely only one of a large number and not even one of the nobility. She determined to put him out of her mind, there was no shortage of personable young men at the Court.

However, this proved to be more difficult than she had thought. It was true that there were many young men crowding the precincts of Whitehall and trying to make themselves noticed for service or preferment. Every morning in the lofty tapestry-hung Presence Chamber they waited in crowds to see the Queen as she made the daily ceremonial progress to the Privy Chamber (where only the most privileged where allowed), accompanied by her ushers, gentlemen, guards, attendants and the full panoply of Court ritual, hoping they might catch her eye so that she would stop and converse with them and remember them for future employment. But in Alice's opinion there were none so handsome or so interesting as Ferdinando Stanley, even without his lineage. Because her eldest sister Anne was married to William Stanley, Lord Monteagle, a distant cousin of the noble family, she knew that Lord Derby had a great estate in the north and indeed owned almost the whole of Lancashire as well as other estates scattered across the country.

It was difficult to keep Lord Strange out of her mind, or to reconcile the young dandy with the enthusiastic companion of travelling players in whose company she had first met him.

The next time Alice encountered him was brief but not without promise. The Queen was taking her customary morning ride with her ladies in St. James's Park when a company of horsemen came to pay respectful homage and amongst the group was Lord Strange. During the short interchange, when Elizabeth called them all by name, the young lord fixed his eyes on Alice and by his expression she knew that she commanded his interest though there was no opportunity to talk. The Queen made a determined effort to keep all her ladies away from any contact with courtiers. Mistress Blanche Parry, one of the Queen's oldest and most trusted attendants, told the girls that Elizabeth considered herself 'in loco parentis' whilst they were in her care and away from their families and held herself responsible for their welfare, but the girls chattered otherwise amongst themselves saying that their mistress was jealous of any competition and wanted to keep the men's admiring attentions only for herself.

When the maids were left to themselves, although ready to be called at a moment's notice, the main topic of current conversation was whether the Queen was considering marriage with the French prince François, Duke of Anjou.

"Why else should Jehan Simier be here, showering her with gifts on behalf of his master and constantly in her company to the exclusion of all else."

"Perhaps he is courting her himself. She certainly plays the coquette with him, smiling enticingly and whispering in his ear."

"There is a rumour that he was seen coming out of her bedchamber." There were muffled giggles from the girls and Catherine Norris whispered, "I heard that he took her nightcap as a present for his master."

"It's all a ploy to make Leicester jealous. His eyes have been straying elsewhere of late," was Anne Carey's pertinent comment.

The maids continued to chatter amongst themselves, not really believing that the Queen was seriously considering marriage at this late stage in her life yet fascinated by her obvious attraction to the Frenchman who was rumoured to be wooing her by proxy on behalf of his master, Anjou. Alice listened with interest, not having the experience to comment herself, but the feeling that romance was in the air was contagious.

In honour of Monsieur Simier the Queen decided to hold a Court ball in March before the sobriety of the Lenten season. Alice was filled with excitement for this would be her first experience of such an event and she secretly hoped it might be an opportunity to meet Ferdinando Stanley, whom she had only glimpsed occasionally in circumstances where it had not been possible to exchange more than a smile of greeting.

On the evening of the ball she entered the Great Hall in company with Eleanor and some of the other maids and stood for a moment in awe at the splendid spectacle. The Great Hall, an enormous space with an arched beamed ceiling and walls covered with glowing Flemish tapestries of classical scenes, was crowded this night with nobles and ladies of all ages. Each strove to outdo the other in the magnificence of their clothes - silks, satins, velvets, brocades - in colours of vibrant intensity with sparkling displays of jewels illuminated by hundreds of candles in wall sconces and candelabra that made the place as bright as day. The maids had been informed they would be able to dress as they chose and Alice was wearing one of the new gowns which Lady Spencer had provided for her acceptance at Court – a vivid emerald satin with sleeves slashed in buttercup yellow and matching long stomacher seeded with pearl beads. A fine tulle ruff framed her face and a pearl-trimmed yellow cap was perched atop her shining hair which fell in waves to her waist.

The Queen had not yet arrived and she was wondering where they were to be seated when to her surprise she found her arm seized by Ferdinando Stanley who whisked her away to a stool near the back of the room while Eleanor was left looking after her in envious astonishment.

"I have been waiting for you," he said, and she made no demur as he seated himself comfortably beside her.

While they waited for the Queen to make a ceremonial entrance they talked easily together, he asking how she liked being at Court, she wanting to know how he passed his time, a reply which was suitably vague.

The Queen's appearance was heralded by trumpets and as she entered the Hall with Monsieur Simier by her side everyone rose to their feet. She was resplendent in silver tissue spangled with diamonds, a huge winged collar of silver lace framing her red hair which was free of all covering apart from a diamond-encrusted circlet resembling a small crown. Then she seated herself on a raised dais of crimson velvet at the top of the room. From a distance she appeared much younger than she really was and the obvious enjoyment in her face enhanced the illusion. Beside her sat Jehan Simier, a small dark man of some forty years old whose brown face lined by the sun had earned the Queen's soubriquet "monkey" in accordance with her habit of awarding affectionate nicknames to her favourites. The Earl of Leicester, seated some distance away, looked both angry and uncomfortable, his sulky florid face causing general amusement amongst the other courtiers. None of the English nobles was happy to see such honour afforded to a Frenchman but to some of them it was worth the experience to see the proud earl so cast down.

When the Queen was seated in state she commanded the masque to begin. With a knowing smile and a simpering acknowledgement to Simier, she announced the theme of the specially composed enactment as being 'Courtship.' A group of six of the most noble ladies made their entrance, amongst whom were Lord Hunsdon's daughters and his daughter-in-law Elizabeth, Alice's sister. They danced together, wearing fantastical gold and silver masks surmounted by curious head tires with symbols of love encased in the constructions – rings, apples, pomegranates, roses, gloves. Then they were approached by six lords who made a dumb show of courting them with gifts and whom the ladies alternately encouraged and refused with dances and mimes.

"Tedious stuff," Ferdinando muttered and Alice dug his ribs playfully.

After much repetition of the same, the dancers were finally matched into six couples who now danced together in a symbol of love and unity.

Under cover of the thunderous applause Ferdinando said, "How much better it would be with words. Some day my players will perform at Court, good plays with excellent actors."

"The music was beautiful," Alice murmured.

"Yes the Bassanos are excellent musicians," he agreed. "You can still have music in plays, but only words can properly convey emotions." His tone was full of enthusiasm and his grey eyes sparkled as Alice realised he was on a subject dear to his heart.

"So you will carry on keeping players?"

"Oh yes," he replied. "A lot of the lords give their name to companies - Leicester, Oxford, Pembroke, Sussex - but with me it is more than a fashionable form of philanthropy. When I was at the University I kept a troupe of jugglers and acrobats but now I support my own small company of actors as you have seen. I intend they shall get bigger and better. Have you heard about the playhouses built in Shoreditch?"

Alice shook her head and he continued, "There are two of them now, the Theatre and the Curtain, only built in the past year or two, but it now means that players do not only have to be travelling companies performing wherever they can but they have places specially built for their needs. Do you know they can hold perhaps three thousand people at a time?"

Alice's eyes widened in astonishment and he revised his opinion, they were green.

He continued, "I'll take you one day. The theatre will be the new entertainment of our time and I intend my players to perform in these new places and at the Court as well, you'll see."

Alice studied him carefully. "I think perhaps you would like to be a player yourself, Lord Strange."

He smiled and was about to reply when dancing was announced and instead he took her hand and led her to the couples gathering now in the space vacated by the masquers. Ferdinando Stanley was an excellent dancer, graceful and athletic and Alice was enjoying the natural rapport they shared when during a particularly energetic Volta she became aware of the Queen's icy glare.

"I don't think we should dance any more together," she said nervously, "the Queen is watching us." Alice was too new at Court not to be afraid of her royal mistress.

"Perhaps you are right, we should look for other partners, just for a time," Ferdinando agreed, following her gaze. "I'm not worried for myself but I do not want to get you into trouble."

The decision was made in any case by the Queen peremptorily ordering the floor to be cleared and taking the hand of her favourite partner, Sir Christopher Hatton who it was said had received his promotion in the Queen's service on the strength of his dancing skills, proceeded to show the assembled company how the Volta should really be danced, glancing now and then to Simier who was showing his obvious admiration at her high leaps and bounds.

As Alice and Ferdinando had separated he had whispered, "I shall seek you again before the evening ends."

Later Alice was approached by her sister Elizabeth, Lady Carey, and she complimented her on her part in the masque. Elizabeth however was looking decidedly out of sorts and said crossly, "I did not perform well, it was all done in haste and we had not enough time to practice. And the stupid headtire was too heavy and kept slipping off my head." Then without preamble she said, "You should not consort so much with Lord Strange."

"Why not? He's surely of a high enough status even for the Spencer girls, his father is Lord Derby," Alice replied sharply.

"He is not in the Queen's favour," Elizabeth snapped.

The statement astounded Alice for the Queen was noticeably fond of the handsome young men who thronged her court. "Because of his association with the players?" she asked.

"What players?" Elizabeth looked perplexed. "It is because he is too close to the throne."

Alice's astonishment was obvious as she stammered, "Too close to the throne?"

"Don't repeat me like a parrot," Elizabeth exclaimed crossly. "His mother, Lady Margaret Stanley, is the granddaughter of the Princess Mary Rose, King Henry's sister and one time Queen of France. The will of King Henry stated that in default of heirs the crown should pass to the descendants of Mary Rose and with the deaths of the Grey sisters Lady Margaret Stanley is now heiress presumptive to the throne. Her son Ferdinando Stanley is next in line."

"I thought that would make him especially amenable to the Queen," Alice stammered, still amazed by the information that Ferdinando had royal blood.

"Don't you know anything, Alice," her sister snapped. "Anyone with royal blood in their veins is anathema to the Queen, she sees them as rivals and potential traitors. Not everyone believes Elizabeth is the rightful Queen and some factions would seek an alternative, especially Catholics."

"Is Ferdinando Stanley a Catholic?" murmured Alice faintly.

"That's debatable." Elizabeth's tone was still curt. "Besides there's the whole matter of the doubtful loyalty of the Earls of Derby. And if you don't know about that then study some history."

"Has George Carey put you up to this?" Alice suddenly exclaimed, seeing behind her sister's ill humour.

Elizabeth remained silent for a moment then said in a softer tone, "He did note it, yes, but I am also concerned for you."

"Are you happy?" Alice asked, suddenly aware of her sister's low spirits.

Again Elizabeth hesitated then replied, "Happy enough. But I get tired of all the rancour and back-biting of the Court, all the triviality of it. I wanted to have a large family and live in the country as we did at Althorp."

Alice could see now how disappointed Elizabeth was that after five years of marriage they had only one child and that a girl and if as in answer to her unspoken question Elizabeth said, "George is becoming increasingly frustrated that I haven't yet given him an heir."

Alice patted her hand reassuringly saying, "There is plenty of time, five years is not long and you are only twenty-five. At least you have proved you can bear children."

Elizabeth smiled and they parted affectionately.

When she had gone, Alice reflected on the conversation, all of which had amazed her. As her knowledge of Ferdinando Stanley increased, so proportionately did her interest. That he should have royal blood in his veins and be a contender for the throne of England should Elizabeth die unmarried was of startling import, also that he could perhaps be a Catholic. A frisson of excitement fluttered along her spine. When he approached her at the close of the evening's entertainment as he had promised she looked at him with new interest and a new sense of awe. He was no longer the friend of the players whom she had first met. However in view of his great lineage it seemed unlikely there could ever be any hope of a permanent relationship between them, even in the heady atmosphere of royal romance.

Yet when they were making their farewells he said, "I want us to continue our acquaintance, Alice Spencer," and she realised his confident boldness, which she had at first surmised to be part of his player's persona, was in reality a product of his aristocratic inheritance. He must be unaware of our family's modest origins she thought. But he continued, "I have to return to Lancashire for a time, my father has commanded my presence at our residence Lathom House as he is planning to visit the Island of Man over which he has lordship. I hope to be back when the Court moves to Greenwich for the summer residence."

Forgetting all the obstacles between them, Alice could not help herself and cried impetuously, "But that is more than three months."

He smiled in satisfaction at her reaction. "Then our next meeting will be all the more pleasurable. Good things are worth the waiting for. You will wait for me won't you?"

Everything Elizabeth Carey had told her passed fleetingly through her head. But the warnings had come too late because Alice Spencer thought she had already fallen in love with Ferdinando Stanley and if he should return her love then she would fear neither their differences of birth nor the Queen's disapproval. Her only fear lay that in the meantime he might forget her and the summer stretched uncertainly ahead. Only a short time ago her desires seemed to have been fulfilled when she had been given the opportunity to live at the Court. Now the promised diversions lacked lustre, and the admiring glances of other young men went unheeded as she waited only for the days to pass until she could see Lord Strange again.

CHAPTER 4

The Suitor

To Alice's surprise the time till Lord Strange's return passed amazingly quickly because the days were filled with activity. In April the Court moved to Windsor Castle for the Garter ceremony on St. George's Day, there was the obligatory picnic and country pursuits on May Day and then the Queen passed a few days at the hunting lodge of Hatfield. All these were novel experiences for Alice and the pervading atmosphere of romance with Simier's continuing wooing of the Queen provided a pleasant ambience for her own romantic dreams.

The Queen's marriage with the Duke of Anjou seemed to becoming progressively more likely and the possibility provided much food for conversation and speculation. Bets were being laid and people were even ordering wedding suits. Simier had put forward the draft of a marriage contract to the Privy Council and the Queen was seen to be increasingly excited as she spent even more time in the French envoy's company.

However not everyone was in agreement with the proposed union. The Puritans were particularly vocal in their opposition to marriage with a French Catholic and spoke against it from their pulpits. The Queen was angered by what she termed unacceptable interference in her private affairs and when the Puritan Philip Stubbes penned his views in a pamphlet she ordered his hand cut off as a warning to others. But some of her councillors were also opposed including the fiercely anti-Catholic Sir Francis Walsingham and, not surprisingly, the Earl of Leicester. The Queen's ladies spent much time discussing the subject but most were not in favour of the marriage, genuinely fearful for the life of their mistress if she should attempt child-bearing at her age. Consequently when Leicester bribed them with gifts and sweetmeats to speak their minds openly to the Queen they were not averse to doing so. The Queen however was furious and warned them in no short measure to mind their own affairs though she suspected that Leicester was behind it for he was popular with most of them.

"He has been spreading it abroad that Simier is giving her magic love potions," Eleanor Bridges giggled to Alice.

But most of the maids were on Leicester's side and pitied him when they heard their mistress screeching to him, making no effort to lower her voice, "Do you think me so unmindful of my royal majesty that in the choice of a husband I would prefer a servant who I myself have raised before the greatest Prince in Christendom?"

However many of the Lords were pleased to see Leicester displaced and the Earl of Sussex was positively helping Jehan Simier with his wooing.

"There is talk that Leicester is planning to kill both Simier and Sussex," Catherine Norris reported.

The rumours, the clandestine manoeuvrings and the frenzied divisions of opinion provided ample diversion for the Queen's ladies, though they found her very difficult to deal with at this time as she alternated between spells of frenetic elation and bouts of deep melancholy, made worse by a severe attack of toothache. So with much to occupy her Alice found the time passing quickly. She did not confide her own romantic aspirations to anyone, not even to her closest friend Eleanor, but at night in the maids' dormitory she let her imagination have free rein and imagined what it would be like to have a closer intimacy with Ferdinando Stanley.

It was August before he returned to the Court which had now moved to the Palace of Greenwich for the summer recess but as soon as he could he sought out Alice. Their first meeting, though it had taken place amongst a crowd of people, was mutually enthusiastic and they both realised that the intervening separation had only increased their pleasure in each other.

Suddenly the Queen's ringing tones broke through the clamorous chatter like a bell commanding sudden silence as she cried, "So, Lord Strange, you have deigned to return to our service. I do not recall we gave our permission for you to stay away so long. I believe you have been to the Island of Man."

Ferdinando approached her, hat in hand, and bowed low before her.

"My most humble apologies, Your Majesty, the winds were contrary and we were delayed by the bad weather. I was in the company of my lord father to whose commands I am subject."

"Are you indeed?" The Queen's tone was ominous, implying that the commands of Lord Derby were less deserving of obedience than those of the monarch. "And was your noble father reasserting his lordship over the island?"

"The Earl of Derby has lordship over the island granted to our ancestors by King Henry IV," Ferdinando said unflinchingly. He resisted the impulse to remind her that the only concession to the English crown was a promise to present the monarch with a pair of falcons on coronation day.

The Queen's mouth tightened and her eyes hardened. People looked on with interest at the confrontation. Some did not understand the import but many nobles knew that the rule of the small independent island in the Irish Sea was a matter of contention with the Sovereign, especially as unofficially Lord Derby was referred to as King of Man. However she let the matter pass, satisfied only in making her disapproval obvious and saying with grim warning in her tone, "I trust you were not plotting mischief with your friends in Lancashire."

"I have no concern with either plots or mischief, Your Majesty. My sole intent is to serve you humbly and I give my life in your service."

She made no attempt to raise him as she said, "But Lancashire is a hotbed of Papism. Know this and impart it to your Catholic neighbours and friends that we will tolerate no disturbance in our realm. We have loyal servants who keep us well informed."

"There is no more loyal servant than I," he replied, not able to keep the belligerence entirely from his tone. "And I am no Papist."

She was silent for a time, surveying the enthralled audience. Then she raised him to his feet saying, "You will stay in London where we are aware of what you are doing and do not leave without our consent."

He retreated backwards from the Queen's presence but as he turned and met Alice's sympathetic gaze, he turned up his eyes in a gesture of frustration.

Later when they were able to talk freely she tried to comfort him by saying, "The Queen is in a difficult mood of late, there's no pleasing her. She's at her wits' end with all this uncertainty about Anjou and last week she was almost killed. She was in the Royal barge with Simier on their way to visit the shipyard at Deptford when a fowler shooting wildfowl at random hit one of the oarsmen by mistake and the shot passed within six feet of the Queen."

"I suppose I should think myself lucky then," he grimaced ruefully. "They are saying that Anjou is coming to Greenwich to visit her at last. Is it true?"

"The answer would seem to be yes, but it is a great secret. No-one is supposed to know, though everyone does," she laughed.

"Well while she is occupied with her suitor we can take advantage and devise more time together. Will you take me as your suitor, Alice?" She searched his face but there was no sign of mockery, only a direct look in his intelligent grey eyes. "I would go down on my knees but there are too many people watching us."

"The suit of Lord Derby's heir is not 'suitable' for the youngest daughter of Sir John Spencer," Alice replied, giving a little grimace of regret. The knowledge about the lordship of an island of which she had never heard had been another surprise.

"Then will Lady Fantastick accept the suit of Lord Strange?" He laughed suddenly. "We can make believe we are players in a comedy."

"That will do well enough while we are here in Greenwich," she agreed.

Their summertime together, their time of holiday, could at least be like a pleasant comedy even if it should last no longer than a tour by travelling players.

Greenwich was the Queen's favourite palace for it was where she was born. The frontage along the river was a long stone edifice broken by square towers and set with mullions, but behind the regular facade a medley of towers and buildings of different shapes and sizes clustered in a world of fantasy reminiscent of an Arthurian romance surrounded by the enchanted woodland of Greenwich Park.

Soon however the pleasant idyll was disrupted by a storm more redolent of tragedy than a pleasant summer comedy. Simier was becoming increasingly irritated by the Queen's reluctance to commit herself to a marriage treaty although she had consented to a visit by her would-be suitor. The Frenchman was suspicious that the Earl of Leicester was undermining her resolve so in a fit of pique he told Elizabeth what many people suspected but what no-one had dared to say - Robert Dudley had found himself a wife. Several months ago he had secretly married the young and beautiful widow of the Earl of Essex, Lettice Knollys, cousin to the Queen. Intent on goading the Queen into action, Simier had no presentiment of the violence of her reaction. Elizabeth was distraught, beside herself with grief and anger, shouting, screaming, crying in turn, vowing vengeance on all within her sight, especially upon Robert Dudley. She had him locked up in the isolated Tower in the Park and was threatening to send him to the Tower of London. Leicester himself was as stricken with grief, vowing his continued loyalty to the Queen and begging for her forgiveness. Most of the courtiers had sympathy for him. For twenty years he had given the Queen all his devotion, suffered her tantrums and humiliations as well as her favour as she vacillated between promising to marry him and spurning his suit, tantalising him with promised delights but never letting him take them. He was a red-blooded man, attractive and virile, with no heirs. No-one could blame him for wanting to marry the beautiful Lettice and put his life on an even keel. No-one but the Queen, who could only see the betrayal of her "dear Robin" and whose life was rocked to its foundation. Everyone felt the brunt of her fury and grief.

Ironically it was Leicester's enemy the Earl of Sussex who persuaded her not to punish him further by sending him to the Tower, pointing out that marriage was hardly a crime. So instead she ordered him to his house at Wanstead, whereupon he took to his bed seeking refuge in illness. When the Queen heard that he was sick she reacted predictably and rushed off to visit him. The stout, red-faced middle-aged man with his brown hair growing sparse was still to her the young man she had loved in the first heady days of her reign. They parted amicably with him promising that nothing would change his affection for her and she ordering that he never bring his wife within her sight.

Once the tumult was over, Court life at Greenwich returned to normal. In the wake of the shock about Leicester's malfede Elizabeth renewed her eagerness to marry her French prince. Simier was exultant over the success of his intervention but most people at Court were of the opinion that it was merely a gesture of defiance as the Queen, still smarting from Leicester's defection, sought to be revenged on her one-time lover.

"She will never marry Anjou," Ferdinando said decidedly. "She has always loved Leicester but would never marry him because she knew it would not please a lot of her people and for the same reason she will never marry a French Catholic. There is too much opposition in England to Papism. She is playing a game and Simier is wasting his time though he doesn't know it."

"You are a good judge of people's motives, Ferdinando," Alice remarked admiringly.

"And their hearts too, I hope?" he said with a questioning grin. "A poet has to understand the heart. I've written a poem for you but I want to set it to music before I give it to you and then I shall serenade you in public."

She giggled happily as a tremor of excitement thrilled down her spine. Many of the young courtiers demonstrated their ability to write verses and musical compositions but to be the subject of one, especially at the hand of such an important lord like Lord Strange, was a great honour.

The Queen finally invited the Duke of Anjou to come to Greenwich to meet her in person although no-one was supposed to know of these arrangements. In order to sustain the secrecy Elizabeth had a number of medieval-styled pavilions erected in the Palace grounds where the two were to meet for the first time clandestinely at night. She had contrived the charade not wanting their first encounter to be official in case they did not like each other and the end result be humiliating after the very public preparations, the Duke was after all eighteen years younger than she was. So the courtiers had to pretend not to notice the pavilions, or at least to assume they were for some entertainment not yet announced.

Everyone was aware of the arrival of the French duke, even though he was hidden away while the Queen went to meet him privately. As the charade continued people talked openly but it soon became obvious that the Queen liked her would-be suitor for her temper improved tremendously and she laughed and frolicked like a young girl. How long this comedy was going to last was a matter of amused speculation by the Court.

In the midst of this heady romantic atmosphere Lord Strange's courtship of his Lady Fantastick progressed to the holding of hands and stolen kisses at every opportunity. Dancing was especially pleasurable because although their stiff clothes and formalised dance steps prevented close physical contact they could communicate with their hands, their eyes, and their eloquent body movements, especially in dances like the Galliards and the provocative Canaries.

A few days after the arrival of Anjou a masque and ball were celebrated in the Great Hall of Greenwich Palace at which all the Court attended, in full awareness that the purpose was to impress the French prince. The hall was magnificently adorned with tapestries and paintings but the dominant feature was a life-size portrait of Elizabeth's father, King Henry VIII, the splendour of which dwarfed all other decoration and beneath which she liked to stand when she greeted foreign ambassadors. Elizabeth was dressed more gloriously than anyone had seen her, in cloth of gold and diamonds, her bodice low-cut, her hair flowing freely, and she danced constantly with all the best dancers so that her own grace and skill could be demonstrated. The fact that the Duke of Anjou was hidden behind a partition to watch was a secret known to all and sundry, especially as the Queen glanced constantly in that direction with coquettish smiles.

Ferdinando sought out Alice where she sat in company with the other maids.

"I've had enough of this play-acting," he whispered. "Meet me near the dolphin fountain. I'll go now, you creep out when there is a lot of activity so you won't be missed."

He gave her no chance to reply and as soon as she could she crept away. When she saw him waiting she gave a little shiver of excitement as she realised they were alone in the darkness, the sounds blurred from within the Palace, the lights filtering through the windows only serving to cast shadows on their expectant faces.

"Come, let's go further amongst the trees where no-one will find us," he said seizing her hand, and as he led the way into the deserted parkland the music and merriment from the palace behind them grew fainter, only discernible in intermittent bursts until finally there was silence.

He stopped and began to kiss her, gently at first then with increasing intensity, his tongue inside her mouth, crushing her to him, and she felt a moment of fear at her first experience of a man's passion. But her heart was beating fast and her loins tingling and her longing for him made resistance impossible as she responded with an eagerness equal to his. His hands moved downwards over her body and he tried to free her breasts from the low neckline of her bodice. When this proved too difficult, exploration restricted by the tight corset, he attempted to lift up her petticoat but was prevented by the padded roll around her hips and the hem of whalebone holding out her skirts.

"Let me unfasten your gown, I can't make love to you in a farthingale," he said.

"We can't," she cried, her eyes rounding in alarm as she realised how far he wanted to go.

"Why not, we love each other. I told you I was your suitor. We are promised to each other aren't we?"

"We are not betrothed," she whispered, the tremors in her body warring against the voices in her head, wanting him but fearful.

He took hold of her hand. "I Ferdinando Stanley do take thee Alice Spencer to be my wedded wife and thereto I plight thee my troth. Now you do the same."

Almost in a dream she replied, "I Alice Spencer do take thee Ferdinando Stanley to be my wedded husband and thereto I plight thee my troth."

"Now we are handfasted," he said. He removed her ruff and headdress so that her hair tumbled down and began to unlace her gown.

It took them a long time to undress and they began to giggle as they struggled with laces and hooks, buttons and trussings, getting cords into knots in their eagerness and Ferdinando swore under his breath. At last they stood in shirt and shift, their whiteness together with Alice's long white stockings making them look like phantoms in the blackness of the night.

The night was warm, the air balmy and fragrant with the woodland scents of evening – musky wild thyme, woodbine and sweet honeysuckle. The lush grass was soft beneath them as they made themselves a bed and the silence of the deserted parkland enveloped them, the only sounds the intermittent squeak of a small creature and the call of an owl to interrupt their moans. Ferdinando was eager but he wanted to savour every moment of his first exploration of his lover's body, and in Alice's initiation into tactile pleasures she was sure that his expert arousal of her virgin flesh demonstrated some prior experience. He was no fumbling novice and in her longing for his kisses and caresses she submitted involuntarily to his complete possession. Afterwards they lay clasped in each other's arms, looking up at the crescent moon and the black velvet sky spangled with stars. The scent of Alice's rose perfume mingled with their sweat and the sickly sweet smell of his seed.

"I want to marry you as soon as possible, Alice," he whispered contentedly.

"How old are you, Ferdinando?" she murmured.

"Twenty. But I'm not of a mind to wait. Especially now we have had our pleasure."

She smiled wryly at the plural but raising herself on one arm to look at him said, "Your family will be displeased."

"My mother won't like it, that's true," he admitted. "She has royal blood and wants me to marry into the highest nobility, perhaps even royalty. But my father and my mother are never in accord about anything, it is not a happy union, they have lived separated for a long time. My father will be less difficult to persuade. Your family might have been farmers not long ago but they are very wealthy now. Yes I have done some research," he confessed as he saw her expression. "My father is short of money. It's a long story and one day I will tell you properly, it has to do partly with the way the monarchs have dealt with us but also both my parents live extravagantly. Besides the upkeep of all our properties my father keeps a mistress and several base-born children and his lifestyle is more expensive than he can afford. That also applies to my mother who believes she should live as royalty and my father has to foot the bill even though they do not live together. Believe me, the fact that your family is very wealthy will be more persuasion for him than impoverished nobility."

"So you are marrying me for my money," Alice said in disappointment and some anger.

"Don't be stupid, I would take you in your shift. I am marrying you because I love you, from the very first moment I think, when you thought me a player at your uncle's house. But I am saying that your family's wealth will be a deciding factor with my father." He leant over to kiss her lingeringly and as his passion began to rise again almost forgot his argument. Then he forced himself to wait, saying, "However the greatest advantage in our favour is that the Queen will be pleased."

"The Queen?" she asked in puzzlement. "I thought the Queen would be even more angry with you."

"Oh no, quite the opposite," he said with some satisfaction. "If I had secretly become affianced to a girl from one of the great noble families as my mother wishes, the Howards, Sussexes, Oxfords for example, especially someone with royal blood in their veins and perhaps Catholic connections, then the Queen would have me in the Tower for she would see me as even more of a threat. But marriage with the daughter of a sheep farmer and a committed Protestant will keep me out of trouble in her eyes. Oh yes, Alice, I think that will be our trump card."

"Ferdinando Stanley, I am almost speechless," Alice said at last.

"An excellent thing in woman," he retorted and as she thumped his chest he caught her in his arms and began to kiss her again until all else was forgotten in a repeat of the consummation of their passion.

It was a long time before they struggled back into their clothes and Alice looked with dismay at the stains on her shift and stockings, while Ferdinando realised he had put the trussing in the wrong holes and his hose hung crookedly.

"I don't think we had better return to the Ball," she giggled as she tried to coax her hair into some sort of order beneath her veil.

"Do you really want to? I have no desire to watch the Queen flirting with her would-be suitor when we have overtaken them."

They giggled again although mention of the Queen made Alice realise she might have to invent an excuse if she had been missed. They crept surreptitiously around the back of the palace and it was only when they had found a door where they could reach their own chambers that she realised her ruff was still lying on the grass. She shrugged carelessly and with a last quick embrace they scampered up quiet stairways hoping no-one had seen them.

When Queen Elizabeth was satisfied that she liked the Duke of Anjou enough to present him to the Court as her official suitor, the masquerade of secrecy was abandoned. She flirted with him openly, kept him always by her side and he showered her with gifts. When the time came for him to return to France they parted with affection and she wrote a poem expressing her sentiments. But no promises had been made and no marriage contract signed. Elizabeth was to continue ruling as the Virgin Queen.

When at the end of the summer the Court returned to Whitehall, one of the Queen's maids at least was no longer a virgin.

CHAPTER 5

Contracted

The young couple stood outside Derby House, the four storey imposing stone mansion on St. Peter's Hill, the bulk of Paul's church standing sentinel to the rear.

"You don't need to be afraid, he isn't an ogre," Ferdinando assured Alice but she looked in trepidation at the massive stone arch, flanked on either side by gatehouses, through which they were about to pass.

Ferdinando had already had one interview with his father, where he had declared his intention of marrying and asked for parental blessing. "This is only a formality, my lord, because we are already wed, having plighted our troth together and enjoyed marital relations," he had announced boldly.

Despite his confident assurance and the knowledge that this was enough to claim legal validity for their union, he was afraid of his father's anger and knew that he could bring about a formal objection on the grounds that he was under age and that there had been no witnesses. Because he had expected opposition he had prepared for all possible objections so that although the interview had been lengthy and not altogether pleasant the final outcome had been that Lord Derby had weakened and invited his son to bring his prospective bride for his approval.

Now they were preparing to enter his presence. As they stood before the arch joining together the two gatehouses, Alice looked up at the eagle carved in the stone. "Our family crest," Ferdinando explained.

"Why is there a child with the eagle?" asked Alice curiously.

Ferdinando laughed. "The story has to do with an ancestor of mine. His wife had not borne him children though he did have an illegitimate son. One day he put the child in a tree and bringing out his wife on a supposedly casual stroll pointed out to her the babe and suggested that since an eagle had fortuitously brought a child in their midst it was obviously a sign that they should adopt him. Whether she believed his story or not, that is what happened and since then it has remained part of our crest."

"I hope you won't play such a trick on me," Alice said light-heartedly, but she had no such fears because she knew she would give him sons.

They entered a courtyard and passed through another stone arch to the front of the four-storey mansion and Ferdinando rang the huge brass bell hanging beside the portal of solid oak studded and bound with decorative iron. It was answered immediately by a manservant in green livery and on recognising the young lord he escorted them across the marble-tiled hall, up a wide oak staircase and along a passageway lined with a succession of narrow lancet windows. On the threshold of Lord Derby's study and library he announced them and they entered a long panelled room almost entirely filled with shelves of leather-bound books yet surprisingly light on account of the large leaded window.

Ferdinando and Alice made their respectful honours and Henry Stanley rose from his seat behind a desk covered with papers and maps. "Queen's business," he said, wafting his hand across the disorder and coming to meet them. He surveyed them gravely then lifted up Alice's chin so that she looked into his eyes. She saw a man of some fifty years, tall and spare with stooping shoulders, thinning receding grey hair and a long narrow face with pouched melancholy eyes and a straggly beard. There was no resemblance whatsoever to Ferdinando. For his part, the sight of the young girl with her copper hair and sparkling blue-green eyes seemed to bring a ray of sunshine into the room and her vivacity touched his world-weary soul and a mind overburdened with state affairs. He noted with approval that though she was dressed well and appropriate to the occasion in a plain gown of blue say-soft, a mixed wool and silk, with a small feathered hat, there was none of the extravagance or affectation of many Court ladies.

("I vow he was seeing my father's gold dancing before his eyes," Alice later laughed to Ferdinando), but she was mistaken in the reasons for his seeming satisfaction.

"So you are Alice Spencer and you are going to marry my son, I believe," he said, surveying them both with a forbidding severity. But by his words they knew that their marriage was now a fait accompli and all that remained were the arrangements to be finalised, legal and financial. They had not yet broached the matter to Sir John and Lady Spencer but it was assumed that once permission had been granted by the Earl of Derby there would be no objections from them to a marriage between their youngest daughter and the heir to the great Lord whose land holdings stretched across the country and beyond. The only matter under consideration would be the amount of her dowry.

"You will be married here in London," Lord Derby stated. "Your lady mother has recently arrived at Court and your brother William will be able to attend now that his term at Oxford is finished."

"I would like that to be as soon as possible," Ferdinando requested.

His father looked at him sharply but then continued, "That is probable because I must leave for Paris shortly, the Queen is sending me as ambassador to King Henri of France. This business with his brother the Duke of Anjou is not done, the Queen is still making a show of considering marriage with him. Would to God it were as simple as your approaching nuptials would seem to be." He sighed and they understood he had no liking for the task that had been imposed upon him. "I will negotiate the Queen's permission for your union, she has reason to be grateful to me at this time," he continued, and Ferdinando heaved a sigh of relief that he would not have to run the gauntlet of his Sovereign's unpredictability. She would indeed be only too eager to gratify Lord Henry at this time, knowing that his embassage to the French Court would cost him a great deal of money for she never paid the expenses of her ambassadors on these costly visits, but both father and son surmised she would be satisfied by the choice of a bride without noble connections. "After your marriage you will live here at Derby House but I would like you to go up to Lancashire and check on the estates in my absence, I do not know how long I shall be away."

When details had been arranged, the betrothed couple were ready to depart for Lord Derby was too busy to spare them any more time. However he studied Alice again carefully. During the short time he had talked with her he had seen signs of her intelligence and the self-confidence she exhibited without any pretensions.

"You seem to be imbued with good sense," he said, "more so than many a pampered daughter of the nobility. I hope that you will be a restraining influence on my son's extravagant tastes and his yearning for a life other than that of a respected overlord of a noble estate."

Alice surmised he was referring to Ferdinando's passion for the Arts although he had told her that his father also patronised a troupe of players.

Then Lord Derby's face softened and he said sadly, "I am happy that you are entering into a marriage based on mutual affection and for that reason I am willing to overlook much. So many of our noble marriages are arranged without thought of personal inclination or compatability of temperament. I have suffered much from such a union."

Then the moment of self-revelation passed and he dismissed them brusquely, turning back to contemplation of the Queen's business evident upon his desk.

Once in the courtyard again the two breathed a united sigh of relief and for a few moments their pent-up anxieties dissolved into peals of laughter.

Then Alice said, "He wasn't an ogre after all. I thought he was kind."

"Don't be misled," Ferdinando warned. "He is much preoccupied with the Queen's affairs at this time which fortunately has worked to our advantage. But it is true that having suffered an unhappy marriage for many years, I told you he and my mother live separately, and having a constant affection for his more humble mistress he would not wish the same for me, no matter how tempting an alternative there might be. I believe he does have a genuine concern for his children, including my four half-siblings. But there is also the matter of your father's wealth," he added mischievously, "I told you that would count with him. He complains about my extravagant lifestyle but he is always in debt himself, not least through service to the Queen. At least he has offered to gain her permission for our marriage, a necessary formality but I do not see how she can refuse him at this time when she is reliant on his service. Now all we have to deal with are your parents, Alice."

Alice thought it wise to confide first in her mother when she made the necessary journey home to Althorp, the first time since she had gone to Court, and broached the subject immediately as her return was unexpected and her mother perplexed by it.

"Are you with child?" Lady Catherine asked immediately, forcing the words from between tight lips and with an ominous scowl on her face as she sat bolt upright in the chair in her private parlour where she had often interviewed her daughters in the past.

"I don't know," Alice stammered, experiencing a return of the old nervousness she had always felt when faced with her mother's disapproval.

"You don't know!" her mother roared. "God's bones, girl, are you so simple that you do not know if you are with child. Have you done the act? I knew no good would come of letting you go off to London and the debaucheries of the Court, I should never have let Thomas persuade me."

"I am not sure if I am with child or not, mother, it is a possibility but you need not worry because my marriage is arranged."

"Alice Spencer, you do not arrange your own marriage. That is a matter for your father and myself to consider. To choose a husband and take matters into your own hands is outside all the bounds of propriety. You have always been too independent but this outrage will make us outcasts in society, after all our efforts to rise in the world and the excellent unions we arranged for your sisters."

Alice allowed her mother to bewail for a while longer, finding a secret enjoyment in her uncharacteristic loss of composure, then when she paused for breath interrupted with, "Not when my future husband is in line to the throne of England and kin to the Queen who has given her consent."

She almost laughed at the expression on the face of Lady Catherine who, after a few moments' consternation, gasped, "The Queen has given her permission for your marriage?"

"Yes, Mother. The Queen's permission is necessary because Lord Strange is in direct line to the throne, his mother is heiress presumptive to the crown of England. The Queen has given her permission for me, your youngest daughter, to marry Lord Derby's heir, a more splendid match than either of my sisters for I shall be a countess and there is even a possibility that one day I might be Queen."

Lady Spencer was almost gasping for breath and as Alice began to unfold the story she could see her mother's anger dissipating and a visible excitement beginning to animate her whole frame. This would be the final accolade for the Kitsons and the Spencers, self-made gentry and now with a foot in the aristocracy, perhaps even royalty.

Alice left her mother to relate the news to her father before the expected summons for herself. Now would come the tedious official proceedings – her parents would go to London to meet Lord Derby, lawyers would be put to work to negotiate financial matters, a dowry and marriage settlements would be agreed upon, not without haggling, then finally a contract would be signed. At least matters would be concluded as quickly as possible under the circumstances and not dragged on for months, even years, as sometimes was the case. As she lay in her old bed in the chamber she had occupied all her life she suddenly thought of the eagle on the Derby crest and the words came into her mind, "They shall mount up with wings as eagles." That was what she was going to do. If the Queen never married, and it did not seem as if she ever would, then there was a possibility that Ferdinando could inherit her crown and she, Alice Spencer, might be Queen of England. It was a heady thought. She couldn't wait to tell Elizabeth and Anne. Elizabeth had married the Lord Chamberlain's son and Ann had married into a lesser branch of the Stanley family but she had found her handsome prince and she loved him, how she loved him. Her sisters had borne their husbands only daughters but she would bear Ferdinando sons, many sons to inherit the great destiny that lay before them. She could not believe that all her dreams had been fulfilled in such a short time.

CHAPTER 6

Premonitions

The marriage was a private affair solemnized at Derby House in the presence of family and close friends. Alice would have liked a Court wedding and Lady Spencer would have preferred Althorp, but circumstances dictated otherwise. Lord Derby was on the point of leaving for France for an indeterminate period of time, Alice knew she was definitely expecting a child, and there would have been the awkward predicament of what to do about the Queen – if she had agreed to attend the expense would have been phenomenal and if she had refused the humiliation would have been unbearable.

Another embarrassment was the enforced reunion of Lord and Lady Derby. Refusing to stay at Derby House with her estranged husband she was dwelling in a house in Clerkenwell that belonged to a kinsman and Ferdinando had taken Alice to meet her there. Alice did not know what to expect from her future mother-in-law, of royal descent and some notoriety in living apart from her husband, (the Queen was opposed to such conduct by married ladies) and felt nervous as she was led into her presence.

Her nervousness did not abate on her first sight of Lady Margaret Stanley who was one of the most beautiful women she had ever encountered. Not yet forty years old, she was tall and slender with a perfect oval face, high forehead and pale creamy complexion, almond eyes beneath finely-arched brows and the hair showing beneath her jewelled cap was a deep auburn. She realised from whom Ferdinando had inherited his own good looks. ("She resembles her grandmother Mary Rose, Queen of France, who was reputed to be very beautiful," he had said.) Her crimson and gold gown of stiff brocade heavily embroidered in gold thread had long hanging sleeves trimmed with sable fur and around her small waist a pomander and jewelled purse swung on a gold chain interlaced with rubies. There were jewels around her neck, on her fingers and in her ears. There was an undeniable regality about her in the way she walked, her graceful gestures, the cool detachment of her gaze. Alice felt unusually intimidated beneath her cool surveillance.

"I must tell you that I would have preferred a different bride for my son," she said in a clear bell-like voice, the economy of the statement implying all the details of the noble union she had wished for. "Nevertheless what is done is done so I bear you no ill will."

Ill will there might not be but Alice had the distinct impression there would be no warmth.

"My son has spoken freely with me and assured me of your mutual affection."

Again she paused and left Alice in no doubt about the words not said - that no girl could resist affection for Ferdinando though she remained puzzled by his own partiality.

However, unknown to the two young people standing anxiously before her, Lady Margaret had given some thought to her grandparents. After being married unwillingly to the ageing King of France, upon his death Mary Rose had chosen with her heart and married the commoner Charles Brandon despite fierce opposition to the love match. She gave no indication of her thoughts but said, "I hope you will find joy in your marriage for it is a blessing not granted to everyone."

When they were dismissed from her presence Alice doubted she would ever feel affection for her mother-in-law nor get close to her, and surmised that Ferdinando must never have known demonstrative maternal love even though he greatly admired his mother. She determined she would make up for any close affection he might have lacked.

Another member of the Stanley family to make her acquaintance was Ferdinando's younger brother William who had been studying at Oxford and to whom she took an instant dislike, perhaps after hearing him say to Ferdinando, "I intend to do better for myself in marriage, I shall not look below the nobility."

Her hurt was alleviated by hearing Ferdinando's infectious laugh as he cried boisterously, "Well I wish you joy then but your happinesss will never be able to rival mine."

William was a younger edition of his father, though not yet eighteen years old. He was tall with the same spare frame and dark brown hair, a dark beard and moustache adorning his long thin face. His eyes were too pale a grey, lacking the expressiveness of Ferdinando's but with a cool intelligent scrutiny. Alice could understand how women might be attracted by the aura of aristocratic arrogance overlaying his narrow features and reminiscent of his mother but intuited that while her husband followed his heart, his brother followed his head.

Even though a private affair, the nuptials were celebrated with all customary luxury at Derby House and Lord and Lady Derby made a semblance of being in accord for the occasion. The bride and groom, together with family and guests, were as sumptuously garbed as for a Court wedding. Alice wore her hair loose for the last time, flowing over the gold brocade gown and only held in place by a circlet of gold set with diamonds, Ferdinando's wedding gift to her. As she revelled in her new husband's admiring glances she thought again how handsome he was in his wedding suit of silver brocade slashed with purple and believed herself to be the most fortunate girl in the world.

After the feasting and drinking and revelry they submitted to the customary ceremony of being put to bed, she throwing her stockings to the maids and he being escorted to the bedchamber with bawdy jests from his inebriated companions, all the time laughing to themselves at the falsity of the ritual and patiently awaiting the time when they could be alone and make love for the first time in a comfortable bed, totally unencumbered.

Soon after the wedding Lord Derby left for Paris as the Queen's ambassador to the French King. He was accompanied by some two hundred attendants and mountains of baggage, dreading equally the personal expense for such a necessary show of importance at the French Court and the sensitivity of the negotiations he must pursue. In his absence Ferdinando and Alice were to take charge at Derby House and the new Lady Strange had to accustom herself to both the honours and responsibilities of heading a noble residence as well as the not altogether welcome presence of William Stanley.

Remembering everything her mother had demonstrated at Althorp, Alice was determined to adjust herself to her new role and set herself to learn everything she could about the Derby household. With her newly dressed 'married head' she felt more mature, though the tight pins made her head ache and she loved the night-time when she could unbind the heavy tresses and her husband could caress them as they made love. However before long the newly-weds were made even more aware of their new responsibilities.

They were seated for the mid-day meal when a servant from Cleveland Row arrived at Derby House with the disturbing news that the Countess of Derby, still in residence there, found herself in serious trouble and her sons were commanded to go to her immediately. The servants halted in their serving and the meal was left unattended as the brothers rose, putting aside their knives and half-eaten meats. Alice anxiously watched them leave in haste, Ferdinando's face creased with worry as he called for horses to be saddled.

When the brothers arrived at Clerkenwell they found Lady Margaret pacing up and down the parlour in a state of agitation, her lips set in a tight line.

"I have this morning been summoned to a private audience with the Queen," she reported, "alone in the Privy Chamber but escorted by Lord Burghley. She accused me of speaking openly my opposition to her marriage with the Duke of Anjou."

"And have you done so?" Ferdinando asked boldly.

The Countess hesitated then said, "Not in so many words, no. In general conversation with the ladies of the Bedchamber I have agreed that it is not a wise thing to do, but so everyone else thinks. I have made no direct statement to the fact, it was merely said in passing, amongst people I considered to be my friends."

"There are few friends at Court, mother, as you should well know," said Ferdinando ruefully. "Everyone is only eager for his own advancement. Do you suspect anyone who might have relayed an exaggerated version to the Queen?"

Lady Margaret hesitated then admitted reluctantly, "Lady Shrewsbury was present. She mistrusts me as a threat to the claims of her granddaughter Arbella Stuart whom she is determined should succeed Elizabeth."

Ferdinando laughed mirthlessly. "Lady Shrewsbury is a ruthless scheming woman with a tendency to make trouble. But the Queen knows this and cannot long believe her word over yours."

"The Queen accused me of trying to prevent her marriage because that would threaten my position as heiress presumptive by her father's will. She accused me of threatening the stability of the State," the Countess confessed miserably. "She has ordered that I be barred from the Court and I must also not leave the house."

Ferdinando felt worried but he said reassuringly, "It was all done on the spur of the moment, you know how her anger flares and then a short time later she has completely forgotten. She is particularly sensitive about her relationship with Anjou and will brook no criticism. She will make an example of you then change her mind about keeping you here. Don't worry, it will soon blow over. And anyway," he added mischievously, "you have always said you are not happy at Court."

Lady Margaret smiled ruefully but said, "That may be true but I mislike the alterative of being confined here in the house."

"We will come and visit you," William promised and Ferdinando suggested, "Why not send the Queen a gift to placate her, you know she is always swayed by gifts."

"Accompanied by my abject apologies," the Countess said bitterly. "But yes you are right, it might serve to eat humble pie."

Her sons exchanged rueful glances for this was a dish their noble mother was unaccustomed to eat.

When they left Cleveland Row they were still perturbed, despite their assurances, and Ferdinando relayed everything to his wife who was waiting in anxious anticipation. "It is always like this when my mother is at Court," he explained. "The Queen commands her presence because she is always uneasy when we are out of sight. She always suspects we are plotting mischief and looks for any excuse to prove it. She also dislikes the fact that my mother and father are separated. Not being married herself, she believes that husbands and wives should stay together under all circumstances and gives the offenders short shrift."

Alice hated to see the carefree Ferdinando troubled and putting her arm affectionately around his shoulders said, "Don't worry, I'm sure the Queen can't be angry for long, we know how quickly her moods change. And you have me now to share your problems, I am part of your family now."

He kissed her lovingly. "I don't want anything to spoil these first few weeks of our marriage but you can see now how the Queen mistrusts us. She has always hated the descendants of Mary Rose and looks for any sign that we may be plotting against her."

Alice began to understand for the first time the delicate position of her husband's mother and matters did not improve. A week later frightening information was brought to Derby House by no less a person than the Queen's principal secretary, Sir Francis Walsingham himself, that Lady Margaret Stanley had attempted to poison the Queen. She had sent a box of Elizabeth's favourite sweetmeats as a gift but fortunately the Queen's taster had discovered a poisonous substance before she had tried them.

"Poison!" Alice had cried, her mouth suddenly dry.

But Ferdinando was furious. "This is all a lie," he cried. "A plot to discredit us. An excuse to remove my mother, as the Queen did with the Grey sisters. Is she to go to the Tower too?"

"Careful," Sir Francis Walsingham warned, "This could be interpreted as treasonous talk." The deep-set watchful eyes in his long saturnine face beneath the black skull cap looked consideringly at the young man. "There was poison discovered in the delicacies, that is a fact."

"Then it was put there on the journey to the Palace, or in the Palace itself," Ferdinando insisted rashly. "The Countess my mother is incapable of such an intention to any living creature, let alone her Sovereign Prince whom she has always served loyally."

"The matter will be investigated thoroughly," Sir Francis said calmly.

The arrival at Derby House of this tall dark middle-aged man, always garbed in black so that the Queen's nickname for him was 'the Moor', had been a shock. He did not use underlings and delegated to no-one, having taken it upon himself single-handedly to be responsible for the Queen's safety. He never let the slightest suspicion go unexplored and his personal appearance demonstrated how seriously the matter was being considered.

"You cannot deny that your lady mother has an interest in alchemy. I have it on good authority that she consorts with 'wizards and cunning men' and keeps a physician skilled in the distillation of various substances," he said.

Ferdinando could not suppress a shiver as he studied the dark impassive face of this man who seemed to know everything about everybody. He was uncomfortably aware of his mother's predilection for sorcerers and fortune tellers, in part a result of her unhappy life, but he said, "The Countess's physician is necessary for her poor health and his special remedies are to alleviate the constant pain in her limbs."

Sir Francis added, "It has also been said that she has had the Queen's horoscope cast."

He paused significantly for there was no need to remind them that this was a treasonable offence. Suddenly a shadow seemed to dim the splendour of the great salon at Derby House with its paintings and colourful hangings, carved oak furniture spread with silk cushions, heavy gold candlesticks.

Sir Francis rose and his tall black figure now appeared menacing. "I have already spoken with Lady Derby," he said. "She has been ordered not to leave her house. I suggest that you also remain in London, Lord Strange."

His leaving of the house was smooth and spectral without even the sound of his footsteps or his long black gown brushing the floor.

When the Secretary had left, Ferdinando called for his valet Ashby, ordering, "Prepare my finest doublet, the black velvet with the gold lace."

"Where are you going?" Alice asked fearfully.

"Where am I going? I am going to the Queen," he cried furiously. "She cannot treat my mother thus, on a trumped up charge of treason that could carry the penalty of death."

Alice paled and seized his arm. "No, you cannot do that. Oh my darling husband you must not anger the Queen any more. If you accuse her of wrong doing she will put you in The Tower. I could not bear that for myself but more importantly it would harm your family and do no good at all."

William added his pleas to hers, "It would serve for nothing but to make matters worse, Ferdinando, you know that."

With a great effort he calmed down but his anger was the more inflamed by the knowledge that he was the one who had suggested the gift to the Queen.

"This is done purposefully with my father away. Why is the Queen so afraid of us when we are the most loyal subjects she has. Who in their right mind would wish to have royal blood in their ancestry. Come," he said to William, "let us go to visit our mother and see if we can speak to her physician."

In the house at Cleveland Row the Countess sat calmly working on a piece of embroidery with a lady-in-waiting but her face was pale and drawn and it was obvious her attention was not on what she was doing. She greeted them tonelessly then said in a helpless voice, "The Queen is determined to put me in the Tower. I shall die there like my cousin Lady Catherine Grey."

"Even the Queen cannot be so heartless," Ferdinando insisted. "She is frightening us. She knows there is no truth in the accusation. It is all a ploy to make sure we know our place, to keep a threat hanging over us so that we never step out of line. Tell me exactly what happened."

Lady Margaret sighed. "I did as you suggested. Knowing the Queen's sweet tooth I had my cook make some sugar confections, he has a particular skill in this, and had them sent to the Queen. He is completely trustworthy, you know he has been with me for a long time."

"Who delivered them?"

"A young serving boy called Alan Fortescue. He is somewhat slow-witted and has neither the years nor the intelligence for treachery."

"But he could have been used by someone."

"It is possible I suppose."

"And your physician with his skill in distilling potions. I would like to speak with him."

"Sir Francis Walsingham has taken away Dr. Randall for questioning."

Ferdinando groaned and looked helplessly at William, then turning to his mother asked, "Is it possible that someone could have subverted him?"

"I do not think so. He has served me for a long time and I have always found him perfectly trustworthy, his medication is of great help to me."

"Then *if* there was poison in the sweetmeats, and I suppose we must acknowledge Walsingham's honesty, it was added later with the certain intention of embroiling us in treason," Ferdinando said grimly. "At the very least by someone wanting to discredit us with the Queen. However although Sir Francis Walsingham is known to be ruthless I believe in his integrity, he will ferret out the truth and we must put our trust in that."

The Countess nodded and smiled weakly, finding some comfort in the assertions of her elder son.

"All we can do then is wait and hope that eventually this farrago will be seen for what it is, a fantasy fit for a playhouse," he added.

"Let us hope it resolves in comedy rather than tragedy then," William commented and was rewarded by a warning look from his brother.

Ferdinando was all too aware that even if the Countess was proved innocent it would not remove the Queen's suspicion of her and before very long there might be another 'incident'. Being in line to the throne meant they walked a permanent tightrope. However the brothers assured their mother they would do all in their power to support her but though they tried to make their farewells as cheerful as possible there was little consolation to be found in the immediate future and they knew it would be a time of worry and uncertainty.

Later Alice asked her husband, "Who do you think might have put poison in the sweetmeats?"

"Who has an interest in trying to be rid of my mother? Either someone who fears her claim to the throne, including the Queen herself, or someone with an interest in promoting the French Catholic marriage. If the poison was put into the sweetmeats before they left Cleveland Row then that would implicate one of the servants and I don't like to worry my mother with that possibility. Not all of them are her own personal attendants, some of them belong to the household of her cousin Thomas Seckart. However if the poison was added later then that would assume prior knowledge that the gift was to be made, unless it was a spontaneous action by someone seizing a fortuitous opportunity."

"Say the Queen herself?"

"I do not like to think of that possibility. My own opinion is that, since the last fiasco when my mother has been confined to the house at Cleveland Row, a spy has been planted there to keep her under surveillance, perhaps by Burghley or Walsingham. Such an infiltrator could have reported the gift being prepared and was either told to meddle with it himself or someone else did so before it reached the Queen."

"Are you saying it could have been arranged by people in authority?" Alice asked fearfully, not wanting to mention any names.

Ferdinando hesitated before replying. "I do not like to go down that road but yes, I think it is a possibility."

"But for what purpose?" Alice was a stranger to the world of political machinations and Ferdinando did not want to worry his wife but neither did he wish to keep her unaware of the perils lying beneath his inheritance. But instead of voicing the possibility that someone might wish to remove the Countess of Derby from the scene he said merely, "It is proof that we are mistrusted and a warning that the government keeps a close watch on us."

The weeks of anxiety were finally brought to an end but not without casualties. The Queen graciously condescended to pardon her dear cousin for any malice that may or may not have been intended "since we are so close in blood and do not desire any lack of trust between us," but still commanded that Lady Margaret should be kept under house arrest with her kinsman until further notice. The hapless physician Dr. Randall had been committed to The Tower for having admitted that he dabbled in poisonous substances for some of his remedies, though he was adamant that none such had found its way into the gift for the Queen.

Ferdinando was furious that his mother had not been completely exonerated.

"Her innocence has not been made clear, a pardon is not a declaration of innocence and this is being used as an excuse to still keep her under house arrest. And why has no attempt been made to find the real poisoner, I'm sure it was within their investigative skills. The matter smells of involvement by a person or people who it is not in the State's interest to investigate. Dr. Randal is being detained in The Tower but Sir Francis Walsingham would have determined that the poison placed in the dish of sweetmeats was not the same as anything used by him so they dare not proceed further with him, it is merely proof that they have taken some action. I do not like to suspect Walsingham or State machinations but it seems to me this affair has been contrived with two purposes in mind – one, to keep my mother out of the way like the Grey sisters and two, to frighten us, to ensure we know our place and don't step out of line."

"It has certainly frightened me," said William feelingly. "So much so that I am going to go abroad as soon as I can. I have no intention of staying here in this climate of suspicion, swung to and fro at the mercy of the Queen's moods and perhaps all of us in danger of being committed to the Tower for some imagined offence. I intend to go and visit father in Paris and finish my studies there. Then I shall travel, as far as possible away from England."

Ferdinando looked wistful for a moment. "You are fortunate you are not the heir," he said quietly. "I must stay here, father has asked me to go to Lancashire and see to the estate."

Before they left London to go their separate ways the brothers went to bid farewell to the Countess and this time Alice accompanied them. As they were led to her parlour they heard the sound of gentle weeping. The men drew back but something prompted Alice to enter. Lady Margaret looked up uneasily, quickly wiping the tears from her eyes with a kerchief, but impulsively Alice knelt down beside her and took the cold hands in hers. The Countess expected to see either pity or embarrassment in the young girl's face but all she saw in the blue-green eyes was a great sadness. She clasped the hands of her daughter-in-law and said softly, "I have always been unhappy. Unhappy in my marriage and unhappy with my inheritance. When I was a young girl the Earl of Northumberland wanted me to marry his son Guildford Dudley. My father would not allow it and instead he married my cousin, Lady Jane Grey. I sometimes think it might have been better if I had and all my sorrows would be ended."

"Then you would not have given me Ferdinando," Alice said softly.

The Countess smiled through her tears and gently touched her face. It was as if for an instant a curtain had lifted on the private world of the noble lady with her dangerous inheritance. Then just as swiftly the curtain fell and her face resumed its expression of impassive hauteur. Without any apology she rose elegantly from her seat so that Alice was forced to rise also and called to her sons in a cool, commanding tone.

They made their farewells formally and listened attentively to their mother's instructions for their future behaviour. But finally Lady Margaret's unease manifested itself as she confessed, "I do wish I could leave here. I hate the thought of being confined to this house and hope and pray it might not be of too long duration."

She could occupy herself with reading, embroidery, music and the offices of religion for a time and the house was large and comfortable with extensive gardens but her sentence was still an imprisonment. She was mercifully unaware that she would never be allowed to leave the house at Clerkenwell and she would never return to Lathom where she had once reigned as queen in all but name.

Later as Alice lay in bed, leaning against Ferdinando with his hands curled comfortably around her waist, she was forced to reconsider her position. Perhaps the life of the Countess of Derby was not to be envied, despite her beauty, her wealth, her lineage. Involuntarily she recalled the earlier words of her sister Elizabeth warning her of the dangers of being associated with anyone close to the throne. She had now personally experienced a demonstration of those dangers. Ferdinando kissed the top of her head and her fears lessened. The difference between her and Lady Margaret was that she had a husband whom she loved from the depths of her being. Soon she would prove that love by bearing him a son and heir.

That certainty propelled her through the unfamiliar experience of carrying a child through the hot London summer, watching her body acquire a grotesque shape, finding small tasks increasingly difficult to perform in the heavy constricting garments, not being able to make love. When she was finally brought to bed the certainty sustained her through the hours of labour where she kept Ferdinando's grateful face constantly before her as the ultimate reward of such an ordeal. Then at last the torture ended and a piercing cry rang out in the chamber followed by the midwife's pronouncement, "It's a girl."

"A girl!" Alice could not believe her ears. "After all that agony, it's only a girl!" Her distraught voice carried all the disappointment and anger surging through her weary body. How could God have allowed her to suffer such torment for the ultimate result to be a girl. She buried her face in the pillows, oblivious to the congratulations being offered by the friends and companions who had shared her hours of labour and were now gathered around the bed. The midwife had ignored her outburst, not unusual amongst the ladies of quality whom she served, and gone to wash the child. Then after the women had been dismissed she called Ferdinando into the darkly curtained room where a blazing fire was burning in the grate even though it was a warm day.

Alice refused to look at him and kept her face buried in the pillows mumbling, "I'm so sorry."

He touched her gently saying, "My darling Alice, we have a child. A healthy child and you have survived, we have much to be thankful for. We are both twenty-one years old, there is plenty of time to have sons." She didn't reply, and he asked, "How shall we name her?"

"Not Elizabeth, anything but Elizabeth," came the sulky reply. "Anne."

"Anne," he repeated in bemusement. "Why Anne?"

"Because it isn't Elizabeth," she cried angrily. Then she turned to look at him saying defiantly, "My sister is called Anne and I like the name."

"Then Anne it shall be." He laughed at her angry sulky face, feeling a rush of emotion that she had survived the ordeal safely as he took her gently in his arms.

Later when she was alone and trying to sleep, difficult to do despite her exhaustion because her body hurt and her head was full of whirling thoughts, she looked back over the past months since her marriage. She had expected so much and in those first heady weeks it seemed she had everything she had always wanted – flying on wings of eagles. But the frightening plot against the family and now the birth of a daughter were not the auguries she had expected for the future.

But Alice was young and resilient. She accepted that these momentary doubts were probably the result of her present weakness. There might well be no more fears and if there were she had Ferdinando to deal with them while there was plenty of time to give him sons.

CHAPTER 7

The Visit

When a manservant informed Lord Strange that a jewel merchant by the name of Master Grantley wished to see him, Alice's eyes rounded with excitement. Perhaps her husband was planning to surprise her with a special gift for her birthday so she made no attempt to accompany him when he followed the servant into the hall where the caller was waiting. Ferdinando however was more concerned that the visitor might have come to demand an outstanding debt but wanted to ascertain the actual purpose of the visit before inviting him into one of the private rooms.

The man standing respectfully in the hall was a stranger. He was about forty years old, tall and elegantly dressed in padded doublet of green braided velvet with close fitting hose, a matching short cape flung casually across one shoulder, a high-crowned hat of black velvet with brooches on his short dark hair tinged with grey. His face was fine-boned with a high forehead and his grey eyes gentle and discerning but with undoubted intelligence in their depths. He was obviously a gentleman of some distinction.

"Lord Strange." He made a low bow.

"Master Grantley?" The stranger merely nodded. "What is your business with me?" Ferdinando asked.

"My business is of a personal nature, my lord. Is it possible to speak in private?"

"Are you a goldsmith? Do you deal in jewels?"

The man smiled. "That is one way of describing my work."

Ferdinando was puzzled and a little uneasy but he was also curious, and he had an instinct that the stranger did not intend harm so after a moment's thought escorted him into one of the small reception parlours leading off from the hall. He motioned him to a seat by the empty firegrate and closed the door, although he himself stood waiting expectantly.

"Forgive the subterfuge, my lord, but I am afraid it is necessary. My true name is Father Edmund Campion of the Jesuit college in Rome. You will be too young to remember me."

Ferdinando's heart lurched uncomfortably. He was too young to remember when Edmund Campion had been an esteemed fellow at Oxford, in great favour with the Queen as an orator, but he knew the story of how the scholar had renounced the Anglican church and converted to Catholocism ten years ago when he had gone to teach at the Catholic college in Douai in northern France.

"I cannot see you have any business with me," Ferdinando said firmly.

"I think I do have business with you, my lord. You are the heir to a great earldom in Lancashire where the old faith is still kept and practised with great fervour by most of your neighbours and tenants, and because many of your family are still true to the faith."

"I am not a Catholic," Ferdinando insisted.

The priest smiled gently. "There are those amongst your acquaintances who are sure that in your heart you are a true believer. We all pray that you will openly accept the faith, as I did myself."

"I am not a Catholic," Ferdinando repeated. "I am a true adherent of the Anglican church and I trust your visit is not merely an attempt to convert me. If so it is futile and dangerous for you are well aware that priests are forbidden in England on pain of death."

"That is the reason I travel disguised. But I am more than an ordinary priest. Together with Father Persons, my superior in the Jesuit order, I have been chosen as the vanguard of a new mission to convert England back to the old faith. We are in England to prepare the way, as John the Baptist did for our Lord, and we will be followed by a great wave of evangelising priests. We are come first to seek the support of lords and notable Catholics for our mission and that is the reason I am come to you. The approval of one of the most powerful lords in the kingdom, lord of a shire that is almost entirely Catholic, would be invaluable. You must recall your lord father's loyalty to Queen Mary Tudor and King Philip of Spain."

"That was in the past," said Ferdinando. "There is now no more loyal subject of the Queen than my father, Lord Derby."

"That is why we look to you," said Father Campion. "We look to you to lead Lancashire. Possibly to play a more important role with your royal descent."

Ferdinando seated himself on the chair opposite, leaning forward to his visitor as he asked, "Do you plan an uprising? If there is a mission to convert England back to the Catholic faith does this go hand in hand with the removal of the Queen?"

"I look no further than a return to the true faith for this my country," the priest said quietly. "What happens afterwards is in the hands of God."

"I will never betray my Queen and my country which is now a Protestant country," said Ferdinando firmly. "You may be assured of that."

Father Campion was silent for a moment then he said, "I do not believe you would betray your Catholic friends either. I am due in Lancashire shortly. I would like to be able to give them the assurance that you will look kindly upon them."

"It is the law of the land to make official note of all recusants," Ferdinando reminded him.

"But I know that you and your father do not always do so," said the priest with a slight smile. "Look in your heart, my lord, and question where your true desire lies."

As Ferdinando said nothing Edmund Campion rose to leave. "I trust you will not repeat any of the words I have said, my lord, or make mention of this visit. I have confidence that you will not betray me. You do not know that I am in England. You have never heard my name other than Master Grantley, a jewel merchant."

Ferdinando hesitated briefly then said, "It shall be so." Then to his unease the priest gave him a blessing, accompanied by the sign of the cross.

He was tempted to lead his visitor to the back entrance but thought that would arouse suspicion if any of the servants were watching so called for Povey, the manservant who had announced the visitor, and asked him to escort Master Grantley to the door as the merchant's business was done.

He did not entirely keep his word. Alice was full of questions about jewels and besides he had no intention of ever keeping secrets from his wife. He was troubled and he needed to unburden himself to her and ask her advice.

She was forceful in her condemnation. "It was very wrong of the priest, who are forbidden in England, to come to you in this way," she fumed. "If it were discovered he had been here then the Queen could accuse you of plotting with the Catholics, she would never believe you were tricked into entertaining him."

"That is what I am afraid of," he admitted. "We must wipe it from our minds. The visit never happened, I have never met Edmund Campion who left England while I was still a boy, and I have never met a jewel merchant called Master Grantley."

"The manservant Povey knows that you did," Alice reminded him.

"And this conversation has never taken place between us," he said fervently.

"Darling, I would never speak of anything to anyone that might in the slightest degree injure you but do not try to shelter me. I am your wife and if there is danger for you I intend to share it," Alice said, aware yet again of perils surrounding them.

Sir Francis Walsingham's network of foreign spies were soon giving him information regarding the "English Mission" as it was termed and Father Edmund Campion and his superior Father Robert Persons, in their many guises and aliases, were being sought with ruthless vigour. As more information was gathered Ferdinando and Alice held their breath in case Edmund Campion's visit to Derby House should be discovered. The priest had been recognised in several places in Lancashire though he had evaded capture, but later in the year he was taken in Berkshire. He was hanged, drawn and quartered in London after lengthy torture but would not reveal the names of any of the people he had contacted. The Queen had tried to save him, remembering his scholarly gifts and courtesy of times past, but he would not recant his Catholic faith nor promise to desist from action which the State considered treasonable saying only, "I would do as God should give me grace."

Ferdinando thought sorrowfully of the gentle kindly visitor as his terrible sentence was announced, to the joy of many Londoners who went to watch his cruel execution. His companion Robert Persons managed to evade capture and returned to France, prepared now to send a wave of Jesuit priests to continue the work he and Edmund Campion had begun.

Later in the summer Ferdinando announced, "I think it is time I paid a visit to Lathom House as my father wished. The weather is good for a ride north."

"Then I'm coming with you!" Alice said decidedly. London was hot, dirty and riotous, the sultry weather encouraging stinking debris and frayed tempers, and besides she was ready for a break from domestic duties though she took little interest in the child who was cared for by a wet nurse and several nursery maids.

"It's a long way, two hundred miles on horseback, five days hard riding," her husband said.

Alice laughed dismissively. "When we went to Deptford to see 'The Golden Hind' do you remember how amazed we were that Drake could have gone all around the world in such a little ship. What is two hundred miles compared to that! And what are five nights on the road compared to three years aboard that little space."

Earlier that year Francis Drake had arrived triumphantly back in London after his three year voyage round the world, bringing with him a horde of precious treasure of which Elizabeth received a substantial proportion. Furious at his plundering of Spanish ships, King Philip ordered the Queen to have him executed. Instead she went to Deptford and knighted him on board his own ship, levelling a personal insult to the Spanish king whom she believed was behind all the attempts to make England a Catholic country again. Lord and Lady Strange had gone with many others to see the now famous ship docked at Deptford.

Ferdinando was no longer surprised by his young wife's spirit and enjoyment of life but he said mischievously, "I thought you would have preferred London life and the Court with all its entertainments and diversions. And perhaps the opportunity for a little flirtation while I am away."

But he was secretly glad that he was to have her company, especially when she thumped him playfully in the ribs saying, "I don't want anyone but you, and one reason I want to accompany you is to make sure you have no-one but me. And besides I want to see your house where one day I shall live."

"Yes I want very much for you to see Lathom House," he replied.

The five days riding were not too tiresome as Alice relished the chance to see a large part of England that she had only heard about, not having previously travelled beyond Northamptonshire, Suffolk and London. They were accompanied by a body of attendants and servants, they stayed in adequate inns at night and the weather was fine, cloudy and cooler on the road but free of rain. Her only complaint was at having to ride side-saddle. "I don't see why women cannot ride astride with more suitable clothing," she grumbled, but she was a competent horsewoman and was able to keep pace with the men without great difficulty.

One of their stops on the road was at the little walled town of Coventry where they discovered the Earl of Leicester's Men on tour. Coventry was a popular venue for players as it stood on the main road to the north-west and was a thriving market town with the promise of large audiences. When it was known that Lord and Lady Strange had arrived in the town with an escort of courtiers the mayor cordially invited them to the Drapers' Hall for the evening entertainment which, in accordance with general practice, was 'the mayor's play', acted before an invited audience of civic dignitaries and their guests in order to gain official approval for subsequent per-formances to the general public. Ferdinando and Alice were made much of by the mayor and aldermen and given the chairs of honour where they were plied with an exceptionally good Burgundy wine. For Alice it brought back memories of the performance at Hengrave when she had first met Ferdinando, although this company comprised some dozen players and musicians and they performed on a wooden stage which they had erected at the top of the hall.

"Leicester's Men are one of the best companies of players," Ferdinando explained. "I would like to poach some of their actors though the popular James Burbage isn't with them on this tour. He is part-owner of the

Theatre in Shoreditch so I suppose his duties are keeping him there."

'Robin of the Greenwoode' was an apt play for the midland shires and was warmly received by the audience. In appreciation the mayor rewarded them with a sum of money and gave permission for them to play for a general audience on the following day.

"This is a means for the town authorities to ingratiate themselves with the players' patron, Leicester, who wields considerable influence here in his own domains," Ferdinando further explained to Alice, rewarding the players himself and publicly voicing his appreciation.

His own players were somewhere on the road but they had seen no sight of them by the time they arrived in Lancashire. They crossed into the shire by means of the stone bridge over the River Mersey at Warrington, the only bridge across the wide river and which Ferdinando said had been built by one of his ancestors. From there it was less than an hour to the busy market town of Wigan on the River Douglas.

"The Douglas runs close by Lathom," Ferdinando explained as they clattered through the market place, having to make their way through the throngs of people gossiping by the market cross and doing business at the Moot Hall in front of the church. They were forced to give them passage but all the townspeople stopped in their activities to survey the rich cavalcade which they recognised from regular visits. Once out of the town through the Standish gate the road began to rise gradually as they rode through open countryside, the river meandering in the valley below, until after a further two miles they came to Standish, another little market town astride an important crossroads. "Preston is straight ahead, Manchester to the east," Ferdinando said, but their road lay westwards. They were now into open countryside again and he pointed out a black and white manor house just visible on a plateau behind a copse of beech trees. "That's Standish Hall, home of the Standish family, close in the opposite direction is Langtree Hall and beyond that Park Hall, home of the Hoghton family. Further eastwards is Duxbury Hall, owned also by the Standish family, then Astley Hall, home of the Charnocks. We shall shortly pass Wrightington Hall where the Wrightington family live then Parbold Hall, home of the Lathom family. All these are our neighbours and the Earl of Derby is their overlord as Lord Lieutenant of the shire. All are Catholics."

"What a lot of Halls so close together," Alice commented in surprise. "And they are all Catholics you say?"

"They are not magnificent manors, quite modest by the standards of Althorp and Hengrave," Ferdinando said mischievously. "Their owners on the whole are knighted gentry, but they are closely bound together by ties of marriage and..," he paused significantly, "by religion."

After they had passed Wrightington Hall with its lake, closely followed by Parbold Hall, both timber and plaster modest manors, the road began to rise gradually and became stony until it levelled out and here Ferdinando reined in his horse and halted.

"Marry gypee!" Alice exclaimed in amazement. The trees had thinned out and the road dropped steeply to a flat plain at the bottom of which the River Douglas threaded its meandering path. The view stretched for miles in all directions, low hills to the north, valleys and peaks with higher hills on the southern horizon, while in front of them to the west was the flat plain which stretched as far as the eye could see. "Is that the sea?" she asked, wrinkling her eyes at a silver ribbon of light in the far distance.

"It is indeed the Lancashire coast and to the far left you can just make out the outlines of the mountains of Wales. But from the bottom of this hill to the sea are treacherous marshes which are difficult to cross without personal experience or a guide to lead you. But look there, in the near distance to your left, you can see Lathom House."

Alice followed his pointing finger and after a few minutes' consideration could make out a huge, sprawling, turreted building that looked like a castle set on a wide plateau. "God's bones, that's no house," she exclaimed, "it's a castle."

Ferdinando just smiled and as they made their way down the steep stony hill, the horses clattering and slipping, the size of the building became more obvious, covering about five acres. The road levelled out as they passed a set of stocks occupied by a dejected young man on the edge of what seemed to be a small hamlet, then crossed a narrow stone bridge over the River Douglas beside which stood a thatched tavern. Then the road began to rise again as they passed through the little village of Newburgh.

"How are the baggage carts to manage this road?" she asked.

"There is another road but it's longer and the view is better this way," he replied.

Taking the higher road by the village green they left the village behind them and were in open countryside again, flat and obviously marshy with clumps of sedge, ragwort and pennywort while wild orchids flowered beside the narrow road which was lined with willow and alder. Now the castle could be clearly seen in all its splendour, its great size becoming ever more formidable as they rode nearer. The high surrounding wall was encircled by a moat more than twenty feet wide across which straddled a barbican flanked by two towers. Nine more tall stone towers were set at intervals on the walls, boldly proclaiming the defensive aspect. Alice gasped in astonishment as before proceeding through the gatehouse Ferdinando paused to let her savour the size and grandeur of the exterior. Then saluted by the guards on duty they passed into an inner courtyard where people were busily going about their business – maids carrying buckets and tubs, some carpenters sawing wood and she could hear the ring of an anvil. Here they were faced by the imposing entrance to the castle itself. Even so, they had to pass through yet another range of defensive buildings into a second courtyard where servants crossed to and fro before they arrived at the Derby living quarters, a series of buildings of varied shapes and sizes constructed of brick and stone but mostly with lath and plaster above. These were linked into a homogeneous whole by stone walls on which stood nine more towers. In the centre was a tower higher than the rest. "The Eagle Tower", said Ferdinando, smiling in amusement as he watched Alice's reaction.

"You never told me the truth," she said to him in half-reproach. "You always called it a house. Instead it's one of the largest castles I have ever seen. Why," she exclaimed in a sudden moment of revelation, "it's like Richmond Palace."

"Richmond Palace was built as a copy of Lathom," her husband said proudly. "Henry Tudor, King Henry

VII, was step-son to my ancestor the first Lord Derby and when he came here he was so impressed that he built his new London palace, Richmond, in the same style."

Alice sat stupefied as she absorbed the size and magnificence of her husband's home and realised that one day she would be mistress here. She loved Ferdinando with all her heart. She loved him because he was young and handsome. Lying in bed in the morning she would gaze on him when he slept, his chestnut hair waving on the pillow, a light stubble on his face before he trimmed his moustache and small pointed beard. She loved him because he was intelligent and witty, good-natured and amusing, and she would rather share his company than anyone else's. She loved him because he was talented, writing poetry and music and scenes for plays. But as well as all that, he had given her for her home the most amazing castle over which one day she would preside as Countess of Derby, almost a queen in her own realm.

"Why do you call it Lathom House and not Lathom Castle, which it surely is," she asked.

He laughed again, his grey eyes sparkling mischievously. "It wouldn't do. Only kings have castles."

She realised now the significance of the rumours she had heard, that Lord Derby was almost a king here in Lancashire.

"Of course it isn't always comfortable inside," Ferdinando warned. "As a matter of fact my father prefers to be at our new house in the deer park, he nearly always entertains there in greater luxury and comfort, or at our house at Knowsley."

But Alice was thinking that she would far rather be mistress of this imposing castle, though she was beginning to have some understanding of the great expense under which Earl Henry laboured with so many splendid establishments to keep.

"Come, let us go into the house and I will show you everything. When we are settled we will arrange banquets and hunting parties and my players should arrive shortly when all the local gentry will be invited to watch them perform," Ferdinando was saying, excited at the prospect, his face animated with joy at the completion of their long journey and Alice's obvious admiration of his ancestral home.

Everyone was happy to see the young lord and make the acquaintance of his lovely wife and Alice found herself the object of admiring curiosity from the multitude of servants and retainers who thronged Lathom House, her position as mistress elevated in the absence of the Countess. Invitations were soon on the way to all the local gentry, some of them carried personally by their hosts as Fedinando made visits to neighbouring halls, partly to keep his pulse on what his tenants were up to and partly to proudly exhibit Alice.

One afternoon they were returning from a visit to the Bradshaighs at their manor house on the far side of Standish when on returning to the small town they could hear laughter and music coming from the market place.

"I believe my players have arrived," Ferdinando cried joyfully and they made their way towards the market cross in front of the church of St. Lawrence where a huge crowd had gathered. The plain-garbed townsfolk nudged each other and pointed to the group of flamboyant courtiers including the Lord and Lady Strange whom they recognised immediately, enviously noting the silks, satins and velvets in vivid colours of blue, crimson, gold, green, the feathered and jewelled hats, the mettlesome horses. But after a swift perusal they turned their attention back to the antics of the half-dozen actors frolicking before a painted cloth hung before their wagon, behind which they disappeared from time to time to change hats and masks and bring out different properties.

"They are performing an interlude," Ferdinando explained. "This is usual for a market place where a full-length play would not be practical without seats and with uncertain weather. Also in some places the authorities are likely to come and move them on before they could finish a long play, although they seldom do that in Lancashire, knowing that the players have my protection. But sometimes an interlude is used as an advertisement to whet people's appetite for a subsequent performance in an indoor space like a guildhall or a school, for which there will be a charge."

The performance also included some tumbling to the delight of the audience, especially the enthralled children. The noble company stayed on horseback until the performance had ended, adding their applause to that of the townsfolk who had been happy to have an excuse to leave their work for a brief spell. When the actors carried around baskets for some reward Ferdinando threw in a gold angel but most of the spectators were suddenly in haste to be gone though when Ferdinando called in a loud voice, softening it with a charming smile, "Nay good people of Standish, surely you can find a penny for an excellent entertainment," a few of them shame-facedly returned to drop in a half-penny or a farthing.

"Can you be at Lathom to entertain us this evening?" Ferdinando asked his players after they had made their courtesies to him and he had praised their performance of the comic interlude, one of several in their repertoire suitable for playing on the road.

"It takes a long time to manoeuvre the cart down Parbold Hill, my lord," Dick Chapman, the leader of the players, said deferentially.

"Yes of course, I forget it is different for us on horseback," Ferdinando replied easily. "Play for us on the morrow. Accommodate yourselves in one of the outhouses as usual and there will be plenty of food for you in the kitchen."

Ferdinando was happy to have his players at Lathom and the following evening they entertained the household in the Great Hall. The vast space had thick colourful tapestries of hunting scenes covering the stone walls and an enormous stone fireplace carved with the Stanley heraldic emblems, the eagle in central place, almost filled one wall. From the hammer-beamed ceiling hung numerous candelabra, some of them holding as many as fifty candles. At the top of the hall was a raised dais for the Earl and his family to sit on ceremonial occasions but this evening the players used it as a stage and instead Lord and Lady Strange occupied the throne-like chairs placed on the stone floor. In her elevated role as mistress of an ancient castle, surrounded by numerous attendants, Alice couldn't help comparing herself to Queen Elizabeth at the Whitehall entertainments when she, Alice Spencer, had been one of the lowly spectators.

The scene was repeated on the following evening with the addition of many of the Lancashire gentry to watch the performance which had been preceded by a sumptuous feast. Lord and Lady Strange were dressed in the latest Court fashions - stiffly padded, richly decorated with gold braid and jewelry, elaborate ruffs of gossamer lace - and were regarded with admiring attention. The clothes of their companions, although of the best quality, were outdated to London eyes and more reminiscent of King Henry's reign than his daughter's.

Ferdinando had explained to Alice, "Display is a means of enhancing our prestige though I have to inform Master Farrington, the household comptroller, of all expenses for the household books as he is extremely diligent in reporting every detail. But my father is of the opinion that the Earls of Derby must be seen to live like princes." Looking at his face Alice was undecided whether he was jesting or not.

During the evening Ferdinando was in talk with one of their neighbours, Sir Thomas Hesketh of Rufford Hall. A big, bluff, red-faced elderly man, he humbly invited Lord and Lady Strange to a supper at his Hall after which he would be pleased to offer an entertainment by his own players. Ferdinando was aware that Sir Thomas had recently been imprisoned for recusancy at the instigation of Lord Derby, even though he was related to the Stanleys through marriage, and wondered if this was an attempt to gauge the feelings of Lord Derby's heir on this matter. However an opportunity to watch a company of players was too good to miss and he accepted the invitation graciously.

Rufford Hall was some five miles to the west of Lathom, a timber-framed manor house with a striking pattern of white chevrons and crosses on the blackened timbers, a characteristic feature of Halls in Lancashire. The manor was of modest proportions but the Great Hall, once the medieval living quarters, was impressive with five bays and a huge oriel window overlooking formal gardens. It was ideal for theatrical performances because its fifteen foot length was bigger than many house spaces and the old-fashioned carved oak screen which separated the hall from the kitchens served as a backdrop for the action and from where the players could make their exits and entrances. Above it was a gallery for musicians and during the plentiful meal a small music consort - a lutenist, a viol player and a recorder player – had been ensconced there. The company was polite and deferential and besides Sir Thomas Hesketh and his wife included their eldest son Robert together with his wife, a relative of the Stanleys from nearby Crosshall, and a man in early middle age by the name of Bartholomew Hesketh. He introduced himself as being the son of Gabriel Hesketh of Aughton, a cousin of Sir Thomas.

When the meal had been cleared away, seats were then set for the entertainment with Lord and Lady Strange seated in the places of honour on carved chairs facing the imposing screen. Sir Thomas and his family were ranged on either side with the household servants behind on benches. To Ferdinando's surprise Sir Thomas Hesketh's half dozen players enacted an old miracle play of Daniel and Nebuchadnezzar in which the central theme illustrated the persistence of faith despite persecution. There was no doubt that the faith intended was the Catholic religion for the sacrament of penance and absolution was incorporated at one point. Alice turned towards her husband, her eyebrows arched questioningly. He replied by raising his eyes to the roof beams and drawing her attention to where the five wounds of Christ were prominently displayed in company with hovering wooden angels.

They listened attentively however and when the play was ended Ferdinando complimented the players (though their performance had been rustic and Alice had found some of their Lancashire speech difficult to understand), giving them a generous donation which they received enthusiastically. Then when Sir Thomas was serving them with cups of wine, Ferdinando said carefully to his host, "You are aware, Sir Thomas, that the miracle plays have been forbidden since Elizabeth came to the throne?"

"Does it matter if we still perform them here in our own homes, so far from the Court?" he replied challengingly. "They are a part of our faith, of the old faith. We still hold to that faith in our private worship."

"It is against the law," Ferdinando said firmly. "When your players travel to other houses, do they also perform these plays?"

"Sometimes, together with interludes. You cannot be unaware, my lord, that most people in these parts hold to the old faith privately even while keeping the laws publicly."

"So your players do not perform such plays publicly, in the street or the market place, as they used to do on the old festivals like the feast of Corpus Christi?"

"Now that is a forbidden festival, my lord. We do not dare anything in public."

Ferdinando knew that Sir Thomas had equivocated instead of answering the question and realised that the older man was deliberately challenging him. He remained thoughtful as Thomas Hesketh continued, "You must understand, my lord, that my players are not like yours, performing at Court and having licences for travelling the length and breadth of the country due to your patronage. My players are local men, men who work at their trades for most of the time, performing when the need arises as they used to do in the old days when the Bible plays involved the whole community on festival days. Their repertoire is not large and the old plays are those with which they are most familiar. As a keeper of players yourself, surely you do not begrudge these men the opportunity to earn a few pence. I myself cannot support them in a manner to guarantee their livelihood and they are not licenced to travel on the road."

Ferdinando knew now that his host had been deliberately testing him but he had no intention of entering into a discussion, either about the cost of keeping players or of the persistence of the old faith in these parts. However he felt the need to issue a warning nonetheless and said, "If I were you, Sir Thomas, I would encourage my players to widen their repertoire or return to their trades. Or even entertain us with music, as they did so ably over supper."

He considered the conversation now to be ended amicably but then Sir Thomas surprised him by saying, "I trust you were as grieved as we were by the terrible death afforded to Father Campion."

"I prayed for him, as for any man forced to endure such a cruel end."

"He made himself greatly beloved here in this area."

"I would prefer to know nothing of this, Sir Thomas, as priests are forbidden in England. You know Lord Derby's position as Lord Lieutenant of the shire and in his absence that duty falls to me."

"Father Campion told us he had visited you and you received him kindly," Sir Thomas continued boldly.

Ferdinando felt a cold hand clutch his heart and cried, fiercer and louder than he had intended, "I keep the laws of the land and would advise you to do so also lest you find yourself again experiencing the unfortunate penalties."

Alice turned her head on hearing her husband's uncharacteristic outburst and sensing some discord crossed over to them smiling and saying calmly, "I have just received from Lady Hesketh a most welcome receipt for relieving children's coughs, useful for our own little Anne. Now may I thank you once again, Sir Thomas, for a most pleasant evening in every way."

Both men smiled at her gratefully and grasped the opportunity to exchange courteous farewells. But when their horses were saddled and they were mounted with their attendants waiting to lead the way home to Lathom, Ferdinando took a last look back at Rufford Hall. With the house shrouded in darkness the white chevrons and crosses gleamed through the blackness and he saw Sir Thomas and his cousin Benjamin Hesketh outlined in the light from the open door. For some unaccountable reason a shiver of apprehension tickled his spine.

CHAPTER 8

Gatherings

Alice had given birth to another daughter. She was inconsolable even though Ferdinando made no complaint, assuring her that he welcomed a companion for three year old Anne and the only matter of importance was the health and safety of both mother and child. But she was overcome with disappointment and a sense of failure, feeling she was no better than her sisters at bearing sons when she had been so confident she could better them. She refused to have anything to do with the little girl and Ferdinando's attempts to name her after either of their mothers fell on deaf ears.

"We have to give her a name," he insisted.

"Frances."

"Why Frances? It isn't a family name. We don't know anyone called Frances."

"I like the name," she said stubbornly.

She seemed determined not to bestow family names on her daughters, whom she considered evidences of her failure to produce the necessary son and heir, and Ferdinando sighed as he reluctantly agreed. He visited the nursery, amused by little Anne's precocious development, but Alice showed scant interest, leaving the children in the care of their nursery maids unless friends and family came to call and then she would display them in their infant finery.

Apart from the disappointment of having borne two girls, Alice was enjoying life. Lord and Lady Strange were often at Court where Ferdinando was esteemed for his talents and his generosity and his wife basked in his popularity. His verses were passed around his acquaintances and he was always willing to give encouragement and financial assistance to young writers. His latest protégée was Robert Greene, a flamboyant character whose egocentric behaviour was complemented by his appearance - bright red hair which he wore long and greased to a point on top of his head with an equally long beard which he never trimmed. He was a university man of scholarship and after travelling extensively in Europe he had taken up writing on his return and had come to Ferdinando's notice when he dedicated his 'Mirror of Modesty' to the Countess of Derby. He was now busy writing romances and pamphlets of contemporary life and it was his sharp wit and keen eye for the vagaries of Londoners that led Ferdinando to think he had the makings of a playwright and was therefore encouraging him to write plays, there being a shortage of writers for the theatre. Lord Strange's own company of players was popular and when in London often entertained at Derby House and the houses of other noblemen. The Earl of Leicester was a friend and they sometimes shared their players, occasionally performing together at Leicester House in the Strand and at the Earl's house in Wanstead when he was able to live with his wife Lettice away from the eyes of the Queen. He also had living with him a new poet by the name of Edmund Spenser whom he introduced to the Court where the young man found immediate popularity with his 'Shepherds' Calendar' and long pastoral entitled 'Colin Clout's Come Home Again'. Copies sold out immediately and he was greatly in demand to make readings from his poems. He was feted by the nobility who clamoured for his presence in their houses and hoped to receive a mention in his poems and Alice found her own independent prestige by the fact that he claimed kinship with her family and dedicated some of his verses to the Spencer sisters. Most noble ladies were honoured by poets at some time but to be favoured by the finest poet of the age was a great distinction.

Ferdinando had also struck up an acquaintance with another newcomer to the Court by the name of Walter Raleigh. A West-Country squire of modest background, Raleigh had found favour with the Queen because of his good looks and fine figure, his eloquent tongue that could flatter easily and his undoubted charm, and she appeared to have chosen him as her new favourite. Ferdinando liked him because he wrote accomplished verses and was a man of diverse talents. Raleigh's interests were not only literary and he could talk knowledgeably about philosophy and alchemy, exploration and colonialism, medicine and the new sciences. A group of like-minded men met regularly at his house for discussion and argument and to carry out experiments, some of them noblemen like Lord Strange, the Earl of Northumberland and the young Earl of Southampton. One member was an Italian named Giordano Bruno, a specialist in the occult, whom Ferdinando had met when he had gone to Oxford in company with other lords to hear the Italian give a series of lectures there. He was a very small man, (it was said he had a name longer than his body) waving his arms around like a juggler doing tricks, but the controversy circling around him centred on his controversial opinions, especially with regard to religion. It was rumoured that the Privy Council was keeping an eye on Raleigh's circle because of the dangerous ideas being circulated but the members laughed and continued their gatherings.

The lifestyle of Lord and Lady Strange was expensive and Alice knew that they were living above the means granted to them by Lord Derby. At first she had made sure that their household comptroller showed her the accounts but now she preferred to be in ignorance of how much they were in debt and buried her head in the sand. She had occasionally raised the matter tentatively to her husband, pointing out to him that his expenses for clothes and shoes were higher than hers and intimating that he spent too much on his players. But Ferdinando would only shrug unconcernedly, saying lightly, "We have to live up to the prestige of our name."

Alice understood that at Court it was necessary to cut a fine figure and not be outshone by lesser nobles. She took as much enjoyment as Ferdinando did in choosing new clothes in the height of fashion and of the richest materials, silks and brocades from Italy and France, new ruffs and gossamer fine linen that was always spotless, expensive head tires of gold and silver wire with jewelled ornamentation and cobweb veils, in imitation of the Queen. But she had been raised with the careful housekeeping of Catherine Kitson and though her mother had believed fervently that the Spencers should impress on every level with their new wealth, she had nonetheless kept strict records for her housekeeping and had made her daughters account for every penny of their expenditure. She shuddered to think what would be her mother's reaction to the Strange's way of living.

"I shall be able to pay back our debts when I inherit the Earldom," Ferdinando said easily.

"But that could be years ahead, your father is not old," Alice reminded her husband. "And I thought you said your father was in debt also."

"When you are of the nobility it is necessary to have some debts," he replied unconcernedly. "To pay all your debts is a bourgeois attitude. I can always sell some of our land when I am Lord Derby, it is what our family has always done. We have so much in so many different places."

Alice easily resigned herself to the fact that if her husband was unperturbed then it was no concern of hers.

One day she was seated in one of the parlours finishing some embroidery on a partlet for the low-cut bodice of a new gown while one of her ladies was playing some favourite tunes on the lute. Suddenly Ferdinando strode into the room with uncharacteristic abruptness, an angry frown on his face and his grey eyes stormy as he cried, "You will never guess what has happened."

Alice's maid, Lucy, stood and Alice nodded for her to put down the lute and withdraw before she asked, "What has made you so angry? It isn't like you to be in such a fret."

Her husband sank down on the padded settle beneath the window so that he faced her. "The Queen has revived her company of players."

Alice felt like laughing. "I expected some national disaster," she said coolly, a smile hovering on her lips.

"It is a disaster," he cried fiercely. "By founding a troupe of players herself, they will be given precedence over all others. No-one else will play at Court and they will have the pick of all the most prestigious venues. And that isn't all," he continued, his lips set in a grim line, "she has demanded that all of us with companies of players should surrender our best actors to her. She has taken three from the Earl of Leicester – John Heminges, Will Kemp and Thomas Pope - she wants Augustine Philips from me, Edward Alleyn from Worcester's Men and Richard Tarleton from the Earl of Oxford, his noted comedian who can draw an audience anywhere. Pembroke says he is thinking of dissolving his company and Warwick's Men have already broken up as you know. She had her own company in the early days when she was first made Queen but it lapsed fifteen years ago. Now she intends to revive it with new players, or more accurately, poaching ours."

"Yes that does seem serious. But why has she decided this now?" Alice mused.

Ferdinando was still angry. "It's to ensure that central government has more control over the companies."

Despite having great lords as patrons offering them a measure of protection, companies of players were not immune from the legislation of the Privy Council. Their plays had to be read and approved by the Master of the Revels and if there was anything he considered to be offensive, to be outside the authorised representation of religion and politics and to question Tudor legitimacy, then it was ordered to be removed.

"The Queen and the Privy Council believe that we who have companies of travelling players make use of them for our own purposes. It is beyond their comprehension that we consider our money well spent by providing entertainment for ourselves and for others. They believe that the only reason we patronise players is to encourage them to propagate our own political ideas, ideas that are not always in accord with government policy – too Puritan, too Catholic, too inflammatory, too sympathetic to regional administration. They are worried because when the players are on the road away from London the government has no control or knowledge over the material they produce."

"That is true," Alice commented. "I have heard you say that Leicester promotes himself through his players." She did not dare to say that despite her husband's genuine love of the theatre, the Derby family looked upon their players as a means of enhancing their influence. Instead she said, "We saw what Sir Thomas Hesketh was doing with his players and isn't it possible there are more like him?"

"There have been rumours about the old Miracle plays being presented in some country areas, especially in the north as we witnessed at Rufford Hall, and this is seen as propagating Papism," Ferdinando admitted. "However this latest move is an attempt to control the nobles' companies by moving a large share into royal hands and therefore curtailing our playing. I am not happy about this official interference in entertainment. Let us hope we don't revert to the old practice of only having local tradesmen putting on plays at festivals and celebrations."

Alice went to sit beside her husband, putting her arm around him consolingly.

"It might only be a temporary whim," she said. "I think the Queen would far rather let her nobles entertain her than have the responsibility of her own troupe."

"She won't have any personal involvement," Ferdinando laughed. "The company will be run by the Master of the Revels but they will be given priority over everyone else and who knows how many more of our best actors she might demand. I'm going to get my players on the road immediately, send them up to Lancashire where they can't be reached."

From the corner of her eye Alice thought she caught a glimpse of movement near the open door and rose swiftly. When she reached the threshold she could see one of the servants almost disappearing from sight down the passageway and she frowned.

"What is the matter?" Ferdinando asked.

"Nothing," she shrugged. It seemed too vague a suspicion to bother him with and he was still wrapped in his vexation. But recently she had been plagued by the notion that they were being spied upon, though with no firm evidence to support the fact. I must be allowing the current atmosphere of mistrust to get to me, she thought. But her suspicions had fixed upon a fairly recent member of their household servants, a young man named Piers Neville who performed various personal tasks for Ferdinando, and she set to watching him carefully but unobtrusively.

One afternoon she saw him leave the house in a manner she considered furtive and on an impulse decided to follow him. She had no time to find a cloak but the spring weather was mild and having spent all morning with the maids in the still-room preparing balms and perfumed waters she was dressed plainly enough not to attract attention. She resisted the impulse to run as the young man's strides were long and purposeful but had difficulty keeping him in her sights as she dodged market stalls, carts, noisy urchins and stray dogs through Paul's churchyard and into Cheapside. However she saw in the distance the courtyard into which he turned and when she arrived there she could see it led to nowhere but the residence of Master Secretary Walsingham whose house she knew. There was no further sight of him so she slowly retraced her steps, deep in thought.

From her private parlour adjacent to the bedchamber she watched for his return, for the window overlooked the back of Derby House from where she could see Paul's church and his obvious route through the yard. Then she sent a servant to command his presence in Lord Derby's study. She considered this room, redolent with the authority of the Earl himself, to be a more suitable place for an interview than her private parlour with its aura of femininity. She had also changed into a formal gown of black and silver taffeta. When Piers Neville entered, surprised at the summons, she was seated in Lord Derby's chair behind his desk, straight-backed with her hands placed upon the papers and seals on the leather-covered surface, symbols of the Earl's authority.

"For what purpose did you visit the house of Master Secretary Walsingham a few hours ago?" she demanded without preamble.

He was taken aback by the sudden question, flustered and caught off guard, his face flushed, his eyes avoiding hers. "I....I.....I had a message, my lady," he stammered.

"From whom?" she asked coolly.

His confidence re-asserted itself and he said boldly, "With respect, Lady Strange, I believe I have the right to make visits to whom I please when I am not on duty."

"You were on duty in our service I may remind you, Piers," she retorted. "And I would not think such a modest servant as yourself would count an important personage like Master Secretary Walsingham among your acquaintances for a private visit."

"It was not Master Walsingham I went to see. It was one of his maidservants, I have an affection for her, but I have to visit her secretly."

Alice sensed by his fixed gaze that he was lying so she took a chance and risked saying, "Then would you not have sneaked in the back way instead of boldly rapping on the entrance door and being formally admitted." He hung his head and she continued, "I have watched you for some time and I believe you have been spying on my husband and relating information to Master Walsingham."

"I have reported nothing to his discredit, my lady," he insisted. "Everything that I have said has been in my lord's favour."

His eyes were expressive now and Alice believed he was speaking the truth but she asked, "Why did Master Walsingham ask you to forward information to him?"

"It had to do with the plot by Francis Throckmorton," the young man replied, knowing he must now tell the truth.

There had recently been another plot to rescue Mary Stuart, kept in captivity for the past fifteen years under the guardianship of the Earl and Countess of Shrewsbury. A Staffordshire Catholic by the name of Francis Throckmorton had been caught carrying letters to Mary from France promising Spanish forces for an invasion of England and the substitution of Mary for Elizabeth as queen. Under torture Throckmorton had confessed his guilt and been hanged, drawn and quartered, and others had suffered in the backlash. Plots against Mary made all Catholics potential traitors and those 'doubtful' Catholics, amongst whom were included the Stanleys, were also viewed with distrust.

"Some of the conspirators in France are kin and Lancashire acquaintances of Lord Strange," Piers said.

Alice knew that two of Ferdinando's uncles had been the leaders of a previous plot to rescue the Scottish queen and take her to the safety of the Isle of Man. "Also the Earl of Northumberland is a companion of Lord Strange," Piers continued.

The Catholic Henry Percy, Earl of Northumberland, had been arrested and questioned about his possible involvement in the plot and was well-known to Ferdinando through his inclusion in the circle of Waler Raleigh.

"Master Walsingham wished me to forward any evidence of suspicious dealings with my lord - messengers, meetings with strangers, people of doubtful reputation. I would not recognise any such of course" he added hastily, "but Master Walsingham knows all when their names are given to him. He has so many people like me, my lady, in all the noble houses but especially in the houses of Catholics. And anyone who travels abroad, students, visitors, merchants, - he uses all of them to convey information."

Alice knew this was true. When her brother-in-law William had applied for a licence to travel it had been granted on the assurance that they would inform Sir Francis of their whereabouts and his tutor Richard Lloyd would supply information on the religious situation wherever they resided. She also remembered that when Lady Derby was accused of trying to poison the Queen, Ferdinando had broached the possibility of a spy being placed in her house.

"How were you recommended to us, Piers?" Alice asked in surprise.

"I was in the service of the Earl of Northumberland. One of Master Walsingham's informers at Syon House involved me in like work and I came recommended from there. But you must be assured, Lady Strange, that everything I have forwarded from this house has been to confirm my lord's reputation as an honest man, a loyal subject of the Queen with no taint of rebellion, no leanings towards Papism. In actual fact I have done you a great service by re-inforcing my lord's credit with the State. The only thing is......," he hesitated.

"Yes," Alice prompted.

"Walsingham has Sir Walter Raleigh's circle under surveillance because he believes they have radical opinions not in accord with the stability of the State. He has a spy in their midst, I'm not sure but I have heard rumours that the Italian, Signor Bruno, is in his pay. But this information has not come from me, I can assure you. Everything that I have done is to confirm Lord Strange's integrity."

"That may well be," said Alice drily, "but we can harbour no spies in our house. You will have to leave our service."

"Yes I expected that. But I do not know where I shall be able to go. And my usefulness to Master Walsingham will be at an end."

"No doubt you will lack his remuneration," Alice said harshly, refusing to feel sympathy for him.

"He pays us very little," said Piers. "And then we must wait for it."

Alice dismissed him but warned him to expect a summons from Lord Strange.

When he had gone she put her head in her hands as she leant over Lord Derby's desk. What a burden to be under surveillance all the time. She shuddered to think what might have happened if Piers Neville had been in their household when Edmund Campion had visited them. Once again her sister Elizabeth's warnings came to her mind.

Alone with Ferdinando that evening she related to him everything that had passed. To her surprise her husband roared with laughter.

"Well that serves Walsingham right doesn't it! If his spies cannot discover any mischief surrounding me then surely he might be convinced. I reckon we should let this Piers Neville stay in our service, he won't be able to find similar employment elsewhere so he might as well work in our favour and we can play Walsingham at his own game."

"Darling, I can't possibly live in a house where we are being spied upon," Alice cried in horror.

"Better to have ones we know," her husband warned. "But I wish the powers that be would make up their minds about what they want to fix on me. Half the time they are fretting about me having pretensions to the Crown for myself and the other half they are suspecting me of trying to put Mary Stuart on the throne and bring back the Catholic religion. Surely they can't have it both ways."

"You must give up meeting with Raleigh and his associates at these gatherings. Walsingham knows everything that goes on there, as I told you, and talking about atheism and the occult sciences is very dangerous. And there are rumours of other things," she hinted in embarrassment.

"If the State wants to find in our intellectual discussions evidences of wizadry, atheism and sodomy then that's their problem. I shall most certainly not curtail honest intellectual activity for fear of intimidation. As a matter of fact I think atheism is probably the better choice, considering all the trouble different religious practices are causing in this time."

"That's dangerous talk, Ferdinando Stanley," his wife said, shaking her fiery head in resignation. She went to kiss him. How she loved him but, against all that she had previously dreamt of, she wished he was a country squire like her uncle Thomas at Hengrave.

CHAPTER 9

Foiled hopes

The Earl of Derby was home from his three year long sojourn as ambassador in Paris, where he had been entrusted with granting the Order of the Garter to the French King. At least he did not have to concern himself further with the troublesome matter of the Queen's marriage as the Duke of Anjou had unexpectedly died of a tertian fever aged only twenty nine years. The Queen expressed her deep sorrow but it was generally understood that she was relieved to be extricated from an embarrassing situation. Lord Derby was vociferous in complaining of how much it had cost him, not surprising since he had been accompanied by an entourage of more than two hundred people. The Queen did not offer any help with expenses but in gratitude for his services made him a member of the Privy Council.

William came home with his father after travelling extensively, first in France then on to Spain, Italy and Germany. His father related proudly to Ferdinando and Alice how his younger son had found much favour at the court of the French King Henri, but Alice wondered sourly how much it had all cost. She did not relish having William permanently at Derby House but Ferdinando was eager to hear of all his adventures and each day brought forth a new instalment – the duels he had fought, the beautiful ladies he had seduced under the noses of their chaperones, his travels in Italy disguised as a friar.

"Do you think it is all true?" Alice enquired sceptically.

Ferdinando laughed however, saying, "Well if it isn't, it makes a good story. I shall pass some of the anecdotes on to my players, see what they can do with them."

William enjoyed a period of popularity at Court relating to them the same tales, further embellished with each telling, then when the novelty had waned he decided to take himself off to Lancashire, to Lathom and Knowsley, where he knew he would find a willing audience of admirers amongst the less sophisticated country gentry. He looked almost handsome with his thin face tanned by a kinder sun, his beard cut short in the Italian style and his clothes showing the elegance of French fashions.

"Give hospitality to my players," Ferdinando commanded him. "They are on the road somewhere."

"I believe Leicester has taken his players with him to the Low Countries," William remarked and Alice noted the affectation of a slight French accent in his speech.

The States of Holland were locked in conflict with Spain who already ruled the Catholic Spanish Netherlands and were now trying to subdue the Protestant States of William of Orange. England had recently sent an army to aid them and the Queen had placed the Earl of Leicester in command even though he was not in good health.

"The Queen's allowed him to take a few players, including Will Kemp whom she poached for her own company," Ferdinando concurred. "I suppose it helps to while away the time between periods of action and at the same time instil patriotic fervour into the army as the Queen will have commanded heroic plays, though they will be hard pressed to mount The Famous victories of Henry V," he laughed.

"Leicester has Philip Sidney and the Earl of Essex with him so perhaps they will take parts. Sidney has a silver tongue and Essex is good at posturing," William said somewhat maliciously.

"I like Essex, he's very handsome and he's always courteous," Alice said pointedly. "And I think Sidney a romantic character, writing such beautiful poems to Essex's sister, even though she married someone else instead of him."

"Here's a slice of romantic news for you, Alice, knowing how much you like gossip," her husband said mischievously. "Leicester's wife accompanied him and apparently was parading herself in Holland like a queen, but when our Queen discovered it she was furious and ordered poor Lettice back to England. A true drama."

Later however there was more tragic drama relayed from the campaign in the Low Countries. Philip Sidney had been mortally wounded at the Battle of Zutphen. His body was returned to London in a ship with black sails and a memorial service held in Paul's church at which the Stranges attended in company with all the Court and most of London, for the young noble was greatly admired for his literary talents, his prowess at all knightly pursuits and his defence of the Protestant religion.

This event was however soon to be followed by another more personal to the Stanleys, and of more dramatic import. It concerned their cousin Sir William Stanley. Sir William had fought for the Queen in Ireland where he had been knighted for his services then led a regiment to the Low Countries under the command of the Earl of Leicester who had said "he was worth his weight in pearl." He had fought at the Battle of Zutphen but when Leicester's ill health forced him to return to England, Stanley changed his allegiance. He handed back to the Spanish the important city of Deventer which had been captured by the English after a hard battle. He then entered into the service of Spain, taking with him some two thirds of his regiment, a total of six hundred men. This caused consternation in the English army while the Dutch placed a price of three thousand florins on his head.

Ferdinando was devastated when the news arrived in England. Stanley was denounced as a traitor and renegade and a pamphlet entitled 'A Short Admonition on Detestable Treason' was hastily rushed into print. The Earl of Derby and William were up in Lancashire and Ferdinando had to bear the brunt of malicious talk and renewed suspicion at Court.

"William always manages to be away when there is trouble," he sighed enviously, though Alice knew envy was not in his nature. She hated to see his usual good spirits cast down and his happy temperament disturbed.

"You cannot be held responsible for the actions of your relatives," she consoled him, though she had come to understand that anything concerning the Stanleys had more than familial consequences and it was opined in some circles that all the Stanleys were traitors. "Even though his actions have caused a sensation, the shock will abate in time and people will forget."

But Ferdinando was not so sure and wondered what mischief Sir William would continue to work now he was in the pay of Catholic Spain.

Alice soon had family griefs of her own when a messenger arrived to inform her of her father's death. Her husband accompanied her to Althorp for the funeral together with their two small daughters. It was several years since the Spencer family had been united on a single occasion but now there was only an atmosphere of great sadness. Lady Catherine bore herself with firm control, shedding no tears in public and organising the funeral meats with her customary efficiency. But her three daughters shed copious tears, not only for the loss of their father whom they remembered more as a distant and stern figure than as a dispenser of affection, but for the end of their youthful life when Althorp Manor under the secure governance of their parents had provided everything they needed – their sustenance, their fellowship, their dreams.

Anne was now a widow with only two daughters and the occasion brought back her own loss, not that she had known a great love for her elderly husband but because a widow's life was lonely and she had not borne a son and heir to continue the line. Alice was sorry to see her so sad. She had never been as close to her elder sister as to Elizabeth but had always looked for her support and her gentle kindness had often shielded Alice from their mother's sharp tongue.

Elizabeth's face had become more gaunt and taken on a dissatisfied cast and when Alice praised the beauty and accomplishments of her ten year old daughter she said sadly, "She is growing up too soon. All George can think about is a prestigious marriage for her which he intends as soon as possible. It would have been different if I could have borne him sons."

"Perhaps it is not too late," Alice murmured, even though believing otherwise.

Elizabeth shook her head. "It is too late. George is diseased." At her sister's startled expression she continued, "He seeks his pleasure elsewhere. He has grown tired of me."

Alice looked over to where Ferdinando was talking with Sir Thomas Kitson and realised again how fortunate she was to have a husband who loved her and was faithful to her, of that she was sure. Her dear uncle Thomas had recently suffered his own loss with the death of his only children, both his daughters Margaret and Mary with whom she had shared the Queen's visit at Hengrave. Loss of children in infancy was commonplace but how hard it must have been for him and his wife Eliza to lose their daughters by smallpox at fifteen and twelve when they were almost full grown. Now her uncle had no heirs to inherit the wealth and position he had striven so hard to attain. She glanced again at Ferdinando and made a silent prayer, "Please, please, let me give him a son." Anne and Frances had been made much of by their grandmother and their aunts but there was an underlying disappointment in the family that all the Spencer girls had only produced daughters.

Before they left Althorp she had wandered alone through rooms that once were so familiar to her, recollecting the happy times – laughter, gossip and dreams with her sisters in the pink canopied bed in their bedchamber overlooking the knot garden, family feasts and entertainments in the dining hall, reprimands for some misdemeanour in her mother's parlour, helping her mother in the stillroom and watching her oversee the servants in the kitchens, lessons with her brothers' tutors in the library and with the music master in the long gallery. She wandered outside to the gardens and in her mind's eye imagined her first rides on her pony, her early attempts at archery and bowls with her brothers John, Richard and William. She knew that John would keep Althorp safe and prosperous in her father's place but it seemed as if an era was ended.

"What are you doing?" Ferdinando's voice sounded in her ear and she felt his arms around her waist. "Are you regretting marrying me?"

"Not at all," she said fervently. "I was reminiscing that is all, memories are part of us aren't they, we can't shut them out. Seeing how unhappy my family is at this time makes me realise even more how happy I am."

She turned to face him, kissing him on the lips. Nothing else mattered except having him. But as she surveyed the comfortable wealth of Althorp Manor she could not help but be reminded of the splendour of Lathom House over which one day she would be mistress. If only her mother and sisters could see this great princely fortress. Perhaps one day they would come and visit her there and see for themselves the good fortune of the youngest Spencer girl.

On the way back to London she and Ferdinando rode together on horseback while the maids with the children and baggage rode more slowly in the carriage. As they approached the city and rode through Bishopsgate where the clamour of bells, raucous cries from the street-sellers and impatient cart-drivers, the deafening clangour of workshops and the general turbulence of a seething mass of humanity overwhelmed them she said, "I hope that is the end of deaths for a while."

Alice's hopes were not realised. Another plot to rescue the captive Queen of Scots had been discovered by Sir Francis Walsingham's agents. Anthony Babington was the twenty-four year old son of a rich Derbyshire squire, a keen Catholic who had assisted priests in the Midlands and been involved in minor Catholic activity. While he had been a page in the household of Lord Shrewsbury he had met Mary Stuart and like many of those who were in contact with her he had fallen under her spell. He had been caught carrying messages to and from the captive queen but these were no mere expressions of loyalty. They detailed plans by Spain for the rescue of Mary, a foreign Catholic invasion of England with English Catholics to aid them and join them, and "the despatch of the usurper Queen Elizabeth by six noble gentlemen." Babington was hanged, drawn and quartered, although throughout his torture and trial he always insisted that he did not know the names of these noble gentlemen. That however was not of immediate importance to Sir Francis Walsingham because he had got what he had long desired and worked for - proof of Mary Stuart's direct involvement by her signature on the letters. Now there was enough evidence to bring her to trial with execution a foregone conclusion.

To those with knowledge of Master Walsingham's methods some doubt hovered around the truth of these disclosures. The process of delivery of the letters in empty beer kegs from the Earl of Essex's Chartley Manor where Mary was being kept seemed a most unsophisticated method of espionage, while the letters themselves had been deciphered by Walsingham's master decoder Thomas Phelippes. But if doubts remained about the naivety of the postal system or the accuracy of the translation they were promptly stifled. All those in positions of authority who had experience of the disturbances caused by the presence of Mary Stuart in England realised the necessity of being rid of the most powerful focus of Catholic rebellion and they now had the means to achieve this.

Ferdinando's intelligence and his personal experience of Court paranoia did not allow him to accept the truth at face value but apart from voicing his doubts to Alice he kept them to himself. A flicker of unease disturbing his consciousness however was the awareness that with the removal of Mary Stuart he himself was now a step closer to the succession, while his mother was again in the midst of speculation. He had tried unsuccessfully to gain her release from her house arrest but it now seemed unlikely that the Queen would agree to such a move in the near future.

He and Alice had also been distressed by the involvement of John Charnock, one of their Lancashire neighbours. He was sentenced to a brutal execution as one of the conspirators and they remembered their visit to Astley Hall near Chorley and the pleasant time they had passed there with John's brother, Sir Robert Charnock. No doubt they would be in mourning at Astley and the neighbouring halls but Ferdinando was also aware that this particular participant would fuel the suspicions of the Queen and the Privy Council regarding the Lancashire gentry.

As a member of the Privy Council Lord Derby was commanded to sit as one of the judges at Mary's trial, a task he did not relish. However the Queen had a personal interest in his participation. His brothers, Thomas and Edward Stanley, had earlier been involved in a plot to rescue the Scottish queen and take her to the Isle of Man. Queen Elizabeth was determined that Lord Derby should confirm his loyalty and prove that he had no sympathy with Mary Stuart.

Her execution at Fotheringay castle did not however end the problem of resistance to Elizabeth because it was soon known that in retaliation King Philip of Spain was preparing a great Armada for the invasion of England, the largest fleet of ships ever known. The Queen ordered Lord Derby to go to the Low Countries to negotiate a peace treaty with the Spanish regent, the Duke of Parma. She had chosen Henry Stanley deliberately. He was being sent to where the treachery of Sir William Stanley had taken place and she was proclaiming to all and sundry that she had not forgotten. Everyone, including the Earl, knew this was a futile mission, an empty gesture, but the allegiance of Lord Derby was being tested within the context of his family's uncertain loyalties.

As expected, attempts at negotiation were fruitless and preparations for defence began in the City and in all the coastal towns of England, the militia trained, beacons set on all the hills, messengers with fast horses set to depart at short notice. Young men all over the country were volunteering for service, only too eager to exchange their spades for pikes and put their scythes and pitchforks to martial use, while the nobles petitioned the Queen for commissions to command them. Ferdinando, in company with his peers, sought audience with her.

Elizabeth was in conference with Lord Burghley and the Earl of Leicester when he was ushered into one of the small rooms at Whitehall set apart for official business. The Queen was seated in a broad-armed chair of carved oak in front of a table covered with papers and maps, in the process of signing documents with a quill from a silver inkpot set beside a matching inkwell and sander on an embossed silver tray. She was wearing a high-necked closed gown with huge padded sleeves, of russet brocade closely worked with gold thread. Her ruff was small and a gold circlet set with amethysts and fastened to a short veil held back her hair. She looked efficient and purposeful and it was well known that she worked long hours on official business, often keeping Burghley up into the small hours then wakening him early in the morning. He was standing beside her now together with the Earl of Leicester.

Ferdinando bowed low and the Queen welcomed him courteously, listening attentively as he made his request to go to Lancashire and organise the militia there in preparation for an invasion by Spain with the possibility that the fleet could attempt a landing on the Lancashire coast.

"I understand your desire to serve us, Lord Strange, and I am mindful of your eagerness in this matter. I have work for you to do in this enterprise but I would rather it be here in London. I prefer that your lord father should command the operations in the north, aided by your brother whom I believe is at present resident there. Your duties will be here under the command of Lord Leicester and Lord Hunsdon who are responsible for the protection of the City."

Ferdinando tried to suppress his anger but could not refrain from saying unsteadily, "Do you not trust me, Your Majesty?"

Burghley gave him a warning glance but the Queen replied smoothly, "Your loyalty is not in question, Lord Strange. It has come to my ears that your cousin, the traitor Sir William Stanley, is relaying information to Spain regarding our naval dispositions and is suggesting a landing on the Lancashire coast, but I have no reason to believe you would support him in any way, any more than would other members of your family. As you are no doubt aware, the priest William Allen in his traitorous 'Admonition to the Nobility and People of England' is encouraging Catholics to support Spain and asks his fellow Lancastrians to offer them a landing on the Fylde coast. I trust with all my heart that they will not do so." She paused and the momentary silence left Ferdinando in no doubt of the warning underlying her words, as was her intention. "I merely consider you would be more useful to us here in London where you can help to organise the defence of the City which is our priority. Also I would have thought you happy to be close to your wife during this time."

Ferdinando gave his assent, voicing the customary expressions of gratitude but aware of Leicester's sympathising gaze.

When he arrived back at Derby House he could at last give vent to his anger in Alice's presence. "She doesn't trust me," he fumed. "She thinks the Lancashire Catholics will welcome the Spaniards and I will aid them."

"Will they?" Alice asked innocently. "Welcome the Spaniards I mean."

"No they won't," he cried. "Because the majority of my friends, neighbours and tenants keep the old faith it does not signify that they are any less loyal to the Queen despite what Cardinal Allen commands. The Pope put them in an intolerable position when he excommunicated the Queen and forced English Catholics to choose between their sovereign and their faith. Most of them are true Englishmen whose first duty is to their country and their queen and the way they worship is an entirely different issue."

"There is still the example of Lancashire Catholics like Cardinal Allen, Sir William Stanley, your uncles, and

John Charnock," Alice mentioned, with an apologetic half-smile.

"The majority are tainted with the actions of a few," her husband agreed.

"Don't let it trouble you," Alice said comfortingly. "I'm sure there will be much opportunity to distinguish yourself here in London." She was well aware of his reputation at Court as a swordsman and had seen his success in the annual Court jousts. "And I am glad to have you with me at this time."

She was pregnant again and had made every effort to keep well in the hope of bearing the longed-for son but she was anxious about the ordeal that lay ahead.

All through the summer Alice's expectations were reflected in the City at large as people awaited anxiously the coming of the great Armada. As her belly swelled with a mix of hope and fear so did the hearts of the citizens. News reached them of the Spanish fleet's departure, then its return to port damaged by a great storm, then its re-embarcation. Then followed weeks of uncertainty as no-one knew how close was the great Armada, ploughing its way towards them. Ferdinando was busy with his military command, working with Essex and Leicester under the overall supervision of Lord Hunsdon, while Alice sat listlessly sewing or reading or playing the virginals, too tired to wander out into the hot, dirty, crowded streets, and waiting for him to return home with the latest news, more reliable than the rumours being passed around the City.

At last came the news that the Spanish fleet had been sighted passing the Lizard but when the Armada approached the Channel the English fleet under Drake and Lord Admiral Effingham were marooned in port by bad weather. Anticipation was at fever pitch but the Spaniards unaccountably delayed their approach and the weather, unpredictable as ever, changed to allow the English fleet to advance towards their enemy. Then came three days of fierce fighting and as the outcome lay in doubt, the English ships so small and few compared to the Spanish, Alice's own struggle began. The child refused to come easily into the world and in consort with the ships tossing and heaving in the English Channel so Alice's bed became a sea of her own misery. Ferdinando was distraught, torn between the country's danger and his wife's suffering. Finally the great Armada lay broken and beaten, half the ships lost and the rest blown off course around the shores of England, and Alice heard the cries of her new babe.

"Is it a boy?" she gasped.

Outside the drawn curtains of the bed, stifling in the summer heat with the windows shut, the room enclosed in the customary birthing drapes and a fire burning in the grate, the maids and friends waited with bated breath.

"It's a girl, my lady," the midwife pronounced. "Lusty and healthy and like to live," she added as Alice's weary sobs of despair filled the confined space.

"Take her away, I don't want to see her. And don't let my husband come to me," she cried, and a flood of hysteria convulsed her weary body in a new wave of pain.

When Ferdinando arrived he looked at her sorrowfully. Her copper hair had been brushed and lay spread over the white pillow embroidered with the Derby insignia like all their linen while tears glistened on her pale cheeks.

He took her hand. "Yes I am disappointed," he admitted and she admired him for his honesty. "But it isn't a great tragedy, it's an occasion for rejoicing, a new child and my dear wife safely preserved, that is everything to me."

"I tried so hard," she whispered, filled with remorse. Why could none of the Spencer girls bear sons.

The midwife brought the child and Ferdinando took her in his arms. "This time I am going to name her. She will be called Elizabeth. At this time of rejoicing everyone is regaling the Queen with gifts in honour of the occasion, brooches and necklets. But we will commend her by naming our child in her honour. Look, she even has red hair," he said, moving aside the coverlet.

It was true. Anne had her father's chestnut hair which waved naturally and Frances a lighter shade with golden tints but the down on the head of this new child was of Alice's own colouring, like the Queen.

The birth of another daughter was the culmination of a period which had brought disappointment. All the Spencer sisters had experienced failed hopes, coupled with the loss of their father. Shadows of unease had brushed the fringes of the Strange's lives by the treachery of Sir William Stanley and the execution of Mary Stuart which had nudged Ferdinando closer to the throne. Yet there was great joy and relief that the Armada had been defeated without plunging England into a disastrous war, and the esteem to the country by the overthrow of Spain was universally acknowledged. The Stranges' little Elizabeth would be a permanent reminder of this great national event.

But even Queen Elizabeth's exhilaration was tinged with sadness for in the midst of the celebrations Robert Dudley, Earl of Leicester, died. She was bereft of the one man who had truly loved her and served her for so long and her sorrow was overwhelming. She was noticeably grieving at the great memorial service held for him in St. Paul's church. Ferdinando and Alice were amongst the noble company and as they walked together back to the nearby Derby House they reminisced about his life and his devotion to the Queen.

"I really liked him. He wasn't popular with everyone but he was always a good friend to me," Ferdinando said. Then a thought suddenly struck him and he mused, "I wonder what will happen to his players."

CHAPTER 10

Encounters

The relief after the defeat of the Armada was evident everywhere in the City and celebrations were never-ending. The relief for Alice was two-fold for despite being disappointed by another girl the thankfulness that she was alive and well gave a heightened awareness to the joy around her. She saw the world with new eyes and relished the freedom of being delivered from the heavy burden she had carried all through the hot summer, enjoying being able to lace herself into fashionable gowns again and pleased to see she had gained little weight.

"We are going to Lathom," Ferdinando announced one morning. "They will be having great celebrations there and I think it will be good for us to get away from Derby House and London for a time – I want to be away from the stresses and strains we have experienced of late, and fresh air and a change of scene will wipe away all your bad memories, darling."

She leapt at the chance to be free from the house after being confined for so long and welcomed the unexpected release from domestic routine. Leaving the children in the care of nursery maids and a wet nurse they were soon in the saddle and galloping north, relishing the fine weather even though the roads were rutted and dusty. The summer was past its best and there was a definite hint of autumn in the air with morning dew, a tinge of orange and gold in the leaves and a faint waft of woodsmoke on the breeze, all of which made the long journey pleasant enough. Alice now knew what to expect of the road but when they reached the top of Parbold Hill and she saw the great bulk of Lathom House in the distance, it tall towers dominating the countryside for miles, she felt the same thrill of excitement as on her first visit.

They were greeted formally but warmly by the steward, Master Rigby, who informed them that Lord Henry was in residence at Knowsley whilst William was in Chester. "He seems to have taken a great liking to the place," he said.

"No doubt it suits him to be free for his wenching and carousing," Ferdinando laughed tolerantly to Alice later. "There's a cockpit there that he likes to frequent."

Alice was to learn that the Earls of Derby were also lords of Chester, the important port with its dominance in the fur trade, though the port on the river Dee was beginning to silt up.

Once they had toured the castle and made their presence known they settled into their rooms in the Round Tower. Alice loved the circular bedchamber with its canopied bed furnished in red and gold velvet, the bright rugs on the stone floor, the silk-padded seats and the beautifully carved chests, together with wide views from the four windows set in the walls of the tower from where it was possible to see green hills on one side and the flat marshy land reaching to the sea on the other.

Ferdinando's mind was already concentrated on what celebrations he could put into motion. Lord Derby had previously commemorated the Armada victory for his neighbours and tenants at Knowsley and Lathom with feasting and the arrival of various troupes of players, and there had been food and drink in the grounds for the humbler folk together with piping, dancing and rush-bearing. Ferdinando was pleased to learn from Master Rigby that the Earl of Leicester's players were still at Knowsley and set about sending messages to the neighbouring gentry with invitations to more entertainments and hunting parties and passing word around to the townsfolk of Ormskirk and the surrounding villages that they were welcome to come and watch the plays. His first intention was to find his own players and by having his messengers enquire where they might be he ascertained they were with the Hoghtons either at their manor house at Lea or at Hoghton Tower and he ordered them back to Lathom as quickly as possible.

In the meantime he decided to pay a visit with his wife to Knowsley. They rode the seven miles or so from Lathom across flat fields until they came to the woods enclosing the vast area of parkland.

"The port of Liverpool is about another seven miles away," Ferdinando explained as they rode up the long gravelled driveway towards the house. Not so large and magnificent as Lathom, it was still an imposing building with battlements and towers and above the castellated entrance the Derby arms boldly displayed. Studying the eagle and child once again, Alice was poignantly reminded of the first time she had seen the crest and how she had confidently believed she would bear sons for the Earldom.

Sensing her thoughts, her husband diverted her by saying light-heartedly, "Around here the common folk call the crest 'the brid and babby' and sometimes use it for one of their alehouse signs."

As soon as they were sighted grooms were running to take their horses, and attendants hurried to escort them into the house where they were welcomed by Lord Henry in his customary abstracted manner.

"You are in time to watch a performance by the Earl of Leicester's players this afternoon," he said. "They were on the road when they heard of the Earl's death, no-one knows what's going to happen to them now so they are dragging out their time here as long as they can. William is also expected to arrive from Chester."

During the extensive mid-day meal father and son were able to exchange news, Lord Henry eager to know all that had happened in London during the Armada crisis and Ferdinando equally interested in what had been happening in Lancashire.

"William acquitted himself well in organising the militia and riding all over the shire to oversee preparations and keep an eye on our neighbours," the Earl said proudly, helping himself to small quantities from all the dishes of various meats spread before them. "There was a real fear at one time that the Armada might try the Lancashire coast as being the only safe landing place between Milford Haven and Carlisle."

Alice knew that her husband was still feeling sore about having been banned from Lancashire and knowing he would not magnify his own part in securing London said, "Ferdinando was praised by the Queen for his efforts in guarding the City. He was tireless in helping Lord Hunsdon with the city defences, especially with regard to the river and the blockade they constructed, and he took over a lot of the responsibility for Lord Leicester's command, the Earl being sick."

Lord Derby nodded his satisfaction, saying, "I was sorry to hear of Leicester's passing, he had many detractors but he served the Queen well. And sorry also to hear of the birth of another daughter," he added pointedly. Lady Margaret had borne him four sons though two had died young.

Alice's cheeks coloured and she turned her face away on the pretext of asking an attendant to pour more wine, but her husband leapt to her defence by insisting, "We are young, there is plenty of time for sons. And all our daughters are healthy and beautiful."

But Alice had felt humiliated and it was a subject harped upon with some malice when William arrived in grand style and with a large entourage, refusing a meal saying that they had dined at an inn on the road.

"If you don't have sons I will be the next heir," he said wickedly and Alice's eyes flashed dangerously. Ferdinando's grandfather had entailed the Stanley estates on male heirs only.

William seemed to take satisfaction in tormenting Alice but her husband appeared not to notice and enjoyed exchanging news with his brother, as he had with his father. He would have liked to have talked with the players but he understood they would be too occupied with preparing for the coming performance and they would have no inclination to break their concentration at this time.

"I will show you my treasure afterwards," William said, his eyes flickering between Alice and Ferdinando.

"Have they found gold again on the Isle of Man?" his brother asked half-facetiously, for the Stanleys had benefitted personally from a previous cache a few years earlier.

"This is a treasure of a different sort," William smiled. "She will be here to watch the players but I don't flaunt her in front of our father, even though he has Jane with him."

For the performance the hall was packed with friends and the large number of household servants. The players performed a version of 'King Arthur and the Paladins' as patriotic plays were much in vogue in the aftermath of the victory over Spain and all Englishmen were in the mood for taking pride in their history. As was customary, Lord Derby had allowed them to borrow arms for the production so that they fought with real swords. Ferdinando's attention was concentrated on the spectacle for he was always interested in the capability of the actors and the calibre of the writing, but Alice found opportunity to cast covert glances at Lord Derby and William. The Earl was seated beside a plump gentle-featured woman, richly but restrainedly dressed in a mulberry-coloured gown, a small bonnet called a pipkin worn over a net which covered her faded fair hair. In contrast the girl seated beside William Stanley would have drawn attention in any crowd. Even from a distance Alice could see the bright flamboyance of her gown and her uncovered ebony hair.

When the play was finished the actors mingled amongst the spectators for a time, relishing the praise bestowed on them and hoping for some small coin above the donation Lord Derby would give them.

William approached his brother and Alice and introduced his companion, "This is Marguerite, I met her in Chester but she is French."

The girl made a semblance of an honour though her gaze was bold and challenging as she met Ferdinando's. She could not have been more than eighteen years old but her eyes spoke of experience beyond her years. Her gown of scarlet and carnation satin striped with black braid followed the natural lines of her buxom figure for she was not wearing a farthingale. The stomacher was cut low and only the briefest edging of her shift covered her round breasts while the tight carnation sleeves had dropped below her shoulders to reveal a tiny brown mole on the white skin. Her thin face with its pointed chin was not beautiful but her jet-black hair, thick and curly, tumbled to her waist in glorious profusion and was left uncovered in defiance of convention. She spoke to them in French and Alice made a spirited response, mentally thanking her French tutor for his severe discipline. Ferdinando smiled in amusement but his command of the language was also sufficient though both Alice and William saw his eyes lingering on the girl's exposed bosom.

"Speak English, you naughty girl," William commanded, then smacking her on the rump he said, "Go and amuse yourself while I speak with my brother." She pouted and turned away petulantly. "She's quite a find isn't she! She certainly knows how to please a man," he said with a wink at Ferdinando and a leer at Alice. "She's a witch, did you see the witch's mark above her breast, yes I'm sure you did. She's coy about her past but I believe she was with a troupe of travelling entertainers. Do you know they have women to act in plays in France and Italy?"

"So I believe," Ferdinando confirmed. "An interesting innovation though I doubt it will be allowed here."

"I've set her up in a cottage on the estate," William confirmed. "I don't intend returning to London for some time and she will help to make my residence here even more pleasant."

"I thought you didn't consort with commoners," Alice remarked tartly.

William only laughed. "I said I do not marry commoners. But they do well as divertissement."

Ferdinando excused himself to go and talk with the players who were busy packing up their costumes and properties into the travelling chests, for these were their most valuable possessions and it was their first task to see them carefully checked and stored before availing themselves of the meats and drinks Lord Derby had provided for them. When they saw Lord Strange they stopped and made their honours. He complimented them on their performance and asked, "What are you going to do now?"

"We are on our way to Prescot next," said Henry Condell. "We always go on to the cockpit there when we have played at Knowsley, the people of Prescot expect us and we don't have to get the permission of the burgesses seeing we have come directly from Lord Derby."

"Yes I know," Ferdinando replied. The little town of Prescot was only two miles from Knowsley and the cockpit was ideal for use as a theatre when the travelling companies visited. "But I meant what are you going to do now that the Earl of Leicester has died?"

The actors looked glum, shrugging their shoulders, and it was Henry Condell who said, "We don't know. We were on the road when we heard of the Earl's death so decided to finish our tour, but we do not know what will happen when we return to London. I suppose we might have to disband like Sussex's players. Some of us might be able to find a place with another troupe but it will be the end of our company as it is and you know, my lord, how much easier it is to work as a company with actors you know."

Ferdinando had been thinking of the possibility ever since they had left London so it was no snap decision as he said, "What do you think of combining with my players?"

The actors looked as if they had not heard aright, then smiles began to spread over their faces and a wave of excitement convulsed them.

"Do you mean *you* would be willing to be our patron, my lord?" asked Henry Condell with an air of disbelief at such good fortune.

"I am offering to be your patron," he confirmed. "You would unite with my players and be known from now as Lord Strange's men."

The actors were unable to contain their joy and began to throw their caps into the air, seizing each other by the arm and dancing a jig as people passing looked on in amazement and Ferdinando smiled at their excitement.

"When you are done at Prescot make your way to Lathom House," he commanded.

As they pushed their loaded cart the two miles to Prescot, the players of Lord Leicester's company were hardly able to believe their good fortune in the realisation they would not be without employment or be labelled rogues and vagabonds with all the subsequent penalties because they had no official patron. They sang ribald songs as they trudged along, proud now to have exchanged the patronage of one great lord for another, higher in the rank of nobility and with all the grandeur of the Earls of Derby as his inheritance.

Alice was not so thrilled when later that night back at Lathom Ferdinando informed her of what he had done. "It's going to be expensive," she said, but he could only see the advantages of having a larger company of players, especially experienced and talented actors.

"What did you think of Marguerite?" she asked, taking off her jewels and putting them away carefully into her jewel case before calling for her maids to help her undress. "I saw you gazing on her with a lascivious look in your eyes. No doubt if she were one of your players I would have something to worry about, thank God they don't allow women here in England."

"Nonsense," he retorted. "I am not attracted to women of that sort, I prefer elegance and culture. And besides, I have never wanted anyone but you Alice Spencer since the moment I first set eyes on you. Now call for your maids and let's go to bed where I will show you how much I am still enthralled by you."

"I didn't like her," persisted Alice, "and that isn't merely feminine jealousy. I think she really is a witch. There was a malevolence in her eyes, I think she could do us harm."

"She is nothing to us and I'm sure William can take care of himself. He will soon tire of her, that's for sure. It's the novelty of having someone French when he's just come from that country, he's still in love with continental fashions. So long as you do not get yourself a cavalier servente, my darling, that's all that matters to me."

The month at Lathom was full of activity with a seemingly endless round of entertainments and feasting. Another travelling company made their way there, no less than the Queen's Men who had come directly from

Stratford on hearing of the revels held by Lord Derby, and Ferdinando welcomed them wholeheartedly, appreciating their high standard having some of the best actors in their troupe.

"We have a new player, my lord," John Heminges said. "We had some trouble at Whitney, unfortunately some of the troupe drank too much and a brawl ensued afterwards with some low fellows who had tried to get in without paying. One of our members was killed in the ensuing fracas. This put us in a great straits at Stratford for there was no-one to learn his parts at such short notice and besides we were already doubling roles to our full capacity. Word must have got around about our predicament because while we were lodging at the White Hart this young man approached us saying he knew the parts in most of the plays in our repertoire. He said he had been watching the players for years, he was fascinated by theatre and knew most of the parts by heart having a naturally retentive memory so if we were willing he would step in the breach while we were in Stratford. We were somewhat sceptical at first, he was twenty-four years old and not a player by trade, but we were desperate so decided to give him a try, thinking we could later find someone else to join us permanently. However to our amazement he was decidedly competent. His memory was excellent, he could learn lines very quickly, and he had a natural ability for stage technique, having an instinctive feel for the right moves and gestures. We didn't expect him to stay with us when we left Stratford, he was a married man with a young family, but we were loath to lose him and when we asked him if he would continue as a member of our troupe he leapt at the chance, bade his wife and children farewell and here he is. May I bring him to your acquaintance, my lord?"

"I am most eager to meet such a worthy acquisition," Ferdinando said warmly.

John Heminges brought to him a diffident young man of medium height and slim build with a pleasant open face, shoulder-length brown hair that was already starting to recede above a high forehead and warm brown eyes that showed both humour and intelligence. The mouth beneath the slim moustache was full and sensual and a trim beard adorned the firm chin. Ferdinando thought him an ideal personage for a company actor, an appearance without any striking features who could take on whatever character was required.

"This is William Shakespeare," John Heminges introduced him.

"I am honoured to meet your acquaintance, my lord," said the young man, his speech pleasantly tuned with warm overtones and the faint trace of a country accent.

"What makes you want to be a player, Will?" Ferdinando asked curiously. "I believe you are not of that metier."

William Shakespeare had found to his surprise that Lord Strange was only a little older than he was and sensing his genuine interest he replied, "I have been working as a clerk to a lawyer in Stratford but 'tis tedious labour. Before my marriage I was helping my father with his business – he's a glover, a whittawer, a farmer, a dealer in wool and other commodities. I did not attend the universities because at the time I came of age our family was in financial difficulties." He seemed about to say more but thought better of it and continued,

"I became fascinated by the players the first time I saw them, it was the Queen's players too and they came to perform in the Guildhall when my father was chief alderman. I was five years old and he took me with him to watch them. From that moment the idea of performing plays and entertaining people seemed the ideal life to me but I never thought it possible until a few weeks ago."

"You have a wife and children in Stratford, do you intend going back there when the players return?" Ferdinando asked directly.

The young man coloured and hesitated a moment. Then he fixed his eyes steadily on the lord's face as he replied, "If the company still wants me when we get back to Stratford then I want to stay with them. I know some people will condemn me for this but I feel it is what I must do. For the first time in my life I feel truly fulfilled, that this is the life I was meant to have. I can't explain it because there is no precedent in our family – solid gentry, farmers and modest landowners. But it burns inside me like a fire. I want to make people laugh and cry, to think and ponder, I want to take them out of their tedious lives and into a world of enchantment if only for the space of two hours."

He stopped in some embarrassment at his own enthusiasm but Ferdinando was nodding eagerly, "Do you know I feel the same. That is why I am the patron of my own troupe of players. I would gladly leave all this," he waved his hand at the great hall with its rich furnishings, "to be a player and wander the roads in complete freedom."

Will Shakespeare laughed out loud and confident of the young lord's friendship dared to say, "No you wouldn't, my lord. Not when it's raining, as it often is, and you are walking miles pulling a cart, not sure if you will find somewhere you can afford to stay the night and whether the town will give you permission to perform; having to learn lines all the time and when you have finished a performance and you are exhausted, having to pack everything away and hope you have made enough money to buy a meal and a bed for the night."

"Well perhaps not," Ferdinando admitted ruefully. "I must confess I like my comforts and perhaps the way in which I indulge my passion is more suited to me. I can sit back and enjoy the entertainment, provide some financial assistance, and if I can occasionally contribute with a few lines, an idea perhaps, then that helps me feel I have a share."

"I would really like to write plays," said the young man. "There aren't enough new plays and people get tired of seeing the same ones. Also I think you have to be an actor yourself to know what really works on stage, not like some of the university poets who compose in the isolation of their studies. You have to have personal experience of the sort of material an actor needs and which dramatic effects work well both for the player and the audience."

"A novel idea," said Ferdinando, impressed by the young man's obvious enthusiasm. "Write a chronicle play about the Earls of Derby, there's no lack of material."

When the two parted it was with the realisation that they had each made a friend, a bond of shared interest in the unlikely alliance of a great lord and a country clerk turned travelling player.

Later when Ferdinando related the encounter to Alice she was thoughtful. "I wonder about his marriage," she pondered. "It can't be a happy marriage or he would not wish to leave home and family for the life of a travelling player. Perhaps it was an arranged marriage that did not please him or perhaps", her eyes sparkling as her imagination took flight, "he got a girl with child and was forced to wed her, even though it was against his inclination."

Ferdinando was laughing. "Alice, you ought to write plays yourself, you certainly have a mine of invention. But if you like, I'll ask him one day. It will be interesting to see if he does set quill to paper and can give birth to his ideas."

"Did you mean it when you told him to write a play about the Earls of Derby?"

"Yes of course. Everyone writes in praise of the Queen, why not us?"

His expression was mischievous but once again Alice was not sure whether her husband was joking or not.

But she did indeed feel like a queen at Lathom, enjoying the respect they were afforded by all and sundry and knowing her rich fashionable gowns were a source of wonder. Before she had come to Lancashire she had thought the Court the apex of ambition, and the fulfilment of her dreams was to mix with the rich and famous on equal terms. But there was ruthless competition at Court and it was difficult to outshine so many noble, beautiful and wealthy ladies, besides which they were all only satellites to the Queen who allowed no-one to challenge her superiority. Here at Lathom she was the acknowledged leader of fashion and society and with the Countess of Derby far away in London she was the mistress of Lathom House. When she had first married she had anticipated spending time at her husband's "house" in Lancashire as an unavoidable trial, buried in the depths of a county which she had been told was remote and rustic, less interesting even than Althorp. Instead the reality had been the entrance into an enchanted world of which she, not Elizabeth, was queen. The constant presence of all the Lancashire gentry at Lathom House and Knowsley was a confirmation of the esteem in which the Earls of Derby were held throughout the shire, though the generous profligacy of the hospitality offered to the Lancastrians was a powerful incentive to their allegiance.

It was at one such gathering that Ferdinando was approached deferentially by a middle-aged gentleman who bowed and introduced himself as "Thomas Standish of Duxbury."

Ferdinando acknowledged him graciously and stopped to listen, saying with his habitual courtesy, "I know of you, sir, though I have never had the pleasure of visiting your house."

"Tis but a small manor, my lord," Master Standish said, "But we are kin to the Standishes of Standish Hall and my wife is of the Hoghton family."

Ferdinando nodded his understanding, being familiar with most of the Lancashire gentry and their connections, and asked his visitor, "Do you seek my assistance in some way?"

"I trust I do not presume too much on your beneficence, my lord," the man replied in the broad accents of Lancashire, "but I was wondering if you could find a place for my younger son, Leonard, in your service. He is fifteen years old and would benefit greatly from a time serving you in some way. My other son, Alexander, is heir to the manor of Duxbury and so is occupied with learning the management of the estate and knowing something of the law."

"Bring your son to me then, Master Standish," Ferdinando offered, and when he was informed that both boys were present with their father he waited with Alice by his side.

Thomas Standish hastened away and returning shortly with his sons presented them to Lord and Lady Strange.

"This is Alexander, my lord, my eldest son, and this is Leonard, the younger. My stepsons in actual fact but indeed they are like sons to me."

Ferdinando greeted them while Alice looked on. They were handsome boys. Alexander was tall and well built with fair hair that was beginning to darken and a small neatly-trimmed fair beard. Leonard was smaller and darker with only the beginnings of stubble on his face. They were obviously dressed in their best clothes, doublet and hose of good quality dark wool with shirts of fine linen, though to Lord and Lady Strange with their customary Court fashions the hand of a country tailor was clearly discernible.

"So you are Alexander Standish," Ferdinando said to the elder. "How old are you Alexander?"

"I'm seventeen, my lord." His speech had the same northern inflexions as his father's but his voice was firm and there was a confidence in his stance and in the direct gaze of his astonishingly deep blue eyes.

"And learning the management of your estate I am told. Do you find the work interesting?"

"Yes, my lord. I want to be a good landlord like my father and," with a quick apologetic glance at Thomas, "to make improvements where I can."

Ferdinando smiled his approval and turned to the younger brother. "You are fifteen I believe, Leonard, and would like a post in my service here at Lathom. What can you do?"

There was a challenge in his eyes but also a hint of laughter and the boy answered bravely, "I can turn my hand to most things, my lord."

"Can you write a fair hand?"

"Yes my lord, I have been complimented on such."

"Are you good with horses?"

"Oh yes, my lord." His tone conveyed his enthusiasm.

While his brother was being interviewed Alexander Standish's eyes had been fixed upon Alice who now asked merrily, "Can you play music and dance, Leonard?"

The boy blushed in confusion and stammered, "I play the lute but not very well, I am better on the pipes, and I am afraid I only know the country measures that we dance at festivals."

"Well we shall have to teach you to dance, both of you," she said, turning to Alexander whose gaze had never wavered from her face and who now dropped his eyes in embarrassment.

"I am sure we can find you some employment somewhere, Leonard. Something that you will both enjoy and find useful in time to come," Ferdinando promised. Many of the younger sons of the local gentry, sometimes the gentry themselves, found service at Lathom and Knowsley. William Farrington, comptroller of the household, was master of Worden Hall. "Attend me here by ten of the clock tomorrow."

While Thomas Standish and his younger son made their thanks to Ferdinando, Alice turned to Alexander, aware of his intent gaze. "We hope to see you also here at Lathom, Alexander," she said, holding out her hand to him.

Later when all their guests had departed and they were alone together Ferdinando said, "Well, Alice, it would seem you have made a great conquest of young

Alexander Standish. He couldn't take his eyes away from you."

Alice looked at her husband in surprise, saying, "Don't be silly, he's only seventeen and I'm an old married woman of nearly thirty and mother to three children."

Ferdinando studied his wife and saw what Alexander Standish had seen – a beautiful woman with shining copper hair and sparkling blue-green eyes, elegantly dressed in a farthingale of luminous pearl-grey satin heavily embroidered in silver thread, smelling of roses and with a lilting courtly speech. To the Lancashire boy from a small country manor she must have seemed like a vision from another world.

"I think you have found yourself a cavalier servente," he teased. "It's fortunate he's only seventeen years old."

Accustomed to admiration, Alice laughed in genuine amusement and the encounter was buried amongst the mass of new faces which greeted her every day.

As the weeks passed Alice thought that Ferdinando was intending spending the Yuletide season at Lathom in the company of his family but one chilly day with the threat of winter in the wind he burst in on her while she was seated before the fire in one of the small private chambers overlooking the inner courtyard, reading a new copy of Edmund Spenser's poems which her husband had bought for her.

"We are returning to London," he said, and when she put down her book in surprise, he continued, "I have just heard some interesting news."

She looked at him questioningly, surmising some important development at Court or at Derby House for him to make such an impromptu decision and feeling a slight tremor of alarm.

"I have just heard that the Queen's players are to be disbanded," he said. "After the Yuletide festivities at Court they will play no more. It seems the Queen has now lost interest in a troupe of her own, especially since her favourite comedian Dick Tarleton has recently died."

Alice's alarm had now turned to puzzlement as she asked, "And what is that to do with us? Why the sudden urge to return to London? Is it merely because you wish to watch them perform together one last time? Is that enough to warrant a long journey at this time of year?"

Her husband looked at her as if she had asked a very stupid question. "I want them for myself, before anyone else like Pembroke or Oxford can take them," he said.

"You can't possibly be thinking of taking on the Queen's players as well as Leicester's," Alice cried in disbelief.

"Not all of them. Just the best. I want Will Kemp and John Heminges. And Will Shakespeare too." His eyes narrowed speculatively. "He's going to write a play about the Earls of Derby."

Through the leaded window where the winter sun's weak rays were glancing on the pages of her discarded book Alice could see the Eagle Tower soaring aloft and the words of the psalmist came involuntarily into her mind – "They shall mount up with wings as eagles." It was no coincidence that the Earls of Derby had chosen the eagle as their emblem. But a sudden flicker of apprehension touched her thoughts as she wondered if they might fly too high and an image of Dedalus came into her mind.

CHAPTER 11

Soaring High

Ferdinando had made the acquaintance of a new member of Walter Raleigh's circle, an enigmatic young man called Christopher Marlowe who was causing a sensation in the theatre world despite being only twenty four years old. He had written a play called 'Tamburlaine' which was unlike anything previously seen on a stage, a story of hubris and violence with a powerful command of language and imagery that up to now no English writer of plays had achieved. Ferdinando had been overwhelmed by the total effect, especially as he had seen it performed in a newly-built playhouse called The Rose on the south bank of the river near the pleasure gardens. An enterprising businessman named Philip Henslowe had noted the success of the other two theatres and considered such a venture might prove a sound financial investment. But as he did not wish to risk too close competition with the Shoreditch playhouses he had chosen the south bank of the Thames for his site, the pleasure gardens there already being a popular outing for Londoners with hundreds of ferry boats making the crossing easy, and his foresight had been rewarded by full houses. Henslowe hired out The Rose to various companies of players but the most frequent users were The Lord Admiral's Men, recognised as the best company in London, and they had performed 'Tamburlaine' there with their leading actor Edward Alleyn in the title role. Ferdinando had been so impressed that he decided to take Alice with him when the peformance was repeated.

Despite her husband's fascination with the theatrical world Alice had never before been to a playhouse. When he visited The Theatre and The Curtain he had gone in company with other lords, riding to Shoreditch then leaving their horses to be looked after by urchins eager to earn a penny, while inside the playhouses they hired what were termed 'gentlemen's rooms', privately curtained areas in the second gallery with the best view of the stage. Some lords demanded stools on the stage itself but Ferdinando vehemently opposed this practice as it distracted the actors, especially when the noble spectators talked amongst themselves or drew attention to themselves by outrageous behaviour.

Alice had always been led to believe that the playhouses were unsavoury places attended only by men and the lower class of citizens together with women of doubtful repute, an opinion loudly proclaimed by Puritan preachers and not always contradicted by men who liked to avail themselves of alternative company for the afternoon, often in the privacy of the 'gentlemen's rooms.' Similarly when the players performed in the inn yards (Lord Strange's Men frequented the Cross Keys in Bishopsgate) the performances were often rowdy with a vast amount of drink being consumed. The companies played more often in the inn yards as there was a shortage of permanent theatres, and the incentive for the landlords to hire out their premises lay in the amount of drink they were able to sell on such afternoons but this fact did not encourage the presence of too many upper-class ladies. Like other ladies of her class Alice had been content to see entertainments at Court or private performances in the houses of nobles and gentlemen and Ferdinando had never pressed for her company, not because he was ever tempted by the availability of other women but because his sole concentration was fixed on the plays and the actors. Now however he wanted her to see this amazing play in a playhouse where it could be shown to full effect on a large stage with all the available mechanical effects not possible elsewhere.

Attended by their personal servants, they crossed the Thames in their own private barge accoutered in green velvet with the Derby insignia, and willing hands came rushing to help as the boat found a mooring immediately in front of The Rose. Alice was amazed at the size of the octagonal structure with its walls of white plaster and timber, its thatch roof surmounted by a square hut on which flew the flag advertising the day's performance. Crowds of people were pouring through the several doors in the building, pushing, talking, laughing, jostling in a seemingly uncontrollable mass, but Philip Henslowe himself was waiting to escort them up a flight of stairs to the second gallery and a privately curtained area. Alice and her maid Lucy were both wearing black velvet masks but as her eyes raked the interior of the building from behind the slits she could see there was a wide variety of spectators, by no means only the meaner sort. The standing area in front and around the jutting stage was indeed crowded with menial workers in their rough clothing together with cropped-haired apprentices and some garishly dressed women with dyed hair and exposed breasts, but in all three of the galleries were seated well-dressed merchants and city wives in their discreet finery. The atmosphere was noisy and smoky and vendors pushed their way amongst the groundlings selling fruit and pies and mugs of ale but when the trumpets blew for the start of the performance and the actors made their entrances from behind the curtained recess at the back of the stage a hush descended on the previously clamorous throng of some three thousand people.

Alice did not enjoy the play as much as her husband, finding it too violent, often repetitious, and in her opinion it lacked romance. But she had enjoyed the frisson of the unique atmosphere on her first visit to a playhouse and was enthusiastic about the young Edward Alleyn, tall and black haired with expressively handsome features and a rich, powerful voice that rang around the huge space with resonant grandeur.

"I would like him for my own players," Ferdinando said wistfully. "I would also like Christopher Marlowe to write something for us".

"I thought you were expecting William Shakespeare to do that," said Alice with a trace of mischief.

"Yes I must remind him about it, he has already collaborated with others on adapting some old plays. But I also want to know Marlowe better. He sometimes comes to the gatherings at Raleigh's house, Raleigh seems to be very friendly with him." He did not tell Alice that Marlowe's controversial opinions often shocked even the most liberal thinkers in the circle. "What did you think of your first visit to a playhouse? Do you remember when we first met I told you I would take you one day."

"Interesting. But I think I prefer private performances. At least the seats are more comfortable," she laughed. "Even with the provision of a cushion these wooden benches are too hard and narrow for my taste. Look, there's Aemilia Bassano, Lord Hunsdon's paramour," she said suddenly, pointing out a tall slender young woman, dressed in a vibrant red and blue gown, her black wavy hair long and glossy beneath her red felt high-crowned hat. For a moment she thought of Marguerite, William Stanley's French mistress.

"She's often at the playhouses, and at the inns too," Ferdinando said. "She seems to be very fond of plays, I see her sometimes at the Cross Keys."

"Do you indeed," his wife said warningly. "She's very beautiful."

Aemilia turned and noticing Ferdinando smiled and lifted her hand in greeting to which he responded with a small bow. Seeing his wife's raised eyebrows he said, "Lord Hunsdon's property. He makes that very clear. He might well be past sixty but Aemilia is his precious possession."

Alice had seen Aemilia occasionally at Court where Lord Hunsdon's great influence ensured her acceptance. Many of the lords had mistresses, her sister Elizabeth had hinted as much about her husband, Lord Hunsdon's son, and the Earl of Oxford had recently earned the Queen's wrath by getting one of her maids with child. Alice thought again of how fortunate she was to have Ferdinando faithful to her after ten years. She was sometimes exasperated by his obsession with the theatre but at least it helped to fill the often empty hours of the sons of the nobility when they had nothing more to do than idle at Court and get into mischief.

It was only a short time later that news got around that Christopher Marlowe had been arrested and put into Newgate gaol for being involved in the death of a man in a brawl in the notorious district of Cripplegate where many theatre people lived.

"Well I suppose that's the end of him writing plays," Ferdinando surmised, for it was general opinion that his sentence would end at the gallows.

His disappointment however was allayed by William Shakespeare announcing to him that he had written a play about King Henry VI which included the ancestors of both the Earls of Derby and the Cliffords (Lady Margaret Stanley's family). On reading it Ferdinando was impressed by the way his ancestors had been heroically represented and looked forward to seeing the play.

The playhouse free at the time was The Curtain which had recently been taken over by James Burbage in addition to the adjacent Theatre which he had built and part-owned. Like Philip Henslowe he rented out his buildings to different companies and as an actor himself worked with whoever was using his properties at the time, sometimes joining with Strange's Men. 'Henry VI' proved such a popular success that it had to be repeated and Ferdinando was delighted with the response and the appearance on stage of his ancestors. This proof of a fledgling playwright amongst Lord Strange's Men provoked the opinion that they might be set to rival the Lord Admiral's Men, especially as they seemed to have lost their playwright.

Then to everyone's amazement Christopher Marlowe walked out of Newgate and continued his life as a writer of plays. Ferdinando pondered carefully on his unexpected release especially when his friend Walter

Raleigh told him it was through the intervention of the Privy Council. They discussed together the mysteries surrounding Marlowe. Raleigh said he had heard on good authority that Marlowe had been missing for two years while a student at Cambridge but when the masters wanted to withhold his degree the Privy Council over-ruled them. Ferdinando had earlier informed his friend of Piers Neville's assertion that Raleigh's circle was under surveillance and how he had suggested that perhaps the Italian Giordano Bruno had been passing on information. He wondered to himself if Marlowe could possibly be serving the same purpose now that Bruno had returned to Italy, he often seemed to be leading the talk into dangerous paths. But he did not voice his thoughts aloud as Sir Francis Walsingham had recently died and the situation could have changed. However he felt a little uneasy in Marlowe's company even though he appreciated his undoubted talent. Marlowe's enigmatic expression, his watchful eyes that seemed to notice everything but gave nothing away himself, were characteristics alien to his own open nature.

However his misgivings were overcome when Marlowe produced his next play, 'The Jew of Malta', and the leading actor Edward Alleyn invited Lord Strange's Men to collaborate in the production to be presented at The Rose. Lord Strange's Men were going from strength to strength and were sometimes invited to perform at Court. Now this joint enterprise with the leading players of the day set the seal on their excellence and because the first collaboration was such a success it led to others in all the three playhouses as Marlowe's plays had large casts. However it was the presence in the Lord Admiral's Company of Edward Alleyn, London's best and most popular actor, that drew large audiences and Ferdinando mused enviously, "I wish I could find an actor as good as Ned Alleyn."

In the summer the Stranges made their annual visit to Lathom House, a period which Alice had grown to anticipate with pleasure. Their residence followed the usual round of entertainments, feasting, and visiting, as the local gentry demonstrated their regard with gifts and invitations of hospitality. In return the Stranges offered them the bounties of Lathom, for Lord Derby had now decided to make Knowsley his permanent home and the Countess was still confined at her house arrest in London. Ferdinando did not forget his more humble tenants in the surrounding villages as well as the townsfolk of Ormskirk, riding out with Alice to see and be seen, scattering coins as they passed and talking companionably to workers who stopped to watch. He invited them to plays at the House, was present at their local festivals and arranged for at least one day's holiday during the time they were in residence so he was generally popular.

The Earl of Derby had declared his intention of never more living in London and was now settled permanently at Knowsley Hall. On their frequent visits to him they noticed he looked tired and considerably aged but he seemed to be content with his books and the company of his mistress Jane Halsall, though continuing to fulfil his obligations as Lord Lieutenant of the shire with all the legal and administrative duties that entailed. William divided his time between Knowsley, Lathom and his own house at Chester, his favourite residence. Marguerite did not appear so much in evidence and it seemed William was losing interest in her though she still lived in a cottage on the estate and he sometimes took her with him to Chester.

"She seems very discontented with William's neglect of her," Alice said to Ferdinando after watching the two together at an afternoon of games and sports at Knowsley. William had been more interested in beating his brother at archery and skittles and when he looked for approval for his victory it was to where a pretty country girl with fair curls and a round rosy face was gazing in admiration. Marguerite in a gaudy flame-coloured gown was leaning against a tree in obvious boredom and with a sulky pout until she strode defiantly to where a group of young men were only too willing to welcome her into their company.

"He has told me he has found another mistress in Chester," Ferdinando acknowledged, "a merchant's daughter who is both intelligent and refined."

"I think there might be trouble brewing," Alice ventured and when her husband asked, "Woman's intuition?" she nodded knowingly.

One morning Alice decided to take a ride around the countryside and although Ferdinando appreciated her interest in the Lathom domains he did not like her to ride alone so she agreed to accept one of the grooms as an escort. When she arrived at the stables she found Marguerite there looking for a horse, dressed for riding in a crimson habit with a feathered hat. She nodded nonchanantly to Alice before mounting a grey palfrey one of the stable boys had recommended for her and trotting away with her head held high.

"She has taken enough time in deciding," he grumbled, after he had saluted Lady Strange and gone to find her horse, a strong chestnut with a shiny coat and bright eyes, lively but amenable.

"She appeared to be deliberately wasting time," a voice behind her said and turning she saw a boy standing in the shadows. "Good day to you, my lady," he said respectfully, making a low bow.

"Alexander Standish is it not?" Alice said smiling.

He acknowledged his name, flushing with pleasure that she should remember him.

"What are you doing here, Alexander?" she asked.

"I came to visit my brother Leonard, my lady. I come from time to time to see him."

"And is he happy here?"

"Very much so, my lady. He is working with Master Farrington the Household Comptroller and is learning many useful things. I have come to collect my horse," he said in explanation of his presence.

Alice bade him farewell and went to mount her horse but when she was in the saddle he began to rear and prance nervously, neighing and snorting, and when she leaned forward, putting her gloved hand on his neck to quieten him, he reared the more so that she was finding it difficult to keep her seat. Alexander Standish ran towards her and seizing the reins with one hand he tried to pull the horse under control while at the same time feeling under the saddle with his other hand. He took from there a small object and holding it in his palm Alice saw that it was a burr.

"When you mounted, the pressure on the saddle pushed it into his flesh," he said throwing it on the ground and flattening it with his foot. "You could at least have been thrown, my lady."

Humiliating at least, causing injury at most, Alice thought, saying, "It couldn't have been accidental could it," not wishing to go further and voice her suspicions to the young man.

Alexander's blue eyes showed the same reluctance to accuse but his idolisation of Lady Strange and the possibility that someone might wish her ill forced him to say, "I saw the French girl hovering close when the stable boy was saddling your horse, my lady. She was asking if you were coming to ride today, she hung around a long time, not being able to decide what she wanted, and I saw her spend time stroking your horse."

Alice nodded. The vindictiveness would be in keeping with Marguerite but why she should vent her resentment on her she had no idea, apart from jealousy.

"Thankyou Alexander, I am grateful to you for your help and foresight."

She still felt a little unsettled from the incident though the horse was calm again now and eager to be out of the stables and enjoying his exercise.

"Do you have to leave immediately?" she asked him.

Alexander looked bemused and he stammered, "I don't have to be back home at any set time, my lady. Is there something you wish me to do for you?"

Alice smiled at his earnestness and said, "I was wondering if you would care to accompany me on my ride. My lord husband does not like me to ride alone so one of the grooms usually accompanies me but I would like your attendance today if you are not engaged elsewhere."

An expression of joy crossed the young man's face and he could hardly control his eagerness as he cried, "I would be honoured to do so, my lady."

"Then let us be on our way."

Before he returned to his own horse she leant towards him saying, "And not so much of 'my lady'. Just once is quite enough for I am assured of your respect, Alex. May I call you Alex, Alexander is quite a mouthful."

"I would be greatly honoured, my lady." Then he laughed and looked embarrassed, but she smiled encouragingly as they trotted together out of the castle precincts and onto the open road.

When they returned to Lathom House after a pleasant ride around the flat countryside to the ruins of the old priory and then through the tiny villages scattered in the lee of Parbold Hill, Alice insisted that he stay and eat dinner with them and his cup was full of happiness, though his awe of his hosts and their surroundings rendered him speechless unless he was directly addressed. Before he made his way home to Duxbury Hall Lady Strange had extracted from him a promise (eagerly given) that if he ever had cause to visit Lathom he would accompany her on her daily ride.

Afterwards Ferdinando teased her about her "Lancashire cavalier."

"I thought you would be pleased," she replied, her eyes sparkingly green, "since you are always complaining when I ride alone." She considered it wise not to mention Marguerite's supposed mischief.

"He must be coming up to eighteen now, almost a man," Ferdinando said with mock severity, but he was always happy when people admired his wife and the great lord knew he had nothing to fear. Alice Stanley liked luxury, expensive fashions, living in great houses and castles, a noble name that commanded respect, and he was happy that he had been able to give her these. But above all he loved her with all his heart and he knew she returned his passionate love with as much ardour as when they had first given themselves to each other in the park at Greenwich Palace.

Lady Strange did indeed bask in the respect and admiration accorded to her husband both at Lathom and in London. As she sat with the nobility in the royal enclosure for the annual Accession Day tournament she knew she was the focus of much interested observation. The stands surrounding the tiltyard at Whitehall were packed with spectators, from the richest nobles to merchants and their wives, apprentices, and even the working sort, for the entertainment was open to all who could afford the expensive tickets as the Queen wanted the anniversary of her accession to be remembered and thankfully commemorated by all Londoners. Lord Strange usually jousted in this competition together with most of the nobility young and fit enough to do so. It was a matter of prestige to have the richest clothes and armour, to have a large escort of personal retainers dressed accordingly, and to perform successfully enough to gain the admiration of the crowd and, most importantly, win the Queen's favour.

For the first time Alice had brought with her the ten year old Anne to watch her father in the tournament. Both were wrapped in cloaks of flame-coloured velvet lined and trimmed with beaver fur for the November day was chilly, but whereas Alice's coils of copper hair were covered by a low-crowned hat with jewelled brooches, Anne Stanley's chestnut waves flowed over her shoulders from beneath the velvet pancake cap and her features already resembled her father's. She leant over the barrier of the royal enclosure in absorbed excitement and once again Alice wished she had been a boy taking careful note of the procedures for when it would be his turn. Anne was unaware of her mother's thoughts, exhilarated by the opportunity to be included in the Court and committing to memory every detail of the occasion so that on her return home she could glory in it to her sisters who would be waiting eagerly. Seven year old Frances had been disappointed about being omitted from the excursion but her mother had explained that it was now time for Anne, as heiress, to be introduced to the life of the Court and she had accepted this with her usual good nature despite Anne's flaunting of her superiority.

All the nobles jousted in turn, their opponents being chosen by lots, and the spectators made bets on the eventual winner of the tournament. The contestants paraded first around the arena, flaunting their finery and the size of their accompanying retinue with their armorial bearings proudly displayed on pennants and shields and wearing their lady's favour in their hats. Lord Strange was clothed entirely in silver, the silver thread in his brocade surcoat dazzling with sparks of light as he moved. His shield and pennants bore the crest of three stags' heads and an eagle with the impresa 'sans changer', and of course he was carrying his wife's favour in his elaborate silver helm. The jousting commenced on horseback with lances then they fought on foot with shields. One by one Ferdinando overcame his opponents and the crowd began to cheer encouragingly as it seemed he would be the champion, for he was popular both with the Court and with the general public who appreciated his support of the playhouses. The final encounter was with the Queen's champion, his own uncle George Clifford.

Clifford was only two years older than Ferdinando, the son of the Earl of Cumberland's second wife and therefore half-brother to Lady Margaret Stanley. He had always been a favourite of the Queen for he was the sort of man she liked, bold, reckless, red-blooded. He had commanded a ship during the Armada battle, had fought bravely in the Spanish campaigns and, unlike his half-sister, had no royal blood in his veins. Because the Queen could not fight personally in the tournaments as her father had done, she had a champion to represent her and when Sir Henry Lee had died the year previously she had granted the honour to George Clifford. Garbed ostentatiously in blue and gold with gold stars on his armour, he carried the Queen's glove prominently in his plumed helmet. He was an experienced soldier, an accomplished jouster and he had the incentive of fighting for the Queen. But finally he was overcome by his kinsman, the patron of poets and playwrights.

The crowd cheered their approval but the Queen was not pleased. Ferdinando rode first to where Alice was seated and taking her favour from his helmet he waved it aloft before presenting it to her. She smiled adoringly at him knowing that the eyes of the vast crowd were upon her, while his daughter was almost bursting with pride. Then he rode towards the Queen and made his obeisance to her. It was all in accord with knightly protocol but Elizabeth's eyes flashed angrily.

The crowd were happy however for there had not been such a popular champion since Sir Philip Sidney. All Londoners knew of Lord Strange's Players who entertained them often and well, both in the playhouses and in the inn yards, and whose entertainments enriched their mundane lives. His support for the theatre loved so much by Londoners, and his known patronage of writers and musicians, made him one of the most popular noblemen and they showed their approval by throwing their caps into the air and shouting "A Strange, a Strange, a Strange for champion."

When the Queen awarded him the prize she smiled, but the smile did not reach her eyes. Lord Burghley and his son Robert Cecil had recently captured a priest travelling from Madrid with letters from Father Persons who was consorting with Sir William Stanley, and Lord Strange's name had been mentioned as a focus for a Catholic rebellion being planned by exiles on the Continent.

CHAPTER 12

Respite

Ferdinando believed that his mother should take an interest in her eldest granddaughter as Anne Stanley would inherit her claim to the Crown if no sons should be born, a likely possibility after twelve years of marriage and no further child since Elizabeth four years ago. Lady Margaret had never shown any interest in her grandchildren and Alice knew that she was disappointed they had not provided sons for the Earldom as she had done.

Anne and Frances were escorted by their parents to Cleveland Row and grandmother and granddaughters had their first glimpse of each other. The children curtseyed low and as they raised their heads Lady Margaret saw her son's features reflected in Anne's face, his grey eyes and waving chestnut hair, but in Frances she saw a picture of herself as a child. Although Anne resembled her father, the features that made Ferdinando Stanley a handsome man were not so striking in the female form, presenting only a pleasant regularity, but Frances's oval face, almond eyes and golden hair promised the beauty of her grandmother. Anne was overawed by the elegant figure with her cool confident demeanour and regally rich clothes. Seated on a black velvet chair embroidered with pearls with a matching footstool that almost gave the impression of a throne, Lady Margaret was wearing a gown of purple velvet trimmed with ermine and a crescent-shaped cap of purple velvet and gold wire framed her beautiful face. Frances however seemed to unconsciously absorb her likeness to this vision and smiled winningly with the assurance of one who, even so young, was aware of her own attractiveness. Lady Margaret took an instant liking to her younger granddaughter and Alice and Ferdinando realised that it was Frances who had won her heart. She was polite to Anne but the eleven year old girl knew that she had been superceded and did not have the instinctive charm to remedy it, while her sibling was naturally responsive without realising she was overshadowing Anne.

The two girls continued to visit their grandmother occasionally. She would talk with them and together they would walk in the extensive gardens when it was fine weather, but Anne could never easily converse with the Countess while Frances chatted happily. One day Anne did not feel well and Frances went alone. Afterwards she appeared relieved when it was only her younger sister who was invited to visit and Frances accepted this as a matter of course. She was happy in her grandmother's company. Lady Margaret found pleasure in advising the child on her needlework for she was an expert, having much time on her hands to practise, and liked to listen to her playing the lute and singing, while Frances who was particularly fond of poetry enjoyed reading to her grandmother. Ferdinando and Alice were disturbed that the Countess was showing preferential treatment to Frances but Anne seemed not to take offence and showed relief that the duty of such an exacting task had been transferred from her.

The Countess's situation both worried and angered Ferdinando as her confinement continued without any signs of a change of heart by the Queen although he made regular appeals on her behalf. Soon however the occasional visits to Clerkenwell were temporarily brought to an end by an unwelcome visitor to London, not entirely unexpected in the heat of the summer months – the plague. There were always cases reported in the summer due to the stinking garbage of the streets, the overcrowded tenements, the insanitary conditions in which most people lived, and the difficulty of keeping food from going bad in the heat. However the year 1592 brought a particularly virulent epidemic. Emergency precautions had to be put into place in the City including a complete ban on theatrical performances anywhere until further notice

The London theatre companies had already suffered a setback earlier in the year when a riot by apprentices in front of the Rose had resulted in the Privy Council temporarily banning all theatre performances. The civic authorities did not like theatre. They considered the players to be of dubious reputation, their plays encouraging dissident opinions and unsociable behaviour, and the overcrowded venues with the easy availability of drink providing ample scope for cutpurses, tricksters and whores. They were always eager to look for infringements of the laws governing performances and seized on any opportunity to close the playhouses and sometimes imprison the actors. Such an opportunity arose when a riot begun by apprentices, disappointed because they could not get into the Rose as it was full, spread into

Southwark where it was implemented by many malefactors only too eager to join the fight. In reprisal all theatres were closed for three months.

Lord Strange's Men were bitterly disappointed by the edict for June was the beginning of their best season, the weather suitable for open-air performances and when they stood to make the most money. They were now beginning to rival The Lord Admiral's Men. William Shakespeare's sequel to his history chronicle of King Henry VI and a comedy called 'The Comedy of Errors' had ensured his notice as a promising playwright and the company had also found themselves a leading actor. Richard Burbage was the twenty year old son of James Burbage and had made his first appearance in Lord Strange's company when they were performing 'The Seven Deadly Sins' at his father's theatre in Shoreditch. With his sturdy figure and curly hair he had a projection and a charismatic stage presence that thrilled everyone and he was already challenging Edward Alleyn in the esteem of London's theatre-goers.

The edict of the Privy Council meant the players would have to go on tour and although they were assured of a warm welcome in the provinces and the houses of regular patrons it was neither as comfortable nor as lucrative as being in London. However by the time the theatres were scheduled to re-open and the players were on the way back to London tragedy struck again when the plague reached such dangerous proportions that the theatres were ordered to remain closed for an indefinite period. The players had to continue touring the provinces.

William Shakespeare did not travel in the company of Lord Strange's Men. He said he was busy writing something important and despite the plague he preferred to stay at his Bishopsgate lodgings. His last two plays had pleased both the general public and the theatre managers who were always glad of full houses. A Roman saga called 'Titus Andronicus' took advantage of the current fashion for revenge tragedies and the London playgoers' appetite for violence and blood-lust, and he had followed this by a comedy entitled 'The Taming of the Shrew' which showed how versatile a writer he was becoming. So there was general anticipation about what he was going to produce next though his companions and his patron were sorry to be without him.

Rumours of the plague had been known since the spring when the first cases had been found in the City but this was not unusual in the warm weather. Alice had insisted that the house be kept fumigated and hung daily with fresh herbs and anyone venturing into the City to the shops and markets must wear a mask and carry a cloth soaked in vinegar and on their return wash themselves thoroughly. The children were kept in the house and visitors limited. But as summer progressed the weather became unusually hot and as the number of victims increased steadily an aura of anxiety began to pervade London.

Alice and Ferdinando were as worried as everyone else for although most of the victims were the poorer sort, Derby House was in the centre of the City, close by Paul's church, and Ferdinando insisted that Alice take the three children to Althorp Manor. Alice was eager to have the girls removed to safety but asked, "Can't we go to Lathom?"

Ferdinando was not averse to the suggestion because the Queen had decided to progress early to Oxford and Bath and most of the nobles were now moving to their country houses, partly for safety and partly because without the Queen the social life was much depleted. However he said, "Lathom is too long a journey for the children. You go to Althorp with them and I'll proceed to Lancashire."

Alice knew that her sisters Elizabeth and Anne would be at Althorp with their daughters. Into her mind flashed a picture of the turreted moated castle in the flat Lancashire countryside and the honour she received there. A domestic sojourn at her old home with young children and her mother and sisters who still considered it their right to interfere in her affairs was decidedly less attractive.

"Let us both go to Lathom," she said. "I don't want to be without you and we could take Anne with us while the younger ones go to Althorp with the maids. I think it's time she saw where she will live one day and she's old enough for the journey now if she goes by coach."

Ferdinando had not wished to be separated from his wife for such a long time so it was not difficult for him to be persuaded into this arrangement. Eight year old Frances and four year old Elizabeth were dispatched to Althorp with a large company of nursemaids, all eager to escape from the plague-infested city, while Lord and Lady Strange set off for Lathom with their excited elder daughter. Anne was to travel by coach in company with a body of attendants and her personal maid while her parents rode on horseback.

Lord and Lady Strange arrived at Lathom several days before their daughter even though they had stopped at Coventry and Stratford to watch players. The plague had forced all the companies on the road on one or other of the acknowledged circuits, some choosing the south-east, others the south-west where the Queen would be, but the north-west route was always popular. Lancashire was mercifully free of all signs of the plague and Alice relished again the tranquillity of the flat countryside with its scattering of villages and its cool air in contrast to the stifling heat of London at this time. They were given a warm welcome and people were morbidly fascinated by tales of the plague-stricken capital where casualties had now risen to thousands. When they rode over to Knowsley to see Lord Derby they informed him that even Bartholomew Fair had been cancelled, the Londoners' great holiday celebration to which the working people looked forward to as the highlight of their year.

They had been settled at Lathom for almost a week when a message arrived that Lady Anne's party had reached Standish and Ferdinando rode out to meet his daughter, taking with him a pony he had bought for her, because he wanted to see her reaction as they approached Lathom House. He had been informed they were resting at The Red Lion inn in the market place and when he arrived he found a small crowd of people, mostly women with young children, who had paused in their morning shopping and were waiting with interest to see the noble company, especially on learning that Lord Strange's little daughter was making her first visit to Lancashire.

Anne looked tired but her face was flushed with excitement and she curtseyed to her father after which he took her in his arms. He wanted to know all the details of the journey but once he was satisfied that all had gone well he said, "Are you too tired to ride the last part of the way, darling, I've brought a pony for you."

"Oh no, father, I would love to ride, I am so weary of the coach," she cried eagerly, especially when she saw the little grey that was waiting for her. As she mounted, the waiting women and children waved to her and called greetings and she waved back regally, her face aglow with the respect she was receiving. Ferdinando repeated the first journey he had made with Alice, pointing out all the local sights as he rode beside his daughter. Once again he halted at the top of Parbold Hill to let her see the vast panorama spread out below and directing her gaze to Lathom House in the near distance. He enjoyed seeing her amazement, especially as they rode nearer to the House and the great castle began to unfold its magnificence before her wondering eyes.

Her fascination with the castle never waned and though she welcomed the safety of the quiet countryside in contrast to the dirty, noisy, plague-ridden streets of London, it was in exploring the vastness of Lathom House and enjoying the respectful service she received that her real enjoyment lay. Watching her delight in the greatness of her inheritance, Alice was once again filled with remorse that it wasn't a son inspecting his patrimony. She was bitterly disappointed that there had been no further child since Elizabeth four years ago but still hoping for a son and heir.

"It isn't as if we only make love occasionally," she said as she nestled beside her husband in bed. They shared a bedchamber and a bed in contrast to most nobles of their acquaintance whose custom was to have their own apartments with the husband visiting his wife's chamber only when he wished.

"There's still time," he reassured her. "We are only thirty-two. Perhaps I should try harder," he grinned, pulling her to him.

While at Lathom, Alice had ridden out once or twice in company with Alexander Standish on the occasions when he had arrived at the House on some excuse and one day he said hesitantly, "I would like to take you riding over Anglezarke one day if Lord Strange would give his permission."

"What a strange name. Where is this Anglezarke?" Alice asked.

"It isn't far from my home at Duxbury, over the moors towards Bolton," he replied. "I often ride over there, it's one of my favourite places, and I would like you to see it. Lord Derby owns the manor there."

"Does he! I have never known my husband mention it. It's a strange name," she said.

"It's a Viking name. The Vikings invaded this part of Lancashire in the tenth century. They had a base in Ireland, in Dublin, and they crossed from there to the Lancashire coast which is flat and sandy. Duxbury Hall was originally the settlement of a Viking chieftain."

"You are well informed of your history, Alex," she said in surprise.

"I like history," he said, flushing a little in embarrassment. "Especially the history of these parts. If Lord Strange gave his permission, do you think you would come?.......my lady," he added.

"I would like to see this place with a strange name," she confirmed.

When Alexander Standish made his hesitant request to Lord Strange, Ferdinando said, smiling at his earnestness, "I am sure you will take great care of Lady Strange who has already expressed her wish to see this place. I know it is one of Lord Derby's manors but I have never been there myself. Perhaps my wife will enlighten me on her return."

The day was set, providing the weather was fine, and at the appointed time Alexander arrived at Lathom and he and Alice set off towards Parbold Hill. At the top they turned in a northerly direction along a leafy lane instead of taking the road to Standish. The road turned and twisted, becoming flat again as they rode along fields of wheat and oats, the outline of misty hills in the distance.

"This is the Yarrow brook," he said as they rode now through woods alongside a river, "and to the right amid the trees is my home, Duxbury Hall, you can just see the top of the pele."

Alice expressed her interest but he seemed disinclined to go nearer, instead crossing a highway which he said was the road from Chorley to Bolton.

"We shall soon be on the moors."

In a short time the broad track led onto a stony path that seemed to be going north and soon they were amongst wild moorland, riding now across rough grass dotted with heather and gorse. There was little sign of habitation, just the odd farmstead scattered amongst the wild terrain with sheep grazing. There was a brooding silence with only the sound of curlew and plover and the soft distant baaing of the sheep.

"This is Anglezarke moor and in front of us is Winter Hill, the highest point," Alexander said. "There isn't a village here but soon you will see Anglezarke Manor."

He led the way across the moorland until they found a path leading to a small manor house of stone and black timber, half way between the wooded valley and the rugged hills, backed by sheltering rowan and ash but with its face to a rolling vista stretching for miles.

"So Lord Derby owns this," Alice said.

"He lets it out to tenants," Alexander said. He was silent for a time while Alice surveyed the scene then continued shyly, "I would like to live there. If I wasn't the eldest son I would ask if I could be the tenant."

"You would like to live in such a wild and isolated place?" Alice asked in amusement.

"It isn't really so isolated. You can see Chorley town there to the north and Duxbury is almost in a direct line, I can be here in less than a half hour. I attended the grammar school at Rivington which is just over the hill. There's nothing threatening or menacing about this place like there is with some lonely places, just space and freedom, nothing but an awareness of how big the world is, how beautiful nature is. It's my favourite place, I come here often. I feel I could almost fly like a bird when I'm up here, like an eagle." His blue eyes were narrowed into the light and his fair hair, darkened in places like damp wheat, was ruffling in the breeze.

She smiled at his whimsical turn of thought but understood what he meant as her gaze roved over the undulating landscape, black peaty moors of the Pennine range to the east but then gentler vistas of fields and woods as the land fell to the north and the river Yarrow, and below them in the valleys gurgling streams and leafy glades. She thought of the eagle soaring aloft on the Derby crest and asked, "Do you have ambitions to rise, Alex?"

He laughed, shaking his head as he replied, "I'm not ambitious, Lady Strange, not in a worldly way. When Duxbury Hall belongs to me I intend to improve it and increase our land-holdings. My ambition is to build a new Hall. From what I have heard about the Court I have no desire to go to London and be a courtier, I would not be happy with the suspicion, the back-biting, the constant struggle to be better than anyone else. I'm happy here, this is where I belong. And we don't have the plague here."

He turned from the ridge with its extensive views and began to lead the way down to a more sheltered leafy vale with the moors rising above them and here he stopped, deciding this was where they would eat the picnic that had been provided for them in the castle kitchens. He unstrapped the pannier carrying the basket of food and laid down the blanket on the grass. They ate in companionable silence, relishing the meats and cheeses, the newly baked bread, pastries and fresh fruit, for the ride had made them hungry. Alice thought in some amusement how different it was from when she participated in the May Day picnics Queen Elizabeth always arranged, when a hundred courtiers travelled on horseback to some picturesque spot with dozens of carts carrying banquets of food with fine linen and glasses, and musicians played while they ate in a pretence of country living. Here in this isolated place there was no sound but the shuffling of their horses and the crying of birds soaring on the heights, no movement except the breeze ruffling the canopy of trees. With the bare moors rolling around them it could have been a melancholy place but instead there was an overwhelming sense of peace with wispy white clouds floating in a sky the colour of a pigeon's wing, the intermittent sun shadowing the grass. London with its plague-ridden streets seemed a million miles away, another world.

"It's beautiful, Alex," she said. "I like this place very much."

He studied her in her russet velvet riding habit, almost the colour of her hair glowing in the sun's rays for her small low-crowned riding hat of black velvet lay on the grass beside her, and felt greatly privileged to be alone in her company.

"Was Lord Derby very angry over the affray at Lea Hall?" he asked suddenly.

"What makes you ask that, Alex?" she said in surprise.

"It was my uncle, my mother's brother Thomas Hoghton who owned the Hall and who was one of the men killed. Did you not know?"

"No I am not familiar with all the relationships around here. All I know is that it was a fight over some cows with so many people wounded and two men killed that the Queen felt bound to voice her displeasure. Yes, Lord Derby was angry when she accused him of not doing enough to keep his tenants in order. And Lord Strange was disturbed because it gave the Queen and the Privy Council reason yet again to see Lancashire as a wild and lawless place."

"I'm very sorry that the affair began with my family," Alexander said miserably.

"You cannot be held responsible for the actions of your relatives," Alice said gently, remembering she had said the same to Ferdinando. "I'm sure Lord Strange will not hold it against you. But how could a brawl of such magnitude occur over a herd of cows?"

"Cows are very valuable here, my lady, especially as the farming land is not good in many places. It is not the first time there has been disputes over the ownership of cattle. This one happened to be of great proportions with large bands of armed men on either side. But it was a great sorrow to our family when my uncle was killed. I hope Lord Strange will understand our regret."

Alice smiled at his anxiety and re-assured him that no displeasure would fall on him personally and with a sigh of relief he rose and began to collect the remains of the picnic and store them away again in his pannier.

As they made their way up from the valley and halted again on the heights to take a last look at the vista around them, Alexander said, "I'm getting married soon."

Alice was surprised and asked, "How old are you, Alex?"

"I shall be twenty by then. Do you think that is too young?"

Looking at his boyish face, untouched by life's misfortunes, Alice considered he *was* too young for the responsibilities of marriage and a family, but instead she said, "Lord Strange and I were both only twenty when we married and we have been very happy together. Are you in love with her?"

He hesitated then said, "She seems to be a very pleasant girl. I have only seen her a couple of times. It has been arranged by my parents. I think my father is feeling his mortality of late, he has recently made his will and would like to see me settled before he dies as I am the heir. Her name is Alice. Alice Assheton, she is of Whalley."

Alice studied him carefully and for an agonizing moment he feared she could see into the reaches of his mind and would know that the girl's name had attracted him because he could murmur it in his lovemaking.

Alice however had no suspicion of his thoughts as she said, "I hope you will be as happy as Lord Strange and I have been for we have always loved each other from the moment we met."

Alexander Standish thought for a moment that his heart would break with envy. When they had left the moors and were back on the Chorley road, Alice asked, "Would you like to show me your home, Alex, as we pass so close by Duxbury."

He appeared ill at ease as he said, "It is not a place of great luxury, my lady. I live in the pele while my parents and my youngest sister Ellen, she is twenty-five but unmarried, live at the Hall together with Leonard when he is not at Lathom. The Hall has not really changed since medieval times."

"I am not so concerned with luxury that I would scorn the acquaintance of our neighbours," she said gently. "I am only a great lady because I am the wife of Lord Strange. My father's family the Spencers were sheep farmers a hundred years ago and my mother's family the Kitsons were merchants."

Alexander looked surprised but she intuited that this was not the time to press him so said, "Perhaps next time I am in this direction you will warn your parents so that I may pay my respects to them. But as it has grown late I suppose it will be best if we return to Lathom."

Back at Lathom, Alice invited Alexander to join them at supper, the evening meal usually taken at five, but he courteously refused saying that he had to return home. However when he was persuaded to take a fresh horse from the stables he did not desist as it gave him an excuse to return to the House another time to collect his own mount.

Over supper Alice described Anglezarke to her husband then asked him about the disturbance at Lea Hall. "Where is this Hall?" she asked.

"On the banks of the river Ribble, near the town of Preston," he replied. "It is owned by the Hoghton family as well as the Tower near Blackburn. I don't think we heard the whole of the affair, it was more likely about land than cows. Thomas Langton of Walton was the aggressor and is being brought to justice. What I don't understand is that they are all Catholics, both Langton and the Hoghtons have been suspected of harbouring priests, and they usually all stick together."

Alice told him about Alexander's anxiety asking, "Are the Standishes of Duxbury Catholics?"

Ferdinando shook his head, "No, they are one of the few Protestant families around here though nearly all their kinsfolk are Papists." He smiled suddenly, "Is young Alexander afraid I will forbid him your company if any shadow of disrepute touches him? It is well I am not a jealous man or I might seek this opportunity to deprive my wife of her cavalier servente."

Alice laughed and crossing over to her husband whispered in his ear, "Come to bed early tonight."

Only when it was certain that the plague in London had worn itself out did the Stranges depart from Lathom and once again Alice found herself loath to leave the Lancashire stronghold. The servants and retainers lined their path as they rode through the inner courtyard and noticing Leonard Standish among them she leaned from the saddle to say, "Give my best wishes to your brother Alexander for his nuptials." Then they were away, clattering through the gatehouse and across the moat on their long journey back to London.

When they did arrive in the City they found it poorer than when they departed. The plague was over now the weather was cooler and winter on its way but it had left behind a total of 15,000 dead. A great proportion of the poorer working people had been victims, businesses had been affected, great houses had been left without adequate supervision, theft and vandalism had been rife and ships sat at anchor in the Thames. Playhouses had stood empty, inns depleted of their custom with their yards closed to entertainment, and many of the poorer tenements were without their tenants and in a state of neglect and decay. It was a sober emigrant population that returned from the countryside to find sober citizens taking stock of their city.

Alice set the servants to cleaning and purifying, washing and polishing, so that all vestiges of miasma were removed in a vigorous upheaval, and the party returned from Althorp, the children eager to rival Anne's elation with their own stories from their mother's old home. Frances renewed her acquaintance with her grandmother and Anne also was invited to pay a visit to Clerkenwell as the Countess was eager to learn her impressions of Lathom House. The Countess also began to broach the idea of her future marriage, insisting to her parents that now was the time to look for a suitable husband.

"She is yet too young," Ferdinando demurred but his mother over-ruled him.

"Leave it too long and all the prime suitors will have been taken," she declared. "The Earl of Southampton and the Earl of Pembroke's son are much in demand, the latter being sought by your brother-in-law George Carey for his daughter. Some parents of noble girls arrange their marriages in their cradles as you well know. She must be affianced before she is of an age to have opinions of her own, it is easier this way for she cannot be allowed to let romantic feelings over-ride her duty to her noble lineage."

The statement was accompanied by a glare at her son and daughter-in-law and Alice wondered how she could voice such a sentiment in the light of her own unhappy experience. Nevertheless Ferdinando agreed, somewhat unwillingly, to search out possible suitors now they were returned to London.

In the City the thankful survivors set to work to revive their lives and before long London was once again pulsing with energy, the houses with open windows, the markets bustling with trade, the inns welcoming their customers with fresh bushes and new-painted signs. The players returned and the playhouses opened to great acclamation and a spate of new plays written by the playwrights while in enforced retirement. To everyone's surprise William Shakespeare had not been writing plays in the interim. He had produced a long narrative poem entitled 'Venus and Adonis' which he dedicated to the wealthy young Earl of Southampton and which was so successful that it sold out immediately.

Alice made herself ready to join her friends at Court again and to exchange all the experiences of their enforced separation. Ferdinando rushed out to buy a copy of 'Venus and Adonis' which he discussed avidly with his friends. They all agreed on the literary excellence of the work, proclaiming the young Shakespeare equal to Spenser as a poet. Although agreeing with the commendation, Lord Strange hoped that this particular member of his Company would not desert the theatre for a poetic career and determined to persuade him to write another play as quickly as possible.

CHAPTER 13

Conspiracies

The meetings at Walter Raleigh's house were disbanded for the simple reason that he was imprisoned in the Tower. The Queen had taken him as her favourite in preference to the Earl of Essex and had showered him with gifts, houses, lands and a knighthood, but had expected in return his total devotion – he was after all forty years old and unmarried. But he had betrayed her by getting one of her ladies with child and had compounded the offence by marrying her secretly. The Queen was furious and had imprisoned them both.

"I'm sorry Raleigh is out of circulation," Ferdinando said when he heard the news. He knew that his friend would not be imprisoned in the harshest of circumstances, he would have a room with a fire, be permitted to send out for food as he was not short of money, be able to enjoy his books and his writing and have friends to visit. Nonetheless it was by no means as comfortable as being at home and lonely for much of the time.

"I must try to go and see him." He knew Raleigh would welcome the opportunity to carry on his intellectual discussions.

"Be careful," Alice warned. "He's most certainly out of favour and anyone showing him friendship will earn the wrath of the Queen."

"Do you think that is enough to warrant my discarding friends when they are in trouble," he retorted. "God's lights, he's only got a woman with child and done the right thing by marrying her, not exactly treason. In fact it could have happened to me," he added with a grin.

However the Raleigh circle was soon missing another of its members, more permanently than a sojourn in the Tower for Christopher Marlowe was dead. It was Alice who first heard the news as she had gone on a shopping excursion to the Exchange with her maid Lucy and two of the male house attendants to escort them. The Exchange had been built twenty years earlier on the model of the Bourse in the Flemish town of Antwerp by Sir Thomas Gresham, a mercer and financial agent to the Crown. Besides being a financial centre where the merchants gathered twice a day, the balconied upper floor on marble pillars above the quadrangle consisted of a hundred small shops and Alice loved to visit the jewellers, haberdashers and mercers. Afterwards they would enjoy strolling through the piazzas with covered walkways lined with statues of English kings and it was here that she heard the news being passed around.

"Marlowe dead!" Ferdinando exclaimed in disbelief when his wife returned with the news. "In what way? He wasn't yet thirty years old and was in the best of health as far as I know."

"They were talking about him being involved in an argument at an inn in Deptford," she replied.

Ferdinando recalled how Marlowe had been involved in fights before, some of them not wholly explicable, so the news was believable. But he was disturbed and hastened off immediately to try and find out more details. Marlowe was indispensable to the players. He had now written three more plays which had ensured full houses at the Rose, especially with Edward Alleyn in the leading roles, and 'The Massacre of Paris' had been written specifically for Strange's Men. 'Edward II' and 'Dr. Faustus', with aspects of homosexuality and the Black Arts, had been more controversial and though they had pleased the London playgoers, the authorities had been disturbed.

His death was the talk of London and the story was that he had been killed over an argument concerning a bill at a Deptford inn where he had shared a meal with three friends. While acknowledging that this could have been a possible consequence of an afternoon's drinking, Ferdinando was not completely convinced that something else did not lie behind it. He admired Marlowe as a gifted playwright but he had always been wary of his opinions and suspicious of his activities beyond the range of the theatre. He thought it was time to pay a visit to Sir Walter Raleigh.

He was admitted into the Tower without hesitation though he slipped a gold coin into the warden's hand as he was escorted to where Raleigh had been given an apartment. The room was of a sizeable proportion with a window overlooking an inner courtyard and a door led into an adjoining bedchamber. But the stone walls gave off a chill that the early summer sun could not dispel and it was dark and gloomy. The royal prisoner was seated in a tall-backed chair at a table covered with books and maps and he rose joyfully when Lord Strange was admitted. He was dressed with his usual elegance in a flame-coloured velvet doublet heavily embossed with gold thread but over it he wore a thick fur-lined mantle and beneath his padded hose he wore canions and long boots.

"Inclined to be chilly," he said, then he clasped Ferdinando's hand in a warm grasp. "You are most welcome, Lord Strange, and I thank you for your consideration. I thought I was persona non grata."

"Not with everyone. Do you need anything?"

"Only my freedom," Raleigh smiled mirthlessly. "I thought the Queen would have released me by now."

"Do you not get out at all?"

"I'm allowed to walk in the gardens sometimes. Fortunately I have my books." He gestured to where piles of books were stacked on the floor. "But I am not of a nature to be cooped up. You know I was at sea when the Queen discovered Bess's condition. She had me brought back from Panama. Here take my seat, there's only the one I'm afraid."

"No, I'll perch on the chest," Ferdinando said, seating himself on the large seaman's chest which was the only other furniture in the room and which obviously held Raleigh's belongings. He didn't like to ask personal questions about Raleigh's predicament and instead he said, "I suppose you have heard the news of Marlowe's death?"

"Cecil!"

Ferdinando was startled at the vehemence of the word and looked puzzled.

Raleigh continued, "I wouldn't be surprised if Robert Cecil isn't behind this somewhere. I've suspected for some time that Marlowe has been used to gather information, especially on his trips abroad. You know he was arrested for coining money in the Low Countries, a hanging offence, yet no prosecution was made. He always had more money than his writing warranted, his father was only a shoemaker."

Ferdinando knew that Marlowe had spent some time in the Low Countries. This was the ambience of Sir William Stanley and other Lancashire Catholic exiles. The name of Lord Strange was bandied about in continental Catholic circles as a likely supporter of Papist plots, Father Campion had said as much, and it was an uncomfortable thought that the playwright might have used their professional partnership as an entree into circles where Ferdinando's reputation was compromised and then passed on information.

"Perhaps he stepped out of line somewhere," Raleigh suggested, "you know he was no follower of rules."

"You can't really believe that, Walter," Ferdinando said.

"I know Robert Cecil has inherited Walsingham's mantle for espionage, or the security of the state as they prefer to call it. And he's just as ruthless in getting rid of inconvenient obstacles. He hates me." Once again Ferdinando was startled by the vehemence and he saw Raleigh's handsome face harden and his lips set into a grim line. "He seeks to blacken my name, not openly but by hints and insinuations." His West-Country accent became stronger in his anger.

Ferdinando thought Raleigh could hardly blame Cecil for the predicament he now found himself in and as if guessing his thoughts he continued, "Popular report is that I seduced Mistress Throckmorton, accusing me of a 'brutish offence', but it isn't true. We were both willing partners, she is no young maiden, she is almost as old as I am."

Ferdinando knew that Alice's opinion was that Bess Throckmorton was more likely to have seduced the handsome seafarer, saying that not only was she one of the oldest of the Queen's ladies but also one of the plainest, and Raleigh had been known to boast that despite his conquests there was no-one he wanted to be fastened to.

"When she found herself with child I did the honourable thing and married her, where is the offence in that?"

Ferdinando felt bound to say gently, "By marrying in secret. Why didn't you be honest and ask the Queen's permission?"

"I feared her anger. And her disillusion," he added honestly. "You know, Ferdinando, that it's common opinion I have used the Queen to raise myself, cloaking naked ambition with flattery and sycophancy, but it isn't true. I have a genuine affection for her. I admire her with every part of my being, I enjoy her company, I am lost without her." There were tears in his eyes. "I heard she was passing in her barge the other day and I begged George Carew, Lieutenant of the Tower, to let me out for a time so that I could see her but he didn't dare even though he is my cousin. I was so distraught I took a dagger to myself but he prevented me from doing harm. I fear I shall go insane if she doesn't restore her favour to me. It will all go to Essex now."

Ferdinando did not know how to respond to this display of unexpected emotion but rose and put his hand on his friend's shoulder.

Sir Walter looked up at him saying, "In marrying young, Ferdinando, you escaped the Queen's possessiveness. You have always had a good head on your shoulders."

"Pray God I keep it there," Ferdinando said in an attempt at lightheartedness.

"Me too," said Sir Walter Raleigh.

A brooding silence hung between them for a while.

It was soon relayed to Lord Strange by his friends at Court that the Queen was displeased with him for consorting with the disgraced favourite.

"I am not going to discard my friends because they are out of favour with the Queen," he said staunchly. "She rules the country, and our hearts they say, but she does not rule my life to the extent of choosing my friends."

"I do wish you would not be so outspoken, I am afraid of your getting into trouble," Alice said, a worried frown creasing her brow, though secretly she was proud that he was no sycophant as a lot of the courtiers were.

It was getting time for the general summer exodus from the City and the Queen had already gone on progress. However before she left she released Sir Walter Raleigh from the Tower because she needed him for a special commission. A Spanish treasure ship laden with gold and jewels had been captured but when it was towed into Dartmouth the sailors and local people had already plundered much of it despite George Clifford being sent to appropriate a large share for the Queen herself. Knowing Raleigh's esteem amongst sailors she ordered him to go and stop the riot and ensure the booty was divided fairly, in other words to claim a large proportion of it for herself. Despite his success he was not allowed to return to Court and although she did not send him back to the Tower she ordered that he remain at his country estate in Dorset.

The Stranges decided it was time for their annual excursion to their estates in Lancashire, especially as they had received word that the Earl of Derby was not well. Once again their eldest daughter Anne accompanied them while the two younger girls were sent to Althorp, a not unwelcome alternative for Lady Spencer bestowed more affection on them than did their mother. Alice had discovered to her surprise that the strict governance of her childhood, when she and her sisters had stood in awe of their mother, was relaxed for her granddaughters and she seemed to genuinely enjoy the novelty of the children's company.

It was August when they arrived in Lancashire and they were shocked to see the deterioration in the health of Lord Derby. He looked frail, his eyes sunken and more pouched than ever, his skin yellow. William said he didn't leave Knowsley and New Park. Although Alice had no wish to see Earl Henry dead, for she had always had kind feelings towards him since he had not opposed her marriage to his son, nevertheless she could not help thoughts creeping into her mind that she might be Countess of Derby sooner than she had expected for the Earl was only just sixty years old.

It was William however who broached the subject openly saying to his brother, "It seems you might be Lord Derby soon," a trace of envy in his voice. He was rewarded by a withering look.

In the weeks that followed Ferdinando attempted to spend as much time as he could with his father though in their talks together he was aware that the Earl was preparing him for the task which now seemed increasingly imminent. Alice found herself with time on her hands. She paid visits to their neighbours and took her maids to the weekly market in Ormskirk where they enjoyed examining the surprising variety of goods, some brought from ships trading at Liverpool, as well as the interested reverence they received from the local people. She rode out every day though she was now familiar with the landscape around Lathom and was suddenly filled with a desire to see the wild moorland of Anglezarke again. One day at the market she had purchased a finely-crafted glass bowl. There had been glass manufacturers in Lathom for some time, supplying the needs of Lord Derby's households, and they were beginning to learn new skills with merchants introducing examples of Venetian glassware for them to emulate. On an impulse she decided to visit Duxbury Hall and present it to young Alexander Standish and his new wife as a wedding gift.

Receiving her husband's permission for the visit and escorted by two grooms she set off one September morning on the way to Duxbury, following the road through the countryside from Parbold as on her previous visit. Remembering how Alexander had pointed out to her the path by the side of the river which he had said led to the Hall she led the way through the trees to the tower visible above them. After a time the path became gravelled and ended at a large timbered and stone farmhouse behind which a stone pele tower three storeys high was built on an eminence. The house was surrounded by barns and outbuildings and a paved courtyard fronted a low studded entrance door beneath a wide triangular porch of dressed stone. The building was only two storeys high but gabled at one end and the irregular aspect was further characterized by small-paned windows unevenly distributed across the facade. Animal sounds of hens, geese and pigs could be heard and a young lad appeared from a stable to ask their business, obviously overawed by the splendidly dressed company on their fine-bred horses. Alice remained seated in the background whilst one of the grooms asked to be introduced to Thomas and Mistress Standish and at that moment the front door was opened by a young maidservant, neatly dressed in a grey wool skirt and bodice with a clean white apron and coif. She dropped a low curtsey and on hearing their business invited them into the house, saying she would call her master and mistress immediately.

They were led into a low hall with smoke-blackened beams, stone flagged and dominated by a large stone fireplace in which a huge log glowed red, but it was well furnished with a long oak table, some high-backed chairs and a livery cupboard, obviously made by a local craftsman but with expertly carved stags' heads in the panelling.

Alice seated herself on one of the chairs with the grooms beside her and immediately there was the sound of running footsteps and Thomas Standish bustled into the hall followed by his wife Margaret. Thomas was red-faced with embarrassment and Margaret flustered to the extent of panic by the surprise visit of the great Lady Strange now seated comfortably in their hall. Margaret Standish, a woman of some sixty years like her husband, was very conscious of her working gown of brown wool with a linen coif, in contrast to Lady Strange's fashionable riding habit of russet velvet with gold lacings and buttons. They made deep honours and speaking together he was offering his apologies for not being prepared while his wife was stammering that she would immediately order refreshments for them. Alice had seen them once at a festival at Lathom House and smiling graciously calmed their apprehensions by apologising for her unexpected appearance and explaining that she really wished to see their son Alexander. Thomas immediately offered to call for him, saying he was over at the pele, while Margaret returned with a young woman bearing a silver tray on which stood pewter cups of wine and a dish of jumble biscuits.

"This is my youngest daughter, Ellen, my lady," she said, and Alice accepted her formal curtsey with polite acknowledgements while she studied Alexander's sister, remembering that he had said she was twenty five years old. She wasn't a beauty but had a pleasant open face and blue eyes reminiscent of her brother while her complexion boasted of fresh air and good country food.

"My other three daughters are all wed," Margaret Standish explained, then encouraged by Lady Strange's ease of manner continued, "four girls until we were blessed by two sons."

Perhaps there is hope for me after all, Alice thought to herself.

When Alexander Standish entered with his father his delight was evident in his face as she stood to greet him, holding out her hand. He was accompanied by a very young girl wearing a closed woollen gown the colour of bluebells with a lawn chemise drawn into a ruffle around her neck. Her brown hair was just visible beneath her neat coif, her fair skin was flushed and her large brown eyes had the look of a nervous spaniel.

"This is my wife Alice," he said.

Alice Stanley smiled encouragingly at her young namesake and said, "I have brought you a gift, somewhat belated, for your marriage."

One of the grooms handed over the cloth-wrapped parcel and when the crystal bowl was revealed there was a concerted gasp of admiration as the glass twinkled in the rays of the sunbeams filtering through the casement.

"I shall treasure it ... we shall treasure it all our lives," Alexander cried while his wife held the bowl in trembling amazement and his parents were overwhelmed at the honour shown to their family by Lord and Lady Strange.

"I also came to ask if you would accompany me to Anglezarke, Alexander," Alice said, "if you are not otherwise occupied. I doubt I could find the way to direct my attendants. Your wife also if she should wish."

"I am not occupied, my lady, I would be honoured to do so. But my wife is expecting our child so I doubt it would be wise for her to ride," he answered promptly.

The girl was blushing furiously and Lady Alice said, "Then Mistress Alice would you mind if I borrowed your husband for an hour or two."

"Not at all, my lady, I am honoured that you should honour my husband in this way." She looked up at him with adoration in her brown eyes.

They were soon in the saddle and on their way to the moors, Alexander and Alice leading the way with the two grooms somewhat reluctantly riding behind. As they began to climb towards Anglezarke Alice glanced back to where the grooms were muttering to themselves and looking distinctly unhappy and with a conspiratorial look on her face whispered to Alexander, "Can't we lose these two somewhere. I don't suppose there's a tavern where we could leave them for a time, they are obviously not enjoying this."

"As a matter of fact there is," he replied. "A little further along the road to Bolton is a small village called

Adlington and there is an inn there called The Green
Man."

When Alice suggested they should resort there until
called for and Alexander gave them the directions they
thankfully obeyed and Alexander felt a great soaring of
his heart as he realised he was alone with his countess in
his favourite place. She let her young escort lead the way
to further exploration, passing Anglezarke Manor
again until at last they rested on the crest, seated on their
horses with the landscape spread out before them in all
its autumn shades of brown and gold and misty mauve,
the fresh breeze kissing their cheeks and ruffling their
hair. She wanted him to point out all the details of the
geography, listening with interest to his history of the
area, and he knew the names of the birds that flew above
and landed beside them, identifying their different calls.

"Are you happy in your marriage, Alex?" she asked.

"Oh yes, my lady," he replied enthusiastically, then he
blushed and she smiled. Young Alice Assheton was indeed
fortunate to have such a handsome young husband,
physically in the prime of his life and who had so quickly
given her a child. She thought back to the early days of her
marriage when she and Ferdinando had been so carefree.
He was worried at the moment by his father's ill-health
and the anticipation of the great responsibility soon to be
laid upon him. In that hour of perfect tranquillity when
the space between earth and sky seemed to be empty of all
but the two riders she had no presentiment of how that
peace would soon be shattered.

They collected the grooms from The Green Man and
then at the crossroads to Chorley she bade Alexander
Standish farewell with thanks for indulging her whim
and salutations to his parents and wife, especially with

regard to the forthcoming child. Then they turned by the Yarrow brook to make their way back through the fields, ready for harvesting, to Lathom.

When they arrived back at the castle she was met by her maid Lucy who informed her that Lord Strange had a visitor who would be joining them for supper. Ferdinando certainly hadn't been expecting anyone when she left and she wondered who it might be.

"Is it someone important?" she enquired, but the girl knew nothing further except that Lord Strange had told her to warn his wife and tell her that he himself would be occupied with the visitor until the time to eat. Alice dressed in a gown neither too plain nor too grand, not knowing the status of the stranger, and went to join her husband in the dining hall at the appointed time.

Ferdinando acknowledged her presence but she thought he looked somewhat distracted as he introduced the man beside him, "This is Richard Hesketh. My wife, Lady Strange."

Alice saw a stout man in his late thirties with yellow hair and beard and holding out her hand asked, "Are you of the Heskeths of Rufford Hall? I don't believe we have met before."

"I am a cousin of Sir Robert, my lady, whom I believe you know well. My father was Gabriel Hesketh of Aughton." Alice knew the village near Ormskirk. "I believe you once encountered my brother Bartholomew Hesketh at Rufford Hall." Searching her memory she recalled the black-bearded man they had seen when Sir Thomas had entertained them with his miracle play.

"I am a merchant and for the last five years I have been out of England, in the Low Countries and lately in Prague," the stranger continued.

She wondered what business he might have with them though surmised a matter of some merchandise in Ferdinando's interest. However the conversation during the meal touched on no such subject, dealing only with banal observations on the state of the country, the quality of the harvest and the acquaintances they had in common. Alice was puzzled by her usually loquacious husband seeming disinclined to talk, even when his players were mentioned, a subject which usually roused him to vivacious enthusiasm. She sensed a great tension hovering between them for some unaccountable reason and was relieved when the uncomfortable meal ended. Richard Hesketh made to leave immediately and Ferdinando seemed eager to have him go.

As they parted the visitor said in a low voice, though still audible to Alice, "I trust to have a favourable response from you as quickly as possible, my lord. You know where to find me but I must return to London shortly and then back to Prague as soon as I can."

"What was all that about?" Alice asked when the visitor had left them.

She expected her husband to laugh about an awkward encounter, about having to refuse one of the many favours he was always plied with, but instead, with a quick look around at the servants who were still about their business in the hall, he took her arm saying, "Come into our chamber where we can talk without being overheard."

In the seclusion of their bedroom in the Round Tower Ferdinando first turned the key in the lock while Alice stood waiting expectantly, puzzled and not a little anxious. Still he did not speak, walking restlessly the length of the chamber, biting his lip, his brow furrowed, and she burst out, "For God's sake, tell me what the matter is, what has happened to put you in this state."

"Sit down," he said, leading her to a chair while he continued to stand. "I don't know where to start." She waited expectantly, her heart beating fast, and at last he made a great effort. "To be brief, Richard Hesketh has come on an embassage from Catholic exiles in Prague. As you know, there are many of them residing there at the Court of the Holy Roman Emperor, several Lancashire Catholics, some of my relations including William Stanley. They are in communication with other exiles in Madrid, France and the Low Countries as Edmund Campion reminded me and the arch-priest Persons continues to mobilise them. Richard Hesketh has delivered a letter signed by a selection of representatives asking me to head a rebellion in England to reinstate the Catholic religion and," he paused, "for me to take Elizabeth's place when she is deposed."

"Well that's easy," she retorted, "you have nothing to do with it, you refuse as you have done before, as you did with Edmund Campion. Unless," a thought struck her, "you are actually considering it."

"Alice, surely to God you know me better than that," he almost shouted. "Never in all my life has there been thought in my mind not to be loyal to the Queen. If the Queen and my mother were both dead, if there were no better claimants to the Crown than I and if I were chosen by the people of England to be their King then I would consider it my destiny. But under no other circumstances would I act."

"Then what is the problem? You ignore it and we pretend Richard Hesketh never paid us a visit, as we did with Edmund Campion."

He sighed heavily. "It isn't as simple as that. In the first place this involves a lot of people, a lot of Catholics I know personally, for example Father John Gerard son of the Gerards of Bryn." (Alice knew that John Gerard had narrowly evaded capture when some of his Lancashire associates had been taken and executed at Tyburn, either as traitors or martyrs depending on opinion.) "I now have in my possession a letter signed by several people, some of them known to me from Lancashire families."

"Then burn it," she shrieked. "I would have thought you had already done so."

"I thought about doing so the moment he gave it to me," he replied evenly. "But two considerations prevented me. In the first place there are probably copies and I don't know where they are. In the second place I do not discount the possibility that the plot is already known, or at least suspected, in government circles. As you know, Robert Cecil has taken on the mantle of Francis Walsingham as head of state security and he has spies all over the Continent, as Walsingham had, to infiltrate gatherings of Catholic exiles and plant informers. Raleigh hinted that Christopher Marlowe had been used in this way on his sojourns abroad, periods of residence that seemed to have no useful purpose for the playwright. I suspect he used to use my name as an entree into certain circles but whether as a fellow theatre enthusiast or a clandestine rebel I do not know. You are aware that I have always been looked upon with suspicion by the Queen and the Privy Council. They suspect I am a secret Papist and a potential rebel even though I have never given them cause to believe either. I really do not know who is trying to use me here, the Catholics with the support of Spain or the government of my own country."

"Surely that is all the more reason to destroy the letter and forget everything that has happened."

"No darling, think about it. If the plot is discovered, or already known, then the fact that I cannot produce the communication will imply that I was willing to concur, or at least that I was willing to cover up the evidence."

Alice sighed, beginning to realise the complexity of the situation in which they now unexpectedly found themselves. "The only solution is to take the letter to the Privy Council," she said at last.

"Exactly! And what will happen then? Richard Hesketh and probably more of our neighbours and people who look upon me as their liege lord will face the utmost penalties and I shall have been the one to betray them. I shall be looked upon in Lancashire as the betrayer of the faith by which many of them live. It is no coincidence that this has happened when I shall soon be Lord Derby. And it doesn't necessarily mean that I shall be cleared by the Privy Council. If they do already have wind of such a plot then it is conceivable they might think I have confessed only when information has been leaked from other sources and I shall still be accused of treason and put to death. The plots surrounding Mary Stuart are still fresh in people's memories and you know what happened to anyone suspected of being a conspirator, suspected, not necessarily proven."

Alice sighed heavily, suddenly feeling a great fear consume her. She rose and went to take her husband's hand saying, "So what are you going to do?"

He released her hand gently and went to look out of the window, surveying the vast collection of assorted buildings and towers that was Lathom House and watching people about their business in the courtyard below – carrying buckets of water and baskets of linen, workmen with bags of tools, servants scurrying with messages and grooms leading horses.

"I suppose there is no alternative but to go to the Queen and the Privy Council," he murmured at last. Then he turned back to his wife saying sadly, "But I feel sick at heart at the knowledge that I shall be sending people to their deaths."

A death that had upset him recently was of a Catholic householder, Richard Ashton, from the nearby village of Croston who had been executed in London only because he had asked for a dispensation from the Holy See in Rome to marry a Catholic lady who was also his cousin, and the Privy Council had seen this as a treasonable act.

"The alternative could well be your death, darling, and I couldn't bear that," she said softly. "You must do this for me, for your own conscience, and for the honour of the Earls of Derby."

"Yes you are right, yet I do not feel I can do anything in haste, my thoughts are too confused. I must still study all the implications. But I cannot see a solution that will not bring great harm to someone."

"One thing I cannot understand is why in this dangerous situation you should have been handed a letter. Anyone could have intercepted it and it concerns written proof of treason. Surely the wisest move would have been to send a verbal message with Hesketh."

"That puzzles me also. There are many peculiar aspects about this affair that I find confusing. The only reason for the letter must be to convince me of the sincerity of the rebels, by signing their names they have left no doubt of their commitment in a way a reported invitation could not. But by sending a letter instead of a verbal communication they have also compromised me in a way that makes it impossible for me to manoeuvre," Ferdinando said, a feeling of foreboding overwhelming him.

Later lying in bed with her arms around her husband, comforting him and finding solace for herself in his nearness, Alice looked back on the peaceful hours she had spent at Anglezarke. She had once thought how wonderful it was to be rising in the world on the wings of an eagle. Now she wished she was flying like a wild bird above the lonely moorland with no frightening worries to pull her down to earth.

The turmoil into which they had been plunged did not abate over the next few days. Ferdinando was distracted, spending hours alone agonising about how he was going to resolve his dilemma while Alice shared his misery and tried to keep some semblance of normality in the household so that no-one would suspect anything was amiss. They had heard nothing further from Richard Hesketh and it was not known if he had left the area or not. Then Lord Derby had taken a turn for the worse and Ferdinando had spent another week by his bedside. It was almost three weeks before he arrived in London. When his father had rallied he had finally made the decision to leave for London, making an excuse of urgent business to his steward and leaving behind a very anxious Alice wondering how she could bear the interim until he returned. But though he had ridden hard for long periods of time, only stopping to change horses and sleep briefly, it was late into the night of the fourth day before he arrived back in the City, to the surprise of his servants at Derby House. The next morning he requested an interview with Lord Burghley but it was the afternoon of the following day before he was admitted to the Lord Treasurer's office at Whitehall.

He had passed another anxious day preparing how to explain himself and continued going over things in his mind as he progressed through the familiar maze of corridors and ante-rooms that made up the palace until at last he was admitted into the office of Lord Burghley. The Lord Treasurer's seventy years hung heavily on him with the burden of the affairs of state and the recent loss of his wife. His shoulders stooped, his face was creased with lines and his long beard completely grey, though the intelligent grey eyes fixed upon Lord Strange were as discerning as ever. Ferdinando explained his predicament as clearly as he could while trying his best to inculpate as few people as possible. Burghley listened attentively but his impassive reaction revealed nothing of his thoughts and he made no comment except to declare that the story must be put personally to the Queen. He ordered him to return the following day and Ferdinando left his presence, feeling no easier in his mind and wishing that the Lord Treasurer had given him some indication as to his opinion.

He spent another sleepless night, wishing he had Alice's company. Early next morning he repeated the long walk through the warren of Whitehall and though in the past he had sometimes felt trepidation when summoned into the Queen's presence he could not remember ever having felt so fearful and so alone.

When he was ushered into a private chamber he found the Queen seated in a red velvet chair before a table on which he could see his letter prominently displayed.

By her side stood Lord Burghley and his son Robert Cecil, now Secretary of State. After greeting him as Lord Strange she invited him to be seated, also beckoning the Lord Treasurer to a seat while Robert Cecil, a thin, hunch-backed young man of about thirty, remained standing.

"Lord Burghley has acquainted me of the matter in hand, Lord Strange," she said in her usual direct manner, placing her long white fingers upon the letter. "I am rather perturbed as to why it has taken you so long to bring this information to our attention." Her small dark eyes in her alabaster face, made whiter by the contrast of the severe high-necked gown of black embossed velvet, surveyed him coldly.

"I was in residence at Lathom House, your Majesty, it is several days' journey."

"But hardly three weeks," she replied promptly. "Was the delay to enable you to give warning to the conspirators? Or have you been considering the proposition?"

Her white face remained impassive but he felt her eyes boring into the inner reaches of his being and he felt a shiver of fear along his spine. However he forced himself to remain calm and replied stoutly, "Lord Derby is gravely ill. I was loath to leave him until I was assured of some improvement in his condition. I gave no thought to any other considerations. I have always been a most loyal subject of your Majesty and will continue to be so as long as I live."

Elizabeth said nothing but continued to look closely at him as if trying to read his thoughts. Finally she said, "I heard of your lord father's ill-health and I am sorry for it, he is not an old man. So it seems you may inherit the earldom sooner than anticipated, a fact not unrelated to the matter in hand."

"When that does happen, your Majesty, I assure you I shall continue to be your most loyal servant, as I have always been."

She remained silent for what seemed a long time and Ferdinando was aware of Robert Cecil's rapt attention, wondering if he could hear the beating of his heart which seemed to be drumming loudly.

Then Elizabeth said, "I am glad you have brought this matter to our notice. Be assured the perpetrators will be dealt with accordingly, as will all those who seek to undermine the stability of the State. Remember to remind your tenants in Lancashire of this. I am sure your conduct in this present matter will serve to give them an example of your own loyalty and your willingness to enforce the laws of this country with regard to religion."

Her warning was unmistakeable. Ferdinando continued to profess his undying loyalty to his sovereign and a small cynical smile appeared at the corner of her mouth.

"I think it might be an apposite time for the Countess of Derby to be released from our custody so that she can go to Lathom and say her farewells to her husband," she said.

Ferdinando said nothing. He was aware of a certain amount of sympathy from Lord Burghley, who had no doubt paved the way for this audience, but could feel nothing but coldness emanating from Robert Cecil's impassive gaze.

The Queen brought the interview to an end, confirming with the two Cecils that the treason would be rooted out promptly and due retribution fall on the traitors. After abasing himself to the limits of his endurance Ferdinando found himself once again in the corridors of Whitehall.

He could hardly constrain himself from running to the water stairs as anger, shame and a still-present fear consumed him. He could not bear to remain in London a day longer. Stopping only to eat a light meal at Derby House he ordered his bags to be packed and a horse saddled and he was away north at a furious pace, to Lathom and Alice.

Back home he confided all the details of the interview to his wife at the earliest opportunity. "I had the feeling she still didn't trust me. She didn't thank me for my loyalty or give thought to the sacrifices I had been forced to make," he said sadly. "She also made it abundantly clear that I had to be diligent in prosecuting the Catholics here. Burghley was sympathetic but Cecil seemed to be enjoying the confrontation. I don't trust him and I'm beginning to be of the opinion of Raleigh." He then went on to relate how the Queen had released Lady Margaret from her house arrest. "She has been looking for some excuse to release her, she cannot keep her confined for ever on such slight charges and my father's mortal illness has provided an opportunity. I am sure my mother will be relieved but the fact that she has been set free only for this reason will anger her. It's the Queen making mischief again because she knows my mother will not wish to visit my father and besides she is not in a fit state of health to be able to make the long journey to Lancashire. How is my father? I must go to see him as soon as possible."

"He is worse," Alice replied. "He will be happy to see you. And so am I. I'm so glad to have you back home with no further repercussions. Let us hope that is the end of the matter."

However despite their hopes they both knew that the consequences still had to be faced. There would be no relief as enquiries began, the conspirators hounded down, the trials instigated and the executions performed. It was a time of great distress for Lord and Lady Strange as news of the plot became public knowledge and rumour, accusation, and suspicion rebounded around Lancashire and London. The background to the drama was the worsening state of Lord Henry's health. They seemed to be living in a limbo of uncertainty, not knowing what each day might bring. Finally on the November day that Richard Hesketh was hanged, drawn and quartered at St. Alban's, Henry Stanley, 4th Earl of Derby died.

CHAPTER 14

Earl of Derby

In November 1593, aged thirty-three, Alice Spencer became a countess with a coronet and robes of ermine. Lady Margaret Stanley was relegated to Dowager Countess of Derby. Alice had outsoared all her family and believed that her dreams had come true, and as if to put the final touch to her achievement she now knew that she was pregnant again. She fervently believed that this time it must be an heir for the Earldom of Derby.

"I feel different this time to when I was carrying the girls. I know within myself that this child will be a son," she told Ferdinando confidently.

Lord Henry was interred with great pomp in the chapel his father had built specially in Ormskirk church for the tombs of the future Earls of Derby. A long procession of black-draped coaches and walkers in elaborate mourning clothes made their way from Lathom House to Ormskirk where the townspeople lined the streets in reverence and the Parish church was packed with neighbours and tenants.

When the funeral celebrations were done, the new Lord and Lady Derby were installed at Lathom with all the customary magnificence. People came from far and wide to pay their respects, offer their allegiance, and fix themselves in the remembrance of the young Earl. Only Robert Hesketh was noticeably missing. He sent word that he was sick. It was a time of feasting and merriment – "the King is dead, long live the King" – carried through enthusiastically into the Yuletide season.

Ferdinando's players, still named Lord Strange's but ready to change their name, arrived to give a continuous series of performances, among them William Shakespeare's play of Richard III extolling the first Lord Derby, and a comedy entitled 'The Two Gentlemen of Verona' which had played to great acclaim in London.

"I shall need to borrow a dog," Will had said, "preferably one that is well-behaved."

The new earl had been amused and mystified. "I know you often borrow swords and other artefacts, sometimes furniture, but I have never been asked for a dog before," he commented but told the playwright to have a word with one of the grooms.

However Alice said, "Why not Anne's spaniel, she would be very excited to have her pet in a performance."

All the girls had been brought to Lathom, nine year old Frances and five year old Elizabeth as excited as their elder sister had been by their first experience of living in the great castle which had now become their home.

Will Shakespeare had grave reservations about the suggestion. Crab was supposed to be an unimpressive mongrel and Lady Anne's mollycoddled spaniel hardly fitted the role but it was important to keep his patron happy and he had confidence that the comedian Will Kemp would improvise accordingly, he always did, much to Will's annoyance as he witnessed his carefully-composed lines being ruthlessly adapted. The play was a great success and the audience laughed uproariously at the animal's obvious unsuitability for the role and Kemp's frenetic attempts to coach some life out of the lapdog's passivity.

The celebrations continued without pause. The winter weather was fortunately mild and dry and the new Lord and Lady Derby rode about their vast domains surveying their lands, introducing themselves to their tenants, and receiving public acclamations in the streets, civic buildings and churches. Alice had never found her time so occupied or herself such a centre of attention. In the evenings Lathom House revelled in feasting and entertainment and Alice had her first experience of hearing the Lancashire toast proclaimed publicly as her husband's health was drunk – "God bless the Earl of Derby and the Queen" – wondering what Elizabeth would think of the priority.

On his father's death William had made Knowsley his permanent home, his status increasing to heir presumptive to the Earldom of Derby should his brother and sister-in-law not produce an heir though Alice was convinced that their forthcoming child would be a boy. William himself was fearful that it might be. On taking up residence at Knowsley he had stated his intention of looking for a wife and had at last given Marguerite, whose ties on his affections had been weakening for some time, her marching orders.

"Will you inform her that it is not according to your wishes now that you are the Earl," he asked his brother.

But Ferdinando refused saying, "You must make the break yourself. Tell her honestly that such relationships can only ever be temporary and although you have valued the relationship in the past you have now reached a point where you wish it to end. Be firm but courteous."

William grimaced. "You do not know her temperament, I have often told her she has something of the witch in her. I am afraid what scenes she will make and that she might seek some public revenge. This is why I thought she would respect your authority."

But his brother refused to be moved saying, "Make it quite clear she must leave the cottage and the estate but provide her with sufficient funds to set herself up comfortably elsewhere. That is the least you can do but give her warning that if she does not abide by these conditions then the money will not be forthcoming. Most girls of that sort are ruled by financial considerations."

Alice was not so sure about her husband's cynicism, believing the French girl had had a genuine affection for William Stanley, not excluding the allurement of his status.

The new earl liked to encourage local participation in festivities and one evening invited a combination of the Ormskirk and Prescot town waites, each being but small groups, to play at Lathom. Their music was loud with shawms and pipes for they usually performed outdoors but the size of the great hall could contain the sound and they played vigorously, dressed in their blue cloaks with red sleeves and peaked caps. Their repertoire comprised both ceremonial music and rustic tunes to which the country measures could be danced to the delight of the country gentry, and the Earl and Countess mingled merrily with the large throng. They joined the dancers and noting Alexander Standish with his brother Leonard amongst the company Alice greeted them and joined their group in the line being formed for Dargason. When the dance had finished she stopped in talk for a time, asking of both of them how their present situation stood.

"My wife has just given birth to our son," Alexander said shyly, "named Thomas after my father. She is at present with her mother at Whalley which is why I am alone with my brother."

Alice congratulated him warmly saying, "You are fortunate to have an heir so quickly, Alex. I too am with child again and hoping to provide an heir for the Earldom of Derby."

"I hope you will have your desire, my lady, and that you will remain safe and healthy," he stammered, honoured by her confidences.

"Will you dance an Almaine with me?" she asked as she heard the music change.

"I would be greatly honoured, my lady, but is it safe for you to dance?" he asked deferentially.

"Perhaps not the Volta," she laughed, "but a stately Almaine or a not too vigorous country measure is quite within my remit. Come!"

As she took his hand Alexander Standish thought his heart would burst with pride. His nervousness vanished for he forgot she was one of the noblest ladies in the land and he was modest gentry, savouring only the fact that she was the most beautiful woman in the hall and she had chosen him for her partner. Her farthingale of gold brocade enhanced her red-gold hair encircled by a small gold coronet, and the standing ruff of gossamer tulle and lace framed her face which glowed with the radiance of early pregnancy. He danced competently for there were several travelling dancing masters who visited the Lancashire gentry and his tall well-proportioned figure gave him a natural dignity.

"I don't suppose you will now require my services to attend your riding, my lady," he said when the dance was ended.

Alice was unsure whether he meant because of her elevated status or her pregnancy but she took him to mean the latter and answered, "Not for the next few months I'm afraid, I intend to take no risks. But I am sure I shall have need of your services in the future and in the meantime please convey my good wishes to your wife on the birth of your son, I am sure this must be a time of great rejoicing for all your family."

"I think my father is satisfied now that he knows our line is secured," the young man agreed.

When his countess bade him farewell he thought this had been the most wonderful evening of his life and that it would stay always in his memory.

The dancing master for the Ladies Anne and Frances Stanley had been brought from London to Lathom so that they might continue their daily lessons. The children had been installed at the New Park, the fine house of more recent construction in the deer park. Much smaller in size than Lathom or Knowsley it was nonetheless moated and castellated but it was more comfortably appointed with a large walled garden. The six year old Lady Elizabeth was now counted old enough to begin her dance tuition and Alice often made her way over to the house to supervise their lessons.

One afternoon she was making her way back to Lathom House when she was met by their personal physician, Doctor Moore, with the news that Ferdinando had been taken ill.

"What is the matter with him?" Alice asked in alarm.

"He seems to have eaten something that has disagreed with him," the physician replied. "He cannot stop vomiting."

Alice hurried to her husband's chamber where she found him seated beside a bowl with a napkin around his neck, looking white and shaken. Several attendants and his valet were gathered around him ready to give any assistance, to remove the bowl after each attack and replace it with a fresh one.

"Don't worry," he said to Alice when she arrived, "it must be something I ate last night. No doubt when my stomach has emptied I shall be better."

"Did you eat anything that the rest of us didn't eat?" Alice queried. "I don't believe you did."

Ferdinando was about to agree when another attack of vomiting overcame him. However after that he appeared to improve. The physician gave him some brandy in hot water and suggested he retired to bed to rest. He offered to sleep in a separate chamber that night but Alice over-ruled him, saying she would only sit by his side to watch over him so he capitulated and they retired as usual to the bed they normally shared.

In the early hours he was awakened by another attack, he was pouring with sweat and said that his eyes couldn't focus clearly. In a panic Alice called for attendants and ordered them to fetch Doctor Moore immediately.

"What is it? What is happening to him?" she cried frantically. "He has never been so ill before, he is strong and is always in the best of health."

"It is something he has eaten," the physician insisted. "Because his constitution is so robust the ill substance is taking longer than usual to be eliminated from his body. I will provide a tartar emetic that will hasten the process."

However the drastic attempt to empty his body of all contamination served for nothing but to weaken the

Earl further. It was not unexpected when his stomach began to be racked by severe pains and his body burned with fever. Alice refused to leave him, and even though his darkened chamber was filled with servants and attendants, she wiped his body herself with fresh linen soaked in cold water and put vinegar rags on his forehead. She ordered that more physicians should be called for, sending horsemen to the neighbouring towns even as far as Preston to seek out help, and they gathered as quickly as they could.

The succeeding days began to take on the semblance of a nightmare as Ferdinando's condition showed no improvement despite all the physicians' varied remedies from emetics to bleeding and the compilation of their own esoteric concoctions – electuaries, cordials, essences, salves. Postules had appeared on his body and his sight was blurred. All efforts were made to keep him clean but it was a constant battle against vomit and excreta.

"It is not fitting for you to see him in this condition," Alice was told by all and sundry but she refused to leave her husband, only departing from his side for meals she did not want and futile attempts at sleep because they insisted it was essential she kept up her strength for herself and for the child she was carrying.

The girls had now been told of their father's illness and were crying to see him but no-one considered this a wise option. Only Ferdinando's brother William was allowed to visit him apart from necessary servitors. By now the news was circulating around Lathom and beyond of the mysterious illness of the Earl of Derby. Messengers and professions of concern were arriving every hour from neighbours and tenants who had heard the news, and all but essential business had been suspended as normal routine hung in abeyance. There seemed to be no reason for the young Earl's sudden collapse and whispers began circulating that perhaps he might have been poisoned.

The hours dragged on and day followed day without respite to his suffering so that his carers were overcome with despair. He drifted in and out of consciousness and began to suffer hallucinations that made him tremble and shout out in fear, sometimes uttering words that were incomprehensible but which included mentions of the Devil. All Alice could do was to hold him and try to comfort him, holding back her tears so as not to distress him further.

Then one day a servant made a frightening discovery. Hidden in a corner of the room he came upon a small cloth figure that seemed to be an image of Ferdinando. A semblance had been made of his features, the head bore real hair of the right colour and the poppet was clothed in a copy of a suit the Earl had been known to wear. But around the body cords were tightly bound and pins stuck through the belly. The onlookers were horrified. Ferdinando's chaplain, who was in constant attendance, made a prayer over the grotesque image before throwing it into the fire, then he prayed with his lord.

"He is bewitched," was the concerted opinion, followed by the expressed hope that he would recover now that the image had been discovered and destroyed. Their hopes were short-lived for Ferdinando did not improve and the physicians reverted to their original opinion that the Earl of Derby had been poisoned.

During one of Alice's short periods of rest when she was lying on her bed in her chamber but not sleeping, her maid Lucy approached her gently saying that one of the porters had apprehended a woman trying to enter the house and claiming she was a witch who was responsible for putting a spell on Lord Derby. Alice almost leapt from her bed and followed the house servant down the stairs and across the inner and outer courtyards to the west gate which straddled the moat and led through to the Ormskirk road where stood the old chapel and the almshouses. She already knew she would find Marguerite there.

"I didn't expect the great Lady Derby to appear in person," the French girl said with a mocking smirk on her face.

"What are you doing here? You know you were forbidden entrance to the House," Alice demanded furiously. "And what is the meaning of his nonsense?"

"I put a spell on Lord Derby," Marguerite answered impertinently. "Do you deny that he is grievously sick with no known cause? Look in his chamber and you will find a mascot made to look like him, even with his own hair on the head, bound about with cords, its body spotted and pins in its belly. Do you deny that he has these pains and postules?"

Alice's heart lurched sickeningly and Marguerite said, "You know I am a witch. Ask William."

"I could understand it if it were William you wished to bewitch. But what have you against my husband?" Alice asked.

Marguerite's thin sly face turned to a mask of fury as she shouted, "Because it was your husband who ordered William to cast me off, who turned me out of my house and forbade me entrance to Lathom and Knowsley. William told me so."

Alice was filled with rage as she said coldly, "That is a lie. Lord Derby had nothing to do with the matter, it was Lord William's wish entirely. He has lied to you."

"That I do not believe," Marguerite cried vehemently. "Well I have had my revenge on Lord Derby. Now William will be Earl and he will keep me in great state and will always be grateful when he sees what I have done for him."

"You are deranged," Alice said scornfully. "It is madness not magic that moves you. You are a shrew but no witch. I do not believe in witchcraft. Lord Derby's illness is not a product of witchcraft and you certainly do not have the power to destroy him." But remembering the grotesque image in his chamber she could not help a tremor of fear. Then as visions of Ferdinando's sufferings came into her mind a storm of anger overtook her. Lunging towards Marguerite she grabbed her long black hair and forcing her head back she banged it continuously against the stone wall of the gate while the girl cried in pain.

"Leave this area now, go far away from Ormskirk, leave the country, or I will declare you a witch before the authorities. You think you have supernatural powers to bewitch men in more ways than one, but believe me the reality is not so romantic if it should reach the ears of the civil or religious authorities. I do not believe you have anything to do with my husband's sickness but I will accuse you publicly and you will surely die for it. I am warning you, if you are ever seen in this vicinity again I swear you will hang on the gallows."

Marguerite was genuinely frightened by the violence of Alice's reaction and whimpering now she picked up her skirts and fled through the gate without a backward glance. Alice was shaking from the ferocity of her emotions and had to lean on the wall for support. Then tears ran down her cheeks as she realised she could not unburden herself to Ferdinando.

The physicians now began to talk openly of poison as the only source of Lord Derby's mysterious illness, something they had long suspected but feared to admit to anyone but themselves.

"There can be no other answer," they reluctantly concurred, though some people still muttered about witchcraft.

"Poison!" Alice felt as if she was going to faint as the chamber reeled around her. "Who would want to poison him? He is liked and respected by so many. I cannot believe anyone would murder him."

The Hesketh plot! The thought came suddenly into her mind. He had been afraid of the consequences, of having to be the betrayer of secrets. Was it possible that someone, or some people, had taken revenge upon him. Were there those around him whose Catholic faith was so strong that they would be revenged on those they believed to have betrayed it.

"He's going to die isn't he?" she said, understanding now the hopelessness of his recovery.

There were half-hearted denials and murmurings about there being still time to stop the venom from reaching his heart but Alice knew that he was going to die. She knelt beside the bed putting her arms gently around his emaciated body and leaning her face against his postuled cheeks burning with fiery heat, a travesty of her handsome, vital husband with his vivacious smile and laughing eyes. She would give everything she had, everything she had ever wished for - wealth, titles, honour - just to keep him with her.

"Fight, darling, oh fight as you have never fought before. Do not give up, don't leave me, I cannot live without you. Remember the eagle on the crest, darling. They shall mount up with wings as eagles, they shall run and not be weary, they shall walk and not faint."

His eyelashes fluttered against her tears as he whispered hoarsely and with great effort, "I love you. I always have."

His chaplain had been with him constantly for the last few days and calling for Ferdinando's secretary said, "Make your last testament, my lord, while there is time."

When Richard Greave arrived with pen and parchment they tried to raise the young lord against the pillows. When Ferdinando understood what he had to do he said with great effort, his voice faint and hoarse, "I bequeath everything I have - lands and monies - to my wife and daughters," but when they attempted to put the pen into his hand to sign the statement that Master Greave had written for him it was beyond his capacity to do so.

It had taken Ferdinando Stanley, the 5th Lord Derby, eleven days in all to die. He was thirty four years old and had been Earl for just seven months. Alice felt her heart riven in two and the pain consumed her utterly, but only in the dark hours in the privacy of her bed did she allow herself the outpourings of the grief which racked her body. It somehow seemed disloyal to him to let people see a fraction of the loss she felt and let them think that was the whole. Since she had first met him she had loved him with a love that was all-encompassing. They had been friends and companions as well as passionate lovers and all the blessings of her life had been multiplied because she had shared them with him. There was an emptiness where her heart had been and a deep fear convulsed her at the thought of having to live without him. She forced herself into comforting her daughters who were inconsolable, unable to comprehend that their beloved father had been taken from them so swiftly and unexpectedly. Alice had never given them much attention, always regretting they were girls. Now as she took them in her arms she realised they were the only survivals of her husband. Anne was thirteen, Frances ten and Elizabeth six. They all resembled their father in some way and would always be a permanent reminder to Alice of what she had lost. She would have to care for them now, give them affection on behalf of their father who had always loved them, be responsible for their future welfare, arrange marriages for them. She wondered how she could do it alone. Her only hope was in the child she carried who, if a boy, would inherit the Earldom and carry on Ferdinando's line.

The late Lord Derby was to be buried in the Parish church in Ormskirk, in the chapel built by his grandfather, beside his father who had only so recently been laid there.

"He should have been buried in the abbey at Westminster with all the pomp requisite for his status," William said, and at first Alice had thought so too, knowing that crowds of his friends and admirers in the Court and in the City would have gathered to pay their respects. But now she had changed her mind.

"His heart was always at Lathom," she said. "He is near home at Ormskirk."

She did not know how she could bear the burden of the funeral, having to publicly make her last farewell, comfort her little daughters and accept the condolences of so many people who would attend.

The strain of the last two weeks proved too much for her – unsupportable worry and grief, lack of sleep and food, anxiety about her daughters, fears for the future. Having borne three children Alice knew her child was announcing his arrival, two months too soon. She bore the pain stoically, even gladly as she remembered her husband's sufferings and sought to recompense him a little by bearing him a son. It was indeed a son, born a few days after his father's death. But it was a still-born son.

Her grief was unbearable. She feared she was descending into madness as thoughts of what might have been racked her mind without respite, tortured by the fact that at last she had borne a son for her beloved husband but they were both dead. She wanted to die herself and it was only concern for her daughters that gave her the will to carry on living.

"If all this had not happened, the child would have been born healthy and full term," was all she could repeat over and over again. The cruel tragedy of Ferdinando's death had brought about the death of their son also. He would have been the next Earl of Derby. Instead it was to be William.

Alice was too weak to attend her husband's funeral. Crowds came to pay their respects and people wept as his coffin was borne through Ormskirk and into the church. After his three young daughters, holding hands and weeping inconsolably, the chief mourner was the new Lord Derby, William Stanley.

CHAPTER 15

Aftermath

The new Dowager Countess of Derby took a long time to recover from the unexpected death of her husband and the loss of her baby son. Weakened both physically and emotionally she had no energy left to think about her changed position and the implications of the future. She could not face people with their expressions of sympathy and the constant visitors proffering condolences were courteously turned away. Messages were continually flying between London and Lathom and she read the letters from her family and friends, and from Queen Elizabeth herself, asking the secretaries to reply for her. Her mother at Althorp and her two sisters in London pleaded with her to go to them but she had no desire to leave Lathom unless she was forced to do so. Only with her daughters did she find some solace. United in their grief they were closer than they had ever been and they could weep together and share their memories.

"What will happen to us now? Will we have to leave Lathom House?" Anne asked.

"Not unless we wish to," her mother replied firmly. "Your uncle William is now Lord Derby because girls cannot inherit the title. But you, Anne, have inherited your father's claim to the crown of England and are now heiress presumptive after your lady grandmother. Your father bequeathed all his monies and lands to us so everything must still belong to us when all the legalities have been confirmed."

"It won't be the same living here without father," Frances whispered and Elizabeth began to cry. Alice gathered them all in her arms.

One warm May morning she was lying on a day bed in one of her favourite parlours when her maid Lucy entered quietly. The large-paned window faced south-east so it was light and sunny and the sun's rays burnished the wood panelling to a golden glow, an effect enhanced by gold silk cushions and padded stools, while a bowl of yellow roses was set on a chest covered by a rug of bright oriental design. She had laid aside her book, not having the patience to concentrate on spiritual meditations, and was gazing apathetically through the open door which led onto a little paved courtyard hedged with aromatic box with stone urns of rosemary and lavender perfuming the air and above the walls the misty shape of hills defined the far distance.

"I beg pardon for disturbing you, my lady," Lucy murmured apologetically, "but there is someone wishing to see you. I told him you were not entertaining visitors but he was very insistent, saying that he had an important message for you. He has in fact made his way past the guards, the porters and the house servants so he obviously proved acceptable to them."

"Do you know his name?" she asked.

"Master Standish. Master Alexander Standish."

Alice's sad eyes brightened though she was puzzled as to what kind of a message he might have for her. "You may show him in, Lucy," she consented.

When he arrived he stood hesitantly on the threshold, holding his hat in his hands, shy and embarrassed now by what he had done.

"Well Alex, what can I do for you?" she asked.

He hesitated then stammered, "I just wanted to tell you personally how sorry I am."

She saw the unease in his face though his blue eyes were regarding her directly.

"You did not need to tell a lie in order to see me," she reprimanded him gently and a faint flush rose in his cheeks. "But come, draw up a stool and sit beside me."

He did as he was bidden and edged himself onto the delicate seat, looking at the Countess and not able to keep the sympathy from his eyes as he noted how she was changed from the last time they had met. She was thin, her day gown of perpetuana hung loose on her shoulders, the soft dove-grey of the glossy woollen cloth emphasizing her pale face, and her blue-green eyes were swollen with weeping. Her red hair was unconfined, tied with a silk ribbon.

"I'm so sorry," he said again, and she could sense the emotion in his words.

Suddenly it was as if a great dam had cracked inside her. She had controlled herself in the face of all those others who had offered their condolences, some sincere, some formalities, but always with the respect of tenants, underlings, officers, servants, and she had kept her dignity as wife to their liege lord. Now the naked emotion in the eyes of her young friend broke her restraint and a torrent of weeping shook her body. "I loved him, oh how I loved him. We loved each other from the moment we met. He was my life, my joy, my friend and companion. Without him I am only half a creature. I do not know how I can live without him."

Alexander dropped from the stool and knelt beside her, holding her hands in his but saying nothing, not attempting to voice platitudes as so many felt bound to do and Alice could feel his compassion as she gripped his hands tighter.

"Oh Alex I don't know what I shall do now, whether I shall be able to stay here. Of what use shall I be as Dowager Countess of Derby. William will be in charge, he will marry and there will be a new family here in this place I love so much. If only my son could have lived. It was a son, did you know? I bore Lord Derby a son at last. If this terrible thing hadn't have happened, my child would not have died, I know that. We would have had a son together and Ferdinando's line would have been ensured. I cannot bear to think about it, it is driving me mad."

"I don't know what to say," he whispered sadly. "I know I cannot comfort you. I can only offer you my devotion and my service. If there is ever anything I can do for you, you only need to call me."

Alice nodded, trying to stem her torrent of weeping. "Thank you Alex, I know I can always rely on you," she said, removing her hands at last from his.

There was silence for a time then as Alice stopped weeping and assumed her habitual dignified mode he returned to his seat and asked tentatively, "Are the rumours true that Lord Derby was poisoned?"

A shadow crossed her face again but she replied, "It would seem to be the only answer, incredible as it is. How could someone poison him without affecting others who ate the same dishes. And if it was a less sinister reason, merely food that had become contaminated, why did not others suffer."

"I am going to find out. I did not really lie when I said I had a message for you. The message is that I intend to investigate the matter, to find out how the food reached Lord Derby's plate only, who the servants were who touched it at any stage, if there were any strangers seen in the vicinity. I do not understand why no-one has done this, why the new Lord Derby has not instigated proceedings."

"Dear Alex, there are many things you do not understand. I am sure it all stems from the message brought to Lord Derby by Richard Hesketh and which he was forced to relay to the Privy Council. You know, as does all Lancashire, about the Catholic plot for which his participation was sought."

After some hesitation Alexander said, "Are you aware, my lady, that I am kin to Richard Hesketh? My aunt is Richard Hesketh's half-sister."

Alice looked confused and he continued, "She married my mother's brother, Alexander Hoghton."

"I did not know that, I know little of these Lancashire family relationships," she admitted. "But it is merely a relationship by marriage, not blood, and you must not feel you are in any way to blame for the actions of your kinsfolk. You are not a Catholic."

"But my uncles the Hoghtons are. I feel our family is tainted by this plot and I would like to find out why it has resulted in this tragedy."

"There are many issues here, some of them with national and political significance and Lord Derby feared them, rightly so. I do not understand who is behind this but to take the matter further will be to stir up a hornets' nest. You must not make any enquiries into this affair. Promise me."

"Please do not make me promise," he said earnestly. "It is a matter of honour to Lord Derby, to you my lady, and to my family that I should discover his murderer."

"Promise me that you will not," she said sternly. "Let sleeping dogs lie. The matter is finished, Lord Derby is dead and nothing will bring him back. It will serve for nothing but to endanger you. Go home to Duxbury Hall and care for your wife and child, Thomas is it not?"

"Yes, my lady." He capitulated unwillingly, his mouth set in a stubborn line, saying, "I will keep my promise only because you ask it of me." He stood, feeling she was ready to dismiss him, but asked, "Will you leave here, my lady?"

"Probably. I do not know."

Although Ferdinando had left Lathom and Knowsley in her possession, Alice was mindful that William would not be willing to let them go.

As Alexander was taking his leave she surprised him by saying, "When I am well will you take me to Anglezarke again." She looked out onto the courtyard where the sun was dappling the stones. "I have a great longing to be riding free over the moors."

A joyful smile crossed his handsome features. "That would be a great pleasure, my lady. When you send me word I will come immediately."

When he had gone Alice felt more at ease than she had done previously for it had been a relief to unburden herself and talk freely. Surprisingly she felt no embarrassment at having wept before him, confident he would never reveal her flood of emotion and warmed by his sympathy. She wondered if she ought to have let him pursue enquiries into her husband's mysterious death but she had more experience than he of the political machinations surrounding the Stanleys and now that Ferdinando was dead she was fearful of any further dangers for her family and for her young friend.

Her interview with her brother-in-law William, now Earl of Derby, was not so pleasant. She had been putting off seeing him with the excuse that she was not well enough but as her strength returned so did her resilience. After enquiring politely about her health and the children he broached the subject in which he was most interested.

"I suppose you realise, Alice, that Ferdinando's will cannot be honoured."

"In what way?" she enquired, being prepared for such an objection.

"It is completely beyond question that the title and estates of the Earldom of Derby should be separated," he replied.

"My husband's last testament willed his monies and lands to me and the children," she stated firmly.

"He never signed the will," the new Earl pointed out.

"If it can be proved that this was the genuine desire of the testator at the time of death then the will is still legal," she insisted.

"But can that be proved? The people present all had a personal interest, especially yourself. Perhaps my brother did not sign purposefully because he knew that the next earl could not possibly take on the inheritance without the estate belonging to it."

"My son was not dead at that time. I could have provided the next heir," Alice reminded him.

"But for all Ferdinando knew, it could have been another girl," he countered.

"And he wished to ensure that his daughters' inheritance was secure," Alice retorted spiritedly. "They need to be provided for, especially Lady Anne who, after your lady mother, is heiress presumptive to the English crown. They cannot inherit the title but there is no reason their inheritance should still not be intact."

"My grandfather entailed the Derby estates on males only and Ferdinando cannot over-rule that," William stated. "No court in the land would uphold it. Don't be stupid, Alice, surely you must realise that I cannot take on the responsibility and expense of the earldom without the means by which it exists. As it is, I am taking on a heavy burden of debt accrued by my father and my brother. I intend to make the earldom financially viable again but I need to do it by careful management of our estates, something that you and your daughters could never do."

Alice bit her lip as she realised there was some truth in what he said. Ferdinando had always lived beyond his means but this was one reason why they would need the Derby lands to continue to live in the state to which she had been accustomed for so long.

"You may continue to live at Lathom for as long as you wish as Dowager Countess and I will allow you enough for your maintenance," William stated coolly. "I myself prefer Knowsley as you know and when I am married, as I intend to be shortly, I shall make that our principal residence together with Derby House in London."

Alice had no intention of living at Lathom as a pensioner while William and his new wife lorded it at Knowsley. The castle was her own, it belonged to her by the terms of her husband's will as did Knowsley and New Park and Derby House, with enough land to provide upkeep for themselves and their properties, the Stanleys owned land in fifteen counties. She would employ managers to run the estates until her daughters were old enough to marry into noble families who would then bring their own land holdings to join with those of the Stanleys. It had happened before. The largest part of the Derby empire had been brought into the Stanley family by the marriage of the 14th century Sir John Stanley to the heiress Isabel de Lathom.

As if guessing her thoughts William said, "And if you think I would allow our lands to fall into the hands of other noble families then you are much mistaken. I shall keep them, and I shall keep them intact as my trust to our family."

"I will take the matter to court, William," Alice warned.

"No court in the country will rule in your favour."

"We'll see about that. I shall hire the best lawyers in the land. I will go to the very top, to the Attorney-General."

William laughed. "You do that! All that will happen is that you will be poorer for it. You are a shrew, Alice Spencer, a money-grabbing farmer's daughter whose ambition was to join the aristocracy and live in great state. You snared my brother but you won't trap me."

The Earl of Derby left the room with a curt farewell and Alice found herself shaking with a mix of anger and despair. Most hurtful to her was the refusal to acknowledge the passionate binding love that she and Ferdinando had shared, irrespective of all other considerations. She admitted that she had wanted to rise in the world, to be rich and respected and the title of Countess of Derby had been the seal on all her desires, but it had been an extra, a wonderful bonus to the relationship she had shared with Ferdinando Stanley.

If only he could be still alive it would not matter to her if he was a travelling player. She was going to fight now not for herself, for without him she considered her life meaningless, but for his children whose right it was to have what he had left them. They were all she had now and she was not going to fail them or her husband who had left them in her care. She would have to go to London and find the best lawyer she could to fight her case.

She knew she could not delay too long but before departing she renewed her intention to make a last visit to Anglezarke and sent a message to Alexander Standish at Duxbury Hall. He came immediately to Lathom and they set off together along the now familiar path through the summer fields springing with new wheat and colourful carpets of wild flowers – golden buttercups and cowslips, blue flax and periwinkle, pink-tipped daisies and creamy white meadowsweet and in the hedgerows the rosy blush of dog roses. The sun warmed their faces as they approached Duxbury and the Yarrow then turned to cross Rivington moors.

"We'll go further this time, I'll take you to Winter Hill where there are the widest views across the Pennine hills and you can see Bolton-le-Moors in the hollow, I was baptised in the parish church there," Alexander said.

They rode at a gentle pace and he told her stories and anecdotes from the past, revealing his knowledge of history, and directed her attention to all the features of the wide-ranging landscape.

"Just below Bolton, amongst the woods there, is Smithills Hall where the Bartons live. It was a favourite stopping place for Lord Strange's players," he said, then realising he was probably revoking unhappy memories he continued on a different subject. "In the reign of

Queen Mary a local man called George Marsh who was one of the first Potestants was tried for heresy at Smithills and later burnt at the stake. You can still see his footprint stamped into the floor in the Hall where he fervently declared his Protestant faith."

"You have a lot of local knowledge, Alex," she said admiringly. "Why are you not a Catholic like most of your neighbours?"

"My father changed his religion when Elizabeth became Queen," he said. "He considered it a mark of his loyalty but many of our friends and kinsfolk continued to hold to the old faith."

They sat their horses looking out over the wide panorama, sunlit in the day's summer weather, a patchwork of variegated greens and spreads of purple heather as the land rose and fell. They could see the old stone and timbered manor house nestling amongst the trees. Alice forgot for a time the sorrows and worries emprisoning her as she watched the birds whirling above in the milky blue sky dotted with wispy clouds and a feeling of release loosened the burden of all her problems.

"I have been thinking about what happened to Lord Derby," Alexander said carefully, and her brief spell of escape ended. She looked at him sharply but he continued, "Because he was poisoned and no-one else was, then the poison could not have been administered in the kitchens and put into the food on the table. It could only have been put directly onto Lord Derby's plate once the food had been served to him."

Despite herself Alice was interested and said, "But that is impossible. It would have been noticed - a servant leaning over him and adding something to his dish."

"Not entirely impossible if he was engaged in conversation and his attention diverted, but yes not likely and too unpredictable because the right moment might never have come. That is why I think the poison must have been put into his wine. Lord Derby had his own individual goblet didn't he?"

"Yes a silver goblet with the Derby arms and his initials in an intricate design."

"So no-one else would use it and it could not be mistaken."

"But if the poison was placed first in the goblet it would be noticed, and how could he be served wine that no-one else would drink?" Alice did not want to think about the matter but she was intrigued despite herself.

"Someone, a servant, waiting with a jug of wine holding only enough for one measure and containing the poison. Hovering close enough to see when Lord Derby's goblet was empty, there would be enough serving men to make his individual presence not remarkable wouldn't there?" When Alice agreed, he continued, "Once he had filled up the goblet then he would return to the buttery for another jug and no-one would suspect anything."

Alice remained silent for a time then said, "This idea of yours means that one of our servants was his murderer."

Alexander shook his head. "Not necessarily though it is possible. A serving man could have been implicated in some way if only by accepting a bribe to take the wine jug into the dining hall without knowing about the contents. Or someone could have been planted just for the occasion, with so many servants an extra one would not cause any comment. If only I could discover who was responsible for serving the wine and if he was contacted by anyone previously."

"Alex you promised me you would not pursue this matter," Alice said sternly. "Have you broken your word to me?"

"No, my lady, I haven't. I swear to you. I have only been thinking about it and before you made me promise I had already discovered from talking to the kitchen maids that a stranger had arrived that day from London, a groom whom they had noticed hanging around in the kitchens begging for a parcel of food to be packed up for him because he had to return to London immediately. I am only surmising that the poison could have been brought by him and a servant only guilty by following instructions he did not understand."

"So you are saying the poison could have come from London?"

"Possibly."

"Is it possible that revenge came from the Catholic exiles abroad who were behind the Hesketh plot?"

"Yes of course it is, and possibly from them via London. But don't you see the murder is unlikely to have been planned by Lancashire Catholics. Despite the differences in religion they loved and served Lord Derby. Let me go to London, my lady, and try to solve this mystery, if only to exonerate my own neighbours and kinsfolk."

"No!" she almost shouted. "I forbade you once and you gave me your word. You are clever, Alexander, and I admire your reasoning. But you would be out of your depth in this imbroglio and you could find yourself in danger."

"I do not care about that."

"Well I do. I don't wish to pursue this any further, nothing can bring back my husband and nothing else matters to me. You concern yourself only with taking care of your wife and son and your estate when it comes to you."

She did not want to look at his crestfallen face and turned her horse to retrace their steps. The clouds had grown bigger and the sun was hidden behind them so that the moor looked gloomy. With the darkening of the scene had come a heaviness between them.

"Is this the last time we shall ride together, my lady?" he asked at last in a subdued voice.

"Probably. I shall be leaving for London shortly. I have much business to do now with lawyers and for this I need the best City lawyers I can find."

"Will you never come back to Lathom?" he asked.

She considered for a time then replied, "I do not know. It depends on what happens in the future."

She was thinking again of all the problems besetting her so she didn't see his face.

"I wish you good fortune, my lady, and hope you will find happiness again," he said. He knew it was not his place to say how much their rides together had meant to him and how his life would never be the same again.

"I wish you joy and success also, Alexander" she said. "Thank you for the loyal service you have given Lord Derby and myself, and thank you also for your companionship. Our rides together have given me much pleasure."

"It has been a great joy to serve you," he replied.

They were both subdued as they turned their back on Anglezarke moor and the sun caught their mood, remaining hidden behind the darkening clouds as they made their descent to the road below.

CHAPTER 16

Settlements

Alice was nothing if not determined. She needed the best lawyer in the land so on her return to London she sought out the Attorney-General himself, Sir Thomas Egerton. She was not unknown to him because he had in the past served Ferdinando's father Lord Henry in some of his affairs though it took her some time to arrange an interview with him. In the meantime she had to settle herself and her daughters in London. Eventually she intended leasing a property but for the immediate present both her sisters Anne and Elizabeth had invited her to stay with them and money was a problem until her finances could be settled.

All the Spencer family had been shocked by the news of the Earl of Derby's untimely death and it was an added burden to Alice's personal loss to have to endure the pity of so many people. For the past fifteen years she had considered herself the most fortunate woman in the world, had basked in the admiration she attracted and the respect afforded to her by virtue of her ennobled status. Now she was merely a dowager countess, a widow on her own, deeply in debt and with the ownership of all her previous homes in dispute.

It was true that for a time her presence in London had been the focus of morbid fascination. Edmund Spenser had written a poem in her honour entitled 'The tears of the Muses' and many other writers had eulogised Ferdinando because he had given his support to so many of them. The actors of his company of players had come en masse to offer her their condolences, obviously very worried about what would happen to them now on their patron's death. It seemed but a short time since Lord Strange had taken over the patronage of Lord Leicester's men when that Earl had died. Alice had promised to continue her support of them in her husband's name for the time being but she did not think she could long do so, financially constrained as she was. It was a time of great worry and apprehension.

She decided to accept her elder sister's offer of hospitality for a time because Anne herself was a widow and during her marriage had been a member of a lesser branch of the Stanley family, her husband Lord Monteagle's domains lying in north Lancashire, so she felt more affinity with her than she had ever done. However it was her second sister Elizabeth, feeling somewhat resentful at Alice's refusal of hospitality when she had been hoping to avail herself of some vicarious distinction, who brought news that both cheered and saddened her at the same time.

"On George's suggestion, his father has decided to take over the patronage of Ferdinando's players," she announced with satisfaction, not able to prevent an expression of smugness from crossing her face. "They are to be renamed the Lord Chamberlain's Men so their future is now assured. They could not hope for a more prestigious patron."

"I am happy for them," Alice said, smoothing the fine black wool of her gown to hide any show of disappointment that her husband's name was to be removed from the company he had built up and loved so much. "It certainly proves their excellence for Lord Hunsdon to give them his name. No doubt they will receive many Court appointments now." She knew Ferdinando would have been pleased so she must show her gratitude. Lord Hunsdon had been the patron of his own troupe of travelling players in his younger days and he had always encouraged dramatic performances at Court. The only reservation was that he was nearly seventy years of age. A current item of Court gossip was that he had recently given up his beautiful young mistress Aemilia Bassano and married her off to a musician by the name of Alfonso Lanier because she was expecting a child, there being some doubt about the father. Alice reflected for a moment on the precarious situation of women who depended on men for their position in life and wondered how Mistress Bassano would feel about her changed circumstances. Then she said, "I hope the arrangement will not be short-lived. Lord Hunsdon is after all an old man and there have been too many deaths with their patrons recently."

"I think it likely that George could consider taking them on when his father dies," Elizabeth replied, enjoying the possibility of stepping into Alice's shoes. Although genuinely fond of her, she had never quite been able to suppress feelings of jealousy at her younger sister's good fortune. Alice knew this would be a practical solution but once again she could not help feeling a sense of disappointment that her sister would be taking her place and her star indeed was falling.

One task she set herself but which she did not relish was to pay a visit to the other dowager Countess of Derby, Lady Margaret Stanley. Taking her daughters with her she took a carriage to Clerkenwell. For some reason unfathomable to Alice, Lady Margaret had continued to live in the house where she had been placed under house arrest for so long, now taking it on lease. It had been built by a distant kinsman of hers but the lease had been acquired by her half-brother, Francis Clifford, and she took advantage of this. It was a fine house, grand and spacious with lofty well-furnished rooms, surrounded by three beautiful extensive gardens with mature trees, shady arbours and cultivated flower beds. Many of the nobility had properties in the village of Clerkenwell for it was a popular site with its green and leafy avenues and parks and the famous well that people visited for its curative properties yet only a short distance from the City. She supposed her mother-in-law had grown accustomed to the place and because she was heavily in debt she probably could not afford to live elsewhere.

They were led formally by a liveried footman into the Countess's private parlour, a long room with a large leaded window overlooking the gardens but which contrived to seem dark because of the oak wainscoting and the Countess's black velvet upholstery. Alice was shocked to see how ill Lady Margaret looked. Her gold brocade gown, though stiff with gold thread and heavily padded, hung on her slender body as if it did not belong to her and although it was a warm spring day she wore an overmantle of fox fur and a tight fitting velvet cap which tied beneath her chin. Her face was pale and drawn, the hollow cheek bones emphasizing her almond eyes, and though still beautiful she looked older than her fifty years. The sudden unexpected loss of her elder son had affected her deeply on top of her other sorrows.

She ordered wine to be brought and apple cordial for the girls and they sat uneasily, Alice not knowing what to say, but just as she steeled herself to begin the conversation the Countess spoke in her musical voice.

"I thank you for your visit but I do not wish to talk about my son. I have heard everything that I need to know which has been too much for me. Sufficient to say that my grief overwhelms me and I know it must be the same for you all. We must bear our sorrow with fortitude and ask for God's grace to help us." Her hand moved involuntarily to the enamelled prayer book which hung on a chain at her waist.

Lady Margaret Stanley had always been aloof and dignified and Alice understood she could not bring herself to say more. She did not wish to hear her daughter-in-law's condolences nor listen to her expressions of loss, for any display of emotion would be distasteful to her. The two women had never been able to forge a relationship. Alice knew the Countess had always been disappointed in her, and it was not going to be any different now even in their shared loss.

Lady Margaret rose with difficulty from her black velvet chair and Alice noted the pain crossing her face as she walked towards her. The outstretched hands were icy cold but when Alice took them in hers the imprisoning grip was like a desperate reaching for an anchor in the shifting sands of her grief and conveyed everything she was unable to speak. She touched the cheeks of all the girls with her long slender fingers then she motioned for one of her waiting women, always hovering discreetly in the background, to lead them out and it was obvious the visit was at an end.

On their way back to London in the carriage Alice attempted an explanation to her daughters who were looking confused and forlorn. "Your lady grandmother is too grieved to say more. You must pardon her seeming unconcern for you. I do not think it is meant, but her life has been one of great sadness."

She did not think the visit had been a success but was surprised a few days later by a message delivered from the Countess asking for Frances to visit her.

Anne scowled at the news and Frances whispered in some distress, "It isn't fair that I should be preferred before Anne when she is the eldest."

"If your lady grandmother has asked for you then you must go to her," her mother said. "The others cannot hold it against you and they must learn that life is not always fair."

Lady Margaret had always preferred Frances and Alice could understand her partiality, for her eleven year old daughter was not only the most beautiful of the three but had a sunny nature, a natural ease of manner and a ready smile that captivated all who met her. She had hoped the Countess would have included Anne in her favour now that she had inherited her grandmother's claim to the Crown on Ferdinando's death, but for some reason it was not to be and Anne was resentful even though she would not have relished the duty. Seeing her eldest daughter's surly expression she wished that Anne could have more of Frances's grace and that she would make an effort to be likeable instead of relying on her high birth. In her features she most resembled her father but she had none of his ease of manner. Little Elizabeth merely wished Frances a pleasant visit, saying seriously that she was glad she was not the one to be chosen. She was always happiest to stay wherever home happened to be and preferred books to toys. Since her father's death she had retreated more into herself and Alice noted how she had taken to reading the Bible and composing little prayers. Frances's visits to her grandmother resumed their earlier pattern and the young girl accepted with her customary charm.

The Attorney-General, Sir Thomas Egerton, finally agreed to see Alice and she went to his chambers in Westminster Hall. The one-time medieval palace by the side of the river was now a rather dilapidated building as the damage done by a fire earlier in the century had never been completely repaired. The rambling structure was a warren of small rooms, ante-chambers and winding corridors but it was the seat of all the major law courts - the court of common pleas, the King's Bench, the Court of Chancery and Star Chamber. Alice was led into the presence of Sir Thomas Egerton by one of his many clerks and after greeting her courteously and offering his condolences on the death of Lord Derby he led her to a seat on the opposite side of his desk and while he settled himself she had time to observe him. He was a handsome man in his fifties, very tall and slim with a long face with high cheekbones, a long nose and deep-set dark eyes beneath high-arched brows. His hair was sandy brown flecked with grey and his beard was neatly cut around his chin. It was said that women went to hear him plead in court mainly to look at him. He had an aristocratic mien but it was common knowledge that he was the illegitimate son of a Cheshire squire who had made him his legal heir and sent him to study law at

Oxford then Lincoln's Inn. From his early years he had become well known as a lawyer, pleading cases in Queen's Bench, Chancery and the Exchequer, but it was when Queen Elizabeth had seen him bringing a case against the Crown that she had made him Queen's Counsellor, saying he would never again plead against her. He had progressed to Solicitor-General then Attorney-General, chief Crown prosecutor, prosecuting Mary Queen of Scots and later bringing the Duke of Norfolk to his death on account of his plotting on behalf of the Scottish queen.

"I don't usually take on personal pleas," he said, spreading his long slim fingers on the top of his desk while he regarded her directly.

"I need the best lawyer in England because everyone tells me my case is hopeless," she replied, undeterred.

Egerton was not immune to flattery or to feminine charms. He studied the woman seated opposite him, her gown of black velvet slashed with black silk contrasted with her red hair and green eyes, the tightly corseted bodice emphasizing her slender figure. The vivacity of her face, warm cream against the pristine whiteness of her ruff, was at one with her spirited tone of voice, but there was also a discernible vulnerability that evoked an inevitable response - his masculine superiority was stirred by this damsel in distress while the challenge of a case deemed impossible was tempting.

"Tell me the whole story," he invited.

He listened carefully, without interruption, as she laid her case before him. Part of his mind was detached as the vehemence of her passion beguiled him but his quicksilver intelligence was reacting to every nuance of the information dispensed.

As he digested the material Alice burst in eagerly, "Is the will legal?"

"I see no reason why the will should not be considered legal," he replied. "However whether Lord Derby your husband was within his rights to make such conditions is another matter. According to the will of Lord Edward, the 3rd Earl of Derby, the lands and estates are entailed on males only and your husband was not in a position to alter this. Also from a practical point of view the claims of the present Earl, Lord William, are valid and would most likely be upheld by a court. It would not be possible for him to sustain his position and fulfil his obligations without the reinforcement of his estates. No nobleman in England would have such an empty title."

Alice's shoulders drooped and her expressive face showed her disappointment. "Are you also telling me my case is hopeless," she whispered.

"No." His emphatic denial brought up her head in surprise. "I say that your attempt to hold on to the estates of the Earldom of Derby is hopeless but I believe you are entitled to some financial compensation for the loss of those estates. Yourself as Countess of Derby, together with your daughters, have the right to be provided for in the noble state to which you are entitled and which would have been yours but for the tragically premature death of your husband. I repeat, Earl William must have his estates but he must pay you for them."

"He will pay nothing. The only concession he has offered is that I may live at Lathom House, which he dislikes, as his pensioner with an allowance he dictates sufficient for my needs." She laughed scornfully.

The Attorney-General said, "He will pay and he will pay you handsomely. This I promise you, Lady Derby, that I will get the best financial settlement anyone could possibly arrange for you. You will continue to live as you always have and your daughters may have no fear for their futures."

Alice felt overwhelmed but still was bound to say, "William will fight. He will not surrender a penny more than he needs to."

"He may fight, but he will not win," said Egerton confidently. "If you are still willing to entrust your case to me then I will bring a plea against Lord Derby on your behalf."

"How much will your charges be?" Alice asked tentatively, half-afraid now she had secured the services of the highest lawyer in the land. "At this moment I have no money. My husband was deeply in debt."

Egerton smiled ironically. "The Earls of Derby are always in debt. This is an appeal Lord William will bring against the indictment but it will be of no avail. As for my costs, fear not, Lady Derby. When I have won the case for you my costs will be as nought."

When details had been settled and further meetings arranged, Alice left the building feeling happier than she had done for some time. She still was not satisfied that some of the Derby estates could not be granted to them and was determined to press Sir Thomas Egerton further on this. She would have loved to have kept Lathom House and her stake in Lancashire but she was honest enough to acknowledge that she could not have lived happily so close to the new Lord Derby who would no doubt have bitter recriminations about her fighting him in the law courts. But the burden of her fight had now been placed upon Sir Thomas Egerton and she was certain she could have left it in no better hands.

Now that William Stanley had inherited the Earldom of Derby he lost no time in seeking a wife for himself as he was past thirty years old and soon preparations were in hand for a sumptuous wedding to be held in the palace at Greenwich with Queen Elizabeth in attendance.

"You cannot possibly not go to the wedding," Elizabeth Carey said in a scandalised voice after relating to Alice the latest Court news.

"That's a double negative," her sister retorted. "And no, I certainly will not attend."

"But it's at Greenwich Palace and the Queen is going to be there."

The venue for the wedding of Lord Derby to Lady Elizabeth de Vere, the Earl of Oxford's daughter, was one of the reasons Alice was determined not to go. She would not admit to her sister her feelings of jealousy that the twenty year old lady-in-waiting would be the new Countess of Derby and William would bask in his good fortune at having secured as his bride a daughter of one of the most prestigious aristocratic families as well as being the granddaughter of Lord Burghley. But she also dreaded returning for such a celebratory occasion to the place where she and Ferdinando had first made love and plighted their troth to each other.

"It will be a great affront to the Queen and Lord Derby," her sister added.

"I shall say I am sick and then no offence can be taken," Alice declared. "Anne can take my place, she is fifteen now and important in her own right."

"When are you going to end your feud with Lord Derby?" Elizabeth sighed.

"When he agrees to my rights regarding Ferdinando's will."

"George thinks you are being unreasonable. He is of the opinion, as are most people, that Lord Derby's claims are justified, the title and the estates cannot be separated and to continue with legal proceedings will be futile and ultimately costly, as well as bringing your name into disrepute as a greedy scheming woman."

"Sir Thomas Egerton, the Attorney General, is taking on my case so he cannot believe it to be futile, though I agree it might well be costly," Alice said. "But I cannot possibly attend William's wedding while there is such bad blood between us. I know he traduces me whenever he can, he always has done, and it is he who spreads the word around that I am greedy and shrewish. Well I wish him joy of his bride because everyone knows the de Veres are shrews. Didn't Southampton say as much when he refused to marry the Lady Elizabeth."

Alice giggled wickedly and Elizabeth joined in, the sisters indulging in malicious Court gossip together as they used to do when they were younger.

"Burghley was furious by Southampton's refusal to take his granddaughter. He'd planned the marriage since they were children and Southampton was his ward."

"Because Southampton was the richest young man in England," said Alice. "Wasn't he fined five thousand pounds for refusing the marriage? I'm afraid William Stanley won't be such a catch, either with money or good looks."

"She isn't such a great beauty herself, is she?" Elizabeth giggled.

Alice stopped laughing. "She will be Countess of Derby in my place." Elizabeth de Vere might be too thin with small eyes and a down-turned mouth but soon she would be receiving all the acclamations of the Lancashire gentry, feasting and entertaining them at Lathom and Knowsley and being entertained by them – the Molyneux and Norrises, the Heskeths and Hoghtons, the Charnocks, the Standishes. She wondered if Alexander Standish would be present at the welcome receptions for the new Earl and his bride who was just twenty years old.

Guessing Alice's thoughts by the glum expression chasing away the laughter, her sister diverted her by saying, "I hope you won't be making excuses not to attend *my* Elizabeth's wedding. Lord Hunsdon is asking William Shakespeare to write a play for the occasion now he has become patron of the company."

"That would be enough incentive for me," Alice said mischievously. But she was glad for her sister that after years of trying to arrange an advantageous marriage for their only child, George Carey had secured Lord Berkeley's heir.

Alice kept to her resolution of not attending the wedding of Lord Derby to Lady Elizabeth de Vere and although there were some whisperings with the Queen herself noting her absence, her sisters were busy informing all and sundry that Lady Alice, Dowager Countess of Derby, was suffering from a summer ague and ensuring that in her place the young Lady Anne Stanley performed her duties graciously. However when Alice was left alone in her sister's house the isolation and boredom overcame her so that she was engulfed in vivid memories which brought a storm of weeping and she wished she had found the courage to go to Greenwich for then the activity and the necessity to play a part would have shielded her from self-pity. As it was she might as well have attended for she was forced to listen for weeks afterwards to so many accounts of how splendid the nuptials had been, how beautiful the bride, how rich the company of great nobles, and how the Queen had personally favoured the young couple – no surprise seeing the bride was the sister of the Secretary of State Robert Cecil and granddaughter of the Queen's beloved Lord Burghley.

On the other hand, resentment for the wedding of Alice's niece to Sir Thomas Berkeley came from Lady Anne Stanley.

"When am I going to be married?" she asked petulantly. "My cousin Elizabeth is only a few years older than I am and her marriage has been arranged for some time."

Alice sighed, realising that this was another responsibility for her to shoulder. She knew from her sister's experience that it had taken George Carey years to find a suitable match for his only child after several futile attempts at negotiations. There were so many pitfalls, not least financial. Until William and she came to a mutual agreement about the Stanley estates her own financial position was precarious and she could not provide her daughters with dowries. But the successful wedding of her niece was enlivened for Alice by a performance at the Blackfriars private theatre afterwards of 'A Midsummer Night's Dream', specially written for the occasion by William Shakespeare, and afterwards she was able to complement the author.

"It was a wonderful play, Will, full of invention and true magic. An inspired idea to set the main plot within the framework of a noble marriage. How my husband would have loved it," she said.

"Thank you, my lady. I think I have improved since I wrote my first play for Lord Strange," said the playwright. Then he added, "We all miss your lord's encouragement and enthusiasm. Lord Hunsdon is a good patron and we were fortunate to be taken up by him but I will never forget that I was first one of Lord Strange's Men."

Alice was moved and after telling him to continue writing plays as good as 'The Dream', promised that she would try and see as many as she could.

Her daughters also loved the play and Frances and Elizabeth couldn't stop talking about it, diverting themselves for days afterwards by acting scenes together, persuading their maids to participate because Anne refused saying it was "silly." She continued in a sulky mood in the aftermath of the wedding, harassing her mother to be more concerned about her own future. Alice was indeed much concerned but as well as financial difficulties there was the position of Anne as heiress presumptive to the Crown after her grandmother. Personal experience had taught her the dangers inherent in such a distinction and she was well aware many prospective suitors would fight shy of entering into a liaison that carried with it so many snares. This aspect of Anne's position in the marriage market was intensified with the death of her grandmother, Dowager Countess of Derby and heiress presumptive to the Crown.

Queen Elizabeth had never liked her kinswoman, had feared Lady Margaret's nearness to the throne and treated her unkindly. But in death she was rewarded with all the honours of her noble birth - descendant of kings and queens - and was splendidly interred in Westminster Abbey. After the Queen the chief mourners were Lord William and Lady Elizabeth, Earl and Countess of Derby, followed by Ferdinando's three daughters together with their mother. Closely following were the Countess's Clifford relations - her half-brothers George and Francis and George's wife Margaret with their young daughter Anne Clifford. The black-clad figures followed the coffin draped in purple and though Alice felt little personal affection for her mother-in-law she sorrowed for her unhappy life and the fact that Ferdinando was not there to lead his mother to her last resting place. She also sorrowed for her children, having to endure another funeral so close after that of their father and who were obviously burdened with memories. Anne walked with an impassive face, her face paler against her black gown, but Frances was desperately trying not to weep and Elizabeth was sniffling as she caught her sister's emotion.

Lady Margaret's testament surprised many. Overwhelmed by debt she had very little to leave but most of it went to her Clifford relatives, her eldest half-brother George being her executor and not her son Lord Derby. George was left the black velvet and pearl suite of furnishings which she had always used in her house in Clerkenwell. William Lord Derby was left only a table and his wife Elizabeth was not even mentioned. Alice's glee served to mitigate the disappointment that Anne, inheriting her grandmother's title as heiress presumptive, was omitted completely. However Frances was left a house and lands in Low Leyton, a village some five miles from London, with the stipulation that it could be used by her daughter-in-law Alice until Frances came of age and needed it for herself.

"Well you now have a house of your own, at least for the present," Sir Thomas Egerton commented on his next consultation with Alice.

"A strange testament though. Her Derby family have almost been forgotten apart from my daughter Lady Frances and this bequest has caused a great deal of ill feeling with my eldest daughter Lady Anne," Alice confessed.

Anne had shouted and railed at her innocent sister, accusing her of flattering their grandmother and turning her mind against her, and Frances had dissolved into floods of tears, insisting she wanted nothing for herself. Alice felt more at a loss than ever at having to bring up her daughters alone without Ferdinando's help. "I cannot understand why Anne received nothing at all and why the Cliffords were preferred before her only son," she continued.

"It stems from her animosity to her husband but I think you must understand how impoverished the Countess was by her overwhelming debts. Her estate was actually put into the hands of the Receiver General and there was very little to spare," said Egerton. Privately he could not understand how the Stanleys with so much potential wealth at their disposal should always be in debt.

"I have a presentiment that my situation could be the same," said Alice. "I fear I shall go the same way as my predecessor. The Dowager Countesses of Derby don't seem to be blessed with good fortune."

A worried frown crossed her brow and Egerton put a hand on her arm.

"Do you doubt my abilities to save you from such a fate? You need not," he said in a soft voice, his hand remaining on her sleeve. "Matters are progressing. Lord Derby is obdurate, as we expected, but I am amassing all the information concerning his estates, his assets and liabilities and his wife's inheritance. I am also collecting the legal documents pertaining to the original distribution of the Derby settlements with their entails and conditions. It won't be a swift victory but be in no doubt of the outcome, Lady Derby."

Alice was always reassured in the presence of the Attorney-General. He exuded power. His elegant figure and quiet voice were deceptively unthreatening but his slim frame was made of steel while his formidable intelligence set him above other men and made him feared in the law courts. His position was soon to be further enhanced by another death.

Queen Elizabeth was grief-sticken at the death of Sir Christopher Hatton, one of her favourite courtiers and her dancing partner, who like Leicester had served her long and loved her. He was also a very able statesman and held the position of Keeper of the Great Seal, the highest political office in the land.

Sir Thomas Egerton was made his replacement, the Queen weeping as she said she thought he would be the last to hold the office for her. His new position also elevated him to the Privy council, that small group of the most powerful nobles and officials who advised the Queen on all matters of policy. Sir Thomas Egerton, the new Keeper of the Great Seal, was now at the head of both the political and legal systems – the most powerful man in the country. When Alice heard the news she thrilled to its import for she knew that with his support she could not fail in her determination to keep her position.

CHAPTER 17

York House

Alice's confidence was justified as the Lord Keeper successfully proceeded against the Earl of Derby who was constrained to offer the Dowager Countess much more in the way of compensation than he had intended. Still Sir Thomas Egerton continued to press for further settlements and Earl William's vilification of the lawyer's dexterity and his sister-in-law's acquisitiveness was spread abroad as he struggled to find money to meet their demands.

"People are talking of you as a greedy shrew, Alice," her sister Elizabeth warned when she went to visit her.

"Who are people? George and his cronies like Robert Cecil, kin now to William?" she retorted. "I'm not willing to give up the life I had, even without Ferdinando, and it is the right of his children. I think Anne should inherit her father's rights to the Island of Man as heiress presumptive to the Crown but Sir Thomas says this is not possible as a woman has never ruled the island."

"You are changing, allowing all this litigation to take over your life. You are no longer the happy carefree person you once were, in fact you are becoming bitter," Elizabeth said sadly, noticing how her younger sister's face often appeared distracted. "Why don't you forget the past and find a new husband for yourself, someone who will continue to give you the life you had with Ferdinando. Look how happy Anne is with her new husband."

After years of widowhood Anne Spencer had secured an advantageous second marriage to Thomas Sackville, Earl of Dorset, a wealthy cultured courtier who wrote verse and was the owner of a beautiful estate at Knole in the county of Kent as well as a noble house in the City. Alice had to admit that Anne had indeed been aglow with happiness when she escorted her through the pleasant rooms of Knole and the extensive landscaped gardens where as well as flowers and herbs her husband was cultivating new fruits like apricots and redcurrants for he had a keen interest in gardening, following the fashion set by Lord Burghley. She had also repeated the advice of her sister Elizabeth saying, "Haven't you thought about marrying again Alice? You are still young, still able to bear sons. It would be good for you to have someone to provide for you, give you a comfortable life."

Seated together under a pergola with the gardens a riot of colour and scents and the gentle splashing of water on stone calming her unsettled spirits, Alice did feel a moment of envy at her sister's good fortune but said, "I've been too busy fighting for our inheritance to give thought to much else. And as far as marriage is concerned, my first priority is to find suitable husbands for my daughters and they seem in short supply."

"My husband's son and heir Richard is near Anne's age. We shall have to see what we can arrange," said her sister with a speculative smile.

"For myself, I don't think I shall marry again," Alice said. "I shall never find anyone like Ferdinando and I won't settle for second best. My fortunes are improving and if I can continue to live in the state and honour of a countess, even a dowager, then that will satisfy me." She always proudly used her title of Countess of Derby and wore gowns of increasing splendour now that her official period of mourning was over, even though her debts were mounting.

Anne studied her younger sister thoughtfully. "You will be lonely without companionship," she warned. "You were very fortunate to marry a man you loved, it happens only rarely. Be thankful for that and treasure your memories but now use your head to find a husband who will give you wealth and security and will be in a position to settle your daughters. There are some earls about, I've found one for myself. You should spend more time at Court. When was the last time you were there?"

"I was there for Yuletide and the Twelfth Night celebrations. Also to celebrate George's investiture as Knight of the Garter."

Her brother-in-law's investiture at Windsor castle as a Knight of the Garter had followed upon his inheriting the title of Baron Hunsdon on his father's death, and as he had also taken on the patronage of the Lord Chamberlain's players William Shakespeare had commemorated the occasion by writing a light-hearted comedy entitled 'The Merry Wives of Windsor.'

"Make an effort to be seen more, Alice. And I'm sure you must miss Court gossip," said Anne. "Listen, I have a snippet that will no doubt amuse you. The last time Lord Dorset and I were at Court the Queen noticed Lady Derby wearing a gold locket around her neck and took it from her, teasing her that it might contain a picture of a lover. Not really expecting it to be true, the Queen opened it only to find no portrait of Lord Derby inside but instead a miniature of Robert Cecil. She promptly tied it to her shoe and paraded around the room with it, much to Lady Derby's discomfiture."

"I heard rumours that she is already tiring of her husband, her name has also been linked with the Earl of Essex," said Alice with a smug smile. She had heard the rumours of Lady Derby's infidelity with satisfaction. William had boasted so openly of making a great match for himself in contrast to his brother but it seemed his noble alliance was not bringing him happiness and there were tales abroad of loud quarrels. She could understand Elizabeth de Vere being attracted to the handsome Essex but not the small hunchbacked Cecil who was also her uncle. It would seem Master Secretary had hidden depths.

However to please her sisters, and because she did miss Court gossip, Alice promised to visit the Court more often. She was never short of invitations to old friends but one evening Sir Thomas Egerton asked her to sup with the family at their newly acquired mansion, York House, their business contacts over the past two years having drawn them into a less formal relationship. The lease of this splendid house in the Strand, with formal gardens at the back leading down to the river, was one of the privileges of the office of Lord Keeper. Alice's daughters accompanied her and they were warmly welcomed by Lady Egerton, another Elizabeth, a grey-haired lady of gracious manner and few words. She was richly dressed though not to the height of fashion, her ruff being half the size of Alice's and her burgundy brocade gown overshadowed by Alice's Spanish farthingale in a vibrant shade of turquoise. She had been a widow, kin to the esteemed More family, when eight years previously she became Sir Thomas's second wife.

It was a very big house but showed its age by the smallness of the many rooms, inter-connecting without passageways but with numerous bays and nooks and crannies, and because the house had been leased by a series of Lord Keepers in Elizabeth's reign the house was a riot of miscellaneous furniture and objects. Tall backed walnut chairs stood beside sturdy oak tables, padded stools beside carved chests, some floors were of polished wood, others of flagged stone, while the walls, some wainscoted others lime washed, showed lighter patches where pictures and wall hangings had been taken down.

"We haven't been here long enough for me to begin making changes as yet," Lady Egerton apologised, "but my husband has already ordered new tapestries and we are expecting furniture from some of our other houses."

"I have several properties as you know, but this is convenient for my work in the City as I am always occupied between Whitehall and Westminster," Sir Thomas said. "I have recently purchased an estate at Tatton in Cheshire but I have no intention of living there – it is intended for my son Thomas."

The household at York House was immensely large. Living there were Egerton's son and heir, Sir Thomas the younger, together with his wife and three daughters; his younger brother John who at twenty years old had just finished his studies at Lincoln's Inn; Lady Egerton's son Francis from her previous marriage; and one of her brother's daughters, fourteen year old Anne More. The Stanleys were introduced to them all, then to another young man whom Egerton introduced as, "My new secretary, Master John Donne."

He was a strikingly handsome young man in his mid-twenties, soberly dressed in a black satin suit but with little ornamentation and a plain linen collar. His black hair hung to his shoulders, his face was long with high cheekbones and a long high-bridged nose, his mouth full and red and sensuous.

During supper Egerton's two sons led the conversation and Sir Thomas was willing to let them do so. It was obvious that though Egerton might be feared in all the law courts he held few terrors for his sons. Thomas resembled his father in appearance and in his restrained manner, enlivened by a wry sense of humour. The younger John was exuberant with a cheerful face that reflected his high spirits and it was he who encouraged the secretary to tell them about his exploits in Cadiz with the Earl of Essex's expedition from which he had just returned, and his visits to the playhouses for which it seemed he had a great partiality.

"Master Donne also writes poetry which is well considered in the Inns of Court," he said.

The secretary answered politely when pressed but seemed reluctant to enlarge on either of these pursuits and Alice intuited it was because his new employer might not consider them suitable accomplishments for the work he had entailed him to do. But although there was a reticence in the young man there was also an arrogance discernible in his sardonic smile and the enigmatic depths of his dark eyes, as if in defiance of appearances he considered himself superior to the rest of the company. But it was a convivial evening with stimulating conversation on a wide range of subjects. Alice noted that Lady Egerton's niece Anne More was not afraid to contribute to the talk and seemed to be a well-educated young lady with a confirmed self confidence as well as an engaging manner. In contrast her own daughters, though prettier, were quietly aloof, speaking only when addressed.

When the Stanley family returned to their own house in the City Frances asked, seemingly off-handedly, "Shall we be able to visit the Egertons again?"

"She likes John Egerton," giggled Elizabeth.

Alice brought to mind the younger son. He was shorter and broader than his father and she surmised he must resemble his mother with his round face and high colour but there was also a distinct resemblance to his father in the dark intelligent eyes beneath the well-defined arched brows. His hair, which reached his shoulders, also had the sandy tint of his father's and his moustache and beard were small and neatly trimmed. His salutation had been courteous without any sign of affectation and when he had taken her hand it had been firm and confident.

"Don't be silly," Frances reproved her sister, but when Alice looked at her sharply she could see she was blushing. Frances was fourteen now and growing even more beautiful with her grandmother's features and her long waving hair with tints of gold when the light caught it.

"With your liking for handsome men I thought you might have preferred Master Donne, especially with your fondness for poesy," Anne remarked.

Frances had been intimidated by John Donne's bold scrutiny of her, preferring John Egerton's boyish spontaneity, but she replied, "I left him for you."

"I would never be attracted by a lowly secretary," Anne said scornfully. "Nor even by someone like John

Egerton. He's only a younger son, he doesn't even have a title and his father was illegitimate."

"Nonetheless the Egertons are very wealthy," her mother reminded her.

"Nobility is more important than wealth," Anne declared.

"Your father didn't think so," Alice snapped. She sighed as she realised once again the burden of having to find suitable husbands for her daughters. They were growing up so quickly, Anne was seventeen and ought to be betrothed by now. At least her financial problems were being slowly eased by Sir Thomas Egerton's continuing success with settlements for her, and the daughters of Ferdinando Stanley, 5th Earl of Derby, would at least have substantial dowries to offer.

Lady Derby and her family continued to visit York House, which became increasingly splendid as time went on with new furniture and tapestries, rugs on the floor and an abundance of silver plate. A new portrait of Sir Thomas in his robes of state was hung over the fireplace in the dining hall. Alice could not help but notice that John Egerton was present at these gatherings and he often contrived to be close to Frances. She was forced to acknowledge that the young man was not immune to her daughter's beauty and attractive personality. It was a pity he was only the younger son without any prospects to inherit or otherwise an alliance with the wealthy Egerton family would not have been unthinkable for her second daughter, although Anne as the eldest must be married first.

The crowded household of York House was soon enlarged by another member, none other than Robert Devereux, Earl of Essex, - an unexpected and unwelcome addition for he was under house arrest by order of the Queen. The Earl had been placed at the head of an army to fight the rebels in Ireland where the situation had been steadily worsening. Many young noblemen and courtiers volunteered to be part of the army, not only for patriotic reasons but because they considered it an opportunity for advancement in Essex's circle at Court. Amongst them had been the Egertons' eldest son and heir, the young Sir Thomas who had left behind his wife and three small daughters, hoping to make his fortune for it was known he lived substantially above his income. However the expedition turned into a humiliating failure. The Egertons learnt from Thomas's communications that the rebels were more numerous than expected, they fought a guerrilla warfare that was suitable for the terrain, (English military strategy being ineffectual in the bogs,) the Irish weather was against them and they soon became short of money and re-inforcements. Casualties were high and one day the Egerton family received word from another source that Thomas had been badly wounded in a skirmish near Dublin but no further news was forthcoming to ease their anxieties.

Being a member of the Privy Council, the Lord Keeper was also kept abreast of the official news. The Earl of Essex as Commander-in-Chief of the English forces bore the brunt of criticism for the failure of the expedition, though the circumstances could hardly be laid to his charge. But some of his more autocratic actions were offensive to the Queen, and his sworn enemy Robert Cecil had been using his absence to blacken his name. He hinted to the Queen that the Earl was comporting himself like a King in Ireland, treating with the rebels and intending to use the army to depose her when they returned to England. Essex rushed home to defend himself against these accusations but instead he was placed under house arrest until he could be put on trial. The house chosen for his confinement was that of the Lord Keeper, York House.

Sir Thomas Egerton was not happy about the arrangement. He had been a colleague of Lord Burghley and through him a friend to Essex, one of Burghley's wards. After the death of the old councillor, the last of those who had served the Queen since the beginning of her reign, Egerton had helped Essex on more than one occasion, notably on that memorable day in the council chamber when Essex had come close to losing his head. After the death of Leicester and Hatton the Queen had taken the young Essex as her favourite, lavishing on him all the affection she had given to Leicester who had been his step-father but still capricious towards him, alternating between cosseting him and humiliating him. During an argument over the grave situation in Ireland Essex's opinions were being disregarded and in temper he turned his back on his sovereign. The Queen immediately struck him a stinging blow across the face whereupon Essex reached for his sword. There was a deathly silence at this treasonable action and the Earl was only saved from the dire consequences by the intervention of Egerton who, taking his arm, persuaded him to make an abject apology. Later he drafted a letter of repentance for him to sign and because of his respect for the Lord Keeper he did so.

In choosing to confine him in the house of the Lord Keeper, the highest law official in the land, Queen Elizabeth was making the statement that she was acting with the support of the legal profession. Egerton himself

heartily disliked being made Essex's gaoler and the fact
that he had shared a friendship with the young Earl was
a barb to the dart. But besides having a liking for Robert
Devereux, Egerton felt that his house was unsuitable
for the purpose. The household was already too large
and rooms too small and cramped for the successful
accommodation of the prisoner. He also had to be fed
and provided for at Egerton's expense for the Queen
never reimbursed the gaolers of her captives and the
Earl of Shrewsbury had lost part of his fortune by his
guardianship of Mary Stuart over fifteen years. A close
watch had to be kept for attempts at escape and this
was a real possibility as the exterior of the house, both
on the Strand side and the gardens which fronted the
riverbank, was crowded with sympathisers noisily
clamouring for his release and threatening riot. Essex, as
was his habit when under stress, suffered a recurrence
of a chronic malady of sickness and griping bowels
which put a further strain on his accommodation. In the
midst of all this inconvenience the Egerton family were
worried about the fate of young Sir Thomas and waiting
anxiously, but vainly, for news of him.

The confinement continued for more than half a
year because even when Essex had been tried by the Privy
Council and the Lord Keeper had successfully commuted
the accusation into one of disrespect and disobedience
instead of the capital charge of treason, the Earl was still
ordered to be kept under surveillance at York House to
the great inconvenience of the occupants. Sir Thomas
was proud of the house, which was a symbol of his
position and used for the exhibition of his wealth and
privilege with entertainment of business associates and
courtiers, and he confided his irritation to Alice saying,

"I am dismayed that my house should be used as a prison for such a long continuance."

She sensed the anger burning beneath his calm exterior, especially when Robert Cecil ignored his appeal to be relieved of the charge on the grounds that he could not carry out his duties efficiently. She sympathised with him, having personal experience of both Cecil's machinations and the Queen's obduracy. As with the Grey sisters and Lady Margaret Stanley, Queen Elizabeth chose house arrest when she could not imprison them in the Tower on such slim evidence. Alice understood his frustration but was surprised to find a chink in his armour in his feelings for Robert Devereux, not unlike the silent affection he gave his sons.

When news concerning the wellbeing of his eldest son and heir finally arrived from Dublin it was to render all other misfortunes superfluous. The young Sir Thomas had died from his wounds. Alice immediately sent a letter of condolence but she could fully understand the grief of the whole household. She knew that the Lord Keeper would be inconsolable even if he did not display open emotion while Lady Egerton had looked upon her stepson as her own.

Frances Stanley thought of John Egerton, saying how sad he must be to lose his only brother and Alice noted that her warm-hearted daughter never considered that the tragedy had raised him to the position of heir, although Anne immediately made note of the fact. There was a widow and three young children to comfort and be provided for and in a further extension of their miseries Lady Egerton was struck by a severe attack of smallpox, her resistance to the disease weakened through the troubles forced upon them of late. When

Alice made a dutiful visit to York House she was entertained courteously by the young Anne More but told apologetically that her aunt did not want to see anyone as her face was so dreadfully scarred and she was still in a very weak state. Alice had seen many such and the Queen's friend and lady of the bedchamber, Mary Sidney, completely lost her beauty through the disease when she nursed the infected Queen Elizabeth who miraculously survived disfigurement. Instinctively she touched her own face as she realised how distressed the whole household must be by this latest misfortune.

The only alleviation of the Egertons' troubles was that the Queen eventually relented and allowed the Earl of Essex to leave his imprisonment at their House. To his anger, instead of a proclamation of innocence he was given only an official pardon and Alice recalled the similar circumstances of Ferdinando's mother, Lady Margaret Stanley. Essex was not allowed to return to his London home but ordered to go to his country residence Chartley Manor – in effect exile from the Court – and some people murmured about further trouble brewing. However York House was now able to return to normality and Alice awaited a further summons from the Lord Keeper in order to resume their periodic assessment of business matters. Hoping that her affairs could now proceed without interruption she was distressed to hear a short time later that Lady Egerton had died. The sorrows and disruptions over a long period of time had left their mark and she never found the strength to recover from the attack of smallpox.

When Alice finally met up with her legal adviser again she was shocked by the changes the unexpected misfortunes had wrought upon him. The steel within his framework held him as upright as ever but the double loss of his wife and eldest son had felled his spirit. His eyes were dull, his face grey and he looked older than his sixty years. It was common talk in Court circles and the higher echelons of the legal profession how surprisingly excessive his reaction was. They saw only his habitual dependence on logic and rational thought. Few people but Alice saw his strong family feelings or understood the melancholy the Essex affair had caused. When he made a hasty decision in the wake of these events people could only speculate that grief had temporarily clouded his judgement, especially when the decision was one that eventually he had cause to regret.

CHAPTER 18

Marriage

In preparation to leave the house she had been leasing in London Alice was busy sorting some of her personal possessions with her maids when a footman announced a visitor asking to see her. "A Lancashire gentleman by the name of Master Alexander Standish," she was informed.

A surprised smile lit her face and telling the servant to show him to her private parlour she made her way there, smoothing the embroidered panel of her forest-green gown and tucking a stray copper strand inside the jewelled net that covered her hair. It was a few moments before the door was opened and she saw the young friend she had not seen for five years.

"My lady countess," he said with a low bow, taking her hand as she held it out to him then absorbing every detail of her elegant appearance.

"Alexander Standish, what a pleasure to see you." There was unmistakeable delight in her voice as she studied him. She had forgotten how blue his eyes were, (not the cold blue of gems but warm like summer pools,) while his fair hair had darkened a little and there was a noticeable maturity in his face. "What brings you to London and how did you know where to find me?"

"I came on business with lawyers. My father has recently died and Duxbury estate now belongs to me so there were various settlements to be made."

Nostalgia overcame her as she heard the broad Lancashire vowels. "I am sorry for the death of Master Thomas," she said, "but I congratulate you on coming into your inheritance." His brown velvet doublet was well cut to his tall strong figure and she suspected he had bought it in London. "So you are ready to make all the improvements you used to talk about?" she said with a smile. "How are your wife and family?"

"Very well, my lady. We have four children now, two boys and two girls."

She noted he still had the same half-apologetic smile as her eyebrows arched.

"Well your responsibilities must keep you occupied," she said.

She seated herself and motioned for him to take the chair opposite and for a time he answered all her questions about the people and their doings in Lancashire. She understood he would not consider it his right to enquire about her circumstances but then he surprised her by saying, "I believe you are to be married to the Lord Keeper."

"Yes I am to marry Sir Thomas Egerton soon. That is the reason I am preparing to quit this house that I have leased for some time."

His expression was unfathomable as he asked abruptly, "Do you love him?"

Her head rose haughtily and she was about to reprimand him for his impudence, but then something stayed her as she recalled how she had asked him the same question when he had informed her of his coming marriage. She tried to gather her thoughts together then said, "I admire and respect him. I am nearly forty years old, I have been a widow for five years and I am tired of being alone. I need companionship. I need someone to help me share the burden of my finances and supervise my daughters - Sir Thomas is arranging marriages for them. He has many properties where I shall be my own mistress again. He is rich and powerful and I shall recover the place at Court that I once had. Isn't that enough?" she added defiantly.

"No it isn't," he said vehemently and she looked at him in surprise. Five years ago he would not have dared to challenge her. "What is wealth and power without love? The Lord Keeper is more than twenty years older than you are."

"Does age matter?" she asked.

"No," he admitted miserably. "If you only want riches and status then I suppose one rich man is as good as another."

"That is quite uncalled for, Master Standish," she said angrily, rising from her seat in accompaniment to the rising of her voice.

He rose also mumbling, "I'm sorry," but she heard the hint of defiance in his voice. "I did not think you would have been so swayed by the lure of wealth when it is common knowledge in Lancashire that Lord Derby has been forced to make you handsome reparation, my lady."

Alice was almost speechless with anger but she cried, "How dare the people of Lancashire judge me for obtaining what is my right and the right of my children."

Alexander shook his head. "No-one judges you, my lady, you are fondly remembered and spoken of."

He hesitated then said, "But it seems you have changed somewhat. I did not think you would have considered marriage for those reasons." He faced her with a direct scrutiny.

She was still angry with him but had to admit that Alexander Standish had certainly grown up. Though there was still admiration in his surveillance of her there was a new critical element and she realised with a pang of disappointment that she no longer held careless sway over him. Suddenly she wanted a return of his devotion, not the devotion of a young boy but of the mature handsome man he had become. She took hold of his arm saying, "Let us not part in anger, Alex. Let us part as friends." She paused while he stood hesitantly. "Do you still ride out to Anglezarke?" she asked at last.

"I don't have too much spare time now but if I have to go to Bolton or Whalley I sometimes take the road over the moors," he answered.

For a moment their minds united as their memories travelled together to the windswept moors with their carpet of heather and the lonely cries of the curlew and the bleating of sheep.

"If you have cause to come to London again then pray visit us," she couldn't help saying, feeling the need to add, "I would like to be kept informed of affairs in Lancashire." Then with a sudden curiosity to know what effect the great city had had on the Lancashire boy she asked, "How did you find London on your first visit?"

"It did not substantially change my opinion," he smiled mischievously. "Too big, too noisy, too dirty and the people too discourteous. But I did get to go to a playhouse, to the new Globe where I watched William

Shakespeare's chronicle of Henry V and that was well worth the journey."

"I saw a performance at Court," she said. "You know my brother-in-law Baron Hunsdon is now patron of what were Lord Strange's players. They don't go up to Lancashire so often now that they play regularly at Court and there are now four playhouses in London in which to perform."

"We still get other travelling players, including Lord Derby's new company, and I go to watch them whenever I can."

"So you still go to Lathom House?" she asked.

"Sometimes. Lord Derby feasts and entertains but it isn't the same. The new Lady Derby is usually in London, she doesn't care for Lancashire, and Lord William spends a lot of his time in Chester."

A wave of longing swept over Alice and suddenly she didn't want to talk with Alexander Standish any longer. She bade him farewell and thanked him for his visit and he made his formal courtesies. She called for a manservant to show him out but before he left the room she said again, "Do not forget to visit me again if you have occasion to come to London."

The marriage of the Dowager Countess of Derby to the Lord Keeper was the subject of much gossip and speculation around the City especially as it occurred so soon after the death of his wife and the fact that it had been performed at the house of Lord Russell without banns or any public announcement, therefore coming under the censure of "clandestine". Comment was made on Egerton's ambitions of aspiring to the nobility by marrying a countess whose children carried royal blood.

There was also talk about how he had contrived to obtain a considerable fortune for the Dowager Countess through the law courts, especially as he had been faced with large debts on behalf of his deceased son. Alice's name also did not escape untarnished as malicious rumours were aired regarding *her* ambition and acquisitiveness, fanned by Lord and Lady Derby. William was not loath to publicise the fact that he had been forced to sell half his estate in order to pay her demands, indeed he had sold an estate in Shropshire to Lord Keeper Egerton. Alice was hurt by the gossip and the coldness she encountered in some quarters, notably from Robert Cecil and his clique, kin and friends of Lord and Lady Derby. Coupled with Alexander Standish's disapproval this had raised doubts in her mind, but her family and friends all approved of her wisdom and good fortune in choosing as her second husband one of the wealthiest and most powerful men in the land and she resolutely squashed any misgivings. For the last few years as a widow with little money and only the title acquired from her deceased husband she had merely been able to live on the fringes of society and she felt increasingly the responsibility for her daughters. As the Lord Keeper's wife and still a countess, a title she intended to keep, she could return to the highest levels of prestige. It was true that it had been a rushed arrangement so soon after the death of Sir Thomas's wife but he had been greatly affected by her loss and seemingly in haste to fill the vacuum afforded by her absence in his household so once he had made the proposal Alice did not think she should refuse the offer. The fact that she did not love Sir Thomas Egerton was a point in favour since it removed any sense of betrayal to Ferdinando, of whom she never ceased to think longingly.

Alice prepared to move into York house with her three daughters and some forty servants, causing a great upheaval as she did so. The secretary John Donne was forced to find himself alternative accommodation in rooms at the Savoy, rented by many young lawyers and secretaries, and Anne More returned to her father's house in the countryside now that she was bereft of her aunt's guardianship. Son Thomas's widow together with her three daughters returned to her family and the stepson Francis moved into lodgings. There was already talk in the City that the Lord Keeper had been forced to rid himself of his household in order to accommodate Lady Derby and her entourage. Only John Egerton remained of the family, much to Frances's delight.

"We shall of course have separate chambers," Egerton had warned her. "I will come to you when I have need."

Alice thought longingly of the closeness she and Ferdinando had shared, sharing a bedchamber and a bed in defiance of convention. However she considered this arrangement would be to her advantage as her new husband was an elderly man and she was not in love with him. On their wedding night she was made aware that the marital rite was a perfunctory act for his sole satisfaction and after releasing her mind to a contemplation of the pargetted ceiling she was relieved by the knowledge it would not be repeated too often. Their marriage had been undertaken not for mutual love but for mutual convenience. Her more mercurial needs were satisfied and for that she would endure the occasional inconvenience of his lovemaking, while her attraction for Sir Thomas Egerton lay in the fact that she was titled, attractive, intelligent and cultured - the perfect wife for a man in his position, an ornament to his office and his household, and sexual satisfaction as it served his needs. It was as a corollary to his prestige that her chief value lay.

It was for reasons of prestige that he now pursued advantageous marriages for his step-daughters. He had put a lot of energy into trying to arrange a match for Anne with Henry Hastings, heir to the earldom of Huntingdon. Henry Hastings was only twenty years old but his father was already dead and it seemed as if he would soon inherit his grandfather's title. The Hastings family also carried royal blood, being descended from the Plantagenet kings, and Anne was beside herself with excitement. Though she had never met Henry Hastings he was young, noble and with royal blood and it was a marriage she had always dreamed of.

However her hopes were to be cruelly dashed. Henry's grandfather refused Anne on account of her being heiress presumptive to the Crown according to the will of King Henry VIII. The Queen was now approaching seventy years old and there was continual speculation about who would succeed her. Anne Stanley was a contender together with Mary Stuart's son King James of Scotland, his cousin Arbella Stuart, and even the Spanish Infanta, backed by some Catholics. The succession might prove debatable and could result in armed conflict. The Earl of Huntingdon had not in the past escaped Queen Elizabeth's mistrust of his royal blood, which had cost him a spell of imprisonment, and there had been a rumour that once in their cups Ferdinando and he had talked about fighting for the Crown. On account of the sensitivity of his inheritance the Earl considered it not wise for his grandson to take Anne and put himself into jeopardy by a double claim.

"The Earl says he is happy for an alliance with the family of Lord Derby but will take the second daughter, Frances," Sir Thomas told Alice. "I say we should accept his offer. I know it is customary for the eldest daughter to be married first but I don't think we should let this very advantageous union pass out of our hands."

Alice sighed. She was sorry that Anne should be disappointed again when her hopes had been so high, especially when Frances would seem to be preferred before her once more. But there was another matter to be considered also.

"Surely you can see that your son John and Frances have developed a deep attachment for each other," she said to her husband. Since John Egerton had climbed into his dead brother's shoes as his father's heir, his brother having only daughters, and recently been knighted by the Queen, Alice had begun to think more kindly about her daughter's preference for him. "They seek each other's company whenever they can and are obviously happy together. It would be a great cruelty to wrench them apart when they are in love."

"What is love?" scoffed Sir Thomas. "Not necessary in marriage and I say we cannot lose this chance of a match with Hastings."

"Would you really like to see John disappointed?" Alice persisted, knowing how fond her husband was of his son, especially since the shock of losing his elder son. She herself would like to see her daughter happy in marriage but not certain how far Sir Thomas's filial affection would outweigh mercurial considerations she dared to add, "It wouldn't be a noble alliance for Frances it is true but wouldn't one of Lord Derby's daughters be a good match for John."

She could see her husband's mind working and finally he said, "Well why not. Why not keep the money in the family. We can try Hastings with Elizabeth."

"But she's only thirteen," Alice cried.

"They can delay the consummation. Let's see what the Earl says."

The Earl of Huntingdon was willing to accept Elizabeth Stanley for his grandson and heir. Egerton was pleased that two of his step-daughters were now safely accounted for but realised there were going to be problems with Anne. Alice had the task of relaying to all of them the news about their future.

Frances was ecstatic, her happiness making her look more beautiful than ever. Though it was probable she could have found a husband more noble than the newly-knighted Sir John Egerton, Alice was sure she could not have found one to make her happier and was satisfied. Frances was only sixteen but she and Ferdinando had married young and she would like at least one of her daughters to have the happiness she had known and not the sad experience of their grandmother's arranged marriage.

Elizabeth was astonished and somewhat fearful when informed she was soon to be married, even before her sister Frances because Egerton was afraid the aged Earl of Huntingdon would die and circumstances change. However the youngest daughter had always been gentle and undemanding. Her tutor had found her an industrious pupil with a genuine enjoyment of books and study rather than the more frivolous pursuits of young girls. She had a naturally religious disposition and accepted without question what she believed to be her destiny. Because she was so young her character would now develop according to her new responsibilities and Alice surmised that as she matured she would grow gracefully into the high position she would attain as Countess of Huntingdon.

Anne was furious, screaming and shouting. "Why should Elizabeth be married before me. She is a mere baby and I am twenty," she cried, throwing hairbrush, mirror and books about the chamber in wild disorder. She continued to rant and rave at both her sisters but they bore her anger patiently, understanding how disappointed she must feel. Alice tried to soothe her by telling her *her* time would soon come but she could not help fearing that it might be difficult to find a husband for her eldest daughter so burdened with a cursed inheritance.

Unlike Ferdinando who had conversed about his doings and shared all his thoughts with his wife, Sir Thomas never spoke of his work in the law courts or the business of the Privy Council. He never told her that the Privy council was using informers to keep the Earl of Essex and his circle under surveillance as they suspected he was plotting rebellion. Essex had never being re-instated in the Queen's favour and it was suspected that his anger about the outcome of his trial, his hatred of Robert Cecil, and his dissatisfaction with the Privy Council and the Parliament over their ordering of the country's affairs, especially with regard to making peace with Spain for which Cecil was a keen advocate, were powerful enough incentives to warrant him taking treasonable action.

One fine Sunday morning in February, seeking her husband to query a matter with him, Alice was informed he had been ordered to Essex House with other Privy Councillors as there was a great disturbance there. York House was close by and it was soon evident to the whole household that an uprising of great proportions was taking place at Essex House as a large company of the Earl's supporters and ex-soldiers from the Irish campaign gathered in the courtyard armed and ready for an attempt to seize London. Most of the servants from York House had gone to see what was happening as well as John Egerton. When he returned it was with the news that his father was being kept hostage there together with the Lord Chief Justice and Essex's uncle, Sir William Knollys. Essex himself had locked them in his library and turned the tables on his one-time custodian.

The household of York House were amongst the first to witness the clamorous procession of the armed company as the rebels proceeded to make their way through the City with Essex riding at the head and calling for the citizens to support him in removing the incompetent and self-seeking government which was ruining the country. However the people of London were not ready for rebellion. No matter how discontented they were with certain aspects of Queen Elizabeth's reign and her advisers, they were not prepared to remove their loyalty from her at this late stage, or even to limit her powers, and Essex's cry for support went unheeded. The abortive coup was soon ended by the aid of the London militia and as the rebels fled the militia followed them to Essex house when they realised the Earl with some of his supporters had retreated there. Windows were broken and stone crumbled as the house was bombarded with cannon and shot.

"What do you think will happen to your father?" Alice asked John Egerton. "Do you think he is in danger?"

"I don't really think so, Essex has too much respect for him and the others, but he is obviously holding them as hostages to bargain with," her stepson replied. "I think the main danger could come from them being accidentally injured in the attack on the house and my father's age and health are not conducive to further alarms."

Alice could not help wondering if the hand of conspiracy would ever cease to touch her.

The Earl however eventually surrendered. The hostages were escorted from the house and taken by barge to Whitehall to report to the Queen. Those rebels who had not managed to flee were taken and dispersed to London's various gaols while the leaders, the Earls of Essex and Southampton, were sent to the Tower.

When Sir Thomas returned home Alice voiced her relief at her husband's release but he merely nodded. She was eager to know everything that had transpired at Essex House but he made no attempt to inform her about what had happened or to confess his feelings about the actions of the Earl with whom he once shared a friendship. Once again she couldn't help remembering how Ferdinando had shared all his thoughts with her. Egerton's comments stopped short of any personal feelings for Robert Devereux, confining himself only to points of law, and when the Earl was executed on Tower Hill on Ash Wednesday he said only "He knew not how to play the malefactor."

Alice found herself with a more personal involvement in the Essex rebellion when she heard that one of the rebels had been her sister Anne's grandson, William

Parker. For a time she had shared her sister's anxiety about the young man's possible fate for he had been imprisoned together with all those rebels who had been successfully captured and she was considering asking her husband to try and secure his release. However after the execution of the leaders the majority of the smaller fry were released and in due course given a pardon by the Queen. There was great relief in the Spencer family but the succeeding lives of the rebels were not left untainted by their involvement.

The first few months of marriage had made Alice realise she was not going to receive close companionship from the union. However the lack of emotional satisfaction was compensated for by material possessions. As a wedding gift her husband bought for her a beautiful large moated manor house at Harefield, in the midst of the fertile rolling countryside of Middlesex and less than 10 miles from London itself. Alice was also pleased to hear that after six years of marriage the new Countess of Derby had presented her husband with their first child – a girl!

CHAPTER 19

Harefield

"The Queen has granted us the honour of a visit to Harefield as part of her summer progress to Bristol," Sir Thomas announced to his wife with evident pride. "I suggest you begin preparations immediately, expense will be of no consequence. The occasion must serve both to impress Her Majesty with our loyal service and to promote our standing in the eyes of our peers. It must be an occasion that will be remembered and spoken of favourably for a long time to come. I will leave the practical arrangements to you but I have some recommendations of my own that I would ask you to respect."

A flurry of thoughts and emotions rushed through Alice's mind, making it difficult to sort out one from the other as she listened to the information relayed by her husband, but later when she had escaped to be alone she could let her feelings have free rein. Her bedchamber she did not consider to be completely her own domain for it was invaded at times by her husband. She had furnished it in the rose hues of Althorp Manor, not wanting anything to remind her of the sumptuous bedchambers she had shared with Ferdinando at Derby House and Lathom House. Her parlour however was her private sanctum and she had chosen one of the sunniest rooms in the house with two large windows revealing wide views of the extensive gardens, now in their summer glory, and furnished sumptuously with velvet upholstered furnishings and rugs in bright yellow with gold trimmings. The walls and plastered ceiling were colour washed in pale saffron to give the room a warm glow of sunshine, even in winter, and because this was a part of the house Sir Thomas never entered she had hung a portrait of Ferdinando on the wall. Seated in a comfortable chair by the window she pondered on the news she had received.

She acknowledged the great honour afforded to them by a visit from the Queen, an honour not granted to the Earls of Derby, which demonstrated how highly esteemed was the Lord Keeper. Their status would be enhanced hereafter as her husband intended. Once again she was aware of how ambitious he was but the scope of his intentions gave her some feelings of anxiety, not only with the great responsibility thrust upon her but the realisation of the enormous cost that would be incurred. Sir Thomas Egerton was a wealthy man but a visit from the Queen had been known to bankrupt greater fortunes and she knew that he would let no such considerations hinder the opportunity to increase his status in the eyes of all those who occupied his world – the world of the law, the government and the Court. He had climbed high but he could never quite discard his humble origins. Alice realised that, despite his words, he had taken her for his wife because of the high status Ferdinando had bestowed upon her and the prestige of having step-children with royal blood. Yet she had to agree that her own soaring ambitions had been no less and her uncle Thomas Kitson had used the honour of a visit from the

Queen to further his aim of nobility. Her memories drifted inevitably back to the last time she had been personally involved in such an event and the happenings of twenty years ago replayed themselves as vividly as if they were yesterday. She was back at Hengrave when her uncle Thomas Kitson had given the Queen the precious jewel and in return received his knighthood and requested her a place at Court. Then, the most poignant memory, her first meeting with Ferdinando. For a time she allowed herself the luxury of happy memories and relived every nuance of that evening, still so bright in her recollection. Then regretfully she closed the book on a life that was past and gone for ever and turned to the practicalities of the future. She began to estimate the tasks facing her and make mental lists before consigning them to paper and allocating to her multitude of servants their individual responsibilities.

Foremost in her mind was the realisation that this could be a golden opportunity for her daughter Anne. Now that Frances and young Elizabeth were seemingly happily accounted for, she was deeply concerned about her eldest daughter, now twenty two years old. The Queen was past seventy and refused to name any possible successor. If the conditions of her father's will were honoured then Anne Stanley would be the next queen of England as being the closest descendant of the Princess Mary Rose. Sometimes Alice allowed herself to fantasise about what it would be like to be the mother of the Queen. She would indulge herself with imagined scenarios although deep within her heart she could not see this becoming reality. When she had broached the possibility to Sir Thomas he had said, "There is no legal authority to accept King Henry's testament above other considerations. When all is said and done, the rightful heirs are the descendants of Margaret Tudor as being the elder sister. That is King James of Scotland."

"But he is the son of Mary Stuart and surely with her history the English people would be loath to accept him."

"He has been carefully reared as a confirmed Protestant and strictly speaking his mother *was* the legal heir after Queen Elizabeth," Thomas reminded her. "In justice to her claim the Crown should belong to him. I would say his greatest disadvantage is in not being English. There are those who do not relish the idea of a Scot ruling England. The other possible claimant is his cousin Arbella Stuart who is English."

"The final choice will be the Queen's," Alice said. "Isn't it probable that she would choose another woman to succeed her rather than an alien Scot, and keep to the wishes of her father whom she admired so much?"

"Has she ever shown any interest in either Anne or Arbella Stuart?" her husband countered. "Ever welcomed them to Court? Ever made an attempt to groom them for her role?"

Alice had remained silent, knowing this to be true. The two prospective heiresses had been completely ignored.

However this visit to Harefield could be the ideal opportunity to remedy that with regard to Anne and later she ventured to voice this possibility to her husband. "In the past the Queen has mistrusted those in a position to succeed her, as everyone knows. But the situation must change now that she is old and cannot reign much longer. Surely she will make her wishes known before too long."

Egerton smiled deprecatingly and shook his head. "You are naive Alice if you believe the final decision will be the Queen's. It will be Robert Cecil's and he is determined King James shall succeed her. He has been treating with the Scottish king secretly for years. And there are many others of his opinion. Even a Scot is preferable to another period of petticoat rule."

In her annoyance Alice taunted him by saying, "Wouldn't you like to be the step-father of a Queen, surely that would be the final crown to your ambition."

"As the first Lord Derby received all his honours by being step-father to a king," he riposted. "Never think that was the reason I married you, Alice. I climb by my own merits and consider the position I have attained to be worth more than an inherited nobility. And don't deny your ambition doesn't match mine. The Spencers and the Egertons come from the same stock."

Alice left him angrily but some of her annoyance stemmed from an acknowledgement of the truth of his final statement, although she only half believed his denials about his reasons for marriage .

However she determined to use the opportunity of the Queen's visit to promote Anne to her notice and at least try to secure a position for her at Court as a maid of honour, as uncle Thomas had succeeded in doing so for herself. In the midst of all the extensive preparations she lavished much attention on her daughter's appearance and behaviour. Knowing how Elizabeth disliked to be outshone she ensured the gown was simple and discreet, though of the richest silk brocade in a deep iris shade so that she would not look too immature, a gauze ruff of moderate size, her only jewellery the sapphires adorning the cap and veil that covered her hair. She had tutored Anne in the necessity of showing a pleasant countenance and making an effort at interesting conversation to all without regard to title and status.

She was looking forward to planning the entertainment they would provide and had indeed thought about asking Will Shakespeare to come to her aid but knew that he never wrote for such ceremonial observances with their necessary excess of flattery. However Thomas had already asked Sir John Davies, one of a set of writers from the Middle Temple with a reputation for intellectual and sophisticated literary tastes, to compose an original entertainment for the occasion. Alice was a little unsure about the choice as Davies often parodied the romantic literature at which Shakespeare was such an expert but her husband was adamant in his intention to employ a fellow lawyer who was highly thought of in the world of the law and admired by the Queen herself. Alice however chose the musicians and knowing that her uncle Thomas often employed the Johnsons at Hengrave she invited them to play at Harefield.

When the day finally arrived for the visit after weeks of preparation and anxiety, Alice felt surprisingly calm. The house was beautiful, the arrangements completed early, the servants efficient, the actors and musicians in readiness. She had the support of her sisters in company with their respected husbands, and her own husband would smooth the Queen's path at every turn as he rode so high in her favour. Alice was twenty years older and no longer intimidated by the monarch, though in honesty she admitted Sir Thomas Egerton's partnership sheltered her more than Ferdinando's equivocal relationship with Elizabeth. The only fly in the ointment was the weather, for it was pouring with rain on this August day. Everyone had been disappointed on rising and being met with grey skies and downpours and it was obvious that the beautiful gardens would not look their best, but it had been a wet summer and on this progress the Queen was no doubt accustomed to less than perfect climatic conditions.

As the Queen's coach and the long following procession entered the grounds of Harefield they were met by two personages impersonating a bailiff and a dairymaid who engaged in a comic dialogue pretending that the identity of the visitor was not known. This called forth much merriment and before continuing along the driveway to the house the Queen was presented with a jewelled rake and fork from the "servants." Then at the entrance to the house the Queen was met by a personification of the House itself – an actor in a parti-coloured robe made to represent bricks who conversed with Father Time on the great honour of the visit, presenting to the Queen another great jewel in the shape of a heart.

When the Queen alighted to enter the house all the customary pageantry could not disguise the fact that she was an old woman. She had to be helped from the elaborate coach lavishly ornamented with the Royal arms and Alice could not help remembering her arrival at Hengrave on a spirited black stallion with the Earl of Leicester and Sir Christopher Hatton riding by her side. Now it was Robert Cecil who assisted her and although the Queen admired his undoubted gifts as a statesman it was known she had no personal liking for him and called him her 'pigmy', a nickname he tolerated only because *She* had given it to him. Alice followed her husband with a low honour but when she lifted up her head it was to see no vision of sovereign majesty at the height of her power. The face beneath the mask of white paint was no longer aglow with vitality but ravaged and wrinkled, the cheeks hollow, the eyes pale and myopic. Instead of the gold-ornamented riding habit she wore a white gown covered in jewels which served only to emphasize her gaunt figure, the inappropriately low neckline revealing withered breasts. Beneath the jewelled headtire her hair had its usual abundance but the burnished copper was now a garish unnatural red and her smile revealed a row of blackened teeth. Alice felt a momentary pity. The greatest wealth and power could not put a stop on the march of time. A shaft of sorrow pierced her as she recalled herself and the Queen twenty years ago at Hengrave. That time was gone forever and nothing could bring back those halcyon days.

The nostalgia was consumed in the flurry of welcome as so many people came to make their honours and if fortunate receive words from the Queen in return, and Alice was warmly received as 'Lady Egerton.' The visit around the gardens had to be abandoned because of the rain so the Queen was escorted by Sir Thomas into the long luminous dining hall with two oriel windows through which the sun often flooded the room, though on this day the dim grey light had to be augmented with candles in the wall sconces.

Sir Thomas had presented all Alice's three daughters to the Queen and this had been an important consideration in the visit as she had still not given her official consent to the marriages of Frances and Elizabeth, both unions having sensitive aspects. The Queen spent some time in conversation with each of them and seemed satisfied by the natural charm of Frances and the gravity of Elizabeth, named in her honour after the Armada victory, but despite Alice's hopes there was no particular interest paid to Anne Stanley.

The music accompanying the lengthy meal greatly pleased Elizabeth. Edward Johnson had written a song especially for her entitled 'Eliza is the fairest Queen' and she had expressed her delight with the composition. During the meal Sir Thomas and her sister Anne's husband, the Earl of Dorset, sat beside the Queen, followed by George Carey then the rest of their respective families. Alice's eyes travelled to her sisters and she was rewarded by looks of approval but she couldn't help noticing the difference in them. Elizabeth was looking increasingly careworn and older than her years whereas Anne was placidly content with her new marriage. Alice studied her husband, listening earnestly to the Queen's discourse. Despite signs of increasing age he was still handsome at sixty and he had already provided her with much that she desired, including the honour of a visit to her new home by the Queen. Even with the absence of mutual love her marriage was fulfilling its early promise of wealth and prestige.

When the time came for the Queen to depart the rain had stopped and an elaborate chair upon a turkey carpet was set for Elizabeth to listen to a dialogue between Place and Time. Place was now garbed in a gown of deepest mourning to lament her departure and presented her with another jewel in the shape of an anchor, one of her appellations being Queen of the Sea. Finally Saint Swithin appeared to apologise for the weather and to everyone's amazement presented a final gift of a rainbow gown of which the sleeves were embroidered with rubies and pearls. The Queen's delight was obvious as the whole company applauded – in honour of the monarch and also of their hosts.

"A successful day," Sir Thomas said with relief when the company had departed in the late afternoon, guests following in the Queen's procession. Together they reviewed the sequence of events and he complimented Alice on her ordering of everything while she expressed her satisfaction with Sir John Davies's surprisingly imaginative entertainment. The only disappointment was that even Sir Thomas Egerton had been unable to persuade the Queen to give his stepdaughter Anne a place at Court, although she had intimated she would make no objection to the marriages of the younger girls, a welcome concession born of her good humour at the day's proceedings. Sir Thomas looked tired with the strain of all his efforts and was no doubt worried about how much the visit had cost him, Alice reckoned some 4,000 pounds. He insisted the investment would bear dividends but privately she had considered the gifts of four costly jewels excessive. He made excuses to retire to his chamber and Alice went to summon the servants and set them about the multifarious tasks necessary in the aftermath.

When she had done she made her way into the gardens to find some quietness for herself. It was damp and chilly but at least the rain had stopped. She knew Anne was disappointed that the Queen had not treated her as she expected but she was exhausted and did not feel she could cope with her daughter's emotions at this time. Her own emotions had been disturbed by the memories the day had raised and a melancholy was beginning to envelop her now that all the excitement was past. Dusk was falling and there was a stillness in the air, broken only by the rustle of a creature in the grass and the whisper of leaves as the breeze touched them. She sat on a stone seat amongst the roses, their petals still dripping moisture, lost in reminiscences. Her thoughts travelled back in time to her young self, full of dreams, filled with excitement when the Queen had offered her a place at Court which she believed was the entry into a magical world. Then she had met Ferdinando when his players had come to perform and she had thought he was a player too. Tears began to roll down her cheeks. If only she could go back in time, make things happen differently, still have him with her.

She looked towards the contours of the house with its solid brick exterior, its tall chimneys dimly silhouetted against the darkening sky. Her life was different now and she must embrace the changes. There was a feeling that life was changing for everyone as the reign of Queen Elizabeth was undoubtedly drawing to a close after nearly fifty years. No-one knew what was to come but the future might hold its own promise. She was no longer young but she had wealth, security and a noble title still. Two of her daughters were now set to enter into successful marriages and if only Anne could be so happily matched she could settle down with her new husband and enjoy a life where she was still important and respected. It had been a long journey between Hengrave and Harefield but she must now let the past go. She said this often to herself and then an image of Ferdinando would intrude into her resolution and she knew she would willingly surrender everything she had striven for in order to have him back with her.

When they returned to York House at the end of the summer it wasn't long before Sir Thomas heard news that disturbed him greatly. His secretary Master John

Donne had eloped with his niece Anne More and married her secretly. "Sir George Moore is in a great fury and has had him committed to the Tower," he told Alice, clamping his lips in a tight line.

"It doesn't seem so great an offence to warrant the Tower," Alice remarked. "I know clandestine marriages are against the law but they are common enough, we ourselves were guilty in that respect," she reminded her husband. "It isn't as if they are nobility with much at stake, like the Earl of Southampton when he was imprisoned by the Queen for marrying Elizabeth Vernon secretly. A great fortune was involved there and he was the ward of Lord Burghley who had intended him for Elizabeth de Vere. Is Anne with child?"

"Not so far as I know," Egerton retorted. "But although they are not nobility, the Mores are very important and wealthy gentry with a long family history. My late wife was the sister of Sir George, as you are aware. And who is John Donne? A mere secretary, a poetaster with no money and no inheritance, and a Catholic to boot."

"They are obviously in love with each other to take such a risk," Alice commented.

"What is love except a romantic delusion," her husband cried scornfully, his usually calm voice rising in anger. "The girl is scarce sixteen, she is underage which compounds the offence. Donne is almost thirty years old. He has obviously seduced her with his fine poetic words and she has not the maturity to withstand his charm. He is hoping for Sir George's fortune and she deserved a more equal partner."

"I think that is unfair of you, Thomas," his wife said. "I must say you are re-acting extremely to a matter which hardly concerns you."

"Alice, are you completely stupid," he said coldly. "How can you say that this hardly concerns me when the man was employed by me and brought into my household where I provided the opportunity for him to meet my niece. Worse than that, it reflects badly on my dear wife Elizabeth. Anne was in her care and this implies she was somewhat lax in her guardianship. The two would seem to have been meeting illicitly over a period of time. What does that say about our household! Sir George More blames us both and this affects my reputation greatly."

"Very well, I can see this aspect of the affair," Alice conceded. "But it is difficult to always be watchful of young lovers, they will find ways to deceive." She thought of herself and Ferdinando at Greenwich but instead said, "Look at your son John with my daughter Frances. York House is an impossible place for constant surveillance with all its nooks and crannies and dark corners. If the couple really are in love then surely Sir George More will come round in time."

"He will never come round to it," Sir Thomas said firmly. "John Donne is in for a long spell in the Tower and if Anne More does not renounce him and renounce the marriage as being performed under duress then her father will disown her."

"Then they will be hard pressed for money. He doesn't earn a lot in your service and his spell in the Tower in the meantime will make matters worse," said Alice.

"It doesn't matter how long he stays in the Tower because he will not return to my employment and I shall make sure no-one else employs him either. John Donne is finished."

She was appalled at his vindictiveness saying, "You cannot mean that."

But her husband stalked away with an implacable expression on his face. Watching his rigid figure depart she remembered a story that was told about him, of how being angry with a plaintiff for being too long-winded and wasting his time in court he had ordered the unfortunate man to be paraded around Westminster with his appeal hung around his neck and afterwards fined heavily. It was said of Sir Thomas Egerton that he was a good man to have on your side but a dangerous man to cross and for a moment a shiver tickled her spine.

As autumn approached sad news came from Hengrave Hall with the notification that Sir Thomas Kitson was dead. Compounding the tragedy was the fact that he had no heirs to inherit his beautiful estate and the position he had built up for himself, his gentility enhanced by the Queen's visit when he had given her a precious jewel and received a knighthood in return. Alice wept for her beloved uncle and for the opportunity he had given her to make a dream come true. In the summer the memories had been refreshed in her mind by the Queen's visit to Harefield. Now they were all buried in the past together with her beloved uncle.

CHAPTER 20

A new reign

"What did I tell you?" Sir Thomas Egerton cried triumphantly to his wife. "There was really no doubt that the Queen would name King James as her successor. Your daughter Anne and Arabella Stuart were merely red herrings to placate the opposition from time to time."

After weeks of illness when everyone knew Queen Elizabeth was dying but she would not accept it, even to the extent of refusing to take to her bed, she had finally relinquished her hold on life on the 24th of March, appropriately the feast of the Assumption of the Blessed Virgin.

"There are rumours abroad that the Queen was too far gone to name anyone specifically and it was Robert Cecil who insisted she had named King James," Alice said stubbornly.

"That is nonsense," retorted her husband. "There were several members of the Privy Council in attendance at the time, including myself as you know. Cecil was not alone."

"And did you hear what she said?" Alice insisted.

He did not answer immediately and she could tell he was annoyed. Then he said, "I believe Cecil and so do most people. In any case it is little to the point because the spectre of armed conflict has been removed and that satisfies the majority, even to a certain reluctance about having a Scot to rule England."

"They didn't give anyone time to question the declaration did they," Alice remarked tartly. It had been George Carey's younger brother Robert who had set off on horseback to the Scottish court only minutes after Queen Elizabeth's death.

"Have you suddenly become a politician?" Egerton said icily, but Alice understood that he was feeling vulnerable with the imminent change of government, fearing that the new king might not ratify his position as Lord Keeper, and she could share his concerns though he had never confided them to her. For herself she was relieved that her daughter Anne was now freed of the burden of her doubtful inheritance and could perhaps find a husband, though she couldn't help thinking of what might have happened if Ferdinando should still be alive. Might the succession have fallen to him? Might the English have chosen him for their king? Could she have been Queen of England? The thought had once crossed her mind when they had been soaring high.

Anne was silent and morose and Alice did not know what was going through her head as she had never found communication easy with her eldest daughter. Perhaps she was thinking of her father, perhaps of herself for she had always nourished ambitions of greatness. Now at last her fate had been sealed after many years of uncertainties regarding her future. At least it might prove easier to find her a suitable husband and Sir Thomas vowed to renew his efforts.

The Egertons were prominent in the funeral procession of the Queen as it progressed from Whitehall

Palace, where she had been lying in state after being transferred on a candlelit barge from Richmond Palace where she had died, to her last resting place in the Abbey at Westminster. All dressed in black every noble and official followed the black velvet-draped hearse with its life-size effigy of the Queen in her robes of state, and every Londoner who could leave their houses went to watch the miles-long procession. Only the dying and the new-born were missing, for even the infirm had been carried to pay their respects to the monarch they had loved and who had ruled over them for so long. Many of the gentry had journeyed from the shires to make their last honours to the only sovereign some of them had ever known and Alice encountered several of her Lancashire acquaintances, though there was no sign of Alexander Standish.

Most of them stayed to welcome the new monarch who was in such great haste to enter into the inheritance to which he had long aspired that even the usual summer visitation of the plague did not deter him. Many holders of positions and benefits under the old Queen, besides the Lord Keeper, were worried that they might not continue to retain them, for the king had brought a multitude of Scots with him in his train and was known to prefer them. Their fears were realised when he showed his obvious favouritism to his fellow-countrymen and assigned to them prestigious positions, antagonising many of the English nobility. But the king also wanted to make use of the expertise of those well-versed in the governing of his new country. Robert Cecil was confirmed in his position as Secretary of State and ennobled as Earl of Salisbury. Sir Thomas Egerton's role as Lord Keeper was enhanced by reviving for him the title of Lord Chancellor, long in abeyance as reminiscent of too powerful a subject, and he was granted a baronetcy. The unexpected honours gave Sir Thomas a new lease of life and everyone commented that he looked several years younger and definitely much happier. He chose for himself the title of Ellesmere after a Shropshire estate with a long and noble history, which ironically he had purchased from the Earl of Derby when he had been forced to sell it to meet Alice's claims, and Alice added a new title to her name.

Her delight in their elevation was only marred by the death of her sister Elizabeth's husband George Carey, the Lord Chamberlain. Elizabeth too had expected great honours from the new king. As a young man of nineteen George had attended the baptism of the Scottish king in Edinburgh in lieu of Queen Elizabeth and he had been a close colleague of Robert Cecil, now the most powerful of the King's ministers. Elizabeth had been expecting a reward for her husband, most likely an earldom, but unlike her two sisters she was to be denied the honour of becoming a countess. George had been ailing for some time and it was rumoured his death was caused by syphilis, a revelation which brought no comfort to his wife. She confided to Alice how she had always longed for sons, the deficit caused she believed by her husband's disease, and having only a daughter, now Lady Berkeley, his title of Lord Hunsdon must pass to his brother. Alice could sympathise personally and was sorry to see her sister so disappointed. She thought sadly of her Christmas wedding at Althorp twenty-five years ago when she had so envied her in her beautiful wedding gown, on the threshold of a glittering life at Court and kinship with the Queen herself. All the Spencer girls had become widows and none of them had been able to bear sons, a trend which seemed likely to continue. Alice's daughter Frances had recently borne her first child safely, much to her mother's relief for she was only 18 years old, but it had been a girl.

One day Sir Thomas Egerton, now Baron Ellesmere, had returned home to York House and seeking out his wife said, "I encountered an old acquaintance of yours from Lancashire in the Chancery court today, a young man by the name of Alexander Standish of Duxbury."

"What was he doing in Chancery?" she asked in surprise.

"I have no idea. Pursuing some claim or other I would guess. I saw him in the passageway as I was passing and recognised him." Sir Thomas's power of recall of both facts and faces was legendary. "I invited him to sup with us this evening as he said he was returning home on the morrow. I thought it might please you to hear some local news as I know you look upon Lancashire with some affection, God knows why – it is a desolate place and a nest of Papists."

She refused to argue with him, saying she would be pleased to entertain Alexander Standish, but experienced a surprising pang of disappointment at the realisation he had visited London without attempting to see her.

He arrived punctually, well dressed in good quality clothes of fine grey wool but without decoration, and a starched cambric collar instead of a ruff. His small pointed beard was newly trimmed and his fair hair cut neatly to his shoulders. He greeted them deferentially and by their titles but without servility and again Alice was struck by the confidence the ensuing years and family responsibilities had bestowed on him. But although their eyes sometimes met across the table there was a necessary formality about the meal and conversation was polite and circumscribed by current events in the new reign. Alice did not think she could ask him personal questions in the presence of her husband but Sir Thomas had no such inhibitions with an inferior and questioned him frankly about his business in Chancery.

"It had to do with the settlement of some land. Appertaining to the affray at Lea many years ago," he explained.

"Yes I remember that, an affair notorious enough to warrant the Queen's interference," the Lord Chancellor said wryly. "If I remember rightly she also turned her anger upon Lord Derby for being unable to control his lawless tenants."

Alexander refused to be drawn and merely smiled, but Alice remembered the affair as being of personal import to him as it had resulted in his uncle's death.

Law cases were always interesting to Sir Thomas Egerton and searching his memory he continued, "Thomas Langton, the self-styled baron of Walton, should have been hanged for his part in the affair but instead Star Chamber ordered him to pay wergild, compensation to the victims."

"My business in Chancery was to do with land transfers relevant to the case," Alexander admitted but refused to elaborate more and Alice seized the opportunity to change the subject.

"Have you begun the improvements at Duxbury that you intended?" she asked.

"Indeed I have. My new hall is in the making. I have found a stonemason who understands my plans and has the expertise to put them into operation. All the old buildings are to be demolished but the hall and centre of the farmhouse is to remain as the heart of the new house, partly because it will lessen the disturbance for my wife and family, we have another child now. There will be two new wings in a combination of timber and stonework so the effect will be an E shape with a large paved courtyard, but I intend it to be finally decorated with the black and white chevrons and crosses as at Rufford Hall."

"And the pele?"

"I haven't decided yet. I may keep it as a memorial to the history of the original building."

"It all sounds very impressive," she said, wondering how he was going to afford it but not feeling it polite to ask.

However Sir Thomas had no such reservations. "I suppose the cost for this project will be covered by the compensation claims for the affair at Lea," he said.

Alice was embarrassed by her husband's impertinency but Alexander merely smiled saying calmly, "My business in Chancery has been relevant to the matter." Then speaking mainly to Alice he said, "I intend it to be a beautiful place for my family to inherit, but it isn't large and won't be luxurious. Just a home that we shall enjoy living in. My parents always made a happy home for me and my brother and sisters but this will have more comforts and new conveniences."

She had intended telling him about her new manor at Harefield but decided the comparison might be too great although Sir Thomas, in lieu of further conversation, described the Queen's visit there. Alexander listened attentively but occasionally a slight smile hovered on his lips and it was not lost on Alice. Her reaction hovered between annoyance that it did not serve to impress him and amusement at his gentle dismissal of Sir Thomas's self-importance.

"Have you been long in the City? Did you come to pay your respects to the new King?" Alice asked, deciding to put him under some pressure.

Alexander laughed as he replied, "Not at all, I am too busy for such flummeries. I came only to settle my affairs and now they are done I am ready for home. What business do I have with the Court and what advantage can I gain from King James?" Then looking directly at Alice with a glint of mischief in his blue eyes that confirmed his intention to be provocative he said, "I believe he is not such a prepossessing figure, a little man with sparse reddish hair and spindly legs. It is said that he wears such heavily padded doublets because he is terrified of an assassin's dagger."

"There speaks a man with the arrogance of youth and a healthy body," Egerton reprimanded him sharply. "The King is known to be extremely learned."

"I believe so, sir. When he is able to be understood, for I have heard his Scots accent is so broad as to be practically unintelligible," returned Alexander, unabashed by the Lord Keeper's censure.

Alice considered it time to change the subject and said hurriedly, "I suppose you have heard that the King has taken over the patronage of the Lord Chamberlain's Men now that Baron Hunsdon has died. To everyone's surprise they are now renamed the King's Men. This rise in their fortunes will doubtless please them greatly, they will be given the opportunity to perform regularly at Court and their new eminence will ensure their position as London's chief theatre company. They walked in the coronation procession as servants of the King wearing his scarlet livery. How surprised Ferdinando would be to see his company so honoured."

"They cannot be any better than when they used to perform in the great hall at Lathom," Alexander insisted. "How we laughed at the silly dog in The Two gentlemen of Verona."

Their eyes met as memories coalesced and they couldn't contain a mutual burst of laughter until Sir Thomas coughed impatiently. Unable to share the reference to times past he was annoyed and had little interest in players.

In the midst of the leave-taking, Alice found herself briefly alone with Alexander. "Were you going to leave without seeing me?" she asked. "You came all the way to London and would have gone home without our meeting."

He looked at her directly, seeing the disappointment in her face, but said, "Yes." She flinched as if he had struck her but he continued, "Our lives are too far apart now."

"I am still the Countess of Derby."

"And Baroness Ellesmere, wife to the Lord Chancellor. Your life is in London now. We can't ride out any more," he added with a sudden wry smile.

Alice searched his face to find out what he was really thinking and trusting her instinct said, "Please don't discard our friendship. Please come to visit me if ever you have need to come to London."

"I shall have few occasions to make the long journey. I have many responsibilities with five children and the building of the new Hall," he said firmly. Then unable to help himself he asked, "Are you happy?"

His rejection had surprised and hurt her. "Of course," she said lightly. "Why should I not be? I have everything I want."

"Then you have no need of me." He gathered up his hat and gloves. "Farewell my lady, and God be with you."

She regretted her words and wanted to be honest with him, to tell him that she still had need of his friendship, but Sir Thomas had arrived in the hall.

"God speed your journey, Master Standish," she said formally.

But when the door had closed behind him she felt disappointment overwhelm her as she realised she might never see him again and her husband's words that he intended visiting her chamber that night went unregarded.

CHAPTER 21

Plots

Any hopes that the peaceful succession of King James to the crown of England would make it easier for Anne Stanley to find a husband were soon dashed by a plot to remove him and replace him with his cousin Arbella Stuart. The details of the plot were obscure and no-one was able to discover the complete truth, not even the Lord Chancellor in his interrogations, because all the people brought in for questioning were blaming some-one else. The official news being broadcast was that Spain was behind the proposal and besides certain minor noblemen being involved Sir Walter Raleigh was branded as chief conspirator. Sir Thomas Egerton took satisfaction in relaying the fact to his wife, well aware of Raleigh's friendship with Ferdinando.

Alice reacted with scorn. "This is ridiculous. Raleigh would never consort with Spain. Why, he has been the strongest advocate in pursuing the war. This smells to me of a plot to destroy him. It is no secret that the King doesn't like him and Robert Cecil has always been his enemy, Ferdinando used to say how much Raleigh mistrusted him."

"You see conspiracies in everything, Alice," her husband said. "And for the wounds of Christ will you never stop talking about Ferdinando Stanley. To you he is perfection personified but in actual fact he hadn't the wit to stay clear of danger. And Raleigh is cut from the same cloth - loose talk on atheism, consorting with men of doubtful loyalty to the State, flouting the King's policy of peace with Spain."

"Then doesn't that prove that he would never join with Spain in a plot to depose the King?"

"On the contrary. If Raleigh can discredit the King's peace policy by proving that Spain still intends the conquest of England then his aim is achieved."

Alice knew it was no use prolonging the argument but understood from everything Ferdinando had told her about his friendship with Raleigh that the outspoken seaman had always been a thorn in the side of the establishment, though largely protected by the Queen. Now it appeared that King James with the assistance of Robert Cecil was set to bring him down because of his vociferous opposition to their plans for a peace treaty with England's long-time enemy.

Sir Walter Raleigh was consequently brought to trial and accused of treason for which the death sentence was proclaimed. However the sentence was commuted to imprisonment in the Tower, on the appeal of Cecil who wanted him removed but whose dislike did not go so far as to want him dead. It seemed likely that his second imprisonment would last longer than his first as his so-called offence was more serious than the seduction of a girl. The girl in question this time, Arbella Stuart, was judged an innocent pawn but the conspiracy demonstrated there was still no guarantee that other claimants to the crown would not be used by unscrupulous factions. The incident served to remind Alice that her worries about her daughter Anne were not over. Neither were plots against the new king and a member of the Stanley family once again found himself a participant in a plot organised by Catholics.

At first King James had tried to make things easier for Catholics by integrating them into positions of trust and lessening the penalties against them imposed by the State. He was also determined to make peace with the old Catholic enemy Spain. People in the governing classes had begun to get worried, remembering that James's mother had been Mary Stuart for whom he was building a magnificent tomb in Westminster Abbey. There were also rumours of Queen Anne's leanings towards Papism. In view of the general opposition to his policies, the King was forced to reinstate recusancy fines and order the expulsion of all priests from the country on pain of death and this was seen by Catholics as a return to the old days of persecution. In retaliation a plot was hatched by some Catholic militants to blow up the houses of Parliament at the beginning of the new session together with the assembled members and the king himself. Fortunately the kegs of gunpowder were discovered at the last minute when one of the perpetrators, Guy Fawkes, was about to light the fuse and so the massacre was prevented. The alarm had been given by William Parker, the grandson of Alice's sister Anne, who had now inherited the title of Lord Monteagle.

Anne Spencer's first husband had been William Stanley, Lord Monteagle, a cousin of the Earls of Derby. Their only child Elizabeth had married Edward Parker and William was their son. Elizabeth had been her father's heiress and in default of a male succession

William Parker had been granted the right to use his grandfather's title of Lord Monteagle on the old man's death.

One of the conspirators in the Powder Plot was Francis Tresham, a Catholic cousin of young Monteagle. He did not want his friend and kinsman, a member of Parliament, to be a victim of the proposed massacre so sent him a letter warning him not to attend the House of Commons on this particular day.

When Alice later heard the full details of the incident from her sister Anne she was surprised to discover how closely her great-nephew's experience had paralleled Ferdinando's. The letter from Francis Tresham had placed him in an identical situation. If he revealed the letter to the Privy Council he would be forced to betray his friends and relations including Tresham who had sent him the warning. If on the other hand he remained silent and merely stayed away from the Houses of Parliament that day, it would then be assumed he was one of the conspirators, or at least sympathetic to them. As far as the government was concerned William Parker did not have a clean record. He had already been imprisoned for taking part in the Earl of Essex's rebellion; he wasn't a Catholic but was known to be a sympathiser, as Ferdinando had been; and he was also a Stanley when it had been said that "all the Stanleys in England are traitors." So the position in which he found himself was full of hazards. However Monteagle informed the Privy Council of the letter and the Powder Treason was discovered and prevented. Those conspirators who had not been killed in flight were barbarously hanged, drawn and quartered. Alice sympathised strongly with her great-nephew, understanding his predicament which had some similarities with Ferdinando's, but instead of incurring the vengeance of those he had betrayed William Parker become a hero and a broadside was printed playing upon his title of Monteagle.

> 'The gallant eagle soaring up on high
> Bears in his beak treason's discovery
> Mount noble eagle with thy happy prey
> And thy rich prize to the king with speed convey.'

There were rumours that Robert Cecil had been aware of the plot all along but had allowed it to go ahead in order to trap the plotters and catch them red-handed. Alice mentioned this possibility to her husband but he was non-committal. But for a time it brought back all the memories of Ferdinando and the Hesketh plot and for several days she was distressed and melancholy. She decided to leave London and go to Harefield for a time.

The fresh air was welcome after the city smog, and the beauty of the manor and the tranquillity of the gardens calmed her spirits. The rooms were light and airy in contrast to the small dark chambers of York House and from time to time she could hear the bell pealing from the adjacent church, not the permanent cacophony as from the countless London steeples but a calm regularity wafting an assurance of permanence across the quiet countryside.

One day she was sitting sewing, a task she always found soothing, listening to the rain pattering on the window panes with a rhythmic staccato, when she was interrupted by a manservant announcing there was a visitor to see her. "Master Standish of Duxbury." She laid down the embroidery frame in amazement, ordering him to be admitted but wondering at his early return, especially in such bad weather and after what he had said.

When he entered, even though the servant had divested him of his dripping cloak and hat, he was still obviously soaked and his hair clung darkly to his head. "I beg pardon for my sorry state, my lady," he apologised, kissing her hand.

"It matters not, you are always welcome, please be seated," she said in some confusion. "But what brings you here in such wet weather and so many miles from London?"

He hesitated and she could sense his unease as he perched gingerly on one of the silk padded chairs, conscious of his damp breeches. But he was direct as always and admitted, "I know I said I would not come to see you again and I am returned within the year. I do not usually go back on my word and I am stricken with doubts now that I have done the right thing. Perhaps I should not have come but I have received some information that I felt I ought to share with you."

Alice was more confused than ever as he hesitated but motioning him to wait for a while she walked to the door and called for heated wine to be brought. While they waited she said, "I am sorry you have had to come all the way to Harefield, it is quite a ride from London."

"No more than an hour, nothing after four days from Lancashire," he smiled ruefully. "I must admit the weather has not been of the best." He had relaxed a little and after drinking the warm ruby red liquor he was more at ease. "I apologise for my unexpected intrusion, I think I have acted with the rashness of youth not the rationality of a man with a large family but I dashed off in haste, not able to keep this to myself, and once on my way it was too late to turn back."

He paused again and though she felt the urge to confess that she was glad of any excuse to see him, she prompted him by asking, "What do you have to tell me?"

"My dear Lady Derby, for that is what you will always be to me, I fear this will hurt you greatly but I believe you ought to know. It concerns the letter from Catholics abroad brought by Richard Hesketh to Lord Ferdinando. From reliable information recently gathered I can tell you that it seems Richard Hesketh did not bring the letter from Prague or Antwerp but it was delivered to him in the City by an unknown hand."

"I don't understand the import of this. What are you saying, Alex?" she asked, trying to make sense of this development.

"I am relating some facts as they have been disclosed to me."

"By whom?"

"Thomas Langton of Walton. As you know from the last time I was in London, I have been involved in some land settlements relating to the affray at Lea when some of his land was taken from him as a penalty for the murder of my uncle. Langton was one of those who supported Richard Hesketh but he is now dying and wished to clear his mind of some of the perplexing aspects of the affair. This is a matter of importance to me also because as you know my aunt was half-sister to Richard Hesketh and so my mother's family, the Hoghtons, are indirectly involved," Alexander said.

"If the letter was penned in London then are you saying it could have been a forgery?" Alice asked. Ferdinando had believed Sir Francis Walsingham led

Catholics into traps, sometimes by the discovery of compromising documents which not everyone believed to be genuine and she recalled how he had voiced his doubts about the letters in the Babington plot which had led to the execution of Mary Stuart.

Alexander shook his head. "I did not say it was penned in London, it would have been difficult to forge all the names on the document. It must have come originally from abroad but Richard Hesketh did not bring it from there."

Alice stared at him then said, "Are you considering other possibilities?"

"I am considering that the Government could have been behind this. That it could have been a Government trap. That they had opened the letter and knew its contents before it was passed to Richard Hesketh. Robert Cecil took on Walsingham's mantle. It is possible that Cecil set the trap for Lancashire Catholics to fall into."

Alice paled and with an unsteady hand put down her goblet of wine on a small table. "Could it be possible that the trap was set for Ferdinando? To see if he would declare himself? He and Walter Raleigh both believed that they were objects of surveillance for their freethinking on religion and other matters. Was he set up by government agents who knew everything beforehand?" A feeling of foreboding consumed her and she couldn't help her hands trembling as she clasped them together in her lap.

"That has crossed my mind," Alexander admitted. "However I am forced to admit that *no matter who* gave Richard Hesketh that message, it must have been a genuine request from Catholics, in exile and otherwise."

"But whatever was in the minds of Catholics, if the authorities knew the contents of the letter and had never allowed it to be delivered then my husband would not have died," she whispered. "If Cecil was testing him, then it was an unnecessary test that cost him his life. Surely after all that time they knew how loyal he was." The tears were beginning to sparkle in her eyes and Alexander had to constrain himself from touching her. Then another thought occurred to her and she continued, "Do you think William was involved in this?" He was after all married to Cecil's niece who had an interest in being Countess of Derby and not merely the wife of an earl's brother.

"No I do not think the present Earl of Derby knew anything, he doesn't have the nature for plotting," Alexander said, adding firmly, "Do not let your dislike of him cloud your judgment, my lady." Alice was aware again of a new critical perception beneath his respect. He paused then said, "There is however something else. Someone else who might have been involved." She looked at him enquiringly and he continued, "Your husband the Lord Chancellor has always been zealous in prosecuting Catholics. You must know how he hounded Mary Stuart, using every legal precedent to trap her. Finally he utilised the law to legitimise her trial and execution where his participation as Attorney-General was essential. Afterwards he was often prosecuting council and judge against many Catholics whose activities fell under increased suspicion in the wake of her execution. In fact you could say he held as much influence regarding the security of the State as did Cecil. Many agents and informers reported back to him as Attorney-General and it was said of him that he would extract confessions and information at any cost."

"Are you saying that Sir Thomas could have been involved in the plot against Lord Ferdinando?" she asked in a shocked whisper.

Alexander shook his head. "I dare not be so definite. But I would say that *if* this plot did originate in government circles or was manipulated by them, then it is almost impossible that Sir Thomas Egerton did not know of it. And he would be as concerned as Cecil to discover exactly what Lord Ferdinando's intentions were once Mary Stuart had been removed from the succession."

Alice remained silent for a time then said desperately, "There is still doubt isn't there? There is still a likely possibility that Richard Hesketh received a bona fide letter from his accomplices which was handed to him in London by one of them. It would have been dangerous for him to have brought it into the country himself from Prague or Antwerp."

"There are many ways of concealing messages, my lady. Couriers, especially priests, are experts at secret hiding places – sewn within the covers of books, in a false shoe sole, in jewellery. One of Sir William Stanley's messengers had information sewn in his buttons. And most clandestine messages are written in a cipher only understandable to sender and recipient. Do not ask me how I know these things but remember that though I am not a Catholic myself I am acquainted with many of them and both my Standish and Hoghton relatives have hidden priests and helped them to escape. One of the strangest aspects of this case has been the existence of such an incriminating letter."

"Alex, tell me your own views, directly and honestly," she appealed.

Her eyes were troubled and afraid but he knew he had to be honest. "I think Lord Ferdinando was set up. That is not to say that plots are not being discussed and even designed by Catholic militants abroad but the plotters are few, disorganised, and their plans are familiar to government agents through informers." Alice knew that Ferdinando together with Raleigh thought that Christopher Marlowe had been used in this way.

Alexander continued, "I believe that Cecil, by means of his spies, encouraged the plot in the first place and knew about the letter which was read in London before being entrusted to Richard Hesketh by another double agent. I believe there was a plot to discredit Catholics in the minds of the general populace, especially Lancashire Catholics, and also to test the new Lord Derby's allegiances, a test which unexpectedly resulted in his death."

Alice felt as if her whole world was crumbling. "Then who killed him?" she whispered.

"I don't know," he admitted. "You forbade me to pursue inquiries. I told you about the mysterious groom who arrived from London at the time but I have now changed my mind about the poisoning being ordered there. I do not honestly think it was a part of State surveillance to kill him. Thomas Langton said he knew nothing about the poisoning but there could have been any one of a hundred or so simple Catholics who knew only half the story and believed Lord Derby had betrayed them – a servant, a tenant, a messenger, all with access to Lathom House. And poison is easy enough to obtain, either in the fields and hedgerows or from an apothecary for the honest purpose of killing vermin. One thing has always puzzled me and that is why under the circumstances of his death no autopsy was performed."

"That was William's wish," Alice said. "He wanted his brother buried quickly with no further repercussions to the affair, he didn't want to start a witch-hunt at the beginning of his lordship. I was too distressed to care, he was dead and nothing could bring him back so nothing else mattered. But perhaps it was Robert Cecil again, afraid that matters had gone too far and who wanted a quick end with no further questions asked. William after all was soon to become a member of the Cecil family."

The rain beat heavier on the window panes as they sat opposite each other, both united and estranged by the confusion of thought. Alice's brow was furrowed and she chewed her lip in distraction. "I have been thinking how there are common elements in this new Powder Plot. My sister's grandson was involved in a similar way," and she began to relate to him the story of William Parker and his letter. "There are rumours that Cecil was aware of the plot and used it to trap the conspirators."

"I wasn't aware of your family's involvement but it is general opinion in Lancashire that this was a deliberate move to discredit Catholics at the start of this new reign. After the King's attempt to make things easier for Catholics the timing is too coincidental not to suspect a little chicanery," Alexander said grimly. "That is not to deny that some militant Catholics intended to assassinate the King and large numbers of the Parliament but the plot was allowed to proceed, even encouraged, so that it could be used as a weapon to strike at all Catholics and brand them traitors. Cecil could very well be behind this and it does lend further substance to the theory that he could have been involved in the same way in the Hesketh plot."

"Why have you told me this? You knew it would distress me. Wouldn't it have been better if I had remained ignorant," Alice said at last, deeply shaken and unable to keep recrimination from her eyes and voice.

For once Alexander was unable to face her directly, not wanting to see the pain marring her features. "I am truly sorry to have distressed you and would do anything to save you unhappiness. But I thought that as Lord Derby's wife you above anyone ought to be in possession of all the facts. I honestly thought this was what you would want. You are strong, my lady."

"No, you are mistaken. People think me hard grained but it is not the truth, sometimes I play the actor, pretending to be what I am not. I had begun to make a new life for myself and thought I could put the past behind me but now you have brought it back to me." She was on the verge of tears again and Alexander had to force himself not to hold her and comfort her. "What has particularly distressed me is the thought that my husband Sir Thomas could have known the circumstances of the letter, perhaps even encouraged the baiting of Ferdinando." Alexander remained silent and something in his face forced her to say, "You did not tell me this in order to turn me against my husband did you?"

"Why should I do that?" he replied calmly though he was aware of an uncomfortable feeling in his stomach as the accusation disturbed him.

She hesitated then compromised by saying, "Because you so admired Lord Ferdinando and you do not think I should have married the Lord Chancellor."

"No I do not. I did not think you would have married for such reasons. You deserve a man who loves you." His gaze was steady and she had to look away. "But you have done so, it is a fait accompli. And believe me, Lady Derby, Lady Ellesmere, all I wish for you now, with all my heart, is that you should be happy and in no way would I wish to destroy that happiness."

"I'm sorry. I'm sorry to have doubted you," she whispered, both hurt and moved by his words. "I cannot say you should not have told me. I do not suppose we shall ever know the complete truth but I am glad for Ferdinando's sake that I can understand as much as is possible. I know you have always tried to serve me to the best of your ability and I thank you for that."

Her face was almost as pale as her lace ruff, seeming whiter against the warm orange-tawny of her gown, and he was loath to leave her though he asked her permission to depart.

She stood saying, "Thank you for coming all this way." Then filled with a longing for him to stay and console her she added, "May I offer you some hospitality here tonight, at least something to eat."

"I thank you but no, my lady. My duty is done. I will return to London where I have accommodation at an inn, the Bell in Bishopsgate, then I will return to Lancashire on the morrow."

When he left, spurring his horse regardless of the pouring rain, he was no longer as sure about his motives for making the long journey. Alice remained at the window looking out at the darkening sky and feeling bereft of all comfort now he had gone. She wondered how much of the conversation she could relate to Sir Thomas, thinking it might be best if she remained silent. However she felt it would be impossible to lie in his bed again until she had satisfied herself that he had had no part in Ferdinando's death. She sighed deeply. She had come to Harefield for peace and quiet but it had been cruelly shattered by the unexpected visit of Alexander Standish.

When she arrived back at York House she found her husband in his study surrounded by his vast collection of books, mainly on law but also geography and history, philosophy and science. He looked up in irritation at being disturbed but she said she had a matter of importance to discuss with him and without preamble seated herself opposite him at his desk. She knew he would not have the patience for small talk and she had no desire to parry with him so she declared herself bluntly.

"Matters have come to my attention regarding the letter delivered by Richard Hesketh to my former husband Lord Derby."

"So?" He looked completely uninterested.

"I have been informed that the letter was only given to Hesketh in London and that it probably came into his hands by means of a government agent."

"And who has provided you with this information? From what source and for what purpose?"

She did not reply but said, "If, as it would appear, the letter was a ploy to catch certain Catholic militants and test my husband's loyalty, I would like to be assured that you were innocent of all involvement."

He tapped his fingers impatiently on the desk as he said, "There is no evidence whatsoever that the said letter was a product of State interference and I deal only in evidence, not speculation. As for myself I fulfil my duties to the best of my ability and when those duties concern the security of the State I do whatever has to be done. Now let that be an end of the matter."

"It will never be an end for me until I know the truth. Lord Ferdinando was never a Catholic and never gave any indication of such."

"It was said of him that he had no religion. In orthodox officialdom that made him more suspect and more open to the influences of unscrupulous factions. He was too tied to his Catholic underlings. Make no mistake, his name was often mentioned in the circles of Catholic exiles and in their correspondence. I was a Catholic once. I was reared a Catholic and continued in this faith for the first few years of my career. Then I was told gently but firmly that if I wanted to rise in my profession I must change my religion. So I did. It was a matter of expediency. Ferdinando Stanley never learnt the nature of expediency."

"He was too open and too honest. He was always his own man, more interested in poetry and music and the theatre than in political posturing," Alice said with tears in her eyes. She stood up but before she quit the room she said, "If I did discover you were involved in these events then that would be an end of our marriage."

Sir Thomas Egerton stood also. He was much taller than she was. "Don't threaten me, Alice. Our marriage would only ever be ended when *I* decided. Do not think you could bring a case against me for divorce in the law courts because I am the best lawyer in England and no-one wins a case against me." He paused to let the message sink in and she stood uncertainly. The he said, "Now go and change for supper, I am expecting the Lord Chief Justice to join us. Remember you are the wife of the Lord Chancellor and enjoy the life I have given you."

Back in her chamber she made an effort to control herself, not intending to weep before any of her maids. Into her mind flashed an image of Alexander Standish with his strong physique and yet his sensitivity, his deep blue eyes that were always honest and direct, his plain speech without guile or flattery. He would now be back in Lancashire. As soon as she could she would return to Harefield.

CHAPTER 22

The Court

At twenty five years old Anne Stanley was still unwed, despite efforts to secure her a suitable husband. Alice and Sir Thomas had believed it would be easy now that James was safely crowned and there were no fears about the succession but that belief had been proved wrong by the Powder Plot and the plot surrounding Arbella Stuart. Soon Arbella was involved in another event which made them realise the King was still overly sensitive about anyone he feared might threaten his permanence.

King James had accepted his cousin at Court and for a time showed her friendship though warning her not to marry without his approval of a suitor. Everyone considered this to be an unlikely event in any case for Arbella was thirty three years old and had neither beauty nor wealth. But love does not look with other people's eyes and to the Court's amazement young William Seymour, not much more than twenty years old, fell in love with her. The snake in their paradise was the fact that he was the grandson of Lady Catherine Grey. The King would never countenance a match between two people both with royal blood and so close to the Crown and forbade any further association between them.

The two contracted a secret marriage but after only two weeks it was discovered and they were both sent to the Tower. It was made clear that there were still difficulties about finding a suitable husband for Anne Stanley.

One disappointment was the refusal of the Earl of Dorset to consider her for his eldest son and heir Richard Sackville, notwithstanding the efforts of his wife on behalf of her niece. "I tried hard to persuade him," Anne insisted to her sister Alice, "but George Clifford is already negotiating with him for *his* daughter and you know how ruthless Clifford is. He obviously has his eye on my husband's fortune. I know Anne Clifford is her father's heiress but he isn't wealthy, having a taste for gaming and loose living, and their lands are far away in the north. I don't understand why my husband is preferring this proposal to ours."

"Anne Clifford has no royal blood to upset the apple cart," Alice said tartly. George Clifford had been more fortunate in his forebears than his half-sister Margaret.

Ann Stanley's disappointment was laced with anger that her competitor was not only a half-cousin but also only fourteen years old. "I shall be too old soon for anyone to want to marry me," she wailed. Her resentment was increased by the fact that it was her sister Frances, happily married to John Egerton, who was the darling of the new Court and King James had kissed her publicly after admiring her dancing.

The Court of King James and Queen Anne was very different to that of Elizabeth. In contrast to the disappointing appearance of the King, the Queen had at first charmed Londoners with her tall statuesque build, fair frizzed hair, rosy complexion and ready smile. But the general lack of decorum and polite behaviour at

Whitehall was soon observed and commented on. Drunkenness was rife and affairs proliferated as the King spent all his time with his male favourites, most of them young and Scottish, and the Queen's only interest lay in enjoying herself as much as possible. The abundance of accessible wealth, the number of beautiful palaces, and the hundreds of gowns in the old Queen's closets provided a paradise for her after the years of austerity in bare cold castles with a sparse budget imposed upon them by the Scottish parliament. There was no shortage of entertainment – balls, maskings, plays by the King's Men, long evenings of childish games and gambling accompanied by much drinking and dallying, and younger courtiers relished the relaxed atmosphere after the strict surveillance of Queen Elizabeth.

Queen Anne did not possess the intellectual abilities and interests of Queen Elizabeth and her liking for childish pastimes and maskings found an outlet in a new form of entertainment. With so many poets and musicians to hand, all eager to present their talents to the attention of the new monarchs, and so many of Queen Elizabeth's gowns that were too old-fashioned to wear but were made from the most luxurious stuffs, the masque was born. Sir Thomas and Lady Egerton had been amongst the privileged audience to watch one of the first of these entertainments, 'The Masque of Blackness,' performed at Whitehall on Twelfth Night.

Egerton had been bored, not having any interest in dramatic entertainments and critical of the cost of such an extravaganza, but Alice, in company with the rest of the noble audience, had been astounded by the innovations of the production. The spectacular scenic effects were the work of a rising young architect called Inigo Jones who created illusions of natural phenomena by elaborate scenery that changed by means of hidden machinery. There were cries of surprise as clouds floated above a forest of wind-swept trees and waves rose and fell in a foam-crested ocean. The only irritant to Alice's enjoyment had been the participation of the Countess of Derby. Although professional actors spoke the speeches, the Queen and her ladies and gentlemen of the Court danced and disported themselves in descriptive tableaux, garbed in fantastical costumes, and Alice was disgruntled to see Elizabeth de Vere as Eucampse in a gown made of silver tissue spangled with crystals.

The innovation of the masque proved a great success with audiences and participants alike and it became a mark of royal favour to be asked to take part. To her surprise Alice was invited to perform in 'The Masque of Queens' together with her youngest daughter Elizabeth, now Countess of Huntingdon at sixteen years old as her husband had recently inherited the earldom on the death of his grandfather and the young couple were considered old enough to consummate their marriage and be husband and wife in more than name. She was taking the place of her popular sister Frances who was near her time with a third child and desperately hoping for a son after two daughters. Once again Anne had been overlooked.

Everyone at Court vied for the honour of being chosen by the Queen to take part in a masque and Sir Thomas Egerton expressed his approval with his wife. But Alice had no idea of the amount of time she would have to spend in rehearsing the songs and dances and the choreography of the tableaux together with hours spent in the company of the seamstresses. The masques had become an obsession with the Queen and the preparations were as enjoyable to her as the final performance. She loved to be dancing and skipping in company with her ladies, most of them very young. The company for this masque included the fourteen year old Anne Clifford, the fifteen year old wife of the Earl of Essex's son, and Alice's sixteen year old daughter. But the Queen's greatest pleasure came from trying on the costumes they were to wear and the ladies stood for hours while Queen Elizabeth's old dresses were cut up, draped around them and pinned into place accompanied by much giggling and exchanging of Court gossip. Some of the costumes were diaphanous, composed of little more than swathes of tissue, and cut short so the girls were screaming at the uncustomary exposure of their white legs and imagining what would be the reaction of the young men. In her maturity Alice found much of this tedious and thought how her time could be better occupied though Sir Thomas expressed his pride in her selection.

The author of the masque was again Ben Jonson who was beginning to rival William Shakespeare as a playwright and had also found a niche for himself with compositions for the Court. When he directed rehearsals they took on a different tone. A short squat man of about Alice's own age, he was bursting with energy, his florid face alight with enthusiasm, his thick curly hair springing from his head with the force of his brain. He worked them tirelessly, making no allowance for delicate sensibilities with his language and his criticisms and Alice enjoyed these times. Jonson was particularly attentive to her, often mentioning Ferdinando's interest in the theatre.

"I think he would have approved of these masques, he was always interested in dramatic innovations,"

Alice said, "but he considered words to be the most important aspect of theatre."

"So do I," Jonson agreed. "I get very angry when my words sink under these flummeries and I have constant arguments with Inigo Jones who tries to make out his mechanical effects matter more than my libretti."

Alice was particularly pleased by the character she had been given - Zenobie Queen of Palmyria. Jonson read to them all the descriptions of their roles, to which he had had some say in the choosing, and which he would then include in the publication of his work. Zenobie was a queen whose noble husband had died and who "continued a long and brave war against the chiefs, lived in a most royal manner and was a chaste woman of most divine spirit and incredible beauty." She hoped that the reference to her "long and brave war against the chiefs" would be recognised as her legal struggles and hoped there would be those percipient enough to recognise the symbolism always inherent in Jonson's works. She had to admit being flattered at having reference made to her beauty when the company on the whole were younger than she was and knew her husband would be pleased with the epithet 'chaste', not one in common usage at the Court.

When the evening for the performance arrived Alice arrived at Whitehall in the company of her daughter Elizabeth, feeling understandably nervous. For the first time she understood how actors must feel and remembered how Ferdinando would never disturb them before a performance.

"I hope I don't make a mistake with the dance steps, or more likely trip over the silly gown with all its floating panels and long train," Elizabeth said, but she was laughing and Alice looked at her with affection. Her youngest daughter had always been the most intelligent of the three, preferring books to more frivolous pastimes, and her disinterest enabled her to view Court life with a detached irony. Her nonchalance steadied Alice and sustained her when they arrived in the dressing room to find the whole company in a state of nervous hysteria, bickering with each other over precedence, panicking about props and accessories mislaid, complaining about the way their hair had been dressed. Inigo Jones and Ben Jonson were carrying on a heated argument about the positioning of some item of scenery using some choice insults that made the girls giggle. Only Queen Anne was unmoved, floating around unconcernedly and returning from time to time to the large glass to make minute adjustments to her fantastical gown and elaborate headdress. Occasionally the door would open and the buzz of excited conversation from the assembling audience could be heard together with the sound of the musicians tuning their instruments.

The entertainment began with the anti-masque of professional actors in their roles of hags and witches depicted in a fearsome representation of Hell's mouth. Then to a loud trumpet blast the scene magically changed to a magnificent building purporting to be the House of Fame and the twelve queens were revealed seated on a silver throne encircled by bright lights. Isolated in the illumination, Alice felt a surge of excitement at the thunder of applause and realised that hundreds of pairs of eyes were focussed on them, the eyes of the greatest and wealthiest people in the kingdom including the king himself. After a speech by Heroic Virtue the scene changed again to the accompaniment of music and the throne disappeared. Fame appeared out of the clouds and called forth the heroic queens one by one. Zenobie was almost the last to make her entrance, only the Queen herself following as the most superior Queen of all, Bel-Anna Queen of the Ocean, a name which Jonson had devised "to honour her in her own person above all women of beauty and virtue on earth." As Alice stepped into the full glare of the light she felt the blood rushing through her body and a sensation of light-headedness at the realisation that in that moment she had the full attention of perhaps a thousand people. This was power. In a flash of illumination she understood the compulsion that drove men to the life of a player with small reward and uncertain employment, the compulsion that drove men like Will Shakespeare to leave his wife and family to create illusion on a stage.

When the evening was finished Alice had to admit that she had found the experience exhilarating. She had often been the centre of attention as Countess of Derby but taking on another personality was a new sensation. In an unexpected way it had brought her closer to Ferdinando, to an understanding of his fascination with the life of a player that she had so often teased him about. As he filled her remembrances again she didn't think she could ever let him out of her life. How she wished he could have seen her as an actor. She was sure he would have been proud of her and so surprised by these new entertainments. However she doubted she would be given another opportunity because there were so many ladies who wished to be honoured by Queen Anne in this way and she used it as a mark of her special favour. Elizabeth Hastings on the other hand expressed herself happy to be excluded from any further performances. Now that her young husband had inherited his patrimony they were to live in his castle at Ashby-de-la-Zouch and she was looking forward to the quiet Leicestershire countryside where she could indulge in her preferred pursuits of reading and writing.

Apart from Court activities where the presence of the Lord Chancellor and his wife was expected, Alice spent much time in company with her sisters, especially Anne who divided her time between the Earl of Dorset's London residence Dorset House and their beautiful country estate at Knole. Alice had become closer to her elder sister over the years and in their long leisure hours when there was little to do except needlework and gossip she could be frank about her less than satisfying union with Sir Thomas Egerton.

"Everyone speaks so highly of him but he is a difficult man to live with. He is completely absorbed in his work so he has little time for aught else and in his private time he likes to be alone in his study with his books so we have little conversation. When we do I often disagree with his opinions and because I have the audacity to tell him so he talks of my shrewish tongue."

Anne's eyebrows raised slightly and a wry smile hovered on her lips. "Ferdinando Stanley always gave you your own way. It was often said of him that he was too accommodating. Perhaps you have need of a man who will impose his will on you from time to time." Alice grimaced and her sister continued, "But do not think your husband is well thought of by everyone. Lord Dorset says he has antagonised both Papists and Puritans, the first by re-enforcing the penal laws against Catholics, and the second by refusing to re-instate those ministers dismissed for their Puritan sympathies, declaring their appeal illegal. Although my husband agrees with him about the union of Scotland with England it is not a proposal popular with everyone. Lord Dorset also says that most people are worried about the way in which Sir Thomas is using the law to support the king's prerogative."

"Yes he will do anything to support the king now that he has been so honoured by him," Alice said with some bitterness, remembering how Ferdinando could never obtain royal approval. "But I suppose if he didn't then all the favours would go to the Scots. There is so much cut-throat competition abroad and if Thomas lost his career then it would be the end of life as far as he is concerned."

"Do you sleep with him?" Anne asked.

"When *he* wishes it. No thought given to *my* inclinations." Alice glanced sideways at her sister and said, "My friend Lady Hay says I should take a lover. Everyone at Court does." She laughed at Anne's scandalised face then relented saying, "Don't worry, I won't. For three reasons. Firstly because at past forty I am unlikely to find someone pleasing enough, secondly because I will not break the wedding vows I made under oath, and thirdly because my husband would be sure to discover it and he would either divorce me or have me killed."

Anne studied her carefully. "The priorities are some-what interesting. If the first objection were overturned would you discount the others? And as your marriage was officially "clandestine" would that not mitigate the second?"

Alice thought for a moment then said, "Despite putting it last, the third objection would probably carry most weight with me. Thomas threatened me with it once, no, I will not tell you the circumstances, but to lose what I have attained would be the end of my life."

Looking at her sister's face Anne considered it was time to change the subject and said, "I am really sorry we could not arrange a match for your Anne with my stepson. Are you any closer to finding a husband for her?"

Alice shook her head. "I am getting to be as despairing as she. She is so difficult to live with these days. She finds an outlet for her disappointment in spending as much money as she can, living above her allowance to Thomas's annoyance, which is another jar between us."

"Send her to live with me for a time. We are often at Court as you know and I am sure she would enjoy Knole."

Anne was pleased with her aunt's suggestion and Alice glad to see her happy though the preparations included many shopping trips and the spending of more money. One afternoon they had been visiting the goldsmiths' shops on London bridge in the company of bored attendants for Anne could not decide between an emerald pendant, a chain of gold links set with rubies and a row of black pearls, eventually choosing the pearls as being the most costly of the three. They took a private barge back down the river to York House and as they disembarked at their own water stairs there was someone standing by the stone gateway leading from the river into the gardens. Alice's heart leapt as she recognised the figure immediately. She dismissed into the house her servants and her daughter who, after a curious glance, was only too happy to escape to her chamber to inspect her new purchases.

"Master Standish why are you standing outside my house?" she asked.

He looked embarrassed. "I was told you were absent and I did not wish to wait inside, I considered it might be inconvenient. So I came down to look at the river. I like to watch all the different boats, the rich in their private barges, the wherries, the ferry boats, merchant ships and fishermen's coracles. I went to Liverpool once and saw all the boats going to and from Ireland, taking foodstuffs and bringing back linen."

She was aware he was wasting time and uneasy about something so said, "Well now I am arrived perhaps we can go into the house if you have come to see me."

They walked through the gate and into the gardens but before they reached the end of the path winding through formal flower beds and statuary he hesitated and said, "May we stay here for a moment."

She stopped, saying, "What is it? What is the matter?"

"My wife is dead. She died two weeks ago. She died in childbirth, the child died also."

"Oh Alex, I am so grievously sorry," she cried, appalled by his revelation. She recalled the girl she had seen at Duxbury Hall, the pretty country girl with her fresh complexion and shining brown hair, the way she had looked with adoration at her young husband.

"She was twenty eight years old. She was too young to die. She was so kind, so loving and had so much to live for, our children, the new Hall. It was my fault. I killed her. She had too many children in a short time and it was too much for her."

His voice broke and her heart went out to him as instinctively she put her arms around him. She could say nothing. How could she say it wasn't his fault – a virile young man with a lovely adoring girl. Death in childbed was a woman's constant fear, all too often realised.

"I'm so sorry," she said again. It was inadequate but she was too close to him to offer platitudes. She would not insult him by making the trite observation that he was only young, he would find someone else.

He could always read her thoughts and breaking away from her embrace he said, "I shall never marry again."

"Don't make that a reparation for your guilt. Don't let guilt spoil your life now," she said gently.

He looked at her steadily as he repeated, "I shall never marry again. The only woman I would ever want is unattainable to me."

Although she had always been aware of his admiration it was the first time he had ever been so explicit and since her marriage she had detected some lessening of the uncritical devotion he had shown her. She was at a loss how to respond and dropped her eyes saying hastily, "What about your children? Who will care for them? Some are very young surely."

He nodded, "Yes they are. But my sister Ellen will help me. You remember Ellen, you met her the day you came to Duxbury. She has never married, has always lived with us. In fact she has been like a second mother to the children, helping Alice. She loves them and will find great satisfaction in caring for them, not having children of her own."

"You are fortunate in having her," Alice said, remembering the homely young woman with her brother's blue eyes.

They remained standing in the garden, the breeze from the river ruffling his hair and trying to lift Alice's hat from her red curls, the sour tang of the mud at the water's edge tickling their nostrils.

"Will you come into the house now?" she asked at last but he shook his head.

"Thankyou but no. I do not feel able to make polite conversation nor accept formal condolences. I have accommodation tonight at the same inn in Bishopsgate then I will return home on the morrow. Thank you for your sympathy,......my lady," he added.

"Will you still visit me if ever you have reason to come to London?"

Alexander almost said that it might be less appropriate with his changed circumstances then thought better of it. When had his being married ever made the slightest difference to his relationship with the Countess of Derby. Instead he said, "If you wish me to come then I will do so."

"I do wish it, Alex. I hope we can remain friends."

He smiled then and she suppressed the desire to embrace him again. Instead she held out her hand and after kissing it he made his departure the way he had come.

She had not noticed Sir Thomas watching from the window of his study but when she encountered him he said drily, "I was not aware you had such an affection for Master Standish."

"He has recently lost his wife," she said, hoping he would understand her demonstration of sympathy.

"It happens to all of us. I've lost two," he said in the tone of voice that implied a wish to have lost a third also.

Alice ignored him saying, "He has six children."

"He will soon find someone else to mother them," Egerton replied.

Alice did not bother to explain but a great weariness overwhelmed her. She remembered how the young Alexander had comforted her when Ferdinando had died and she had lost her baby. Now she had had to comfort him for the same reason. It was strange how life turned in circles. A small unwelcome voice began niggling her consciousness. "Alexander Standish is a free man and he is devoted to you." She closed her ears to the voice. Of what import was it? She was a married woman. "Many married women take lovers. Haven't you been advised to do so," the voice inside her whispered. She struggled to drown out the voice. Alexander Standish was no courtier, he was too honourable to embark on such a course. Besides he was twelve years younger than she was and far beneath her social standing. He was her cavalier servente as he always had been. She could take comfort in that.

CHAPTER 23

Illusions

At twenty eight years old Anne Stanley was the same age as Alice Standish when she died after bearing seven children. But she had at last found a husband. Grey Brydges was also twenty eight and for the last five years, since the death of his father, he had borne the title of Lord Chandos and inherited Sudeley Castle in Worcestershire. But because his father had been involved in Essex's rebellion the inheritance was disputed and he had been forced to carry on a bitter legal struggle with his cousin. It was general opinion that he should marry her to settle the matter but Sir Thomas Egerton had other ideas. After successfully pleading the case for the restitution of his inheritance the Lord Chancellor had persuaded Brydges to accept Lord Derby's eldest daughter, a prestigious match now that there were no longer any doubts about the succession and after all he did owe a debt of gratitude to the Chancellor.

Anne was beside herself with excitement. It mattered not that she had never met Lord Chandos or that he was not at least an Earl. The young man lived in such splendour that he was called "King of the Cotswolds" and she was going to live in a castle. She wiped from her memory all past rejections and paraded herself as a young girl with her first suitor. Her younger sisters were too happy for her to resent her boasting and Alice was filled with relief.

"You look happier these days," her sister Elizabeth noted, happier herself since her only daughter had borne her husband, Lord Berkeley, a son and heir.

"I am so relieved that Anne has found a husband at last. Now all my daughters are well settled and I think Ferdinando would have been satisfied. And to tell truth I am glad to have her off my hands, she has been so difficult these past few years. I only hope she continues to be pleased with her husband and that he does not tire of her."

"You seem happier with Sir Thomas of late. Unless you have found yourself a lover," Elizabeth said archly.

Alice shook her head but couldn't help feeling a momentary regret. "I am learning resignation in dealing with him and relieved about the prospective marriage though the preparations involved are overwhelming. I am planning an entertainment of some kind to celebrate the engagement."

"At York House?"

"No, it isn't suitable. Perhaps at Harefield, perhaps at Frances's house at Ashridge or Elizabeth's at Ashby." The unsuitability of York House had not however been her prime consideration. "It will be a Derby celebration," she said firmly, "the last of Ferdinando's children to be settled even though Thomas has negotiated the match." She knew her husband would not leave his work in London to make a long journey into the countryside.

Alice found herself spending less and less time at York House and more time at Harefield if she wasn't visiting her daughters or her sisters. However she had been in the City when Alexander Standish had made his promised visit. She had had no warning and when his name was announced she was in the middle of doling out spices to the cook. When she arrived in the large parlour he was standing by the fireplace with his arm leaning on the marble mantelpiece, waiting composedly, and an infusion of warmth spread through her body as she saw his familiar figure. He greeted her with his usual formality explaining he was once again involved with legal matters in the Chancery court and had taken the liberty of calling upon her as she had requested. She ordered cups of wine and they sat exchanging news. Alice informed him that Sir Thomas was engaged at Westminster, glad of the fact so they could talk freely. She told him of her relief at Anne's approaching marriage and asked how his children were coping with their mother's death, remembering her own daughters' long period of adjustment when Ferdinando died. He spoke warmly of his sister's care for them and told her how the new Hall was progressing.

Then when current news had been exhausted, including her description of the masque in which she had acted, he said, "I was thinking of visiting one of the playhouses before I return home, something I always look forward to when I am forced to come to London."

"You are as keen as ever on the players," she remarked in amusement.

"Indeed I am. An interest initiated by Lord Strange," he replied. At the mention of the name his thoughts travelled back to the time when as a boy he had dared to ask the Lord's permission to take his wife to Anglezarke and on an impulse asked, "Would you come with me?"

"To a playhouse!" Alice had only ever visited a playhouse once when she had accompanied Ferdinando to the Rose to see Marlowe's Tamburlaine. Although there were now five playhouses in London they were not places visited by noble ladies and Sir Thomas's opinion of them was condemnatory. "Ladies do not frequent the theatres, especially without their husbands," she said, realising she sounded prudish.

"No, you are quite right. It was wrong of me to suggest it. I will go alone. Forget I mentioned it." His broad Lancashire vowels were more pronounced in his apology but there was no sign of the diffidence he had shown when first asking if he might take her to Anglezarke. The characteristic half-smile hovered on his lips as he said, "A common playhouse is not the right environment for the Countess of Derby, Lady Ellesmere."

Alice wasn't sure if there was irony in his words and noting her momentary confusion he continued casually, "It's just that I know how much you too like plays, my lady."

She saw the challenge in his blue eyes and at that moment regretted being a great lady with all the restrictions imposed upon her. She imagined herself a citizen's wife with no more worries than feeding her household and organizing one or two maids, being able to wear simple gowns without the constricting corsets and voluminous farthingales that inhibited free movement, being able to go to the playhouses and the inn yards whenever she wished to see all the new plays by all the prolific new writers. She wanted to go to a playhouse with Alexander Standish. "I'll come with you," she said impetuously, drowning the fear of Sir Thomas's reaction if he should discover it.

He grinned. "Where shall we go? I've read the playbills. There's a play by Will Shakespeare at the Fortune but it would be easier to cross the river to the South Bank than get up to Shoreditch. There's a revenge tragedy at the Globe and an old comedy 'The Shoemaker's Holiday' at the Swan."

"Oh most definitely a comedy."

In her chamber she found a linen petticoat that she was intending to give to one of the maids and a waistcoat that was past its best but which she sometimes wore in the still room. Under a small pipkin of black velvet she tied a linen kerchief like the citizens' wives wore. She still looked a prosperous city wife for the murrey kirtle was circled with braid, the linen waistcoat was embroidered in blackwork and her small ruff was of fine cambric. Alexander smiled when he saw her.

They hurried out of the house like conspirators, hoping they would not be seen by any of the multitude of servants, through the gardens and onto the stairs at the river bank where they hailed a ferry boat to take them across the river to Southwark and the Swan theatre.

The latest playhouse to be built on the South Bank was identical to Alice's remembrance of the Rose, wattle and white daub and octagonal in shape. The neighbouring Rose now stood derelict, in the process of being demolished by Philip Henslowe who was replacing it by a bear-baiting ring. Henslowe disliked the competition from the newer playhouses, the Globe and the Swan, and as he already had the Fortune theatre in Shoreditch he was capitalising on the equally popular entertainment of bear and dog fights. This time the theatre manager was not waiting to welcome them and escort them to specially reserved seats as on her last visit. Instead they joined the noisy thrusting throng jostling through the several entrance doors. Keeping a tight hold of Alice's arm Alexander paid the entrance penny to the gatherers seated at their tables then another few pence at the stairs to the second gallery which gave the best view of the stage and where the benches had cushioned seats. Amongst the vast crowd they were anonymous and able to enjoy the play. Thomas Dekker's comedy was about London and ordinary citizens and although not a new play its periodic revivals were evidence of its continual popularity. They laughed uproariously at the comedy scenes although they were unprepared for one of the plots which dealt with an unacceptable love affair between two people of unequal class, a young lord and the daughter of the mayor. Neither of them commented on it though both imbibed speeches like:-

"Too mean is my poor girl for his high birth,
Poor citizens must not with courtiers wed,
Who will in silks and gay apparel spend
More in one year than I am worth by far."

When the play was finished and they had to join the queues waiting in the squally rain for a ferry back across the Thames, Alice couldn't help wishing their private barge was to hand and realised how much she took for granted the privileges of her status. It had been a pleasant illusion to imagine herself a simple citizen for a short time but she was too reliant on the trappings of wealth. Nonetheless she had enjoyed the afternoon with Alexander Standish more than any experience since acting in the masque. Their companionship had been as on their rides around the Lancashire countryside as they laughed together and discussed the play and the actors. Now she hoped that Sir Thomas would not have returned to York House before she could re-establish herself safely. Removing the kerchief from her hair she strode confidently indoors, only stopping to tell the nearest servant to inform the cook that a visitor would be joining them for supper before hastening to her chamber to change.

Later as she took her place at the dining table she was transformed back into the countess, laced into a brown silk gown with gold facings and tight sleeves of gold brocade, her hair coiled with gold pins by her maids. Sir Thomas was already there in conversation with several more guests he had brought along from the day's business and greeted her in his usual manner so there was no fear he had heard about her escapade. They usually had guests joining them for supper so the presence of Alexander Standish went unremarked and the conversation rolled around general matters including the King's dubious Spanish policy and the commission he had instigated for a new translation of the Bible. Alexander joined in the talk, showing a considerable knowledge of current affairs and determined to demonstrate that the Lancashire gentry with their receipt of regular newsletters and their frequent visits to London were not the backward northerners they were often portrayed.

When all the company had departed and Alice was preparing to retire to her chamber her husband stopped her saying, "I cannot see what business brings Master Standish to the City so often."

"He has business with lawyers and I do not consider twice a year to be often," she replied.

"I would have thought the nature of his business could be adequately conducted by lawyers in Preston, it cannot be of so great importance."

Alice was riled by his scornful dismissal but thought it wise to say nothing.

However Sir Thomas continued, "I think it best if you discourage his visits in future, in view of his situation it is not decorous for you to be seen so often in his company."

"Are you dictating whom I should have as guests in my own home," she enquired, trying to keep her temper.

"When they are unsuitable, yes. York House is *my* house, Alice, granted to me by virtue of my position as Lord Chancellor. I would not have any talk about my wife."

"Are you insinuating there is more between us than a long acquaintance that goes back to him serving Ferdinando?" she enquired in a tight voice.

"Oh no, Alice, I know you better than that. I know you would do nothing to risk losing all the social advantages that matter so much to you. Why, Standish's annual income would not pay for one of your gowns, as I know to my cost. But I would not have the slightest whisper of impropriety touch my name."

Alice turned on her heel and left him. If Alexander Standish should visit again she would ensure she would be at Harefield, indeed she intended spending even less time at York House with Sir Thomas. But she thought wryly of how he had used the same words as the mayor in 'The Shoemaker's Holiday.'

On the following day when Alexander came to pay his respects before leaving for Lancashire she told him half of what Sir Thomas Egerton had said.

"That is only reasonable," he admitted. At supper as he glanced from time to time to where she was seated at the head of the table he could not help but compare the elegant countess encircled by the trappings of wealth and deference with their all too brief illusion of equality in their afternoon excursion. It really would be better for all concerned if he put an end to an association so unequal.

But then she said, "You will come to visit me at Harefield won't you? You always said you would come to me if I needed you. And I do need you, Alex. You brighten my life."

Her green eyes were appealing and he sensed the resonance behind the brief statement for he had noted the cool formality between Sir Thomas Egerton and his wife. And she had deliberately stipulated Harefield, not York House. He hesitated a moment for deception was not in his nature. But from the beginning he had sworn to serve her loyally and there seemed to be no good reason for that to change. The initial adoration of a young boy had developed into a genuine friendship but a friendship was all it could ever be.

"I will come to Harefield, probably in the Autumn," he promised.

"I am going to spend the summer at my daughter's home in Leicestershire, Ashby castle," she said. "I have decided to hold the betrothal celebrations for my eldest daughter Anne there. I have an idea for something different for the ceremony, I will tell you what comes about at our next meeting." She was sure now that he would visit her again for he always kept his word and somehow the knowledge raised her spirits.

She had sent a messenger to seek out William Shakespeare where he would most probably be at the Globe Playhouse with the King's Men, asking him to favour her with a visit to York House. She was aware that it would be in keeping with his character to decline politely saying he was too busy. Unlike Ben Jonson, he took little interest in commissions for the nobility, his main interest being in writing plays for the general public not Court masques or mottos for civic commemorations and she knew that financial reward would not be a consideration.

However one day he surprised her by arriving personally at the Lord Chancellor's house. She greeted him warmly and he addressed her formally as "Lady Ellesmere, Countess of Derby." She served him wine then knowing he would not appreciate his time wasted by flattery came straight to the point. Putting him into the picture by explaining the celebrations for Lady Anne Stanley's betrothal at Ashby castle she said, "I have the idea of making the present-giving in the style of a masque. As each person presents their gift I would like them to speak a short verse in the form of a riddle, appertaining to the circumstances and the present they are giving. I was thinking in the style of the riddles in your play 'The merchant of Venice' where each of the caskets for Portia's suitors contain such verses."

The playwright remained silent and she continued, "I know that you dislike such trivialities and that you do not usually undertake commissions like this, but I do particularly want you, Master Shakespeare, not anyone else, and I am pleading with you to do this for Lord Ferdinando, for his sake and for his memory on this particular occasion which would have meant so much to him."

He thought for a moment then said, "I will accept for Lord Ferdinando, in his memory, and also for you, my lady, who has always attracted praise from poets. Let me know how many verses you want, the names and number of the givers with the gifts they are to present and I will compose something in accordance with each."

Alice was laughing with happiness. "I do thank you sincerely, from the depths of my heart, especially when I understand it is not in your nature to accept such commissions. I am truly honoured that you should make such an exception for me and I need not say how much I have always enjoyed your plays."

"I am thinking of returning to Stratford soon, my lady. I shall continue to write plays but I think my acting days are over and I am tired of all the day to day problems of running a playhouse. Also there are so many new playwrights these days, when I first joined Lord Strange's company there were but a few."

She noticed how he had aged considerably, his figure thickened, his hair receded more from his high forehead, lines on his brow, though his eyes were still bright and intelligent with humour in their depths.

"Do not forsake the theatre completely, Master Shakespeare," she commanded.

Alice made the long journey to Ashby castle in July accompanied by her sister Elizabeth Lady Hunsdon, and Elizabeth's daughter Lady Berkeley. Her sister Anne Countess of Dorset had been forced to refuse the invitation as her husband was gravely ill and she was not willing to leave him. As the coach entered the castle park they were greeted to their surprise by fanfares of trumpets and as they proceeded along the driveway they were met by a consort of musicians serenading them. When they came within sight of the castle they were amazed to see a masque in readiness. On a dais covered in green cloth strewn with wild flowers her three daughters were seated – Anne, Frances with her three small Egerton daughters and Elizabeth, together with John Egerton and Lord Chandos, the prospective bridegroom. Her other son-in-law Lord Hastings was waiting to welcome her and led her to a throne-like chair in centre place where she sat in splendour surrounded by her family. Retainers and friends of the Hastings family were seated on benches set on the grass below, around the space marked out for the entertainment. Lord Hastings had commissioned a masque by the popular writer John Marston, specially composed and presented in honour of the dowager Countess of Derby. Alice felt the tears prickling her eye at the honour accorded her, wishing Ferdinando could have been present to see this gathering of his now-extended family. She sat with her own court, needing no Inigo Jones to supply fantastic effects as the natural beauty of mature trees and plants provided all the scenery necessary for the masque's sylvan theme.

The following day hosted the official betrothal accompanied by lawyers to oversee the signing of the agreement with all the necessary financial settlements. Congratulations and refreshments then filled the hours until the present-giving ceremony. This time Anne sat in pride of place on a dais in the great hall of the castle, her radiance making her almost beautiful in a white gown studded with pearls, her hair flowing loose to her waist, with Lord Chandos beside her. One by one in order of precedence with the Countess of Derby leading, the twelve symbolic givers - family and friends of the Hastings family supplementing the Stanleys - presented their gifts to the betrothed couple and as they did so they recited the enigmatic verses that Will Shakespeare had composed. In final place to symbolise the new generation of Ferdinando Stanley's family came Frances's eldest girl, five year old Elizabeth Egerton, bearing a basket of flowers and repeating her verse with a concentration that made everyone smile.

"It was a great success," Alice said, relating all the happenings in detail to her sister Anne on her return. "It was like being back at Lathom as Countess of Derby. All the family together with only Ferdinando missing."

"Will you never let him go?" Anne said in a tired voice. "Your marriage to Egerton never stood a chance because you are still tied to Ferdinando Stanley after all this time."

Alice did not deny it but said instead, "Thomas didn't have the power to release me. He is a cantankerous old man."

"That is the problem with marrying a man older than you are. I experienced it with Lord Monteagle. And now I am happy with Lord Dorset it seems I shall soon lose him. George Clifford is trying to hasten the marriage of his daughter to young Richard because if my husband dies before Richard is twenty one he will be made a ward of court and his fortune taken out of his hands."

"George Clifford is astute. Thomas says he intends leaving his lands to his brother in default of a son and heir, which is why he is so eager to have the Earl of Dorset's fortune secured for his daughter," said Alice. "What a business it is trying to get our children wed."

However with her eldest daughter settled at last and her youngest daughter having recently produced a son and heir, who to her delight had been christened Ferdinando, Alice could now feel a measure of content. After the success of the summer she felt happier than she had done for some time.

CHAPTER 24

The Gift

Alice's content did not last long. The first cloud on the horizon was the news that the Countess of Derby had been made governor of the Isle of Man and she recollected with resentment that when she had wanted the honour for her daughter Anne she had been told it was impossible for a woman to hold such an office. It was rumoured that the Earl of Derby was leaving the control of his affairs more and more to his wife and spending much of his time alone in Chester distracting himself with writing plays for his players. It was common knowledge that it was not a happy union though the couple obviously passed some time together as proved by Alice's second annoyance. After some years the Countess had borne her husband a son - James, the new Lord Strange - so Earl William's line was secure in the title.

In contrast Frances had borne John Egerton another daughter, her fourth. Alice was fearful that she was following in the line of the Spencer sisters.

Anne, Lady Chandos, was so far childless, a state not likely to be remedied in the near future because shortly after the wedding her husband had taken himself of on a tour of Europe with his friends. This had much displeased his wife and Alice suspected that all was not well with them. After the difficulties of finding a husband for Anne she hoped this was not going to prove an unhappy union and the celebrations at their betrothal an illusion.

Her sister Anne had become a widow again and her stepson Richard Sackville with his new wife Anne Clifford were now Earl and Countess of Dorset, owners of Dorset House and the beautiful Knole so she could no longer visit there.

Sir Thomas Egerton was becoming more irritable, in part because he was tired through his heavy workload and responsibilities even though he employed a large staff. One of his new secretaries was Aemilia Bassano's husband, Alfonso Lanier, who had been forced to give up his position as a Court musician through ill health and now served to help with French and Italian translations. Sir Thomas was continually being advised to retire, especially by his son John, on the grounds that he had worked long enough, but he refused to do so. Alice was torn between wishing him release from his stressful office in the hope this would make him easier to live with, and the fear that they would of necessity spend more time together. She sighed, her troubles were not over. The euphoria of the summer of Anne's wedding and the pleasant residence at Ashby seemed far in the past.

The cold wet Autumn and the signs of returning melancholy led Alice to take herself off to Harefield again, Sir Thomas showing no inclination to dissuade her, and she also expected the promised visit of Alexander Standish. October passed slowly though there were visits to accept and return and constant conferences with craftsmen and seamstresses because she was intent on beautifying the house even more now that it was her principal residence.

One drizzly day Alexander's name was announced and she experienced the familiar lifting of her spirits. She greeted him with pleasure saying, "Now I can take a rest from domestic concerns." Her pleasure in his arrival was further enhanced when he informed her that he need not hasten back as he had a few days to spare. They both acknowledged it would not be fitting for him to stay at the manor so he accommodated himself at the King's Arms on the village green.

The next few days became for both of them an interlude of great content. Tired from his long journey and burdened with the care of his large family and his inevitable loneliness, Alexander found his heart soaring again, while in his company Alice revelled in the companionship and closeness of spirit that she so missed. During the daylight hours they would ride for miles despite the chill and squalls of rain. The ancient name was Harefield moor but the landscape had none of the wildness of Anglezarke moor. It was tranquil fertile countryside and from the top of a short steep hill the land fell to rolling meadows interspersed with wooded groves through which the River Colne meandered slowly. In the freedom of the open air they were kindred spirits, friends and equals with nothing to remind them of their differences.

"In weather like this it would be bleak on Anglezarke," Alexander said. "Here the rain seems softer and the breeze gentler. And yet, apart from your company, I prefer our less cultivated landscape with its raw beauty. It breeds strength and fortitude."

"Do you go there often?"

"As often as I can. I take my eldest sons there to ride and hunt. I often look at the little manor house and ponder the possibility of buying it sometime."

In his company Alice often reminisced about her time in Lancashire and their mutual knowledge of places and people. She found she was able to relive her days as Lady Strange and her life with Ferdinando with the joy of recollection and not the pain of loss, as if his presence made a link between past and present. Alexander Standish was the only person who united the two disparate parts of her life and she felt comfortable in his company. He told her stories about his neighbours' activities, the progress of his children and the imminent completion of his new Hall. In return she described all the little incidents of her life as he listened attentively and made wry comments, while her accounts of the Court took on a flavour of absurdity when she related them to him.

She told him how during a masque that Robert Cecil had commissioned to welcome Queen Anne's brother King Christian of Denmark to London the masquers and musicians were so drunk that they could not stay on their feet. "The Queen of Sheba was supposed to present the King with refreshments of jellies and creams but fell up the dais and poured everything into his lap and when the Danish King attempted to dance with her he fell down and pulled her on top of him. Robert Cecil was said to be mortified," she said, not able to help a smile playing at the corner of her mouth.

Sounds like a comedy in the playhouse," he laughed. "I have no equal diversions from Lancashire with which to regale you."

"The tables have been turned on Cecil of late and it would seem his supremacy is coming to an end. The king's new favourite, a young Scot called Robert Carr, is after his position and the King can refuse him nothing, he has already been given a knighthood, vast amounts of money and many important offices. It's a very different Court to that of Queen Elizabeth."

"What's the difference with how the Queen treated Sir Walter Raleigh?" Alexander asked, with a trace of provocation in his voice.

"The difference is the King is inseparable from him, walking with his arm around his neck, fondling him and embracing him with slobbering kisses," she replied. "Immorality of this sort is openly paraded and drunkenness is seen everywhere."

Alexander looked at her carefully then said, "Do I take it you are getting tired of the Court?"

She didn't reply but then after a time said, "It isn't the same as it used to be."

Her thoughts involuntarily travelled backwards and she realised with a start how often she felt dissatisfied with her life even though she had everything she had always longed for. Alexander's eyes narrowed thoughtfully as he studied her. But in the evenings when they supped together in the luxurious surroundings of Harefield Manor he would be reminded again of the noble state in which Baroness Ellesmere lived, surrounded by a multitude of servants, cocooned by every comfort that money could buy. It was then he felt a great gulf yawning between them and he never dared ask again if she was happy for she appeared to be so. When she spoke of her husband it was always with a cool respect.

Sometimes in the evening they would play music together and one evening he produced a copy of a new song which had recently been published and which he had bought while in London. He played the music on her lute. "It's by Thomas Ford," he said.

"It's a beautiful tune," Alice mused as the soft notes of the instrument picked out the melody.

"My singing isn't equal to my playing," he said, but then he handed her the sheet on which were also written the lyrics and she read them.

"Since first I saw your face I resolved,
To honour and renown you.
If now I be disdained I wish my heart
had never known you.
What I that loved, and you that liked,
Shall we begin to wrangle,
No, no, no, my heart is fixed,
And cannot disentangle.

If I admire or praise you too much,
that fault you may forgive me,
Or if my heart had strayed but a touch,
then justly might you leave me.
Where beauty moves and wit delights,
and signs of kindness bind me,
There, oh there, where'er I go,
I'll leave my heart behind me."

She read them carefully without making comment and he sat in silence. She laid the sheet on her lap but both were aware that the atmosphere in the room had subtly changed. There was a tension between them like a taut cord waiting for a tumbler to find his balance and walk across. Emotion was tangible in the stillness, the only sound the crackling of logs in the grate. The silence seemed to last for ever, heavy with thoughts and feelings and unspoken words, and both felt themselves being drawn into an abyss that drew them they knew not where.

It was Alice who broke the silence. "May I keep it?" she asked, her voice trembling a little but knowing she must speak.

"I would like you to. I have committed to memory both the words and the music," he replied. His voice was calmer than he thought it might be.

The moment had gone. He picked up the lute again and continued to play more tunes.

The next day Alexander Standish began his journey back to Lancashire. They parted formally as they always did and when he declared his intention of coming to London again in the spring she renewed her invitation for him to visit her.

When he had gone Alice was conscious of a loss such as she had not experienced since Ferdinando died. Her mind was in turmoil, her only glimmer of happiness lay in the uncertain possibility of another meeting in half a year. The peace and luxury of Harefield usually satisfied her but instead she felt restless and discontented. Was it true that she was getting tired of the only life she had ever aspired to? Why did she feel so bereft when she had everything she had ever wanted? Over the next few days she decided she must take herself in hand and not let melancholy overtake her just because the visit of a friend had ended. She purposefully filled her thoughts with resolutions for the future, concentrating on her good fortune. She had many other friends who came to Harefield for the entertainments she arranged with players, poets and musicians, all of whom she rewarded well, and she took pleasure in encouraging new young

writers. She would make an effort to go to Court more
often, especially during the coming Yuletide season, even
though it was less appealing than in Queen Elizabeth's
time. At least there was the diversion of the frequent
masques. Her equanimity began to establish itself as she
made plans for the future.

It was very light in the room because the sun was
pouring golden beams through a huge arched window.
But it wasn't a window as there were no panes of glass
to obstruct the vista of summer flowers spreading to a
horizon of incandescent blue and filling the air with
sweet perfume. The bed was large and the flimsy white
curtains billowed and floated like clouds in the soft
breeze that wafted them. She was naked and so was he,
his arms around her, their bodies fusing as he pulled her
close. His even white teeth nibbled her breasts, his strong
brown hands caressed her thighs. She pushed back her
hair, falling in waves over her shoulders, so that she
could look into his blue eyes and see him smile. Her heart
was racing so fast she thought it would burst the confines
of her body as he covered her face and throat with kisses,
moving downwards to her inner sanctum, and she found
it difficult to breathe as he held her tight, pulling her into
him as she moaned with pleasure.

She awoke gasping for breath, her heart beating
painfully, her body drenched in sweat. She lay disorient-
ated, breathing hard, trying to accustom herself to her
surroundings – the darkness of her chamber with the
snuffed candles, the emptiness of her bed, the weight of
the heavy blankets pressing upon her.

There was a light tap on the door and her maid Lucy's
soft voice. "Is anything amiss, my lady, I heard you cry out."

She swallowed hard and her throat was dry as she cried hastily, "All is well with me, it was a dream that is all, I am sorry to have disturbed you."

There was silence again and a wave of shame washed over her. How could she have dreamt such a scenario. She had many times dreamt about being with Ferdinando again but this time he had not been her lover. What desires were in her mind that could have raised such a vision unconsciously? Tears sprang to her eyes but she was unsure if they were tears of shame or regret. She wanted to push the dream out of her remembrance and yet some corner of her mind wanted to hold on to it and the ecstasy she had felt, an acknowledgement causing further shame. You cannot help your dreams, they are unsolicited visitations, she tried to reassure herself. Yet she was disturbed by the possibility that her desires had enacted the scene when her will was temporarily suspended. Tomorrow she would return to York House and busy herself with affairs there. She would submit to the wishes of her husband for he was not in good health and she would make a greater effort to be amenable to him and abide his ill temper. She felt guilty about leaving him so long and vowed to spend less time at Harefield. She would also stop measuring out her days by the occasional visits of Alexander Standish.

She kept to her resolution even though Sir Thomas never showed particular joy at her return. He did not appear to notice her increased concern for his wellbeing and found all his satisfaction in his work. She was therefore as surprised as anyone that when he turned seventy years old he announced that he was going to retire from all his offices. She wondered how he would be able to fill his days when his work had been his life.

No doubt he would spend much time with his books but she supposed she would now see more of him and there would be much entertaining. He would also wish to keep his contacts at the Court even though he was no longer Lord Chancellor. In recognition of the valuable services he had performed over a long time, the King offered him the Earldom of Bridgewater. He declined it, saying he wasn't interested in an earldom at this late stage in his life.

"You should have accepted for the sake of your son John," Alice remonstrated with him.

"So your daughter could be a countess?" he challenged her. "John can make his own way, I have never believed in inherited titles as you know. All my achievements have been by my own merit. And I know it would be worthless to you since you have always continued to call yourself Countess of Derby."

Alice sighed but she knew she could not contradict him.

His retirement also meant they would have to relinquish York House to the new Lord Chancellor, Sir Francis Bacon, and she dreaded the upheaval this would entail as well as understanding her husband's reluctance to do so. He had always preferred their London residence. She expected to have his presence more at Harefield though no doubt he would also wish to visit his other properties in various parts of the country and she could see much travelling ahead.

Alice was aware there would be many difficulties before they could settle down again. However they were not the kind of difficulties she had expected. Twelve days after his retirement Sir Thomas Egerton, one-time Attorney-General and Lord Chancellor, was dead. "I thank God I have never desired long life nor never had less cause to desire it," he said. Without his work he could not exist. It had provided him with the necessary status, honours and prestige. Without it he was nothing.

His death came as a bolt from the blue and Alice was shocked by the suddenness of it. Her second widowhood was as unexpected as her first for although Sir Thomas's health had worsened over the years he had never shown any sign of particular illness. She had had no time to prepare and the confusion into which she was thrown was overwhelming, though John Egerton was a tower of strength, taking on much of the burden of his father's affairs. His testament declared his wish to be buried in his home county of Cheshire and for the next month Alice had little time to think of anything beyond the funeral arrangements, the legal arrangements and the many bequests of his will. There were many letters to write and formal condolences to accept, for several writers eulogised him in print including Ben Jonson who spoke of his 'winged judgements'. There was a constant stream of visitors to York House but one visitor she expected did not come. However she was too occupied to give much thought to anything but immediate concerns and the days sped by on wings. To her fell the enormous task of removing their belongings from York House and re-organising the household. Not everything could be transferred and not all the servants re-employed. Furniture had to be re-allocated, some of it sold and some left for the new incumbent, while she tried to find places for those servants whom she could not employ herself or be used by Francis Bacon.

Finally all business was completed and York House relinquished. Alice felt no particular sadness as she left the house for the last time. As soon as she could do so she would remove herself to Harefield which remained in her possession. Her husband's other properties had been left to his son John and Frances. Harefield would now become her permanent home.

After the frenetic activity of the past weeks the quieter surroundings of the countryside were appealing, though there were still many condolences and visits to endure, from her family and the local gentry. But still one visitor she expected did not come. Even amongst the previous hustle and bustle she had expected every day to hear his name amongst the callers thronging York House. As the days passed and she began to have more time for herself she could not help worrying. Why did he not come? He had comforted her when Ferdinando died and she had done the same on the death of his wife. Perhaps he was occupied with other matters but she found it hard to believe that he had not time to offer his condolences. Perhaps he had sent a letter which would arrive in due course. She had no claims on him. Why should she expect him to leave everything and rush to her side when he was two hundred miles away, responsible for an estate and a large family, just because her husband had died – a fact that did not concern him. He would know that she was hardly prostrate with grief. Also the situation was different now. She was a widow and he could no longer be her 'cavalier servente', the conventions of courtly love dependent on a young man's devoted service to a married woman. The continuing relationship of a widower with a widow was open to gossip, especially considering the difference in their social status. Was it the fear of impropriety that deterred him? Somehow she did not think Alexander Standish would let this consideration over-rule the claims of their friendship because a friendship was all it was. It was never meant to be anything else. She had always kept the distance of class between them, a barrier against close involvement perhaps more protective than her marital status, and their friendship had always been tempered by the differences separating them. She should think of what to do with her life now that she was alone again and rid herself of the dependence she had begun to place on him. She had a wide circle of friends, many of them widows themselves like her sisters. She had money and could continue to show interest and patronage to new writers looking for support. She had the beautiful house, full of comfort and luxury. She had in fact a life many women would envy. What had happened to make her think it was not enough? All she was conscious of was a great disappointment, but she was afraid to delve beneath the tumult of emotions overwhelming her. She told herself she was physically and mentally exhausted by the recent experiences and this was the only reason she was reacting so extremely to the fact that Alexander Standish had not come on one of his visits when she had expected him. When she had recovered from the shock of Sir Thomas's death and all the attendant stresses, the heavy workload increased by financial problems, she would be better able to cope with minor difficulties.

In her restless state the great house often seemed imprisoning and the numerous hovering servants and attendants intrusive so that she often sought solace in the gardens, now showing signs of new life. Blossom was beginning to garland the trees, pink-tipped buds awakening the roses and gillyflowers ready to open their faces to the strengthening sun. Yet this promise of new beginnings only served to intensify her melancholy.

Seated on a bench under an early-flowering cherry tree, the gentle breeze ruffling her hair, her thoughts returned to plague her. Perhaps despite the words that had occasionally betrayed his feelings for her, Alexander had only been playing the part of a cavalier servente after all, play-acting in keeping with their separate roles. There was also the possibility that he could have found someone to love - a young girl of his own class. He was still a young man, a young handsome man with his gentle smile, his blue eyes, the Lancashire accents of his voice as he told a story with his wry sense of humour. Her thoughts took a more personal turn as she remembered the occasional touch of his hand on her arm, the way he always seemed to know what she was thinking. Suddenly she couldn't bear to be reminded of him. The fact that she was no longer young and there was nothing she could do about it filled her with despair. She recollected her pity for the ageing queen at Harefield and how she had realised that wealth and power were no bulwarks against the sands of time. As she mourned the loss of her youth and beauty, the noble life she had always longed for seemed a prize she no longer valued so highly.

She was filled with an unbearable sense of loss and disappointment and tears trickled down her face as she was unable to quell the sobs welling from the depths of her longing. She was vaguely aware of feet running across the grass but in her distress paid no heed to them until a familiar voice said, "Why are you crying? Oh Mother of God, I did not think you would be so unhappy, forgive me, forgive my misjudgement, forgive my lack of understanding. I did not think you would be so grieving." He knelt down beside her, taking her hands in his strong grip.

For a moment she thought she was dreaming, that her need had created an illusion as before, but when she lifted her head and saw his face creased with concern she realised it was no dream.

"I thought you weren't coming," she said in a whisper, removing one hand to wipe her eyes clumsily.

As he saw the tears glistening on her cheeks he realised she was crying for him. He sat down beside her and pulled her to him. "How could you believe I would not come." She leaned her head against his shoulder and he let it remain there, his arm around her. "My dear Alice, surely you did not believe I would not come," he said. It was the first time in all the years they had known each other that he had used her name but she did not notice. "I am so sorry I have been so long and I have grieved you. I have had important business to do in the City and I tried to hasten matters, but if I had known......", he hesitated, "if I had known you needed me so much I would have left it." He lifted her head gently so that he could look at her. "But my business concerned you and I did not want to come until I could tell you my news. Lord Derby had sold Anglezarke Manor to two London merchants. I have bought it from them. I have been busy buying Anglezarke Manor."

"You always said you would like the manor," she said, relief overwhelming her that none of the reasons she had imagined for his absence had been the right ones.

"Yes I did. I have sold some more land in order to buy it. But I have bought it for you, Alice, not for myself. I have bought it as I a gift for you."

He saw amazement and incomprehension in her face as she struggled to make sense of what he was saying.

"It isn't so splendid as the house Sir Thomas Egerton bought for you here, but it's a gift with my love. Yet I must admit some selfishness involved too. I bought it in the hope you might want to come back to Lancashire."

She could find no words to say and he continued, "I know you will not want to leave London and the Court and Harefield Manor permanently but whenever you feel the need to come back to Lancashire for a time, as you used to come to Lathom, you will have a home there. It's for you to use whenever you like, without any conditions," he stated firmly. "It's yours. Will you accept it?"

Into her mind flashed a picture of the wild Lancashire moors with the small black and white manor house nestling against a tree-shaded ridge and she was overwhelmed by what he had done.

"I will be close whenever you have need of me. We would be neighbours, friends," he said. He paused, his eyes fixed on her face. "More, if you should ever wish it."

She was filled with a great surge of emotion for this strong, honest, handsome man who had loved her for so long with a tenacity and a loyalty she had grown to depend on, but she was forced to say, "Alex, I am nearly fifty years old."

She was conscious that the expensive rose oil could not hide the faint lines around her eyes and on her brow, and her hair now needed a little touch of henna.

Alexander Standish saw only the blue-green eyes, the abundant bright hair, the changing expressions on her vivacious face, the ready smile, the slender figure – the same woman who had entranced him as a boy twenty years ago.

He said, "I am not one of your poets who praise you in verse. I am a simple man who cannot versify. But to me you will always be the same as when I first saw you.

And I am not so far short of forty years myself. My eldest sons are now the same age as Leonard and I were when we first came to Lathom and I fell in love with you."

There were lines crinkling around his eyes and mouth when he laughed and the odd grey hair appearing on his temples. It was true he was no longer the boy she had first known but a wise chivalrous man, more attractive now in his maturity. Alexander Standish had more true nobility than many of the courtiers she had known. Suddenly she was tired of the hollow splendour of her existence, the artificiality of the Court, the grasping ambition of her acquaintances and felt a great longing to be back in Lancashire.

"Yes Alex, I'll come," she said, and she realised she also wanted to be close to him. More than anything else she wanted him in her life for without him everything else had ceased to have importance. "I'll come as soon as I can."

CHAPTER 25

On Wings of Eagles

"Are you happy?" he asked. "If you are happy then I am content."

Alexander had ridden over from Duxbury Hall to call for Alice at Anglezarke Manor and together they had ambled over the hills towards Bolton-on-the-Moor. On their return they reined their horses near Winter Hill and sat looking over the wide panorama as they used to, the valley spread below them, the river Yarrow meandering towards where the new Duxbury Hall stood. The years rolled away as they recalled their excursions in the past when he was an earnest lovesick boy and she was Countess of Derby. From a distance it seemed as if they had not changed, dressed for riding in buttoned jackets, hats and boots. But the intervening years had brought many changes, apparent in their faces but hidden from view in the deepest reaches of their souls.

"Yes I am happy," she said, the smile on her face confirming her words. "I'm glad I came. Thankyou for giving me the opportunity to come back here." She realised how truly happy she was, the first time since Ferdinando died. "The manor is beautiful and I can never cease to thank you for this wonderful gift, one of the most precious I have ever been given."

The house was small and cosy with polished wood floors and wall panelling burnished by the mellow rays of the summer sun during the day and at night by the candles aglow on the furniture carefully made by local craftsmen. The beamed ceilings and small-paned windows created an intimate interior protected by the copse of trees. But the frontage faced a vista of rolling hills and wide spaces that belied any illusion of confinement. The small body of servants were efficient and self-effacing, at hand for all Alice's needs, and Alexander had found an excellent cook. Alice did not know how long she would stay there but she knew she could come any time she wished. She could divide her time between London and Lancashire as she used to in the old days when she was Lady Strange and, for a short time, mistress of Lathom. She looked forward to being able to revisit old acquaintances and the places with which she was once so familiar and Alexander would be close whenever she needed him. She realised how much she needed him and thought of the hint he had given her, yet something still held her back.

In the distance she saw a large bird swooping over the hills. "Look, look Alex, it's an eagle," she cried excitedly, and they dismounted, narrowing their eyes into the light. They watched the eagle circling and swooping as if seeking something and Alice thought of the eagle on the crest of the Earls of Derby, of Ferdinando's pride when he had first explained it to her – the eagle an apt symbol for the great Earls with their soaring ambitions. The bird flew above them and in that moment Alice felt as if she too was suspended in time, hovering between past and present on the lonely moorland, almost as if she could be gathered up in its wings. She heard Ferdinando's voice as clearly as if he were beside her. "Let me go, Alice. Be free as I am free. Be free to love again." The eagle circled once more then soared higher and flew away into the distance, disappearing into the light.

She watched it go and as it vanished from sight she felt a great lightening of her heart, purged of guilt and fear, cleansed of regrets, loosened from the bonds that had chained her to the past. Ferdinando had released her to love again. She would never forget him but it was time to move on, to find happiness in a new love with his blessing and she felt as if she too was soaring on wings.

Alexander had been watching her and as she turned towards him he saw the expression on her face and understood. He had always been able to understand her thoughts. He moved towards her and took her in his arms. She linked her arms around his neck and pulled his head down to kiss him and he responded with all the passion she knew he was capable of as the hunger of years of restraint was released. As they kissed ever more greedily and held each other closer she could feel his strength sending the blood pulsating through her veins.

"I love you Alex," she said, when they pulled apart. It was a love that had grown over the years and been held in check, but now in its expression was as overwhelming as first love.

"I have always loved you," he said simply, but with her avowal his heart was soaring with a happiness he thought he could never attain.

He began to kiss her again and their bodies fused as they sought closer contact.

"Long time friends, new lovers?" he whispered. But it wasn't really a question. "I know I can't marry you but we can be lovers."

Alice knew he would be a passionate and sensitive lover. More than anything in the world - riches, status, respect - she wanted to be loved by this man who had given her so much devotion over the years and whom she desired with a passion she believed had gone for ever. "My chamber is waiting," she whispered.

"Then let's go home," he said.

They mounted their horses and turned them in the direction of the manor. They rode fast, hooves pounding on the spongy turf of the moor to where the manor waited, warm and welcoming, full of hope and joy.

FINIS

Historical Note

I have kept as closely as I could to the historical facts, only making minor changes in the interests of clarity or dramatic effect. The unknown parts of the lives of my characters I have filled in with my own imagination.

Alexander Standish died in 1622 and was buried in the Parish Church at Chorley.

Alice Spencer, Baroness Ellesmere and Countess of Derby, died at Harefield in 1637. She was buried in the Parish Church at Harefield in one of the most beautiful tombs in the country. One of the last poets to benefit from her patronage was the young John Milton. The manor of Harefield is no longer there.

Lathom House was completely destroyed by the Roundheads during the Civil War after successfully withstanding an earlier siege. Nothing remains.

The new Duxbury Hall was later remodelled in the 19th century but destroyed by a fire in 1859. It was rebuilt in a "Georgian" style and later bought by Chorley Corporation who demolished it in 1956.

Acknowledgements

I am indebted to Helen Morwood ("Shakespeare in Lancashire") for information regarding Alexander Standish's family, his visits to the Chancery Court and his purchase of Anglezarke Manor for the Countess of Derby.

I am also indebted to Siobhan Keenan ("Travelling Players in Shakespeare's England") for some of the information regarding travelling players.